DULCIE BLIGH

DULCIE BLIGH

By Gail Clark

G. P. Putnam's Sons, New York

Copyright © 1978 by Gail Clark

All rights reserved. This book, or parts thereof, must not
be reproduced in any form without permission. Published
simultaneously in Canada by Longman Canada Limited, Toronto.

SBN: 399-12053-x

Library of Congress Cataloging in Publication Data

Clark, Gail.
Dulcie Bligh.

I. Title.
PZ4.C5926Du 1977 [PR6053.1298] 823'.9'14 77-21672

PRINTED IN THE UNITED STATES OF AMERICA

*For my beloved husband Ron,
without whose gentle bullying and bribery
and unwavering belief
the first word of this or any other story
would never have been written.*

DULCIE BLIGH

Chapter One

A FUGITIVE MOON scurried across the predawn sky. Heavy fog shrouded London, muffling the footsteps of the night creatures who would, at daybreak, creep into their secret crevices, into the ramshackle tenements and stinking alleyways of the dilapidated, verminous rookeries. On the dark Thames, a mournful bell of a riverboat keened.

Through the thick mist slid a furtive figure. He avoided the brilliant beacons of the druggists' globes, deep red, green and blue, and shunned even the dimmer glow of the wrought-iron gaslights. He had no wish to be glimpsed by a member of a Bow Street foot patrol. With pleasure, he inhaled the damp, cold air, so different from the heavily rose-scented atmosphere that he'd recently left behind.

Through cobbled lanes and streets, past dark houses and inns, he moved silently. An ancient watchman leaned heavy-eyed on a pole too stout for him to raise; another dozed within the haven of his sentry box. The safety of the streets was the responsibility of these men. The felon smiled. In grogshop cellars and attics, drunks lay in snoring stupor on bales of stinking straw, waking only to stagger into the taproom to buy more gin.

His footsteps faltered. Unobserved, he paused in a deserted doorway and reached into a pocket of his voluminous coat. Emeralds, sparkling against his glove, lit his eyes with greed.

London began to stir. In a few hours' time these streets would fill with peddlers and pedestrians and carriages. Maroon and black mail coaches would rattle over the cobblestones. Mingled smells of horse manure and sweat would hang heavy in the air. Smiling grimly, the wrongdoer skirted a tall gray-black building with an arched gateway and narrow windows. He would not be caught in the shadow of Newgate by the merciless light of day.

Through rifts in the fog, the Arbuthnot residence in Cavendish Square stood revealed in all its misguided magnificence. Originally built in the neoclassical style, its Greek pediments, porticoes, and colonnades had since then been floridly adorned. As mismatched as Arbuthnot House and its Egyptian, Chinese and Gothic statuaries were Sir William Arbuthnot and Lady Arabella, the dashing widow who had lately become his wife.

The youngest housemaid rose at dawn. Stretching and yawning, she built up the kitchen fire. Countless tasks stretched before her: she had to dust and polish in the breakfast room, prepare the table, attend to the downstairs fireplaces and shine the grates. Pleasant it might be to catch a few more moments' sleep, but it was as much as her job was worth. Lady Arabella would want her morning chocolate, and she was not one to tolerate delay. On her way to the stairs she passed a lower storey window which stood open. On the ground outside it lay a dull brass button, torn from some visitor's coat.

Upstairs in the master bedchamber, a morning breeze ruffled the open draperies. On the massive mahogany bed, hung with deep crimson that matched the damasked walls, the coverlet was still turned back invitingly. The pristine bed, untouched since the little housemaid had made it up the previous day, stood out in stark contrast to the room's shocking disarray. Chairs were overturned and mutilated, their stuffing pouring out like lumpy sawdust from a disintegrating doll. The soft crimson silk that had once draped the dressing table from mirror top to table toe lay shredded on the floor. Hinged glass cosmetic containers were shattered, their contents ground into the Aubusson rug. A wall-safe hung open: from it dangled a broken string of pearls. Thomas Lawrence's portrait of Lady Arabella lay in the fireplace, the exquisite face mutilated and charred. The door to Lady Arabella's dressing-room stood slightly ajar.

Here, too, chaos ruled. The contents of a dainty writing-desk were strewn heedlessly about, the privacy of her ladyship's communications no longer a matter of consequence. A delicate rose-colored chair had been wrenched from its brass paw feet. Supported by intertwined dolphins, sea horses, and eagles, Lady Arabella sprawled on a recamier. Her slender neck was twisted at a grotesque angle, her rich brown curls were in tangled disarray. The perfect features that had led one admirer to compare Arabella to Helen of Troy were contorted in nightmare. Red streaked her dressing gown.

Humming tunelessly, the little housemaid mounted the stair. It was a marvel that Lady Arabella could dance half the night away, yet arise refreshed at such an early hour. The maid suffered a moment's indecision when there was no answer to her gentle tapping on the door. The Arbuthnot retainers stood in awe of their new mistress, whose moods fluctuated rapidly between gentle charm and icy rage.

Holding hard to her courage, the girl balanced her tray with one hand and cautiously pushed open the door. Blinking, she shook her head. Her mouth formed a silent gasp of astonishment as she gazed upon the wreckage; then, as she looked further, into the dressing room, she screamed.

Motes of light danced merrily on the shaft of the silver knife that protruded from Arabella's breast. Rivers of dark liquid made patterns on the rug. The little maid cried out again as her tray clattered to the floor.

Chapter Two

Oaks and elms and beeches surrounded the stately mansion in St. James's Square that was the traditional London residence of the Barons Bligh of Greenwood. The fifth Baron, an eccentric and swashbuckling individual given to exotic explorations, had more than a year past embarked upon an expedition to the Holy Land, where he traveled in a crimson palanquin decorated with six gilt spheres and slept at night in a huge green tent covered with yellow flowers and stars, so only the Baroness was in residence.

Brocade draperies hung at the mullioned windows of the morning room, an exquisite chamber with ceiling and carpet of the palest green and walls papered in a charming floral design. Dulcie Bligh, curled up in a rosewood chair, absently nibbled a piece of toast while scanning the pages of a romantic novel. Her heavy hair, worn in intricate coils from which it forever escaped, was this day a shade of orange that superbly complemented her bronze Rutland half-robe and striped zephyr shawl. Tall and voluptuous, she had an arresting face, both piquant and sensual, with elegantly sculpted cheekbones and a determined chin, an arrogantly aristocratic nose, a generous and seductive mouth.

Lady Bligh was not alone. Across the narrow room her companion, Lavender Lytton, contemplated a vase of flowers as if it might contain the answer to some profound mystery. In a gilded cage a canary named Calypso trilled merrily, watched intently by a huge, battle-scarred, orange-striped cat. Noticing her audience, Calypso hit a note so shrill and uncanary-like that Lavender awoke from her abstraction. "Casanova!" She dislodged the tomcat, not without difficulty, from the arm of a satin-backed chair that stood in uncomfortably close proximity to Calypso's bower. Casanova subsided in her lap, a displeased mass of thwarted hunting instincts and ruffled fur.

"Superb!" announced the Baroness, tossing *Pride and Prejudice* aside. Her flamboyantly youthful appearance belied the fact that more than half a century of history had unfolded under her roguish, enigmatic gaze. "Most delightfully acerbic! I highly recommend it, Lavender." Her dark eyes twinkled. "You will find it vastly edifying, I vow."

"Then by all means I must read it." Livvy's voice was soft and low, as pleasant to hear as its owner was to behold. She was unfashionably thin and much too tall, but these imperfections were far outweighed by classically beautiful features, a curly mop of blue-black hair, and a pair of magnificent lavender eyes. Lady Bligh's only complaint about her current companion, frequently voiced, was that Lavender's emotions were held too firmly in check.

"You've been thinking about your dratted husband." Dulcie's tone held disapproval. "I wish you wouldn't. What did he ever do for you?"

Livvy, by now accustomed to Dulcie's uncanny ability to read her thoughts, regarded her shrewd employer quizzically.

"He shot himself," she retorted, "an incident which, believe me, I do not recall with any great regret." Casanova twitched irritably. "Instead, I was considering my gratitude to you."

"And well you may," the Baroness agreed. Lavender's first position after her husband's death had been as governess to a brood of disobedient and rag-mannered siblings who, due to the uncertainty of their paternity, were known to one and all as "The Miscellany." Her rescue was considered by many to have been one of Lady Bligh's happiest impulses, and by others to have been her greatest folly, since those of uncharitable disposition claimed that Livvy had driven her husband to his premature demise. "That is why I remind you of your indebtedness at least once each day."

Livvy laughed. "Wretch! You do not remind me at all, and I wish you would, for I am in grave danger of forgetting my place. You spoil me atrociously! If you treat all your retainers so well, it is a wonder that they ever leave you." Nonetheless, Lady Bligh's companions were of legendarily short tenure. Those fortunate enough to gain approval were rewarded by being thrust, willy-nilly and despite protest, into whatever lifestyle the Baroness deemed most congenial; while those who earned Dulcie's disapprobation were disposed of among the various hopeful relatives who waited anxiously to hear of the next alteration to her will. Livvy, however, did not wish to join either of these groups. Her lot had been pleasant as neither wife nor governess, but with the Baroness she was well content. Lady Bligh, she knew, nourished mysterious, vaguely hinted-at plans for bringing her forward, schemes which Livvy suspected were markedly unsuitable for an impoverished widow who would soon attain an unenviable thirty years of age, but she was determined to remain, as befit her station, in the background of Dulcie's modish life.

With a sideways look at Livvy, the Baroness balanced a silver butterknife on one finger. She had commanded both devotion and loyalty from the cradle, was adored by her entire huge acquaintance, and was considered by her exasperated family to be a vexatious original. "I've a hunch we shall see that rascal Dickon today."

Livvy idly stroked Casanova, who returned the compliment by enthusiastically kneading her thigh. "Has he been out of town? Your nephew is usually more attentive than he has been of late." This negligence did not displease her; she found Lord Dorset a most vexatious man.

Lady Bligh looked amused. Benedict Trench, the Earl of Dorset, was the only one of Dulcie's innumerable connections for whom the lady professed the least degree of affection. Livvy did not share the sentiment; so strong were her feelings about the provocative Lord Dorset that it was a rare meeting between them when sparks did not fly. "You do not approve of Dickon," said the Baroness. "It is an opinion that many hold."

Because Livvy could not disagree, she remained silent. Lord Dorset was a dangerous, reckless man with a sublime disregard for convention, the niceties of polite behavior, and anything that did not concern himself. Livvy could not fault his attention to his aunt, but his quarrelsome impatience with the rest of the world caused her to think him both arrogant and underbred.

Dulcie frowned, as if beset by a sudden twinge of pain, and let the butterknife clatter to the table-top. "You've a hunch!" cried Livvy, familiar with the signs. She leaned forward, interested—Lady Bligh's instincts invariably proved correct. Aware that he had lost his captor's attention, Casanova slipped heavily to the floor.

"I have, indeed." With the expertise of a master dart-player, Lady Bligh launched the little knife at the butter dish and scored a perfect bullseye.

"What is it?" Livvy's perfect brows rose. "Dulcie, is something amiss?"

The Baroness shook her head, then turned expectantly toward the doorway. Her long and slender fingers tapped impatiently against highly polished wood.

As if summoned by some silent bell, the butler, Gibbon, threw open the door. Gibbon was a startling figure, tall and cadaverous with a shock of white hair. He had been a Bow Street Runner, but even this commendable following had not curbed his passion for picking pockets. Both careers had ended prematurely on the memorable occasion when Gibbon's nimble fingers came into too close contact with the Chief Magistrate's pocket watch. Dulcie had rescued him, and now, like Livvy, he was well content to serve her.

"The Right Honourable," intoned Gibbon in hollow cadences, "Earl of Dorset." Then he stepped back and allowed Dickon to enter the room.

Lord Dorset was a well-formed and muscular man of eight and thirty years, a scant inch under six feet tall, with sun-streaked brown hair and a haughty, dissipated countenance. His usually impatient expression was, on this occasion, wry. "Must Gibbon behave with so much pomp?" he inquired. "He makes me feel like visiting royalty."

Dulcie did not laugh, which struck Livvy forcibly. Though the remainder of the family was constantly aggrieved by Dickon's scandalous exploits, many of which involved ladies of the less respectable variety, Lady Bligh found him a source of amusement and usually greeted with enthusiasm his reappearance after one of his frequent absences from Town.

"You seem to have won his approval." Dulcie gestured toward a chair. Dickon's most recent indiscretion had involved the continuation of a somewhat ill-advised liaison with a newly married lady whose spouse was not complacent. Livvy suspected that, in this instance, the lady was the predator. Lord Dorset, whose conquests were legion, was not inclined to linger long in a jealous husband's territory.

"I cannot imagine how," the Earl replied. Although Dickon's tone admitted an awareness of his innumerable shortcomings, Livvy's opinion of him did not improve. Even were he as handsome of person as was generally acknowledged, his rude and offhand manner was such as must immediately displease. It was incomprehensible that so many women would go to such lengths to secure his attention. All Society had been agog when one high-flyer tried to strangle another, all for a glance from Dickon's weary eyes.

"Nor can I," Dulcie agreed. "It is not for your pleasantness of manner, certainly." This odd pronouncement earned her Dickon's attention and caused Livvy a resurgence of distress. "Dickon, I fear you are in dire straits."

Lord Dorset was less appreciative of Lady Bligh's hunches than was Livvy. "Nonsense," said he, in a manner that conveyed deep boredom. "I am in no difficulty. I daresay there are a number of people who might wish me harm, but I assure you I am quite capable of taking care of myself." His impersonal glance brushed Livvy, who was among his ill-wishers. She liked him even less for the scant interest he showed in Dulcie's concern.

The Baroness persevered. "I am not speaking of your detractors," she snapped, "but of something far more serious." Dickon's retort was lost in a shrill explosion of noise from the far end of the room. Livvy leaped to remove Casanova from his precarious grasp on Calypso's wildly swinging cage. Though Lord Dorset was seldom amused, the sight of his aunt making soothing noises to her canary, while Livvy sought to retain firm grasp on an infuriated tomcat, sent him into peals of merriment.

Dulcie remained unmoved by her nephew's rare and dazzling smile. "It is no laughing matter," she said. "Dickon, I grow increasingly anxious for your safety." She stared at him as if by intense concentration she might look into his mind.

Her piquant features grew serious, her voice hushed. "Dickon, what have you done?"

Before he could speak, the door to the morning room opened once more and Gibbon appeared, the death's-head lines of his face set in disapproval. Livvy experienced a moment of extraordinary clarity, wherein they all seemed actors waiting in the wings for the play to begin. She did not anticipate a comedy.

"There is a person waiting to see Master Benedict," Gibbon announced, in tones of deep displeasure. Livvy concluded from the butler's incredible facial contortions that he meant to warn his mistress against the visitor. "I have told him that his lordship is not here, but he refuses to accept my word."

"And no wonder." Peering cheerfully around Gibbon's stiff and outraged back was a rotund, dapper little man, clad in somber clothing that was enlivened by a carmine satin waistcoat embroidered with gold butterflies. His bald pate, set off by a scant fringe of black hair, gleamed. "I know you of old, laddie, and a terrible liar you are." He beamed upon his audience and bowed to Lady Bligh, whom his unerring eye had instantly singled out as the Baroness.

"I further suggested that information concerning his lordship's whereabouts might be ascertained by inquiring at his lordship's residence." At the corner of Gibbon's mouth, a maddened muscle twitched.

"As if I hadn't already done that very thing," said the little man. "No one needs to tell *me* what proper procedure is."

"If it is your wish, madam," said Gibbon, in the tones of one goaded to the brink of folly, "I would be happy to escort this person to the door."

"Aye, I imagine you would." The stranger retained his cheerful poise. He was quick with his fists, and he was also never without the loaded pistol that currently reposed in his waistband. "I'd just like to see you try it, laddie!"

"Never mind, Gibbon," the Baroness interposed hastily. The cat who had been draped around her shoulders like a strange, furry boa, thudded to the floor and moved to doze upon the hearth. "Do you mind telling me," Lady Bligh inquired of her guest, "precisely who you are? Why have you come here in such determined pursuit of my nephew?"

"Pursuit?" The stranger considered the word. "I'd hardly call it that, not just yet anyway. This is in the nature of being what you might call a friendly visit." He exuded goodwill. "Lord love you, it's not my place to be pursuing a peer of the realm."

Livvy, recovering from her initial surprise, wondered why Dickon allowed this outrageous conversation to go on. The Earl, as was his habit, was seated in the darkest corner of the room. His expression revealed vague interest, nothing more, but Livvy had not missed his initial startled frown. Her curiosity grew.

"As for why I'm here," the intruder continued, rocking forward and back on the balls of his feet, "this is where his lordship's butler said he was most likely to be found."

"It is difficult," Dulcie commented, "to find good help these days." Gibbon subsided into indistinguishable mutterings, his tousled white hair bristled with affront. "It is quite conceivable that my nephew is still abed. Pray continue, Mr.—er?"

"Crump." He swept her a flourishing bow. "It is most urgent that I speak with Lord Dorset on a matter of great importance to him."

"You have been told that Lord Dorset is not to be found on these premises." Lady Bligh exhibited a slight annoyance. "I think, Mr. Crump, that you had best inform us of your precise identity, and of your purpose in seeking my nephew."

Livvy was astonished by the Earl's silence during this exchange. It was shocking that he should leave it to Dulcie to extricate him from his difficulties. She frowned. Much as she disapproved of Dickon, Livvy had to admit that this was unlike him. The Earl was reckless, but not one to shirk the consequences of his misdeeds.

"You mean you don't know?" The stranger's eyes opened wide. "I was sure Gibbon would've told you." He shook his head reprovingly at the enraged butler. "You grow shockingly lax, my lad. I'm sure I don't know what to think."

"Nor do I, Mr. Crump." The Baroness was exasperated. "Would you explain how it is you know my butler by name?"

He did so with stunning simplicity. "I'm from Bow Street." The silence that followed this announcement gave him ample time to observe its effect. The younger woman he passed over quickly, though she was fine as fivepence in her simple, high-necked gown, and gazed upon the quiet gentleman. Dressed in the height of fashion, he wore fawn pantaloon, a pale buff kerseymere waistcoat, and an exquisite cravat, its pristine folds arranged in the intricate Waterfall. Unless Crump was mistaken, those Hessians had been made by Hoby, the famous bootmaker to the *ton,* whose shop was on the corner of Piccadilly and St. James's Street. The gentleman was also wearing a close-fitting coat of brown superfine that had doubtless been fashioned by Weston. In Crump's pocket lay a dull brass button, similar to the ones that adorned that fine garment. He was very curious about the identity of this gentleman.

Lady Bligh grew surprisingly belligerent. "If Gibbon has misbehaved," she said, "I'm sorry for it, but I'm sure all can be set to rights." Her chin jutted forward. "Understand this, my good man: I will not have my butler dragged off to Newgate, or the Fleet, or whatever hovel it is that you propose to put him in!" Gibbon moaned.

"You misunderstand," Crump protested. But the Baroness was not easily dissuaded from the notion that her butler was to be thrown into jail and expressed herself with such vehemence that her hair came tumbling down. In desperation, Crump threw up his hands. "It's not Gibbon I'm after, but Lord Dorset!"

The Baroness broke off in mid-sentence. "Dickon?" She blinked. "Well, that's another matter, to be sure." So vague was her tone that Crump began to wonder if Lady Bligh was right in the head.

Livvy, who had observed these proceedings with increasing understanding, took her cue. Devious indeed was her employer's character. "You remember, Dulcie," she prompted gently, "this gentleman wishes to ask some questions of your nephew."

"What questions?" demanded the Baroness querulously.

Crump began to wish he'd never undertaken this somewhat daring assignment. He was unused to pursuing criminals through the portals of the aristocracy, and Lady Bligh's queer antics made him extremely uncomfortable. "They're of a confidential nature," he replied. "Not the sort of thing I'd want to mention in front of strangers."

"Nonsense," said Dulcie. "I will introduce you. Gibbon, have Mary fetch us some tea." She rose, revealing a statuesque and superbly proportioned physique, and took Crump's arm. "This is my dear friend, Mrs. Lytton. You need not fear speaking in front of *her*. She and my nephew are the dearest of friends, and she is very much in his confidence."

Livvy accepted this blatant falsehood without an eyelid's blink. "You are a Bow Street Runner, Mr. Crump? How fascinating!" She extended her hand. "Isn't it terribly dangerous?"

Crump, pleased, made a rumbling noise. Much censure was cast upon the Runners, and this appreciation was balm. Though Bow Street functioned as best it could with limited numbers and scant funds, many sought to discredit the Runners, and the creation of an adequate police force had long been delayed by jealousy between the City and Westminster.

"King George," commented the Baroness, "once tried to shake hands with an oak tree in Windsor Park. He believed it was one of his kinsmen." Reluctantly, Crump released Livvy. "This is Mrs. Lytton's fiancé, Mr. Urquehart. Perhaps I should explain that dear Lavender is widowed."

"Urquehart, is it?" inquired Crump. His eyes narrowed. "Odd how your Mr. Urquehart fits the description I have of Lord Dorset." At that moment, Mary, the housemaid, appeared with the tea tray. She was a red-haired, pug-nosed, freckled miss with an infinite capacity for mischief and an eye for gentlemen. She deposited the tray on a low table and her saucy glance moved around the room.

Livvy held her breath. She couldn't imagine what Bow Street wanted with Lord Dorset, or why Dickon did not simply disclose his identity, but each word Crump uttered deepened her misgivings. She prayed fervently that Mary wouldn't betray them with an ill-advised remark. One thing was certain: if Dickon in any way caused Dulcie a moment's distress, Livvy was prepared to see him dearly pay.

Despite the seriousness of their predicament, the Baroness gave every evidence of enjoyment: here was a challenge worthy of her skill. "You are correct," she said, almost gaily. "As hundreds of men in London would also fit that description. My nephew is not an exceptional-looking man."

"Thank you," murmured Mr. Urquehart. "It is so flattering to be considered quite in the ordinary way."

"Never mind, darling," Livvy said, smiling seraphically. "It does not in the least alter my feeling for you."

The Baroness ignored them. "Mr. Urquehart is extremely discreet, so you may speak freely in front of him. If nothing else, his devotion to Mrs. Lytton will ensure his silence." With a pert twitch of her hips, a curious glance at Crump, and a warm smile for Dickon, Mary left the room.

"A friendly lass, that one," remarked Crump, not unappreciatively. He had a great weakness for wholesome country girls.

"Believe me, Mr. Crump," retorted Dulcie, with feeling, "she is too much so." Inexorably she led him to an elegant tapestried sofa, and presented him with tea. "Now, where were we?"

"Dickon," prompted Mrs. Lytton, who was carrying the beverage to her newly acquired betrothed. Mr. Urquehart took the cup, set it down on a curved-legged table, and derisively pressed his lips to the inside of her wrist.

"Impetuous boy," commented Lady Bligh as Mrs. Lytton blushed and snatched her hand away. "Have you observed, Mr. Crump, that this younger generation is remarkably hot-blooded? Why, I well recall—"

Crump felt that he had been led far enough down the garden path. Either Lady Bligh was in her dotage or he was being treated to a rare Banbury tale. "That's all well and good," he interrupted firmly, "but it's not getting us anywhere. It's Lord Dorset that I must speak with, and as soon as I may."

"Dickon?" Petulantly, the Baroness plucked at the fabric of the sofa.

"Suppose you tell us, Mr. Crump," said Mrs. Lytton in her gentle voice, "just what it is you wish to discuss with Lord Dorset? It is unfortunate that you did not find him here, but we can inform him of your visit when he next calls." Her smile conveyed her awareness that Crump was a busy man. "I am sure the Earl will be happy to assist you in this matter, whatever it is." Mr. Urquehart wore an impatient look, as if displeased to hear his fiancée speak so knowingly of another man.

"You must swear you will repeat this to no one," said Crump, deciding that Mrs. Lytton was someone he could deal with. The Chief Magistrate might not like his confiding in her, but Crump had not become one of the few Runners to earn handsome amounts of reward money by following strict protocol.

"Of course." Livvy's speaking glance dismissed her companions as negligible. The Baroness was now engaged in dropping fragments of biscuit into her tea.

"The matter concerns the theft," Crump lowered his voice, "of Lady Arabella Arbuthnot's jewels." Again, he watched for their reactions. Mr. Urquehart's frown deepened. Mrs. Lytton looked surprised, and Crump wondered what the widow had expected him to say. On the hearth, the huge cat stretched, then padded across the room and jumped onto Mrs. Lytton's lap.

"Arabella?" The Baroness removed a huge topaz ring, dropped it into her teacup, and began stirring busily. "What's Arabella done now?"

"Never mind, darling." Mrs. Lytton's glance was sad. "She is deteriorating rapidly, alas. Her bursts of lucidity grow farther and farther apart. It is a grievous thing to her family and the reason, I fear, why Lord Dorset's visits grow more and more infrequent."

Crump wondered how he was to report so strange an interview to Bow Street. He had the magistrates' consent to investigate this crime, and permission to use as many men as necessary. Crump intended to employ his best efforts, for he would receive a handsome reward for recovering the stolen jewels, but thus far he had accomplished little beyond wild speculation and useless conjecture. It occurred to him that Lord Dorset might, were he cleared of all suspicion, be sufficiently grateful to offer an additional stipend.

"You were acquainted with Lady Arabella?" Crump's unease grew as the Baroness slid down on the sofa, leaned back her head, and tugged thoughtfully on her luscious lower lip.

"Of course," Mrs. Lytton nodded. "I met her through Lady Bligh."

"Then you will be grieved to hear that Lady Arabella is dead."

This time the widow's reaction was everything Crump might have wished. She gasped and dropped her teacup with a clatter that recalled the Baroness from her reverie and sent the cat, hissing, straight into the air. It landed again in Mrs. Lytton's lap, from which refuge it glared at Crump balefully. The taciturn Mr. Urquehart strode swiftly across the room to stand behind his fiancée, one hand gripping her shoulder while he glowered at Crump.

"My dear Lavender!" chided Lady Bligh. "You've spilled your tea!"

"It's nothing." Livvy hid her trembling hands in Casanova's abundant fur. The game they played had suddenly turned dangerous.

Mr. Urquehart spoke. "Do you understand, Baroness? Lady Arbuthnot has met with a mishap."

"What sort of mishap?" There was nothing vague about the Baroness now; her dark eyes fairly snapped with interest.

"It wasn't exactly an accident." Crump had an unpleasant notion that this investigation had gotten shockingly out of hand. "I'm afraid, ma'am, that Lady Arabella has been murdered."

"I'm sure I don't see," the Baroness commented, "why *you* should be afraid." Mrs. Lytton had turned chalk-white. "What was it, robbery? I told Arabella she should be more careful of her baubles. The way she left them laying about was an invitation to every thief in London, and there are more than a few." Her tone was reproachful. "One would think Bow Street would do something about the appalling amount of crime instead of sending their Runners to frighten innocent children out of their wits." Abruptly, Mr. Urquehart moved to the sideboard and returned with a glass of amber-colored liquid, which he placed in the widow's hand.

Lady Bligh's tone grew more strident. "We shall be murdered in our beds! I know it! What," she demanded of Crump, "are you doing about this atrocity? Soon it will be unsafe to even venture out of doors!"

"What a terrible thing," said Mrs. Lytton. With the liquor, she had regained some of her color. "But what has it to do with us?"

"The Chief Magistrate is most anxious to see the villain caught." A list of the stolen property was already in circulation among the pawnbrokers, and would appear in major newspapers. Rewards were being offered for reliable information. Crump gazed upon Mr. Urquehart, who had resumed his brooding pose behind Livvy's chair. "What about you, guv'nor? Were you acquainted with Lady Arabella?"

"Not to signify." Mr. Urquehart was irritable. "Nor do I see by what authority you have burst in here to upset Mrs. Lytton and Lady Bligh. I suspect your superiors would not approve your methods, Crump."

Livvy was alarmed at Dickon's tone, for he sounded much more the haughty Earl than Mr. Urquehart, the private gentleman. "You must not give in to these nervous excitations, darling," she said quickly, and had the satisfaction of rendering him speechless. "You know you will suffer for it if you allow yourself to become overwrought." For the Runner's benefit, she forced a smile. "We are happy to aid Mr. Crump in his inquiries." It was difficult to accept Arabella's death, and uncomfortably easy to believe that Dickon might be involved. She shivered as she felt his sardonic gaze.

"If you please," the Baroness said suddenly, "I would very much like to know my nephew's position concerning this thing."

"As would Bow Street." Here, Crump knew his role. "It has come to our attention that Lord Dorset was Lady Arabella's paramour." He glanced at Mrs. Lytton, but she exhibited neither shock nor disillusionment.

"So?" Lady Bligh raised a mocking eyebrow. "I think you

are not aware, Mr. Crump, of the habitual immorality of the aristocracy, and of Arabella in particular. She was an odd combination of perfect physical beauty and the most depraved moral laxity! Dickon's association with Arabella is hardly significant." She laughed. "Surely you do not think my nephew would employ this unconventional means to end their relationship?"

"It's facts I'm interested in," Crump retorted woodenly, "and it's my duty to question anyone who might have information that would help with the solving of this case. The fact is, Lady Bligh, that your nephew was intimate with the deceased."

"Since you know so much about Lord Dorset," Mrs. Lytton interposed quietly, "you must also know that his attentions were not confined to Lady Arabella. Surely you do not think he would commit a crime of passion over so lukewarm an *affaire?*"

"It's not for me to think anything, ma'am." Crump knew full well that the association had been far from tepid, at least on the lady's part, and had included countless quarrels and arguments. "I just want to ask the Earl a few simple questions."

"What you want," said the Baroness, suddenly wild-eyed, "is to arrest my nephew. I won't have it, do you hear?" Crump recoiled at her frenzy. "I won't have him hauled off to rot in Newgate, or the Fleet, or wherever it is you mean to take him!"

"Oh, dear." Mrs. Lytton gazed at Crump reproachfully. "You've set her off again." At the window, Mr. Urquehart growled.

"Your nephew," the Runner bellowed, at the end of his patience, "is not suspected of this crime!" Dulcie fell silent, and Crump crammed his hat on his head. "Not that he's in the clear, by a long shot, but the Chief Magistrate was most insistent that I shouldn't upset you." His face was now far from jovial. "Diddled by a greenhorn!" he muttered to himself. "He's gone to ground, or I miss my guess."

"Diddled?" repeated Lady Bligh. "Mr. Crump, you are nothing if not colorful."

"While I sat here," Crump snapped, "listening to a bag of moonshine, Lord Dorset has given me the slip!" Reason reasserted itself. "I beg pardon for using such expressions in your presence." If his superiors ever received a detailed account of this interview, Crump's career might abruptly end. "It is thieves' cant."

"Remarkable. You need not apologize, Mr. Crump." The Baroness plunged her fingers into the teacup and extracted the topaz ring. "What was it you wanted to ask my nephew?"

Crump grimaced. Lady Arabella had been murdered, a fortune in jewels stolen, and Lady Bligh could find no more suitable occupation than splashing in her tea. "I hope your nephew can satisfactorily explain how a knife bearing his initials came to be plunged into Lady Arabella's heart. Otherwise, his predicament will be extremely serious." He did not add the chief medical officer's opinion that this knife was not, in fact, the instrument of death. Turning on his heel, Crump strode from the room.

"Skewered!" mused the Baroness. "Fancy that. Like a witch, Arabella is dead with a stake through her breast."

Hidden in the hallway, Crump peered back into the room. He stared astonished as Lady Bligh peered intently into the depths of her lovely Limoges teacup. Mrs. Lytton, oblivious to this mad pastime, sat staring at her hands. The orange cat stretched and yawned, then rubbed itself against Mr. Urquehart's legs.

The Baroness dropped the cup back in its saucer and briskly clapped her hands. "My dear man," she said to Mr. Urquehart, with every indication of sincerity, "what must you think of us? To find yourself plagued by that ridiculous thieftaker while paying a morning call!"

Crump reflected sourly upon the thankless hazards of his chosen profession. He longed for nothing more than a comfortable chair, a bowlful of pungent tobacco, and a few hours passed in congenial company. Lady Bligh's voice increased in volume. "Mr. Crump!" The thieftaker jumped as if he'd been stung. "You will find your missing pipe in the left corner of the drawer where you keep your hosiery. You placed it there two nights ago after imbibing a substance known, I believe, as blood-and-thunder."

She stood in the doorway, a denunciating preceptress. "If you must indulge in such depraved habits, Mr. Crump, it would behoove you to take appropriate precautions. You might easily have gone up in flames!" Having reduced her adversary to schoolboy size, the Baroness slammed the door in his face.

In disgust, Crump made his exit. It was his unpleasant duty to inform the Chief Magistrate that Lady Bligh had chosen to behave like a raving lunatic, that Mrs. Lytton was unaccountably jittery, and that the Earl was playing least-in-sight.

Crump was a patient man, and not easily brought to a standstill. Why had Lady Bligh shown so little surprise at learning of Arabella Arbuthnot's sad demise? How could she have learned of his fondness for the weed, or of the disappearance of his pipe? Wondering just what else the Baroness knew, Crump melted into the shadows and prepared to wait.

Chapter Three

From beneath the wide brim of her fantastic bonnet, Lady Bligh observed the Chief Magistrate. A man upon whom responsibility weighed heavily, Sir John wore a permanent frown on his deeply lined face. London possessed no official police force, and it was the Chief Magistrate's duty to see justice upheld, despite corrupt state officials who were indifferent to truth and conviction and even guilt. Runners and patrolmen existed on a mere pittance, yet were expected to render assistance to any who requested it, with no fee but the hope of a grateful reward. Sir John lived in the hope of reform—first, of the archaic laws that made it possible for the rich to buy their freedom while the poor rotted in prison for the crime, it sometimes seemed, of simply being alive; and, above all, of the insane process which required that Bow Street could investigate a crime only at a private citizen's request.

"Poor John," said the Baroness, as if she knew of his earlier interview with a superior who had irately denied his request for additional funds. As that gentlemen had pointed out, the Chief Magistrate had access to constables from the parishes, watchmen, beadles and the like; but, Sir John had countered, it was equally true that some parishes had too many of these auxiliaries, and other parishes hardly any at all. He pushed the recollection of that unpleasant interview aside.

"I am sorry to have had to summon you here to Bow Street, Dulcie," said the Chief Magistrate, raising shaggy brows. "But you have been having a May-game with one of my best men." He permitted himself a brief inspection of the Baroness, who had changed little in appearance since their first meeting, countless years before. Full figured and striking, yet with an air of fragility, Dulcie was unquestionably the most beautiful woman he had ever known. She blinked and smiled brilliantly, transporting him to cloud-cuckoo land. "Can it be," he added, "that you do not wish to see justice served?"

"John!" protested the Baroness. Her attitude was as easy as if she were exchanging the latest *on-dits* with other social lions at Holland House. "You are most unfair. Surely you do not think I would connive at letting miscreants run free!"

"I think," retorted Sir John, "that it would depend upon the criminal and his particular offense." He had to force himself to be stern. Lady Bligh brought life into his malodorous chamber, which was haunted by the ghost of many a miserable prisoner. Clad in an ensemble of Pompeian red, with plaitings at the bodice and the wrists, petals on her shoulders and ruchings at the bottom of her skirt, and in a tippet of green satin, Dulcie was as festive as any Christmas tree. Upon her curls, today the palest pink, sat a red confection trimmed with bands and bows of green. Sir John tried again. "Do you care to explain to me the mysterious Mr. Urquehart?"

Lady Bligh bubbled with merriment. "It was the most

diverting thing! Your Mr. Crump was as watchful as a setter with a scent, but dared not accuse us outright of perfidy."

The Chief Magistrate did not share her amusement at Crump's expense. He had an unadmitted soft spot for his Runners, whom the world dismissed as spies who denounced criminals for government reward. Reward! thought Sir John derisively. Precious little money to be earned on Bow Street. There were only two felonies—highway robbery and burglary—that roused the least interest from the government.

Dulcie frowned. "I declare, you have grown deuced serious! I think it is a very good thing that I did not marry you, John. It is obvious that we do not suit."

"So you said at the time." Though he appreciated the Baroness, and once had loved her to distraction, he could not but agree. "Why did you treat poor Crump to such a Banbury tale?"

"I could not help myself," Dulcie sighed. "It was shocking, I know, but you must allow me my small amusements." She grew helpless and frail. "It is little enough that's left to me."

"Rot!" retorted Sir John. He leaned forward, elbows on the battered desk. "Why do you seek to practice your wiles on me? Is there perhaps something you wish to hide?"

"No sense of humor whatsoever," mourned the Baroness. With a deft maneuver of one hand, she helped herself to snuff. "Frankly, I wished to test your perspicacity." She studied him. "You have grown shockingly stuffy, but do not want in wit. How serious do you consider my nephew's involvement in Arabella's death?"

The Chief Magistrate was not surprised by this sudden attack; Dulcie's impetuous manner was not unknown to him. "I cannot tell you that until I learn the truth of yesterday."

"Not cannot, but will not." Dulcie crossed her arms, drawing Sir John's attention to the low-cut neckline of her gown. "Very well." Her manner was confiding. "As you know, my nephew is a trifle wild, although I do not believe his indiscretions have previously brought him afoul of the law."

Only strong affection could lead anyone to refer to the disreputable Earl of Dorset in such mild terms, but it was true that Dickon was not among those aristocrats who deliberately flaunted authority. Even in his youth, Lord Dorset had refrained from such high-spirited pranks as boxing the watch. The Charleys were inefficient night watchmen whose main activities were walking the streets, armed with wooden rattles, and shouting stentoriously every half-hour. It was rare sport among young bloods to steal upon a snoozing Charley and tip his box front downwards, leaving the unfortunate watchman lying in the mud, with his box on top of him, until a good Samaritan arrived to set him right again. "Go on."

"You can imagine my consternation when I found a thief-taker in my morning room!" The Baroness exhibited great indignation. "One would think Dickon was a common felon about to be dragged off to jail."

The Chief Magistrate was long inured to hearing his men spoken of in unappreciative terms. In the 1770's, the government had agreed to finance the foot patrols; yet even now, forty-four years later, Bow Street patrolmen were so little valued that they earned one scant guinea a day. The Runners, except for the few like Crump who earned significant amounts of reward money, took home thirty shillings a week. It was not surprising that some Bow Street men were slightly less than honest; they would starve on official pay. "You should have known better," he remarked. "Were Lord Dorset to be taken into custody, I would not send Crump after him."

"Yes," Dulcie admitted, "but I was mighty curious. Dickon is devilish close-mouthed, and I took the opportunity to learn from Crump what was going on." She smiled ruefully. "I wish

I had not, for this is a pretty kettle of fish. Now, as matriarch, it is incumbent upon me to clear the family name."

Despite himself, Sir John's lips twitched, for a more unlikely matriarch he had never seen. The blushing curls had begun to escape her bonnet, which was decidedly askew.

"John," Dulcie said, with unusual seriousness, "I do not know what to do. It is intolerable that Dickon should be involved in this."

To his surprise, the Chief Magistrate found himself determined that Lady Bligh should be spared any unpleasantness. By some strange magic the Baroness brought enchantment to the most tediously mundane matters, and some trace lingered of the spell that she had cast on him so long ago. She still, at more than fifty years of age, managed to look like one recently arisen, well-satisfied, from a lover's tryst. He tried to resist his feelings, reflecting that she had spent much of the intervening time engaged in the frivolous pursuits so enjoyed by the Upper Ten Thousand, and was furthermore married to an erratic and irreverent Baron who suited her admirably. Though Sir John had been born into its illustrious ranks, he had only contempt for the *haut ton*.

"I wish you would say something," Dulcie remarked petulantly. "It is deuced uncomfortable to sit here while you glower into empty air." Her pose was melancholy. "Do you find so little pleasure in my company?"

The Chief Magistrate rubbed his forehead and thought of the various serious matters that demanded his personal attention, among them the periodic attempts made on his life by frustrated criminals; the imminent advent of the King of Prussia, a gaunt and melancholy man who had to be protected from the enthusiastic interest of the mob; and the impudent antics of a law-scorning highway-robber known as The Gentleman who inspired well-heeled aristocrats with dread. Lady

Bligh was proving a distraction of no small degree; it seemed of paramount importance that he should quiet her unease. "Lord Dorset's involvement," he said carefully, "is circumstantial. Crump wished to question him concerning details that might help us to discover the culprit."

"Circumstantial?" Dulcie sat upright. "When Dickon's knife was utilized?" She wrinkled her brow. "I suppose there is no doubt that it was his knife?"

"None at all." Sir John concentrated on a very uninteresting letter opener. "It is an uncommon piece, one that I myself have seen in his possession. Dulcie, I will confide in you, but I must have your word that what I tell you will not go beyond this room."

"Of course." Lady Bligh was pathetically eager for reassurance.

"That knife was not the instrument of Lady Arbuthnot's death." The Chief Magistrate leaned back in his chair, aware that he was being extremely indiscreet. "She was poisoned."

The Baroness abruptly abandoned her worried pose. "Poison! Administered by whom?"

"If you can answer that, Dulcie, you are far wiser than I." She did not comment. "It was a slow-acting toxin that could have been administered any time that evening."

"Then why," Dulcie frowned, "the knife?"

"It seems that someone was anxious to implicate Dickon. We also found, in the fireplace, letters that he had written to Lady Arbuthnot. They were not completely burned."

"Letters!" The Baroness was rigid with astonishment. "Good God, I am surprised that Dickon put forth so much effort! He didn't care two figs for her, you know."

This was an odd comment to make about a man and his mistress, but Sir John was not unacquainted with their history. Arabella had seen in Lord Dorset an admirable diversion from her tedious marriage to a titled gentleman much older than she. The intrigue had outlasted both the lady's marriage and her bereavement, for even after she was free, the Earl had shown a marked disinclination to make their relationship either honorable or permanent. Nor had the affair ceased when Arabella married Sir William Arbuthnot. Lord Dorset, however, was far from devoted to his inamorata, frequently neglecting her for weeks at a time, and for ladies of far less social standing. The Chief Magistrate suspected Dickon found it amusing to be so relentlessly pursued.

"I've often wondered," Dulcie mused, "if she was anything more to Dickon than a means to annoy Humbug."

"I beg your pardon?" The Chief Magistrate was startled.

Lady Bligh grinned. "As Dickon is my best-loved nephew, Hubert Humboldt is my least." Sir John was not insensitive to the warning. "They exist in a state of most unamiable enmity. Hubert was among Arabella's swains, but she had no time for him when Dickon was around." Her manner was simultaneously whimsical and provocative. "Dickon calls his cousin Humbug, and I fear I've caught the habit. It is such an apt nickname."

Sir John, who was acquainted with Humboldt, offered no dissent. Hubert's preoccupation with matters of fashion and etiquette might be overlooked, if one were charitable enough to tolerate mincing fops, but Hubert also had a malicious tongue, and an audacity of manner that rivalled Brummel himself. The Chief Magistrate, who had once been on the receiving end of that vituperative wit, most unprofessionally considered the possibility of sending Humbug to Newgate.

"We have digressed," the Baroness announced. "The point is, Dickon's involvement with Arabella could not be considered serious."

"I reached the same conclusion." Sir John's agreement was prompted by an epistle found in Arabella's desk, in which Dorset declared, in unmistakably strong language, his determination to accept no further impassioned and perfumed missives from her ladyship.

"What were Arabella's activities," Dulcie inquired, "on the evening of her death?"

The Chief Magistrate, who had not spoken at length with Lady Bligh for many years, had forgotten the quickness of her mind. "Lady Arbuthnot attended a rout," he replied, "from which she departed early. She did not return to Arbuthnot House until a much later hour."

"Where was she in the meantime?"

"We do not know."

"Humph," said the Baroness. "It seems to me, John, that you do not know a great many things, You have an unenviable task ahead of you."

The Chief Magistrate had already received demands from exalted quarters that an arrest be quickly made. It was Sir John's opinion that the murderer would fastest be caught through the tracing of the missing jewels. Crump was invaluable in this regard, for he often disguised himself and worked as a spy among thieves. Once the stolen property was recovered, it was returned to its owner only after both the thief and Bow Street had received a percentage. Such practices brought further censure on Bow Street, and Sir John would have preferred to concentrate his efforts on capturing the criminal instead of recovering the booty. But his opinion, it seemed, carried little weight.

Dulcie sighed, drawing his attention. "I wonder," she murmured, "precisely what Sir William was doing that night. It seems to me that your attention should center on him."

It was common knowledge that Lady Arbuthnot had little time for her spouse, an outspoken and highly opinionated nincompoop. "Sir William," said the Chief Magistrate drily, "has an alibi. He was in attendance at the Cyprians Ball."

This annual function, where courtesans entertained their admirers and protectors, was held at the Argyle Room.

"Unfortunate." Lady Bligh wriggled a foot thoughtfully.

Sir John faced his unpleasant task. "I don't suppose you'd care to discuss your nephew's whereabouts on that particular night?"

"My dear man, you must ask Dickon that." The Baroness smiled. "I suspect he was keeping an assignation with my companion; they are well on the way to being unofficially betrothed. Lavender has an absurd notion that her position renders her ineligible to become a Countess, and an even more ridiculous idea that I would not approve." She adjusted the tippet. "They are most amusing to observe."

The Chief Magistrate was not to be so easily diverted. "The felon entered Arbuthnot House through a lower-story window." He reached into a pocket and drew forth a brass button. "He left this behind."

Dulcie rose to peer over his shoulder. "Fascinating. It appears to be from a gentleman's coat."

"Precisely." Sir John squelched an urge to disregard the proprieties and pull Lady Bligh into his lap. "Lord Dorset is missing a button of the same pattern from an evening coat."

Dulcie did not waste time inquiring how Sir John had become so intimate with her nephew's wardrobe. "It doesn't signify. Dickon was a frequent caller at Arbuthnot House and could have lost it at any time. Nor is the fact that he lost a button conclusive evidence that this button is his."

"True." The Chief Magistrate pocketed the item. To his relief, the Baroness moved away. She was the personification of a world that Sir John seldom entered, the playground of gay and glittering aristocrats devoted to the pursuit of pleasure, an elite and artificial sphere that existed in determined ignorance of stinking poverty and rampant crime. "Crump tells me

Gibbon is a member of your household. I trust he functions more efficiently as a butler than he did in my employ." The Chief Magistrate touched his pocket watch, an item of no small historical significance that had once belonged to Sir Henry Fielding, the great magistrate and author. "Gibbon was the most useless bumbler I have ever known. Bow Street policy, of course, is to set a thief to catch a thief, but Gibbon too often proved reluctant to return stolen property, once he had recovered it."

"He is invaluable to me," Dulcie retorted, "being thoroughly unethical. Gibbon has not totally reformed: he picks the pockets of those callers of whom he does not approve."

Dulcie rose, and the Chief Magistrate realized, with a pang, that his visitor was preparing to depart. "I appreciate your frankness, John; you have set my mind at ease." She smiled wistfully. "It has been too long since we have talked like this. I hope you will allow me to return your hospitality, and will call on me."

"I am kept well occupied here." He indicated the untidy stacks of paper that overflowed the scarred desk. "Before you leave, Dulcie, there is one other thing."

"Yes?" She was all interest.

"Crump was most anxious to understand your knowledge of his missing pipe." Again the letter opener came into play. "I was forced to spend an exhausting half-hour trying to render an explanation, with lamentable results."

Dulcie laughed. "Poor Mr. Crump was all at sea. I assume it was where I said it would be?"

"Of course." Sir John's gaze was speculative. "Just how far does your foresight extend?"

"I know little enough of value." She appeared remarkably innocent. "You will remember that my hunches are unpredictable. You should be grateful for it, John: could I but call upon such gifts at will, your Runners would be out of a job."

"So they would." Sir John was constantly torn between his wish for an adequate city-wide police force and the knowledge that this reform would mean the end of Bow Street. "I must beg you to refrain from such displays in the future. Your flashes of intuition are impossible to explain, and I am a busy man." His smile briefly lifted the weight of years from his tired features. "Crump is convinced that you are most oddly mad."

"Poor John." It was Dulcie's turn to exhibit sympathy. "If you send your Mr. Crump around this afternoon, I will see to it that Dickon answers any questions he may wish to ask. It is the least I can do in atonement for my sins."

"Crump." The heavy eyebrows frowned. "Would you not prefer someone else?"

"I refuse," said Lady Bligh firmly, "to speak with anyone else. Your dedicated little Crump amuses me." She regarded her one-time beau. "I promise, John, that I shall try to cause you no further difficulty."

So far from being reassured was the Chief Magistrate that he grew most uncomfortable. "Dulcie, you must not become further involved in this thing." He had a dreadful vision of the Baroness caught in an unknown killer's toils. "Give me your word that you will not interfere."

"You distrust me." Dulcie tucked escaping tendrils of hair beneath her extravagant bonnet. "I will promise you anything, John, if you will only come to tea." She left the room blithely, as if her purpose had been achieved.

The Chief Magistrate, lost in unwilling memories of the bewitching young creature who had so long ago enslaved him, moved to the window. The Baroness had been an enchanting girl, a well-bred temptress whose dark-eyed glance hinted at intoxicating pleasures of an intoxicating sort. Sir John was shocked to discover that he was still tantalized by those elusive delights.

Lady Bligh stepped into her carriage, her manner quite

carefree, and the Chief Magistrate moved back to his desk. He was well aware that Dulcie had not given him her word.

The West End streets were crammed with carriages—stanhopes as tall as a first-floor window; tilburies, curricles, and tandems; tim-whiskies and phaetons drawn by glossy thoroughbreds. As varied as the vehicles were the men, women, and children who thronged the narrow roads. Mingled with young martial heroes, fresh from triumphs over the French, were sellers of ballads and pamphlets; whores and pickpockets; hawkers of oranges and chestnuts, pasties and tarts, gin and beer. Along the cobbled streets could be found spectacles of every sort: Punch-and-Judy entertainments and performing fleas; traveling fairs with mountebanks, wirewalkers and bearded women; houses of assignation where even ladies of quality could salve their discontent.

Lady Bligh's well-sprung barouche moved past the French restaurants and raffish oyster saloons that thrived around Piccadilly, narrowly avoiding a collision with one of the sisterhood who haunted the neighborhood. The streetwalker raised a menacing fist and mingled colorful curses with the varied cries that filled the air.

Exquisite dandies strolled in St. James's and Piccadilly, joining their less colorful brothers in the gentlemen's clubs, playing faro and macao at Brooks, or looking in at Watier's, where Brummel reigned supreme. Behind the Corinthian pilasters of White's handsome and well-proportioned facade, the rich lords of the Whig aristocracy gambled deep, both night and day. Here, where whist was the game, Lord Dorset had once won £200,000 in a single night. The Earl had never been numbered among those gentlemen whose losses of fortune were the stuff of life to Messrs. Howard and Grubs, much patronized money-lenders to the fashionable world.

Lady Bligh's coachman drew up before a large and unattractive home in Grosvenor Square. Without waiting for assistance, the Baroness stepped down. Set on a long strip of ground running back from the street, with a courtyard behind it and a coach-house in the rear, Arbuthnot House towered over her. A parapet surmounted this graystone structure; crimson brick set off the dingy sash-windows in their recessed frames. Wrought-iron twisted into railings, lamp-holders and link-extinguishers. Dulcie grimaced and applied herself with vigor to the heavy brass door-knocker.

She was ushered by a haughty butler into a small anteroom. "I will ascertain," said he, inspecting her engraved visiting card, "if Madam is receiving visitors."

"As you wish." The Baroness, unperturbed by treatment more suitable to a common tradesman, prepared to wait. "I think you will discover that Luisa dares not refuse to see me." The butler formed the immediate intention of leaving this underbred person to cool her heels as long as he dared.

No sooner had the frigid servitor disappeared from view than Dulcie blithely mounted the circular mahogany staircase that led to the upper floors. The interior of Arbuthnot House, she noted, was lavishly embellished with columns and entablatures, coved recesses and niches, making the inside of the house as grotesque as its exterior. Lady Bligh paused in the upstairs hallway, then moved unerringly toward the master bedroom.

The Baroness blended magnificently with the delicate pinks and startling reds, her gown and hair in perfect accord with the unconventional décor. Though Arabella's chambers had been set to rights, they showed evidence of the sad events that had transpired there. Lady Bligh inhaled the fading scent of roses as her dark eyes moved slowly around the dressing room. Whatever Arabella's shortcomings, her taste, in inanimate objects at least, could not be maligned. Dulcie threw open the wardrobe where expensive gowns hung undisturbed, and fingered the soft folds of a rumpled and stained evening dress of rich-figured French gauze.

Next to catch her attention was the dainty writing-desk. Her nimble fingers pressed a hidden spring and a narrow drawer appeared. Without pausing for inspection, the Baroness stuffed its scant contents into the bodice of her gown and closed the aperture. Her gaze moved to a poorly executed pastoral scene, an incongrous article to find in the boudoir of Arabella Arbuthnot, whom one would hardly expect to nourish a preference for chunky milkmaids and knock-kneed cows. Dulcie removed the painting and detached from its backing a thin piece of parchment which she added to her other contraband. Then she stepped back into the hallway and calmly descended the stair. The butler was waiting in the hallway.

"Madame Arbuthnot will see you now." His voice dripped icicles. Lady Bligh smiled gently and allowed herself to be conducted to the drawing room.

"Luisa," she said. "How delightful to see you again." The two ladies surveyed each other without enthusiasm. Despite her haggish appearance, Madame Arbuthnot had once been a beauty, and had reigned uncontested until Dulcie, many years her junior, had burst upon the *ton* and stolen Luisa's position and her beaux. "You are looking well."

"Fiddle-dee-dee," retorted her hostess, at whose elbow a brandy decanter, barely a quarter full, sat upon a Chippendale table badly splotched with liquor stains. It was common knowledge that Arabella's arrival at Arbuthnot House had caused her mama-in-law frequent recourse to the bottle. A carriage accident, twenty years previous, had left Luisa confined to a wheelchair. "You might as well sit down, since you're here."

"As gracious as ever, I see." The Baroness alighted on an uncomfortable Carolian love-seat. "How do I find you Luisa?" The room reeked of brandy. "Well, I presume?"

"You presume too much," Madame Arbuthnot snorted. "Consider yourself lucky to find me at all, and don't be impertinent." She filled her glass.

"I beg your pardon, Luisa. I did not mean to pry." Madame Arbuthnot had fallen prey to the rigors of time. Scant gray hair straggled past her brightly rouged cheeks; hooded topaz eyes glowered malevolently from gaunt eye sockets that jutted out hideously amid sagging flesh. It was as well that Luisa was a recluse: the sight of her would have inspired many a young miss with an abiding horror of advancing age.

"Don't try and pull the wool over *my* eyes, Dulcie Bligh!" snapped her hostess. "I wasn't born yesterday. You want something or you would never have come here." Luisa cackled. "Brass-faced baggage! It ain't like you have a fondness for me."

The Baroness kept her emotions under remarkable control. "You misjudge me, Luisa." Her tone expressed only concern. "I have come to be with you in your time of need." This generosity was a trifle startling, considering the ladies' long-standing enmity.

"Balderdash." Luisa drained her glass and observed her caller tipsily. "Open your budget and don't waste my time. I believe in blunt speech, you know."

"The whole world knows," Dulcie retorted, then smiled sweetly. "Dear Luisa, I fear you are quite overset by your difficulties."

The dowager roared with laughter. "Difficulties!" She wiped her streaming eyes. "You're speaking of Arabella, of course. The silly twit's death is the best thing that's happened to me for many a long year."

"Poor Luisa. How tedious you have become."

The dowager brandished the decanter angrily. "You didn't know the girl, Dulcie. That damned hussy was set on cuckolding my son. Poor soul, she went to meet her Maker prematurely, and fortunate it was."

Dulcie was undismayed by such vehemence. "Ah!" she said quietly. "Of course. The Arbuthnot fortune."

"To be sure." Madame's topaz eyes were bloodshot. "One thing I'll say for you: you're up to all the rigs. The Arbuthnot millions may've been made in trade, but my son was knighted for his services to the Crown, and it wouldn't be fitting for a bastard to step into his shoes." The *ton* had long ago been induced to overlook the Arbuthnot origins.

"No, indeed." Lady Bligh was fascinated. "Was that a likely eventuality?"

"You don't blab, either," commented her hostess, "so I'll tell you that it was. William was set on having a son." The heavy jowls wobbled with amusement. "Mighty fine he's grown, and means to secure the succession." Malign laughter pealed. "You'd think, from William's carrying-on, that he was born nobility. Even now he's hobnobbing with the swells in one of those dratted clubs."

The Baroness was not disheartened to find Sir William away from home. "Do you not wish for grandchildren, Luisa? Little creatures of joy and delight to dandle upon your knee?"

The dowager choked on her brandy. "No more than you, I'll warrant," she gasped. "Noisy, nasty little things."

Dulcie exhibited little interest in this sidelight on Sir William's nursery days. "Arabella was not eager to oblige?"

"Hah!" Luisa's eyes glittered. "That one was too busy with your devilish nephew to spare her husband even token time." The stooped shoulders heaved. "Not that I bear young Dickon any ill-will, though he's bound for perdition as sure as I'm bound to this chair." She paused to observe Lady Bligh's reaction to this dire prediction, and derived great pleasure from her guest's hastily averted face. "There's little that goes on in this house that I don't know, including my daughter-in-law's reluctance to warm her husband's bed." Madame Arbuthnot turned confiding. "I'll tell you this, Dulcie, my nose for mischief has always been acute."

The Baroness contemplated that magnificent, and somewhat misshapen, appendage. "You cannot deny that Arabella was stunning," she murmured. "I wonder who would wish to do away with her."

The dowager again had recourse to her decanter. "At least half her acquaintance, if not more. Arabella was not of an endearing nature." Luisa obviously had little interest in the matter of Arabella's death. "She surprised a thief and he disposed of her." Large yellowed teeth flashed. "Most conveniently."

"A thief who knew the safe's combination? Come, Luisa, that won't do!"

Madame Arbuthnot raised her goblet. "My son ain't as careful as he should be." The words were slightly slurred. "Nor are servants what they once were." Golden eyes bored into Dulcie. "I know why you're here, you want to clear that rakeshame nephew of yours. You're wasting your time, Dulcie Bligh! I wouldn't help you if I could." The harsh voice ceased abruptly as the dowager's head slumped forward. From the slack lips issued a hearty snore.

Lady Bligh gazed upon the raddled dowager, a gruesome spider squatting in the center of her cluttered web. Jacobean panelling warred with Chinoiserie wall-paper; Geneva velvets mixed indiscriminately with Georgian brocades and Burgundian tapestries. A William and Mary tallboy was adorned with Queen Anne embroidery. In one corner sat an Elizabethan bread cupboard. It was rumored that Madame Arbuthnot never left this chamber, taking her meals at one of the scarred tables and passing her nights on the worn settee which looked far too fragile to support her weight.

Luisa stirred. "You're still here," she remarked, in disappointed tones. One swollen hand moved to her brow. "Sweet Christ, but I've the devil of a head."

"Did you think you'd dreamt me?" Dulcie inquired. "I fear William neglects you, Luisa. You are too much alone. Such excessive solitude often leads to disorders of the mind."

"Think I'm queer in the attic, do you?" The veined hands

shook. "I'll listen to no more nonsense, you insolent chit. You may take your leave."

"Luisa! I have only your best interests in mind." Lady Bligh was unruffled by the old woman's ferocity. "You need a companion, someone to amuse you and run small errands. You would be much more comfortable." Dulcie glanced significantly at the empty decanter.

"Humm." Luisa contemplated such an addition to the household, a hapless creature whom she could bully and torment. A female in unfortunate circumstances would not quickly take offense. "You may be right."

"Of course I am." The Baroness was brisk. "I know just the person, an impoverished female who will suit you perfectly. She was left destitute by her, er, family and has had to seek employment." The account was true, if highly abridged. "Primrose is a good, unassuming girl; I'm sure you'll find her all that you might wish."

The dowager's smile was wolfish. She would derive great satisfaction from abusing Lady Bligh's *protégée*. "You and your unfortunates. Can't you find any better way to pass your time?"

"At my age?" The Baroness was a picture of feebleness. "The pursuits of youth are beyond me. Age has vanquished both of us, alas."

Gratified to consider her rival thus cut down to size, Madame Arbuthnot conceded that Dulcie had lost none of her style. "You've a good heart, Dulcie Bligh," she announced, with rare generosity, "for all you're a flibbertigibbet. Send the wench around."

"Bless you, Luisa." The champion of the underprivileged rose. "You are not so unsympathetic as you would have the world believe."

Madame Arbuthnot remained enchanted by the notion of her old foe now fallen prey to decrepitude. "Stay and have some black pudding with me." She cackled at Dulcie's instinctive revulsion to this horrid, low-cost concoction. "It's better fare than your nephew will have where he's going!"

Lady Bligh was greatly moved by this grim reminder. "I must go," she replied, in muffled tones. "Thank you for seeing me, Luisa. I will arrange to have Primrose call."

"Do that," the dowager agreed cordially. "And give Dorset my regards."

"Your kindness knows no bounds." The Baroness pressed a dainty lace-edged handkerchief to her eyes. "Pray don't trouble yourself; I will find my own way out." She left Luisa shaking with vicious glee.

Once in the hallway, Dulcie's melancholy miraculously disappeared. The bowed shoulders straightened, the grief-stricken features took on brisk determination. Madame Arbuthnot would have been greatly incensed to see her favorite enemy move so youthfully. Rustling faintly, the Baroness strode toward the library, Sir William's private domain.

Chapter Four

DULCIE SAT IN the Grand Saloon, beneath a stained glass window of abstract design, which she claimed was Saint George slaying the dragon and which Dickon irreverently identified as the legendary Sir Philpott Bligh—better-remembered for his alcoholic capacities than for the daring he exhibited during the Crusades—locked in mortal combat with an extremely obstinate mule.

The Baroness took stock of her ill-assorted troops. "It must suffice," she sighed, "though it is not what I would like." She smoothed disheveled curls. "But we shall contrive."

Livvy would have given a great deal to learn precisely how the Baroness had passed her morning; Lady Bligh unmistakably resembled a canary-fed cat. Thus reminded of her duties, Livvy cast an anxious eye upon her charges. Calypso muttered darkly, one wary eye fixed on Casanova, who dozed innocently upon a satin-covered couch. Livvy pondered their presence in the little-used Grand Saloon. The stage was well-set; it remained to discover for whom.

Lord Dorset manifested his customary indifference. Livvy marveled at this imperturbability, an unendearing trait. The Earl looked very well in his coat of bottle green and beige unmentionables, and if he experienced any curiosity about Dulcie's summons, it was not evident. Nor did he display annoyance at being distracted from his usual pursuits, though at this hour Lord Dorset was more often found in the fencing rooms in St. James's Street, in "Gentleman" Jackson's Bond Street boxing saloon, or examining the latest acquisitions at Tattersall's. Dickon cocked an inquiring brow, and Livvy looked hastily away.

"Gibbon," Dulcie said. Her tone made the butler jump as if bee-stung. He had recently appropriated a fine diamond stickpin from an unsuspecting caller, and feared his mistress's eagle eye. "I will not scold you," the Baroness remarked, "but you must try to curb these unbecoming impulses."

Chastened, Gibbon bowed his head. "I assume," his employer continued, arranging a vase of newly cut flowers, "that you have retained your old contacts?"

Gibbon tried desperately for an expression of nonchalance. He succeeded only in looking like one discovered with both paws stuck to the forbidden honey jar.

"Come, come," Lady Bligh prompted, with more than a trace of acerbity. "Don't shilly-shally, Gibbon, we haven't the time! Do you still consort with the criminal element, pawnbrokers and dealers in stolen goods?"

Gibbon flushed scarlet. "Pawnbrokers are not necessarily criminals, my lady, for all they're clutch-fisted misers, to a man."

"Answer me!"

His head hung lower, the white hair lank with shame. "I see

such people occasionally, my lady. Purely in a social context, you understand."

"If you wanted to dispose of some stolen items, I daresay you would know where to go?" Dulcie's tone was wry.

Gibbon was a caricature of affronted innocence. "I, my lady? I have no traffic with fences, and that's a fact."

The Baroness did not bother to dispute this unlikely statement. "You are going to," she announced, and produced a handwritten list. "I want you to discover the whereabouts of these items."

Gibbon goggled at his mistress, who might have been sending him blandly to the local apothecary. "Bow Street will be making similar inquiries, so you must be quick." She handed him a heavy purse. "I doubt they can pay so handsomely for information as I. You must also be discreet; I do not care to have the suspicious Mr. Crump learn of my interest in these gems."

Gibbon digested this comment. So alert became his emaciated features, so jaunty his air, that he might have arisen rejuvenated from his own deathbed. "I will contrive to satisfy your ladyship." He bowed, then succumbed to joy at the opportunity to put the Runner's nose out of joint. "You needn't fear, my lady, that Crump will steal a march on me!"

"I trust not." Dulcie ruminated. "When Crump calls, you will extend him the hospitality of the house." Gibbon, reminded that his nemesis was likely to become a frequent visitor, gagged on his chagrin. "Allow him to wander at will, and make sure you keep a sharp eye on him."

Somewhat assuaged, Gibbon moved toward the door. "Gibbon!" Lady Bligh held out an imperative hand. Gloomily, the butler extended the pilfered stick-pin. "I will see Mary now."

Silently, Livvy and the Earl watched Gibbon shamble to the door. With unusual patience, they awaited Dulcie's explanation of the proceedings. It was not forthcoming.

As Mary stepped into the room, her eye moved appreciatively to Lord Dorset. Livvy reflected that the cheerful little maid had left behind her country upbringing to fast become a connoisseur of gentlemen. The Earl winked.

"Come here, child." Dulcie grasped Mary's chin and forcibly diverted her attention. "I want you to do something for me."

"To be sure, my lady." In Dulcie's household, Mary was allowed to indulge her ambition to be an abigail, with Livvy a willing guinea pig; elsewhere, she could hope at best to be a scullery maid. Mary would do anything for the Baroness, a fine lady and an even kinder mistress, despite her painful habit of pinching Mary's rosy cheeks.

"I wish you to cultivate the habit of gossip." Mary's brown eyes widened.

"Gossip, is it?" She giggled. "That'll be no hardship, ma'am."

"I thought not." The Baroness frowned as Mary's glance wandered again toward the Earl. "I want you to find out all you can about the inhabitants of Arbuthnot House."

Mary abandoned her daydreams, which were of a most titillating variety. "Where the mad old woman lives?"

So pleased was Lady Bligh with this description of Luisa that she laughed aloud. "Precisely. Learn all you can about the mad old woman, Mary, and her immediate family, and I will be well pleased with you."

Mary grinned. When she married, she would have a tidy nest egg set aside, though she had not yet determined whom her lucky bridegroom was to be.

Dulcie's laughter ceased. "There must be no indication that you have any purpose in asking questions. Your curiosity is inspired only by the atrocious crime."

"I'm a ghoulish sort, I am," Mary agreed, more than a little delighted with this variation of her duties. "Don't worry, ma'am; everyone knows my tongue is loose at both ends."

Skillfully, she evaded Dulcie's quick fingers and made her exit.

Through the doorway came Culpepper, Lady Bligh's own abigail. She sniffed dourly. "I don't know what you're up to now," said Culpepper, with the frankness of one privileged to serve the Baroness for thirty years, "but I want no part of it."

"Tsk!" said Dulcie. "Culpepper, your attitude! If I could get along without you, I would turn you out."

Culpepper, a gaunt, black-clad crow, was not intimidated. "Just think what the Baron would say."

"What *would* he say?" inquired Lord Dorset, intrigued. The fifth Baron was not one to mince words.

"It doesn't signify." Dulcie waved an impatient hand. "If I recall correctly, I'm not speaking to him. Culpepper, I've a favor to beg. It concerns that watchman who is so besotted with you."

Culpepper, an unlikely object for infatuation, was visibly gratified. "Encroaching little mushroom," she remarked. "What about him?"

"I wish," said Lady Bligh cautiously, "for you to be conciliating." She forestalled an explosion. "If you are not, Dickon is likely to find himself in Newgate, and that would displease me greatly."

"I can't say I'm surprised. I knew he'd go his length one day." Lord Dorset, under Culpepper's stern regard, managed to look quite engagingly abashed. The basilisk stare returned to Dulcie. "Though I don't see what that oafish watchman can do about it."

"Very little, I imagine," the Baroness agreed, "but you, dear Culpepper, can accomplish a great deal. There is an excellent tavern across from Bow Street headquarters. I expect you to develop a strong craving for beefsteak and oyster sauce, washed down with stout."

Culpepper shuddered. "And to keep alert for whatever I may overhear? Very well." Martyred, she paused in the doorway. "Though I suspect it's you who'll be in Newgate, my lady, and at no far future date!"

Lady Bligh closed the door firmly behind her. "Now for you." She observed her nephew, engrossed in spinning an ornate quizzing-glass. An angry scar slashed the back of his well-shaped hand. "Dickon, I expect you to conduct yourself absolutely normally. You will follow your usual pursuits, but will refrain from either drinking hard or playing deep. You will, in short, do nothing to add credence to your part in this thing."

"Did I not know you better, Aunt, I would suspect you of seeking to reform my way of life."

"Bah!" retorted the Baroness. "I haven't the least interest in your fancy-pieces or even your monstrous wagers." Her delicate nostrils twitched. "I'm not one to spoil sport, Dickon, nor have I any desire to interfere in your debaucheries—it is a way of life to which you are admirably suited."

"Furthermore," murmured Livvy, "Lord Dorset's redemption would prove an arduous, perhaps impossible, task."

"And a thankless one." Dickon was unruffled. "Dulcie, it appears that your companion does not think well of me."

"Lavender," snapped Lady Bligh, "is most discerning." A dainty foot tapped the floor. "Her attitude, however, must speedily change."

Livvy looked up. "It must? I don't agree."

"I pray, Lavender, that you will not prove difficult." Dulcie's tone was sharp. "There are various matters in which I will require your assistance."

Livvy's cheeks burned. Never had she been more forcibly reminded of her status. "I will, of course, do as you say."

"Your part will be the most difficult." Lady Bligh scrutinized her companion, clad in a modest high-waisted yellow gown that boasted only a single flounce. "But there is no one else whom I can send."

Livvy was stricken. "You're sending me away?" Her heart sank to her toes.

"Isn't this a trifle extreme?" The Earl raised his quizzing-glass. "She isn't lively, or of a particularly pleasing disposition, but she seems to suit you well enough."

"I hardly think," said Livvy, goaded, "that your character is so exemplary that it entitles you to comment on mine!"

The Baroness sighed and moved to a rosewood sideboard, with cupboards below, lined with brass inlay with a honeysuckle motif. "Stop it, both of you, and consider our predicament. This incessant quibbling will speedily ruin my plans. Livvy is going briefly as a servant to Arbuthnot House, where she will employ the alias of Primrose." She raised a glass to her lips, then paused motionless. Livvy and the Earl exchanged a puzzled glance.

Dulcie drained the goblet. "Listen carefully; Crump will soon be here." The dark eyes pinned Dickon to his chair. "I have seen fit to provide you with an alibi, and beg that you will not overset my efforts."

"Oh?" Lord Dorset was courteous. "Where did I pass the crucial time?"

"You were trysting with Lavender." Lady Bligh ignored her companion's indignant gasp. "I think that I should tell you that the pair of you are about to become officially betrothed."

Crump paused on the threshold of the Grand Saloon. Tall windows, draped with heavily looped velvet, were thematically linked to doors with pediments and carved architraves. Married to this architectural magnificence was a gay Rococo ceiling. The marble fireplace was topped with Sicilian jasper, and embossed paper adorned the walls. Crump did not know that this was an excellent example of Palladian interior planning and an even more superb demonstration of the absent Baron's taste, which had also run unchecked in the Monk's

Parlor, the Dome, the Crypt and the Picture Room, where folding panels revealed ever more drawings and paintings, one behind the other. He only knew that such overwhelming grandeur somehow diminished him, leaving him unusually unsure.

Crump's reception at the Bligh residence had, today, been unexceptionable, although it had obviously galled Gibbon to be so polite. Crump wondered how long this forbearance would endure.

The Baroness moved forward and extended a gracious hand. "Mr. Crump, how kind of you to call. Sir John has told me I must apologize for my dreadful behavior." Her enchanting countenance was rueful. "Sometimes I am possessed by a spirit of deviltry, and I always heartily regret my pranks afterward, but then of course it is too late."

Crump was not disarmed by this ingenuous speech; instinct warned him to tread carefully. "No apology needed, Baroness," he said, glancing askance at her tea rose hair. "You had your little game with me, and I'm not one to begrudge a little fun." His auditors, in their turn, were put on guard by his mildness. Livvy stared nervously at the Runner's waistcoat, a startling striped creation of various conflicting hues.

"So this is the elusive Earl." Crump hooked his thumbs in the waistcoat, of which he was inordinately proud. Lord Dorset's expression was as bored as if he were observing the dancers at Almack's, an establishment from which he was permanently barred.

The Baroness fluttered around the Runner. "Before we discuss business," and her tone declared this of all things most tedious, "let me offer you refreshment." She was remarkably cheerful for one whose nearest and dearest faced censure and disgrace, if not worse.

Crump allowed himself to be enthroned in a straw-colored French chair and sampled the Madeira. "Very tolerable," he announced, unaware that Lord Bligh prided himself on the excellence of his cellars.

"I am glad it pleases you." The Baroness might have spent a portion of each day hobnobbing with the bourgeoisie. "How may we assist you, Mr. Crump?"

Crump was in no hurry to be on with his questioning. He thought of the dark, blind alleys of St. Giles and the East End, where families slept like rats on bundles of rags, with no hope of an honest living and no comfort except in drink. His task would have been easier if Lord Dorset was among the Bucks who gathered with thieves and cadgers in the back slums of the Holy Land, and who consequently made frequent appearances in Bow Street. Bringing in Lord Dorset was going to be a more delicate campaign, for the Earl, though profligate, was apparently no fool. Allowing the suspense to build, Crump sipped the Madeira, comparing it mentally with the rot-gut gin known widely as Blue Ruin.

His audience showed no tendency to squirm, but suffered the Runner's deliberations indulgently. Only the canary burst into nervous song, due not to Crump's silence but to the stealthy maneuvering of the orange cat, which approached a circular table, inlaid with double rows of brass, that sat parallel to the gilded cage. Disappointed by the coolness of his hosts, Crump set down his glass and brought out his battered Occurrence Book.

"Now," he said importantly, "let us proceed." His bright glance darted toward the saturnine Earl. "Suppose you tell me all you know about the deceased."

"All?" repeated Lord Dorset, horrified. "Have you so little consideration for poor Arabella's reputation?"

"Dickon!" The Baroness toyed with a Sèvres snuff box. "I am sure Mr. Crump does not wish to learn the more intimate details of your *affaire.*"

Livvy threw herself with gusto into her role. "Mr. Crump

may not," she interjected, noting the Runner's shocked face, "but *I* do. Pray continue, Dickon!"

"I am disillusioned," mourned Lord Dorset. "You told me once that such casual encounters would not weigh with you."

"Lavender is most magnanimous," Lady Bligh commented. "The perfect wife for a gazetted rake." She had the air of one bestowing a blessing. "How could you think that I would not approve, you foolish children?"

"Darling Livvy!" The Earl crossed the room in a few enthusiastic strides. Crump stared in amazement as Lord Dorset dropped to one knee and clasped the widow's hands. "There is no longer an obstacle in our way. Say you will be mine!"

Livvy struggled with an overwhelming urge to slap Dickon's mocking face. The Baroness beamed. "It does my heart good to see such happiness," she confided to Crump. "Lavender! You have not said yes."

"Oh." Livvy recollected their situation. "Of course."

"Such maidenly reserve!" applauded Lady Bligh as the Earl rose and brushed his knees. Crump thought Lavender remarkably passionless.

He was incorrect: Livvy seethed with emotion, but not of the gentler variety. The Earl lounged gracefully against the back of her chair. "We digress," she remarked. "Mr. Crump will have little interest in our personal affairs."

Crump, who in fact was planning to strike up an acquaintance with various members of Lady Bligh's household for just that purpose, did not correct her. "I'm sure I wish you happy, ma'am, but time is running short. Any information you can give me regarding Lady Arbuthnot will be most appreciated at Bow Street." He prepared to write. Were it not for the Chief Magistrate's insistence, Crump would not have called a second time on Lady Bligh, from whom he knew he would never learn anything that might prove detrimental to Lord Dorset. Sir

John claimed that the Baroness was an avid enthusiast for justice, but Sir John was clearly deluded.

"I am afraid I will be of little assistance." The Earl displayed regret. "While Arabella and I were, er, on intimate terms, I was not her only cavalier. In truth, I was little more than her cicisbeo." Crump snorted. The Earl did not fit comfortably into that category of gentleman privileged to escort a married woman, paying her assiduous but chaste attention, before returning her untouched to her husband. "Nor do I know who replaced me in her affections."

"You might guess, Dickon," the Baroness prompted. Crump was pleasantly surprised by this helpfulness. He retained strong doubts, however, about Sir John's assertion that Lady Bligh possessed a superior understanding.

"Of course I might." Lord Dorset passed a moment in thought, then named an extensive number of gentlemen who would be highly incensed by intimations of dalliance. Crump wrote rapidly. The list was long, and assured Dulcie and the Earl that the Runner's investigation would not proceed quickly.

"Arabella," the Baroness pointed out, "did have many enemies. But have you ruled out the possibility of simple robbery?"

"Not at all," the Runner lied. "It's the most likely possibility, but Bow Street doesn't like to take any chances with a case like this." He regarded the Earl, who gazed upon his beloved with besotted bliss. The lady did not seem to return the sentiment. Crump wisely concluded that this was to be, on the widow's part, a marriage of convenience.

"Let us begin," he said, "with the knife. Any notion, Earl, as to how it came to be in Lady Arbuthnot's chamber?"

Lord Dorset, among whose wide acquaintance could be found none who dared to address him so offhandedly, raised his brows. "Arabella used it as a letter opener." The derisive mouth twitched. "On one memorable occasion, she offered to use it on me."

"I see." The Earl and Lady Arbuthnot had enjoyed a most unusual relationship. "You wrote her a great many letters, did you?"

"In the first flush of passion." Lord Dorset contemplated a gleaming boot, then treated his interrogator to a roguish grin. "You might consider those letters to be garbage left over from my salad days, and as unpalatable as leftovers usually are."

"Shocking," murmured Livvy. This was not her opinion of Dickon's indiscretion, but of his metaphor.

"I cannot imagine," the Earl continued, "why Arabella kept the wretched notes, unless as a potential source of blackmail."

"I doubt," interrupted the Baroness, "that even Arabella would dare publish her memoirs. Continue, Mr. Crump."

Crump did not resent this waste of his valuable time. The details gleaned from these less than impartial informants were enlightening indeed. "Now, guv'nor, if you'd just tell me where you were on the night of the crime."

"Mr. Crump!" Lady Bligh was aghast. "This sounds positively ominous!"

"It's standard procedure, ma'am." Crump thought of the Chief Magistrate's anger were the Baroness to go off in another of her hey-go-mad humors, and sought hastily to dispel her unease. "We ask as many questions as we can of people likely to know something useful." He brandished the little notebook. "It's all right here: marks on the body and the clothing; statements other people made on the subject. Then we put it all together and presto!" He snapped his fingers. "The guilty party, do you see?"

"I do." Lady Bligh was extraordinarily contemplative. The canary's squawks crescendoed and Lord Dorset stretched out a careless arm to intercept Casanova in mid-pounce. As Livvy scrambled to catch the teetering flower vase, Dickon dropped the hissing cat in his aunt's lap, where it crouched malevolently. If the Baroness noticed Crump's instinctive withdrawal, she refrained from comment.

"On the night in question," Livvy volunteered, with the determination of one who wished to hang, "Lord Dorset was with me." She participated in this charade not for Dickon, but for Dulcie's sake. For all Livvy cared, the Earl might spend the remainder of his days incarcerated in some dark, dank, and, preferably, distant tower.

"Darling!" ejaculated Lord Dorset. "Your courage unmans me."

"I trust not permanently," the Baroness remarked. "Lavender, you are a constant surprise."

Livvy's blush was masterful. "Sometimes," she confessed, "I even startle myself." Bravely, she faced Crump. "Surely you see that Lord Dorset must be free of any blame."

"He is a fortunate man." Crump revised his opinion of Livvy: she was pluck to the backbone.

"I am," the Earl agreed. "I think we should send the announcement of our betrothal to the newspapers without delay."

"Aren't you being," Livvy inquired weakly, "a trifle precipitate?"

"Nonsense!" interrupted the Baroness, smiling serenely as Lord Dorset dropped a reassuring kiss upon his beloved's brow. "Surely, Lavender, you do not propose to make poor Dickon wait?"

Casanova shifted positions and Crump started nervously. The damned cat looked uncommonly ready to pounce. "Do you mind telling me exactly where this assignation took place?"

"Mr. Crump!" The Baroness was shocked.

"It's all right, Dulcie." Lavender, mortified, twisted a blue black curl. "We attended a Vauxhall masquerade."

"Vauxhall!" Lady Bligh had recourse to her hartshorn. The pleasure gardens, with their pavilions and gardens, temples and cascades, were no fit place for a gentlewoman, particularly on masquerade nights when a thousand lamps illuminated the long avenue of trees and musicians performed in the orchestra pavilion, and the most well-brought-up of ladies might be tempted to abandon both principle and decorum.

"And I, Mr. Crump," said the Baroness, recovering herself, "was dining with the Prince Regent on the night in question, at Carlton House. The King is unwell once again. His latest delusion is that all marriages have been dissolved." Her smile was kind. "We were served with chilled champagne, and fruit from silver platters, by an attendant clad in a complete suit of ancient armor. He must have been most uncomfortable, poor man. Walter Scott was also in attendance. I am sure he will vouch for me."

Crump imagined the consequences were he to attempt to verify her statement, and hastened to assure Lady Bligh that he did not doubt her word. Carlton House, where the Regent surrounded himself with an unusual assemblage of odd individuals who pandered to his tastes, lay at the center of the fashionable world. Crump had once received a handsome fee for guarding the Royal Prince during a spectacular fête, and had more appreciation for a public execution than for the remarkable blend of talent and wit, buffoonery and obstinacy, that was the uninhibited First Gentleman. He thought it a pity that the Regent's appetite for music and dancing and amorous adventure was not balanced by a passion for judicious government.

"Lavender," said the Baroness, "you are looking quite pale. You must not fret over Dickon. Like Casanova, he will always land on his feet."

"I trust," retorted Livvy, "that, also like Casanova, he will no longer spend the greater portion of his time in pursuit of pretty songbirds!"

"An, no," the Earl replied, his scarred hand resting heavily at the nape of her neck. "I have reformed."

For the first time, Livvy considered the precariousness of her position, and Lord Dorset's reaction should she betray him. The thought made her shudder. There was no question but that Dickon would have his revenge.

"I am glad to hear you say so," Lady Bligh remarked.

"But of course!" The Earl's dissipated countenance was virtuous. "What is it they say about a bird in the hand?" He smiled upon his newly acquired fiancée, whose expression was mutinous.

Crump could not have later said precisely how it happened, but one moment he was innocently observing a sentimental scene, and the next he was an unwilling participant in a most displeasing fray. Lady Bligh shrieked as Casanova leapt snarling from her lap to land on Crump's shoulder. Claws dug into his coat, a nasty hiss sounded in his ear. Crump leaped quickly to his feet, but the animal refused to be dislodged.

"Dear heaven!" cried Lavender, but Dulcie's meaningful frown anchored her firmly to her chair. Calypso twittered madly as Lord Dorset cautiously approached the combatants. Had Crump been calmer, he might have found it surprising that so famed a sportsman would treat a simple house cat, albeit of a gigantic order, with such excessive care. But Crump, in terror of his life, had closed his eyes in prayer. A rough tongue began to inspect his ear. Convinced that he was to be devoured alive in Lady Bligh's Grand Saloon, Crump embarked upon a manic dance.

The Baroness rose and, with great presence of mind, poured the remainder of the Madeira over her obedient pet. Casanova, orange fur abristle, stalked majestically from the battlefield. His victory had never been in doubt.

"Poor, poor man," murmured Lady Bligh, ineffectually brushing droplets of Madeira from Crump's coat. The Runner declined her aid and, sadly deflated, took quick leave of the home of the Barons Bligh.

As the doors closed behind him, the Baroness turned to gaze benignly upon her co-conspirators, neither of whom appeared particularly gratified by the role he had been called upon to play. "Such a droll little troll is our Mr. Crump." Her serenity was sublime. "Tonight, Casanova shall dine upon beefsteak and cream."

Livvy, considering the treatment that the Runner had received at Dulcie's hands, thought it far more likely that Dickon would dine on starvation rations of water and mouldy bread, and at no far distant date. The notion was quite delightful. Livvy could not know that Crump's tattered Occurrence Book, which many a lawbreaker would have paid a king's ransom to possess, now nestled most snugly in a hidden pocket of Lady Bligh's stylish red gown.

Chapter Five

LIVVY HAD DISCOVERED within herself a hitherto unsuspected flair for make-believe. Oppressed by Sir William's flowery compliments, and his mother's malevolent abuse, Livvy took refuge in riotous imagination, even envisioning Lord Dorset, that fiend in human form, placing his heart at her feet, there to be summarily trod upon. In contrast with her current drudgery, the role of an Earl's betrothed might not be unpleasant, even though it meant tolerating a fiancé as aggravating as Dickon. Such flights of fancy were not to be taken seriously, of course, but they were Livvy's only escape from the brooding, malignant atmosphere of Arbuthnot House. With a dreadful grimace, she removed a cobweb from her path, nearly upending the tray she was carrying to Louisa. On her way, however, she found occasion to stop outside the library door.

It was not to be supposed that Livvy was the sort of inquisitive female who would blithely poke and pry; indeed, were it not for the fact that she was anxious to speedily fulfill her mission and take her leave of Arbuthnot House, and the further circumstance that she heard Crump's unmistakable amiable tones, she would never have stooped to eavesdropping. But, after a severe struggle with her conscience, and a harried inspection of the deserted hallway, stoop she did, applying one lavender eye to the door's keyhole.

Crump, who twirled a gilt-headed baton, stood at a window draped with badly worn damask, looking down at the street. The Runner was not in the most pleasant of moods, having spent the previous evening in a Covent Garden gin shop where one could become drunk for a penny and dead drunk for two. So considerate was the establishment that it provided free beds of straw on which the clientele might sleep off the harrowing effects of Madame Geneva and Strip-me-naked; and, while Crump had not been reduced to such ignominy, he had encountered considerable difficulty in finding his way home. He turned and narrowly avoided collision with a set of library steps, earning Sir William's unvoiced scorn.

Crump cleared his throat. "I've come upon a very painful errand, sir," he said. "Sorry as I am to intrude in your time of sorrow."

With a creak of rigid corsets, Sir William waved a fleshy hand. "Never mind all that." Unlike the Prince Regent, upon whom he modeled himself, the Colonel was neither graceful nor charming, easy nor urbane. "You've come about my missing papers; well, get on with it!"

"Papers?" Crump was taken aback.

"Yes, papers!" Sir William fulminated. "Are your wits wandering, man?" A thought struck him, belatedly. "You're from Bow Street, ain't you?" Somewhat bewildered, Crump admitted the truth of this. "Then you're here about the papers that are missing from my library."

"Valuable papers?" inquired Crump, with a twinge of avarice.

For some strange reason, Sir William exhibited unease. "Not particularly—personal matters. You know how it is."

"Are these papers connected with the sad events that occurred recently on these premises?" Crump knew only that the Quality were full of whims and oddities.

"No, no!" Sir William might have been speaking to a dim-witted two-year-old. "They disappeared at a later date, and from this very desk." It was a handsome piece, ornamented with a brass gallery, with pigeonholes ranged in the form of a shallow horseshoe.

"Then," Crump retorted, indignant at being mistaken for one of sufficiently lowly stature to deal with worthless papers that were doubtless just misplaced, "they're no concern of mine!"

Sir William regarded his visitor belligerently. "If you're not here about the papers," he demanded, "why the devil *are* you here?"

"I'm from Bow Street, like I said." Crump added Sir William to his extensive list of those he'd like to see committed to Newgate to await an unspecified but terrible fate, a roster currently headed by Lord Dorset. "The name is Crump."

Sir William wilted visibly. "A Runner?" he inquired cautiously.

Crump was not unused to this reaction, and most edifying it was. "Aye." If he swaggered slightly, it was forgivable. "I'd like some information, guv'nor, about the unfortunately deceased."

Sir William looked briefly blank, then understanding dawned. "Arabella! I told your superiors all they need to know when I reported the crime. There is nothing further to discuss."

It became clear to Crump that Sir William was of a limited intellect. "Afraid you have no choice, guv'nor. Unless, that is, you wish to accompany me to Bow Street headquarters and talk to the Chief Magistrate." He hooked his thumbs in his mustard-colored waistcoat. "Take your pick, Sir William. I'm sure it makes no difference to me."

Sir William appeared unhappy at having the situation made so plain. There was no doubt that he was greatly affected by his wife's untimely end; his watery gray eyes were bloodshot, his ample flesh an unhealthy hue. "Get on with it," he repeated unappreciatively. "I'm a busy man."

Crump drew forth his Occurrence Book, which had vanished only to innocently reappear atop a cluttered table in Crump's untidy room, an event that had led the Runner to disavow all alcoholic beverages save a dog's nose, a relatively innocuous concoction of warm porter, moist sugar, gin and nutmeg. It was not a resolution that he'd kept long. "First I must tell you that we've not yet found any trace of Lady Arabella's jewels."

Sir William turned his head, no small feat considering the high points of his stiffly starched collar, and glowered at his visitor. "You're not very eager to earn five hundred Yellow Boys!" In the hallway, Livvy gasped at the size of this reward. She wondered cynically if Sir William were more concerned with the entrapment of his wife's killer, or the return of her jewels.

Crump was, in fact, as eager to find the jewels as was Sir William. Crump's nocturnal excursions were not, as they might appear, mere debauchery; nor had he any particular professional interest in the mollishers who sluiced their throats with jackey, or the young pleasure-seeking bucks of the town who woke to find their pockets picked and their breeches gone. In regard to the missing jewels, however, his extensive inquiries had come to naught.

Overlooking Sir William's annoyance, he went on calmly. "That's as may be," he replied, "but before Bow Street returns those sparklers, you and I need to have a heart-to-heart talk."

Sir William's agitation grew. "Talk?" he blustered. "What about? I'm sure I told Sir John all he needs to know!"

So extreme was this reaction that Crump immediately smelled a rat. "Not all." He was extremely bland. "It has come to our attention that you quarrelled with your wife on the night that she was, er, called to her eternal rest."

Sir William was so startled that the vast array of fobs and seals and pins displayed on his well-corseted chest wriggled frantically. "Nonsense! It was a mere disagreement, nothing more!" He assayed a weakly conspiratorial smile. "I'm sure I needn't tell you how these things are, eh, Mr. Crump?"

"I'm afraid," replied the Runner, intent on his quarry, "that you do. Bow Street is most particular about these small details."

Sir William rose abruptly and threw open a window. Clad in a blue coat, crimson waistcoat and canary pantaloons, he resembled nothing so much as a corpulent pouter pigeon. "Deuced close in here!"

It was true that the library was permeated with a strange odor—a mixture of bandoline, perfume and the particularly pungent scent of tobacco that clung to Crump's small person—but the Runner was not to be distracted. "The quarrel, guv'nor?" he prompted. "If you please."

Sir William raised empty hands in a gesture of resignation. "It is a trifle awkward," he sighed. "There is no use trying to wrap it up in clean linen, I suppose." He sat again at his desk, the only pristine area in an otherwise chaotic room, and surveyed his visitor intently. "May I trust you to keep a still tongue in your head?"

"Mum as an oyster!" retorted the Runner, and awaited enlightenment.

Sir William deliberated. "My wife," he said at length, "was much younger than I, and with a taste for gaiety." He was morose. "I was warned—but that's neither here or there. In a nutshell, I soon found that Arabella's interests did not march with mine."

"Ah." Crump exhibited spurious sympathy. According to gossip, Lady Arbuthnot had no sooner become a bride that she'd embarked upon an all-out campaign to plant the antlers on her bridegroom's florid brow.

"It is the way of the world." Sir William sighed heavily. "I tell you in strictest confidence, Crump, that my wife's behavior was not as circumspect as it should have been."

"Ah!" Had Crump not evolved a habit of emotional detachment, he might have pitied this unhappy man. It was Sir William's misfortune to triumph at nothing, even matrimony; vaunting ambition prompted him to spread himself too thin, if such a phrase could be applied to one of such remarkable girth. He excelled not at equestrianism, as did Lord Petersham, Tommy Onslaw, and Sir John Lade; nor in wit, as did Sidney Smith and Luttrell; nor even at gastronomy, a field dominated by Lord Sefton.

"In a word, she was unfaithful to me." Sir William toyed with thick brown side whiskers, which owed their luxuriant appearance to the judicious application of artificial hairpieces. "I taxed her with it, and she immediately got on her high ropes." He appeared to be in the throes of a vast melancholy. "Are you a married man, Crump?"

The Runner was indignant. "Och, I'm too peevy a cove to be caught in a parson's mousetrap!" He recalled the conversation to its original purpose. "So you confronted your wife with her infidelity and a quarrel ensued. What then, guv'nor?"

"There's nothing worse," Sir William commented with feeling, "than a woman in the sullens." He shuddered, an act that made the sagging flesh beneath his chin wobble most disgustingly. "I tell you, they can make life damned uncomfortable."

The pitfalls of Society were many, including vice, profligacy, and extravagance. Crump didn't imagine that Lady Arbuthnot had avoided a single snare. "I take it that your wife refused to give up Lord Dorset?"

Sir William underwent a startling transformation. "Dorset!" His pudgy visage was suffused with color; his eyes threatened to pop out of his head. "Prove that Dorset killed my wife and you shall have *seven* hundred Yellow Boys!"

Even Crump's practiced poise deserted him at this staggering offer, but he knew how ephemeral were the promises of the Quality. "You wouldn't be," he inquired jovially, "trying to bribe a Bow Street officer? I must tell you that's a very serious offense."

Sir William, too, made a fast recovery. "You misunderstood," he said, and dropped his head into his hands. "I want my wife's murderer caught, and to the devil with the cost!"

"Trust Bow Street," Crump replied, without real sympathy. Sir William, whether driving in his racy curricle or mourning his dead wife, remained only a figure of fun. "It will be attended to. Everyone connected with your wife is being closely investigated." His smile was not pleasant. "Very closely indeed."

"I loved my wife." Grim-faced, Sir William might have been confessing to a cardinal sin. "Dorset killed her as sure as I'm sitting here." Crump made soothing noises but Sir William pounded the desk with a vigor that made Livvy, still crouched in the hallway, start nervously. "I tell you, Crump, with or without Bow Street's help, I'll see the villain hang!"

Livvy, whose brief stay at Arbuthnot House had brought her into entirely too much contact with Sir William, could stomach no more. She rose, wincing at the protest of cramped muscles, and stole silently away.

* * *

It was nearing nine o'clock, and a solid stream of carriages reached from Carleton House to the top of Bond Street. The Prince Regent hosted a fete with as much élan as he gave away his heart, an item proferred on many occasions with veritable barrages of *billets-doux,* exchanges of hair, mementoes and trinkets, protestations of undying affection, and hints of an unlikely marriage ceremony. All the Quality were there, and each waited, patiently or impatiently, for his or her coach to approach the doors of Carleton House.

"I hear," said Lady Bligh, inclining her sea green head to the Russian Ambassador and his wife, whose carriage stood nearby, "that nearly two thousand invitations were extended to this affair." Lord Dorset growled. "Shame, Dickon!" protested the Baroness, albeit insincerely. "Can you not drum up a little more enthusiasm? After all, it is no small mark of favor to be recognized despite your current unfortunate situation. The world will take it to mean that Prinny is convinced of your innocence."

Judging from the impatient expression on his haughty features, Dickon regarded this royal vindication with no particular joy. "*Not a fatter fish than he,*" quoth the Earl, "*flounders round the polar sea!*"

"Tsk!" Thus the Baroness disposed of Percy Shelley's efforts. "Do strive for a more pleasant expression, Dickon; we shall be the cynosure of all eyes." Clad properly for so momentous an occasion, Lord Dorset wore a coat and breeches of claret velvet, a frilled shirt, and Florentine waistcoat. He also wore a savage scowl.

Dulcie ignored her nephew's silence, and bestowed a tolerant nod upon Mr. Romeo Coates, a wealthy Tulip of Fashion who possessed a fine diamond collection. The Earl, less broadminded, observed the Tulip's carriage, shaped like a kettledrum and drawn by white horses, upon which was prominently displayed a large brazen cock and the equally brazen motto, "While I live I'll crow." Stung by the Earl's sneer, Mr. Coates reflected that he, for one, would not be the least displeased if Dorset were to hang.

Finally they drew up to the doors of Carleton House and the Baroness alit, presenting a perfect illustration of vain and empty-headed frivolity. "What a marvelous era we live in," she remarked, taking firm hold of Dickon's muscular arm and steering him relentlessly through the courtyard where, in full State regalia, the band of the Guards played. "Think, Dickon! Catalini, Bianchi and Naldi are singing opera; Edmund Kean is acting at Drury Lane." They were received in the octagon-shaped hallway by members of the Prince's household.

"And Byron," the Earl observed a limping, aloof individual with dishevelled curls and a rapt expression, "dines on vinegar and potatoes while Prinny, over cherry brandy, concocts new and grandiose building schemes to transform London into a city equal in splendor to Imperial Rome!" His expression lightened as he regarded his aunt, resplendent in a trained evening dress of lilac silk open in front to expose a decorative petticoat edged with silver fringe and decorated with festoons of green bulrushes tied with silver cords and tassels. Atop her green curls was an elaborate headdress of pearls, amethyst and jade, surmounted by seven lilac-tinted ostrich plumes. "Confess, Dulcie! What secret motive prompted you to drag me here?"

"I considered an evening at Carleton House might prove amusing." The Baroness was bland as custard. They passed down to a suite of rooms on the ground floor, along a large hall hung with Dutch paintings, and into a library. Dulcie's dark eyes became severe. "I cannot think where you came by this extraordinarily disobliging nature."

"Can you not?" The Earl's gaze rested upon a bookcase, in the Gothic style, enlivened with buhl cabinets and miniature sculptures and triumphal arches. "Odd, since you have repeatedly observed that my obstinacy is strongly reminiscent of Max."

"Not obstinate," amended the Baroness, "but stubborn as a jackass!" She smiled sweetly at various curious bystanders, and whisked her nephew into the golden drawing room, where heavily gilded Corinthian pillars were cleverly arranged. "I refer, of course, not to you, but to Bat."

"Of course." The fifth Baron Bligh's unflattering nickname combined his tendency toward flight with his resemblance, in certain more ferocious moods, to Attila the Hun. "Have you received word recently from my uncle?"

"Ah, yes. He has been to Palmyra, the ruined city of Queen Zenobe, where only a handful of European men had previously been seen." An unfathomable gleam appeared in Dulcie's eye. "Accompanying him were seventy Arabs, Bedouin chieftains with ostrich feathers decorating their lances, and twenty-two camels loaded with stores. Thus far fortune continues to smile on Bat, a most regrettable circumstance, since there is no doubt that he deserves, at the very least, to be boiled in oil!"

Lord Dorset's humor was lightening in leaps and bounds. They passed through a small bow room, hung with more Dutch pictures, into a dining room with black and gold doors, scarlet-upholstered furniture, and a ceiling painted to represent a summer sky. "May I inquire what Max has done to incur such grave displeasure?"

"You may not." The Baroness, whose ensemble clashed shockingly with the décor, led the way into a Gothic conservatory that was designed like a cathedral with a nave and two aisles. "The Stanhope woman reached Palmyra before him, and left her name carved in a conspicuous spot on the ruins."

The Earl quite properly vouchsafed no comment. His uncle's friendship with Lady Hester Stanhope, though of long standing, was free of any amorous intent on the part of either party, a fact which Dulcie deplored as unnatural. Dickon's harsh features relaxed as he contemplated the career of a fellow adventurer. There were blots aplenty on the Bligh escutcheon, but the fifth Baron called to mind one distant ancestress who had shared a brief, but dizzying, adventure with a handsome Romany who had come on a horse-thieving expedition, but pillaged the lady of the establishment instead. Long suppressed and much diluted, the profane gipsy blood had resurfaced, tenfold in potency, in Maximilian Bonaventure Bligh.

Hexagonal lanterns hung from the points of the arches. Prinny, clad in his heavily embroidered Field Marshall's uniform, embellished with a magnificent aigrette and the garter star, dominated the huge chamber, not by size alone but by force of personality. "We will be besieged with questions regarding your fiancée," murmured the Baroness thoughtfully, "since the announcement has appeared. I think it best to say she is indisposed."

"Is she?" inquired Dickon, more interested in the stained glass windows that bore the arms of England's various sovereigns than in Livvy's well-being.

"I trust not." Lady Bligh tapped an elegant foot in time with music that issued from another room. "Although if Luisa means to feed her on black pudding, she may soon be. No, I simply mean that no one must discover that Lavender is at Arbuthnot House, where she is masquerading under the name of Primrose."

Dulcie walked on, drawing Dickon along into the gardens, where a long covered walk, erected for the occasion, was decorated with flowers and mirrors. "The devil!" he protested. "What are you up to, Dulcie? Who are you looking for?"

The Baroness adjusted her headdress, which had a tendency to slip to one side. "No one at all, dear Dickon. It is a pity that you possess such a suspicious mind." Her glance was sympathetic. "I daresay it must be quite uncomfortable."

Lord Dorset's mouth twitched. "Don't be thinking," his aunt

added, with startling accuracy, "to abandon me here so that you may indulge in less respectable pursuits. It will not harm you in the least to spend one evening as behooves a gentleman—and, in the eyes of Bow Street, it may do you a great deal of good!"

The Earl glanced around him, as if expecting to encounter Crump's genial blue orbs, but Crump was not one of the Runners assigned to this affair. "Rumor has it," he remarked, "that you are growing damned familiar with Bow Street's Chief Magistrate."

"Rumor also has it," Dulcie retorted, "that you murdered Arabella and made off with her jewels!" Having put her nephew most firmly in his place, she smiled serenely. "Take a lesson from this, Dickon, and henceforth believe not all you hear." The Earl, who habitually ignored all the titillating *on-dits* that flew about the town, a tendency perhaps developed in self-defense since a great deal of that scurrilous gossip concerned him, looked even more saturnine.

It was not to be supposed that Lord Dorset and his aunt passed unremarked through the lordly and celebrated crowd. Heads turned to follow their progress; behind exquisite fans and long white kid gloves, speculation flowed like wine. The *ton* had reached no conclusion concerning Lady Arabella Arbuthnot's abrupt departure from this life, but it was generally conceded that the brusque and impatient Lord Dorset was all too capable of committing the foul deed. Dickon's partiality for loose women and fast company was recalled and zestfully discussed. "Poor Lavender," murmured the Baroness, apropos of nothing at all.

"Poor?" repeated the Earl. "On the contrary, your companion is to be envied. She has a comfortable position and duties that can hardly be considered onerous, coupled with what I'm sure is an overly generous wage."

Lilac plumes quivered wrathfully. "Lavender," Lady Bligh

snapped, "is beyond price! May I remind you, Dickon, that you are speaking of your betrothed?"

"You may not," replied Lord Dorset bluntly. "If you had sought to do so, you could not have shackled me to anyone less to my taste, or to anyone less suitable."

"Fiddlesticks!" Dulcie was preoccupied. "I do not consider Lavender ineligible. Had I set myself to the task, I could have done much worse by you." Her attention was focused on a couple who approached from the gardens. "You are merely piqued that Lavender does not approve of you."

"Humbug!" ejaculated the Earl, with loathing. This expletive was not inspired by his aunt's companion but by the Exquisite who minced toward them. Dickon had not yet recognized the lady who leaned heavily on the gentleman's languid arm.

Hubert Humboldt had all the earmarks of a fop. He was attired in the highest kick of fashion, in silk coat and breeches of midnight blue, a waistcoat with blue spots, pale pink stockings, and a cravat as ample as a tablecloth. Knots of ribbon sprouted from his knee. "Damned man-milliner!" growled Dickon.

Malicious dark eyes glittered in a face that might, in a man less ready to wield a wicked, wounding tongue, have been judged personable. The face was also adorned with sidewhiskers, a daring moustache, and a black silk patch. With a flourish, Dulcie's least-liked nephew kissed her hand.

"Hubert." Lady Bligh might have been dispassionately observing a particularly repulsive reptilian species. "We have not seen you for some time." This lapse did not appear to occasion any regret on Dulcie's part.

So superb was Hubert's self-possession that he exhibited neither wounded sensibilities or dismay. "I stand convicted of neglect." One hand, of a dazzling purity achieved through the application of enamel, touched brown curls arranged in that state of Machiavellian disorder known as the Windswept style. "How remiss of me! Poor Livvy will think me a fickle creature. I trust she does not nourish a broken heart?" Hubert's breath was scented with myrrh.

Lord Dorset was happy to deflate these pretensions. "You really should read the newspapers," he remarked. "I must inform you, cousin, that 'poor Livvy' has agreed to become my wife."

"I might remark," murmured Humbug, waving a highly scented cambric handkerchief, "upon the astonishment engendered in me by so shocking a *mésalliance*. However, I hold a high opinion of Livvy and shall leave such tittle-tattle to my peers. It signifies not to me, after all, if my noble cousin chooses to ally himself with a mere paid companion. Indeed, I am positively smitten with admiration—considering the *débâcle* of your first marriage!—for your bravery!"

"Brave Livvy, *I* should say," offered his companion, moving into view. The Countess Andrassy was a bronze-haired beauty, whose face was marred only by restless discontent. Shadows painted around her slanted eyes gave her a look of interesting exhaustion. "Whoever she may be."

While Lord Dorset struggled mightily for speech, it was left to the Baroness to greet his ex-wife. The scandal attendant upon the dissolution of their union—for divorce was uncommon, and this particular divorce had been outstandingly scurrilous—had for many a long day occupied Polite Society.

"Gwyneth," she stated, with a regal inclination of her head.

"I do not think," observed Hubert, "that the family is overjoyed at your reappearance, Gwyneth dear. Perhaps they will feel differently when you explain your return to London."

"I wouldn't," said Dulcie, "make book on it." Countess Andrassy observed the small fortune in amethysts and jade that was draped about Dulcie's elegant person, and controlled her temper. Lord Dorset, having regained control over his emotions, wore an indifferent mask.

"Aunt!" Hubert protested, with rancorous enjoyment. "It is a very moving tale."

"I'm sure it must be," Dorset remarked, with every indication of boredom. "Gwyneth was ever mistress of the storytelling art."

Emerald eyes flashed. "Ah, you're a fine one to talk, with your forays to the dens of vice and God knows what other depravities. I cannot trust myself to say more!" She rolled her eyes heavenward, as if a familiar figure might be perched, harp in hand, upon some passing cloud. "I haven't slept a wink since I heard of poor Arabella's sad end." For one so grievously stricken with nerves, Gwyneth looked remarkably robust in a dress of semi-transparent and clinging white gauze, striped with blue, that clearly revealed a Junoesque physique undisguised by even a single petticoat. Perched on her bronze curls was a cap of gold net. "Good God, I am so distracted I can say no more!"

"Then don't," advised the Earl.

Lady Bligh, who disapproved of the prevailing taste for semi-nudity, perhaps feeling that it was a practice that should be engaged in by no one but herself, interrupted with a hearty sneeze. "My dear," she remarked, adjusting her plumage, "you should have gone upon the stage." One ostrich plume caressed her unlined brow. "Pray state your reason for accosting us, and with a minimum of histrionics!" Highly entertained, Hubert offered Gwyneth his handkerchief.

"I hastened to England as soon as I heard," Gwyneth persisted, applying this article to her nose, to Hubert's shuddering dismay, "leaving my poor husband to fend for himself. I was sure that I would find that Dickon had been denounced to the Runners, and that my darling child had been turned over to some tyrant who would bully and mistreat him." She clasped her hands. "You can imagine a mother's dismay!"

"To be truthful," commented Dulcie, since both her nephews seemed to be bereft of speech, "I cannot. Your fears were groundless, Gwyneth; as you see, Dickon has not been taken into custody. Therefore, you may safely go away."

"I mean," Gwyneth said stubbornly, with a cautious glance at her ex-husband, "to see my son!" Dramatically, she sobbed. "It is most cruel and unnatural to keep him hidden away like some fairground freak!"

"Monstrous," agreed Lord Dorset, finding his voice, "if that were the case. It is not, however: Austin's company is denied to no one but you."

"Yes, to me, his mother!" Hubert looked faintly nauseated as the handkerchief was next applied to the emerald eyes. "Heaven only knows how Austin must be suffering from the lack of his mother's love." Gwyneth treated her audience to a wistful smile. "We were such dear friends, my son and I, in happier days."

"I'd no notion of that," Lady Bligh remarked, interested. She met Gwyneth's hopeful gaze. "One truly *does* learn something new every day."

"I *will* see my son!" cried Gwyneth, with a remarkable recovery of animation. "You cannot deny me! It is a mother's right."

"Never!" announced Lord Dorset, with a vehemence that made Hubert wince and caused even Prinny's head to turn. The Regent gazed upon Dulcie with marked approval, a circumstance that caused several interested observers to recall his disagreeable taste for ladies of mature years. Although Lady Bligh could not by any stretch of the imagination be called grandmotherly, and despite her wonderfully youthful appearance, which a great many of her less fortunate contemporaries contemplated with sour chagrin, she was undeniably a great-aunt.

"Children!" The Baroness, as nonchalant as if royal admiration was only her due, shepherded the combatants toward a huge supper table, intended for only the principal guests, that extended through both the conservatory and dining room. "This discussion would best be put off until a more private moment." She turned on Hubert who gazed fascinated upon the silver fountain, complete with green moss flowers, fanciful bridges and gold and silver fish, which served as the table's centerpiece. Smartly, she pinched his arm. "Coxcomb!" remarked Lady Bligh. "A word to the wise, nephew: stay away from the bloodsuckers."

Hubert looked startled, as well he might, for what could his aunt know of the moneylenders who battened on those unfortunate enough to lack sufficient funds? It was a condition with which Hubert was well acquainted, for money ran through his well-tended fingers like water through a sieve. "Damned if I know," Hubert muttered, "how you know the things you do."

"Have I impressed you?" inquired Dulcie, with an unfriendly glance. Hubert's slender build made him appear deceptively effeminate. "Had I but the time, I could tell you a great deal more."

Hubert quickly turned her attention to his rival, Dickon. "Who would have thought," he said fastidiously, "that a connection of mine could turn gallows-bait?"

"I knew it all along," commented Gwyneth smugly, ready to resume the quarrel. "How like Dickon to bungle the thing."

"I believe," continued the Baroness, ignoring these intended diversions, "that there is a certain jeweler in Cranbourn Alley with whom you are not unacquainted, Humbug."

Hubert's supercilious countenance darkened. "Hell and the devil confound it!" he exclaimed.

"Yes, yes," said Dulcie. "It's evident that I'm a knowing one. Tell me more about this jeweler, nephew!"

"I'd hoped you wouldn't find out." Hubert was sunk in gloom. "Oh, very well! Sir William Arbuthnot was also one of Hamlet's customers. I learned of it by accident, when I came upon him pledging his gold and silver plate." The Earl wore an arrested look, while Gwyneth stared wide eyed.

Lady Bligh idly twisted a sea green curl. "Playing deep, was he?" she mused. "This puts an entirely different light on the matter. No wonder William is so anxious to recover Arabella's jewels."

"I don't know about that," Hubert said, "but deep basset's been his ruin. Nor is this the first time he's fallen into the hands of a damned cent-per-cent, curse the bloodthirsty breed! Arabella was forever wasting the ready, you know, and William was hard pressed to raise the wind."

Lord Dorset exhibited little gratitude for Hubert's disclosures. "Humbug, too, has had deep dealings lately," he observed indifferently. "Perhaps you should warn him, Dulcie, not to follow William's path."

"Rot!" retorted Hubert. He smiled with a notable absence of warmth. "I have not yet been done up, nor do I expect to be."

"Having," murmured Dulcie, "unexpected resources at your disposal." With grace, she helped herself to snuff. "But I shall warn you anyway, Hubert: take care lest you meddle in matters that are none of your concern. You may speedily find yourself in the suds."

"Lud!" protested Hubert, wrenching his handkerchief from Gwyneth and applying it to his fevered brow. "You sound quite maternal, Dulcie. Can it be that you cherish a sneaking affection for me?"

"You delude yourself." The Baroness tilted her head, to the detriment of her headdress. "You are an irritating creature, but less foolish than you seem." The thoughtful gaze rested on Hubert's startled features, surely paler than the occasion warranted. "All in all, I think I would not care to see you hang."

So intrigued was the Earl by this statement, which implied that his cousin might share a fate with infamous cutthroats and common felons, that his vitriolic features were transformed. "Hubert!" One sardonic eye was applied to his ornate quizzing-glass. "This positively reeks of infamy." Hubert licked dry lips but offered no reply.

It was left to the Countess Andrassy to forestall the questions that hovered thick in the air. With a moan worthy of one doomed to walk the earth for time immeasurable, she sank senseless to the ground.

Chapter Six

"Speak one more word to him," Bertha hissed, "and I'll cut out your miserable tongue!"

Livvy was in a dilemma. There was no doubt that this homely, furious creature meant exactly what she said. "I am a servant in this house," Livvy protested, "just as you are. I cannot bid Sir William go to the devil, much as I might wish to do so!"

"Ah, but *do* you wish to do so, miss?" Bertha squinted balefully. "That's the heart of the matter, it seems to me."

Livvy absently rubbed her backside. "How am I to convince you?" Never had she sported so many bruises on various portions of her anatomy, souvenirs of Sir William's overtures, which invariably began with a hearty pinch. "To be blunt, Sir William is repugnant to me."

They stood in a plain boxed-in staircase that led to the kitchen and the lowest regions of Arbuthnot House. Bertha, scowling, stood with hands on hips, and Livvy hoped fervently that Lady Arabella's one-time abigail would not succumb to an urge to push her rival down the narrow stairs.

To Livvy's surprise, Bertha grinned. "He's a top-lofty clown, William is, and I can see why a lady like yourself would have no liking for him." The smile disappeared. "But he suits *me* well enough!"

Bertha, after Arabella's death, had found a new place: in Sir William's bed. This circumstance would have passed beneath Livvy's notice had not Sir William, led by his amatory success to envision himself a latter-day Don Juan, made it increasingly obvious that he was prepared to transfer his favors to his mother's new companion.

"He'll be casting sheep's eyes at you and making a great cake of himself as long as you remain in this house." Bertha was prepared to defend her position with tooth and nail. "I think, miss, that it would be wise of you to leave."

"But I cannot!" So menacing was Bertha's attitude that Livvy wondered if she was to be dispatched summarily to meet her Maker. "Believe me, Bertha, I would depart this house on the instant if only I could!"

"Why can't you?" Bertha was momentarily distracted from her murderous design. "Don't tell me you're devoted to that evil gorgon because I won't believe a word of it!"

Livvy grimaced. "Heavens, no! Madame Arbuthnot is the most unpleasant individual it has ever been my misfortune to know." She imagined Dickon's scathing, superior comments were she to turn craven and flee. "Nevertheless, there are reasons why I must stay, at least temporarily."

Bertha sniffed. "It sounds havey-cavey to me. You could find a position easy enough, especially with your connections."

"My connections?" Livvy was perplexed.

Bertha wore a sly look. "Why, that Baroness that sent you here. Seems that she could've done better by you, doesn't it? If I were you, I'd tell her so."

A vague notion, staggering in its impact, was forming in Livvy's head. "What do you know of Lady Bligh?"

"She's Lord Dorset's aunt, ain't she?" Blushing, Bertha fiddled with her cap.

"So you know Dickon," Livvy mused. "I should have thought of that. He was a frequent visitor here, was he not?"

"Yes, miss." Bertha was most demure. Livvy marvelled at Dickon's ability to arouse lecherous inclinations in even the most unlikely breast. "It's a pity; he was a fine figure of a man! William says they'll take him to the gallows and string him up as he deserves."

Livvy reached a momentous decision. "Bertha, I am going to confide in you." She grasped the abigail's arm. "Where can we talk privately?"

Bertha's eyes widened, but she led the way to the kitchens without protest. The large chamber was deserted and, considering the quality of the food served at Arbuthnot House, Livvy was not surprised. She moved across the flagged stone floor and stood before the fireplace. A variety of pots, pans, lids, small mops and jugs were arrayed on wooden shelves set in the recess made by the chimney breast. Thick dust attested that these articles were not often used.

Bertha drew a rickety chair to the kitchen table and sat down, propping both elbows on the wooden surface in disregard of bits of food and less wholesome things. "Let's have it! I don't have all day."

Livvy decided upon a dramatic approach. "I am here," she said, in suitably intriguing tones, "under false pretenses! I must tell you that I am not what I seem!"

"Fancy that!" Bertha nibbled on a chunk of overripe cheese.

"I am prepared to take you into my confidence," Livvy went on, "but you must promise to repeat no word of what I am about to say." She stole a glance at Bertha, who appeared adequately intrigued. "Not even to Sir William!"

"You're going a bit too fast, miss." Bertha squashed a maggot with her thumb. "What's in it for me?"

"My departure, as soon as my task is done." Queasy, Livvy leaned against a huge brown-painted dresser with shelves, cup hooks, drawers, and cupboards of a putrid yellow-green. "With your help, it may be accomplished speedily."

Bertha, having devoured the cheese, after dislodging its inhabitants, turned her attention to a hunk of stale bread. "I didn't reckon you for a clutch-fisted sort. A girl like me has to think of herself, for no one else will."

Livvy considered this quite likely; Bertha was hardly an appetizing lass. "I daresay I might be able to spare ten pounds."

"Paltry," pronounced Bertha, revealing herself as no novice to the arts of bribery.

"Very well, twenty-five." Livvy hoped her tone was sufficiently firm. With assumed nonchalance, she moved to the stone sink. It was as unsavory as the table, and Livvy quickly moved away. "I thought you wanted me to leave quickly? My task can be accomplished without your help, but it would take much longer."

Bertha licked her fingers, including the maggot-killing thumb. "I haven't said no."

"You haven't said yes, either," Livvy pointed out irritably. Her efforts at detection had been frustrated at every turn. Even the housemaid who had discovered the body had had little enough to say, merely bursting into hysterical sobs at the mention of Arabella's name. Judging from the state of Arbuthnot House, she also had little enough to do. "I can tell you no more until I have your word."

"Twenty-five pounds." Bertha clasped her hands across her stomach. "Very well, you have it." She leered. "Don't worry about William; he's not interested in what I *think*."

Livvy overlooked this crudity. "I am not a servant at all," she confided, "but Lord Dorset's fiancée!" She hoped she had not misread Bertha's character. "I have come here to do what I may to clear my beloved Dickon's name."

Bertha stared. "I would never have guessed! You don't seem the sort to take his fancy, but there's no telling about the gentlemen."

Sourly, Livvy contemplated this backward compliment. "How right you are, Bertha; they are truly an unpredictable lot."

"That's a kick in the teeth for Arabella!" Bertha laughed. "Lord Dorset played fast and loose with her ladyship while getting himself shackled to you. But there! I knew she wasn't worth a groat to him."

Livvy refrained from asking how Bertha had come to this conclusion, for she suspected she already knew. Lord Dorset had a damnably undiscriminating eye. "Then you'll help me, Bertha?"

"For twenty-five pounds," Bertha retorted cheerfully, "I'd send my own mother to jail. What do you want to know?"

Weak-kneed with success, Livvy sank into a chair. It occurred to her that she had no notion what she was to find out. "Tell me about Arabella," she said, trying to appear more confident than she felt.

"She was a queer one." Bertha drew patterns on the table's filthy surface. "Flirting with every man that came near and leading poor William a merry chase."

"When did Sir William first, er, take an interest in you?"

"Don't you go thinking *I* had anything to do with it!" Bertha leaned across the table, eyes snapping. "William was besotted with his wife and had no eyes for anyone else when she was around."

"I see." Livvy gingerly grasped a filth-encrusted knife and moved it out of the abigail's reach. "Isn't it a trifle odd that he should notice you so belatedly? You were Arabella's dresser; he must have seen you every day."

Bertha's indignation was replaced by an equally unsettling

smugness. "So he did, but I haven't been here over three months, miss. It takes some gentlemen a while to get up their nerve."

"Three months!" Livvy was dismayed. "I thought you were with Lady Arabella during her previous marriage."

Bertha shook her head and frowned. "That's a very fishy thing. She had an abigail who'd been with her for years, but when she married William, she turned the poor creature off without so much as a reference! That's an ungrateful way to act, if you ask me."

"Odd, indeed," murmured Livvy. "Have you any idea where the woman went?"

"None at all." Bertha grew coy. "But I imagine I could find out." Her glance was meaningful.

"Ten more pounds," Livvy prompted, as lavish with Lady Bligh's fortune as Lord Dorset was with his own.

"Done!" Thus inspired, Bertha became even more helpful. "There's something else, miss: Arabella was terrified of someone or something, sure as I'm sitting here. Many's the time I thought she was going to jump right out of her skin."

So intrigued was Livvy that she, too, leaned her elbows on the table. "Who, Bertha, who?"

"That's what I can't figure out." Bertha screwed up her features in unaccustomed thought. "It wasn't William or Lord Dorset, of that I'm sure."

"Luisa, perhaps?" If it was true that Lady Arabella had lived in utmost dread, her foul-tempered mama-in-law was the most likely source.

Bertha shook her head. "I think not. Her ladyship hated Madame, no doubt of that, but you don't deliberately provoke someone you're afraid of, and the two of them were always at it hammer and tongs."

Livvy jerked her elbows off the table and rose to pace the room. She paused near a cast-iron range, obviously never used, and contemplated an iron mantelpiece that held plates, candlesticks, and a large salt shaker, all liberally festooned with cobwebs. "When did all this begin?"

"A man came to see her ladyship about two months ago." Bertha was still engaged in tortuous thought. "I doubt he was a gentleman, for all his fancy dress. He didn't stay long but when he left, Lady Arabella looked like she'd seen a ghost. It was after that she became so queer, going off into the boughs if even a letter came."

"I wonder who he was." Livvy suspected she was being treated to a highly exaggerated account; Arabella had been far from the nervous sort of female who heard danger in every footfall.

"I've no notion," Bertha shrugged. "Her ladyship wasn't one for confidences."

An imperious bell pealed. "Madame," remarked Bertha, "will be wanting her brandy." She rose to fetch dusty bottles, which Livvy accepted cautiously. "I'll be seeing what else I can find out, miss, but the people in this house are a close-mouthed lot."

Of this, Livvy was only too aware. She paused in the doorway and turned. "Thank you for your help, Bertha. I am most grateful."

"No need for thanks," Bertha retorted, moving toward the larder in search of further sustenance. "Just pay up, like you said."

"What if I find out that Sir William was involved in his wife's death?" Belatedly, Livvy realized that she risked having her investigations ruined. "Have you thought of that?"

"I've thought of little else these past several days, and lay with a murderer I will not do." Bertha's expression was self-righteous. "A girl has to draw the line somewhere! If William is a murderer he'll find himself out in the cold, and without a kind word from me."

Livvy thought that Sir William, in such a case, would lose more than the company of his convenient. "And if not?"

Bertha flashed a saucy smile. "If not, miss, he'll find himself standing before a preacher, and in record time!"

Livvy mulled over these disclosures as she reluctantly mounted the stair. Bertha's ambitions were as absurd as they were grandiose, and hardly of a sort to find favor with Madame Arbuthnot, who ruled her son with an iron fist and a guilty whip. Sir William was never allowed to forget that he was responsible for the accident that left his mother imprisoned in her wheelchair. Cautiously, Livvy opened the drawing-room door. The chamber had all the benevolent atmosphere of a prison cell.

Like a magpie, Madame Arbuthnot squatted in her cluttered nest. Her flabby chin rested on her equally flabby chest, and rattling noises issued from her open mouth. Livvy tiptoed into the room, placed a brandy bottle on the table beside Luisa's chair, and cautiously settled onto the hard love seat. Madame's past and character were written on her face, and it surpassed anything a delicately nurtured English lady should have been expected to understand. Livvy wondered if Luisa's crippling accident had also twisted her mind. Were not the old woman a helpless invalid, she would have been capable of any villainy.

Luisa stirred and Livvy held her breath, only to release it when her formidable employer subsided once again into moist, unpleasant snores. Madame, who expected substantial returns from even her most meager investments, would not be pleased to find her paid companion idly taking her ease. It was Livvy's duty not only to provide a meek foil for Luisa's hectoring tongue, but to dress and undress her, a task that filled Livvy with revulsion. Even this was not the worst, for she also had to tend to her employer's most basic needs, emptying slops and rinsing the vessels with scalding water and turpentine. She folded reddened hands in her lap and pondered the eccentricities of fate. Her imprisonment at Arbuthnot House was as horrendous as any that might await the most hardened murderer, but she had committed no transgression of such magnitude to warrant subjection to Sir William's brutish advances and his mother's bullying ways.

"Caught you!" barked Luisa, causing Livvy's heart to stop. "Lazy good-for-nothing chit! I don't pay you to loll about like a lady of leisure!"

"I beg your pardon, ma'am," Livvy replied meekly. Surely the possessor of those beautiful golden eyes could not have been born a gruesome crone. "I only meant to be at hand in case you should wish me to perform some service for you."

"A likely tale!" Luisa reached for her bottle, one in a long succession of which even Livvy had lost count. Not yet prepared to face the day, Luisa was still clad in a gown and petticoat of once fine calico, now torn and stained. A Duke of York's nightcap hid her sparse gray hair. "A more worthless bag of bones I have yet to see."

Livvy suffered this slur in silence, for it was true that she'd grown even thinner during her sojourn at Arbuthnot House.

"No man would ever look twice at a female as scrawny as you," Luisa remarked, in fine fettle, "except my son, who'll chase anything in or out of skirts!" She leered. "Cat got your tongue, Primrose? I know quite well what goes on in my house."

Livvy, with difficulty, maintained her servile attitude. "I hope I know my place, ma'am." It was galling to take such abuse, and for the sake of a man she detested heartily.

"You don't blush, either," remarked her tormentor. "Hardened to impropriety, Primrose?" Luisa raised the bottle to her lips and drank, then passed the back of her hand across her brandy-splattered chin. "I'll wager it's not the first time you've been offered a slip on the shoulder by a handsome gentleman!"

"Sir William," Livvy replied, with lowered eyes, "has made no improper suggestions." She reflected upon the blindness of maternal love, which made a romantic figure of a man fit only to haunt one's dreams, like a hobgoblin.

"He will," retorted Sir William's fond parent. "What will you say then, Primrose? Will you agree to a tumble in the hay?"

"Certainly not!" Livvy would tolerate only so much, even for Lady Bligh. She reconsidered, and looked at the floor. "It sounds exceedingly uncomfortable."

Luisa threw back her head and laughed aloud. "So you *do* have spirit! I couldn't imagine Dulcie championing such a mawkish ninny as you appear to be." The amusement was abruptly gone. "Don't rely on your luck! If you cross me, girl, it'll be the worse for you."

Livvy didn't doubt the truth of this. "I beg pardon, ma'am, if I have presumed." Luisa would probably carry out a vicious vendetta with the greatest style.

"Bear in mind, pea-goose," Luisa had regained her good spirits, "that you're dependent on me." Yellow teeth bared in a smile. "It don't bother me a bit if William has his bit of fun with you, so you needn't worry about that! Although a scrawny thing like you could barely warm a man's bones."

"You misunderstand." Livvy quailed at the thought of being crushed in Sir William's fleshy and malodorous arms. "I am not of a promiscuous nature."

Luisa was interested. "Holding out for marriage? More fool, you!" Her bowed shoulders shook. "One thing's certain: my son will never marry a fubsy-faced old maid. Take care, Primrose, or you'll end up leading apes in hell!"

Livvy refrained from explaining that, no matter how unpleasant her marriage had been, her widowed state absolved her from the fate reserved for unhappy spinsters. Luisa sank into deep thought, raising and lowering her bottle with hypnotic regularity. Madame Arbuthnot was already more than a trifle pie-eyed.

"How," demanded Luisa, so abruptly that Livvy started, "do you know Dulcie Bligh?" It was a question that might have arisen sooner, had Luisa's mind not been pickled in brandy.

Livvy was prepared. "Lady Bligh has been very good to me." She had learned to lie like a trooper in but a few days' time. "She is my god-mama, you see."

Suspicion was written large on Luisa's haggard features. "Dulcie stand godmother to a puking squalling brat? Not likely, Primrose!"

"Is it not?" Livvy countered, interested. "The fact is, she did. I believe there were circumstances which indebted Lady Bligh to my mother."

To Livvy's mingled relief and surprise, Luisa accepted this Banbury tale. "Pulled Dulcie's coals out of the fire, I don't doubt!" She laughed maliciously. "You wouldn't be knowing it now, but Dulcie Bligh was quite a high-stepper in her day." The hooded eyes glittered. "Don't go getting notions into your head, Primrose! You won't be mollycoddled here."

Livvy, fascinated by these disclosures concerning the Baroness, was doomed to hear no more. "Fetch me another bottle!" Luisa demanded, and Livvy moved to the bread cupboard, an item that, like all others in Arbuthnot House, showed signs of long neglect. With newly acquired expertise, she removed the filthy cork.

"I hear my son had a visitor yesterday." Luisa fell upon the bottle as if with a virgin thirst. "Don't hover, nitwit! Sit down."

Livvy spoke around the nervous frog that had leaped into her throat. "I believe so, ma'am." Heaven only knew how Madame would react to the crime of eavesdropping.

"Did you see him?" Luisa demanded. The golden gaze was

intent. "You've got eyes and ears, Primrose! Who was this unexpected visitor?"

"I had but the merest glimpse of him, ma'am," Livvy temporized.

"So there *was* someone!" Madame was as uneasy as if she sat on thorns. "Was he young or old, short or tall? Did he present a rakish appearance, or seem an unsavory specimen of *hoi polloi?*" Her hands trembled, spilling brandy on the soiled gown.

Livvy had an odd notion that Luisa had a definite visitor in mind, perhaps the same mysterious caller who had so upset Arabella. "He was short," she replied, "and rather stout." An image of Crump sprang into her mind. "Beyond that, I could not say."

Luisa relaxed and lost her corpselike hue. "His purpose, Primrose, his purpose! Don't shilly-shally, wench, make a conjecture!"

"I'd guess he was from Bow Street, ma'am," Livvy obliged. "He had the look of a thief-taker." Perhaps now she would learn something of sufficient importance to justify the speedy removal of her mistreated person from Arbuthnot House.

"What would you know of thief-takers, Primrose? Have I been misled in your character?"

"It was a misunderstanding." Ruthlessly, Livvy blackened her reputation, spotless prior to acquaintance with Lady Bligh. "The Runner who apprehended me soon realized his error."

"Light fingered, are you?" inquired Luisa. "Things disappear with damned regularity in this house, but I'll know where to look the next time."

"I have never," Livvy protested indignantly, "done anything illegal, immoral, or even improper in all my life!" Or, she mused to herself, not until recently.

"Sweet Christ! What a dull stick you are. I could almost pity you, Primrose, you've no notion of what you've missed!" With sparkling eye, Luisa determined to investigate her companion's past. "Bow Street," she muttered. "So they've finally decided to make inquiries into Arabella's death, and high time it is!" Livvy held her breath. "But you know all about that, eh? Arabella's name will be on every tongue."

"It must have been a severe blow for Sir William." Livvy oozed false sympathy. "And for you, to lose your daughter-in-law so tragically."

Luisa snorted. "Balderdash! Bow Street should talk to *me!* If I was of a mind, I could outsing a canary." Livvy, with a pang of homesickness, wondered how Calypso fared in the absence of his protector.

Madame Arbuthnot cackled with evil glee. "Dulcie Bligh has trouble aplenty in store! Bow Street will soon enough learn that Arabella was trysting, on the night of her death, with Dulcie's rough diamond of a nephew!" She scrutinized Livvy severely. "What do you think of that, Primrose?"

"Shocking!" Livvy was wooden. "I am unacquainted with the gentleman."

"Best make haste," Luisa advised, "for he'll be the jailer's meat 'ere long!" The bottle was raised once again. "I'm not in my dotage yet, and I shall say no more! Poke your curious nose elsewhere, Primrose. You'll learn nothing from me."

Livvy bowed her head. She knew that a display of either curiosity or offense would arouse Luisa's suspicions. For one so addicted to the bottle, Madame Arbuthnot was at times remarkably astute.

Luisa, her brief gregariousness exhausted, relapsed into snores. There was only one course open to Livvy now, unless she was to reveal herself as a pigeon-hearted creature unable to fulfill her mission. With a heartfelt sigh, Livvy braced herself for Sir William, and a task that was both unpalatable and plain. As stealthy as a woodsman, she stole from the room.

Chapter Seven

THEY WERE GATHERED in Dulcie's private sitting room, more commonly known as The Hymeneal, created by the fifth Baron for his wife upon their return from a honeymoon spent in Greece and Rome. Lord and Lady Bligh were still remembered in those fair isles, most particularly for the occasion when the Baroness had, on a dare, splashed gaily through a fountain of antiquity. The Hymeneal, octagonal in form, was done in shades of black and white and gray. The ceiling was domed, with a fan design; dancing nymphs, winged sphinxes, gryphons and fantastic foliated beasts cavorted on wall panels framed in light moldings.

The Baroness sat at a writing desk with a rising top and fitted sidetrays. Two drawers were inset with Wedgwood plaques representing the Marriage of Cupid and Psyche, and a Sacrifice to Hymen. Scattered sheets of paper, crossed with bold writing, were piled upon the desk and strewn about the floor. Thoughtfully, Dulcie nibbled at her quill.

"Arabella's jewels," she mused, "have not made a reappearance. Why is that, Gibbon?"

The butler, dressed in the customary black that accentuated his pallor, stood as far as possible from the mischievous Mary. "If the thief has a glimmer of sense, he'll lay low. All a chap has to do is flash those sparklers and he'd be hobbled straightaway!"

"Hobbled, Gibbon?" inquired Lady Bligh.

"Taken up and committed for trial, my lady." Gibbon, delighted to thus display his expertise, appeared almost human. Mary listened attentively, while Culpepper looked both disapproving and resigned.

"Were you the thief, Gibbon, what would you do?" The Baroness rose to pace the marble floor. "Let us attempt to reason out this situation."

"I'd hop the twig and keep dubber mum'd until the heat died down," replied the butler promptly. He observed his employer's bewilderment. "I mean, my lady, that I'd depart the vicinity and keep my mouth shut until I could safely dispose of the contraband. Lady Arabella's jewels won't be easy to get rid of; they're widely known, and Bow Street is too interested in their whereabouts."

"More and more curious." Lady Bligh toyed with a chess set in jasper ware, the opposing sides black and white, that depicted famous actors playing *Macbeth.* Charles Kemble as Duncan, and Mrs. Siddons as Lady Macbeth, were the royals. "Are receivers of stolen goods so wary of thief-takers?"

Gibbon grimaced dreadfully. "Fences, my lady, are afraid of no man, but they'll only give a fraction of what something is worth at the best of times, and with Bow Street keeping such a sharp watch it becomes a chancy thing. The stones have to be reset and the metal melted down before the baubles can be resold."

"I see," murmured Dulcie. "Then no immediate profit

would accrue from the theft. Great risk was taken, it seems, for little gain."

"If the thief was unfamiliar with the game," Gibbon added, his pallid brow wrinkled in thought, "it may be he didn't know he'd have to hold on to the gems. Fences will seldom purchase from a new hand without a proper introduction, for fear of a plant."

"My!" said Mary, lecherously. "Ain't you the knowing one!" Gibbon cleared his throat and eyed her nervously.

"Since you are so eager to put in your ha'penny's worth," the Baroness remarked, "you may be next." She seated herself in a massive chair, dark wood ornately carved and upholstered in silver gray Italian velvet that matched the window hangings. The scrolled chair arms terminated in satyr masks, the legs in cloven feet. "Tell me, Mary, what you've learned."

The girl's freckled face was unusually serious. "Not much, my lady, except that Sir William and Lady Arabella quarreled mightily on the night she died."

Dulcie's inquisitive eyes fixed on her pert little housemaid. "Did you ascertain what this argument was about?"

"I did." Mary was smug. "Sir William had learned that his wife had bedded down with Master Dickon—seems to me he must be a proper slow top not to have known it sooner! Lady Arabella made no bones about her partiality."

"Did I ask for your opinion?" inquired the Baroness.

"No, ma'am." Mary grinned, uncowed. "He—Sir William—demanded that she end the relationship, and Lady Arabella laughed in his face. Then he threatened drastic measures, and she said she'd leave him."

"I wonder where she meant to go." Dulcie gazed blankly upon a massive side table with a heavy black-veined marble top found in Titus's Baths in Rome. "Not to Dickon, surely, for he would speedily have sent her to the rightabout."

"That's not all, ma'am!" Mary's freckled cheeks were flushed with excitement. "Sir William said that before he let her leave him, he'd see her dead!"

This announcement did not elicit the response that Mary had foreseen. Gibbon tsk'd with disapproval at such vulgar behavior, Culpepper grew even more severe, and Lady Bligh reflectively twisted a silver curl, careless of her elaborate hairdo.

"He *did* see her dead!" Mary burst forth irrepressively. "Though the servants aren't sure that he did the thing, being one whose bark is worse than his bite, as they say."

"Barking dogs," murmured the Baroness vaguely. "They do bite, you know." Briskly, she rose. "Very good, Mary! You've been a great help. Keep your ears open and report to me anything else you may hear." With a poorly executed curtsey and a saucy wink at Gibbon, Mary left the room.

Dulcie moved to the writing desk and began to fill yet another sheet of foolscap with her large untidy scrawl. "Culpepper! How progresses your romance?"

"I suppose *you*'d call it satisfactory." A dull red spread over the abigail's dour features as she recalled hours passed as the only female customer at the tavern across from Bow Street headquarters. It was an old building constructed partly of brick, now beginning to powder and flake, where the heavy smell of tobacco hung in the motionless blue gray air. When Culpepper closed her eyes to sleep at night, those drab walls appeared to haunt her, with their vast array of ancient advertisements for soap, cure-all pills and physics, snuff, combs, and pomades. "Myself, I hope to never look another oyster in the face!" This sentiment extended to the besotted night watchman, whose growing infatuation rendered him no more agreeable.

"Nonetheless, you will." The Baroness could be extremely ruthless. "What have you learned?"

"There is a rumor," replied Culpepper, immolated on the

altar of duty, "that Sir William didn't spend the entire evening of his wife's death at the Cyprians Ball."

"Aha!" Dulcie ignored the abigail's Friday face. "We progress. How long was he absent, and where did he go?"

"It is gossip only; no one knows." Culpepper's frigid tone indicated her sentiments regarding tale-bearing. "There is also speculation that the robbery was a well-planned thing since there was no evidence of forced entry. Perhaps the thief was granted entrance by someone already in Arbuthnot House."

Cross-eyed with concentration, the Baroness ran thoughtless fingers through her hair. Culpepper moaned and moved to right the damage. "Gibbon!" cried Lady Bligh. "What are the usual means of gaining access to a house that one means to burgle?"

Gibbon twitched with pleasure at this opportunity to further display his knowledge. "A good cracksman, my lady, has a regular arsenal of tools—a crowbar and centre-bit, keys and picklocks, prussic acid or mux vomica."

"Good heavens!" Lady Bligh jerked away from Culpepper's ministering hands. "It's a wonder we all aren't murdered in our beds. What, pray, is mux vomica?"

"Hog's vomit, my lady." Gibbon ignored Culpepper's consternation. "It's used to destroy animals."

"Well it might!" Dulcie frowned. "I see that I am a veritable innocent. How are these various tools utilized?"

"I speak from hearsay only," Gibbon offered cautiously. "Not from direct experience, you understand."

"Quite."

"A crowbar is applied when noise doesn't matter, to wrench open a door. A centre-bit is used to bore holes along the edge of the doorstyle, close to the head of the panel. Then a pocketknife is run from hole to hole and the panel is removed."

"Thus is the entrance effected. Fascinating!" Dulcie winced as Culpepper dug a hairpin into her scalp. "This begins to look deuced odd. It is unlikely that the servants would neglect to secure the windows, even at Arbuthnot House." Dulcie's attendants awaited further observations, but she irritably waved them away.

Left alone, Lady Bligh rose and once more paced the floor, pausing to survey herself intently in a silvered looking glass, as if the mirror might speak. She wore a flowing gown of midnight shade, with long sleeves drawn tight in several places, and a large silken Paisley shawl.

The looking glass remained inarticulate and Dulcie turned away, brooding. She walked to the fireplace and idly touched an exquisite porcelain figurine of a beautiful lady, attended by a blackamoor page, sitting in an ornate chair with an infinitesimal tea table, complete with chocolate pot and cups, by her side. "Bother!" said the Baroness, returning the figurine to its resting place on the mantelpiece. "I simply cannot make sense of this thing." Struck by a sudden thought, she gathered her scattered papers and locked them inside the writing desk, then seated herself again in the satyr-headed chair, from which vantage point she studied the portrait of her spouse.

Maximilian Bonaventure Bligh, as depicted in this painted likeness, was a tall man with strong features weathered by long exposure to the elements. Beneath strongly marked brows glittered seductive, heavy-lidded eyes. It was a strikingly handsome face with an aquiline nose and a sensuous mouth that was disguised by neither moustache nor beard. The raven hair, streaked heavily with gray, was worn unfashionably long. The Baron was shown in burgundy velvet and a frilled shirt open at the throat to reveal a chest as bronzed as his arrogant face—a costume that had led his wife to inquire whether he conducted his adventures half nude. The Baron's reply was not recorded for posterity.

"Bat," remarked Dulcie conversationally, "there are times when I heartily deplore your wanderlust!" She studied her eccentric helpmeet's painted likeness. "Not that you'd be of any practical assistance if you were here, you wretch, for you'd only say that we should leave it to Dickon to extricate himself from this mess." A familiar voice floated down the hall, prompting her to glower most uncordially at the Baron, who was currently off exploring Rosetta, Egypt, famous for its gardens and its fleas.

"Don't bother to announce us," came Hubert's languid drawl. "I daresay my aunt knows our names well enough, although I fear the poor old thing's grown shockingly shatterbrained." This sally was greeted by Gwyneth's high-pitched laughter. Lady Bligh made a hideous face as Hubert minced into the room. "Dulcie, you are alone! It is an ill omen to be caught talking to yourself, dear aunt! It is a sure sign of approaching senility."

"Coxcomb!" retorted the Baroness, without removing her dark eyes from the portrait.

Hubert, too, gazed upon the Baron's likeness, unappreciatively; Bat was the only living being of whom Hubert stood in awe. The Baron's acerbic manner made his waspish nephew appear a mere novice in the fine art of affrontery. "I shall never understand how Uncle Max manages to look simultaneously like a haughty aristocrat and a blood-thirsty buccaneer."

"It is quite simple," the Baroness replied kindly. "Unlike you, Bat doesn't *try* to look like anything."

Gwyneth was not so interested in the Baron's appearance as in the huge blood ruby that flashed from one painted hand, an item even more magnificent than the black opals which the Baroness wore in profusion. Gwyneth positioned herself in a massive chair, the arms of which terminated in an eagle's head with a sharp, savage beak. It was a motif that predominated in the room, seen yet again in a marble-topped console supported by a fierce bird with outstretched wings, and atop the silvered mirror. It seemed to Gwyneth that the birds bore a startling resemblance to the Baron's predatory visage.

Hubert turned away. "An incredible likeness." He seated himself with great consideration for the skirts of his incomparable coat.

"Is it not?" Lady Bligh gazed, with marked distaste, upon the rouge that colored her nephew's cheeks. "You do not approve, Hubert? You think Bat should have been portrayed for later generations in the robes of a peer of the realm?"

"I fear," lamented Hubert, leaning his gold-tasseled cane against the arm of his lion-headed chair, "that no one could mistake dear Uncle Max for a perfect gentleman."

"No, indeed." Dulcie smiled, a reminiscent gleam in one dark eye. "He fits my notion of a perfect husband, however—when I'm speaking to him."

Gwyneth had been too long unheard. She shivered delicately. "How like you to put a brave face on it. I know better! I, too, was doomed to spend a portion of my life married to a reprobate."

Lady Bligh laughed aloud, apparently finding in this a jest of no small order. "Do you picture me imbibing wormwood and gall? Silly chit!" Gwyneth colored unbecomingly. "I have no quarrel with Bat's intemperance. Why should I?" The reminiscent gleam briefly reappeared, even more pronounced. "I have always admired a rake. They make life so interesting." Gwyneth bridled, but bit back the sharp retort that rose to her tongue. Quarrelling with the Baroness would not advance her cause.

Hubert's superior gaze travelled, pained, around the room. Each time the Baron returned from one of his countless voyages, he refurnished a chamber in the Bligh mansion in an appropriate, albeit fanciful, style. "My uncle's taste," Hubert remarked, not with approval, "never fails to amaze me. I shudder to think what may come of his journey to the Holy Land!"

"Why should you?" inquired the Baroness. "You are not required to live among these rooms. You are not even required to visit them."

"I would not neglect you, aunt; how can you think such a thing?" Hubert fixed his quizzing-glass in the socket of one eye and regarded Dulcie's silver curls with an awe equal to that which he accorded her surroundings. "All the same, the worthy Bligh ancestors would rise wroth from their graves if they knew what Uncle Max had wrought in their respectable town mansion."

"It is a compelling argument against the possibility of an afterlife." Dulcie tapped bejewelled fingers against the arm of her chair. "Why this great concern, Humbug? Do you fear that Bat will run through the Bligh fortune?"

"That unworthy thought," Hubert protested, wounded, "has never crossed my mind!"

"It shouldn't: you'll never see a penny of it." The Baroness selected a copy of the *Morning Post* from a pile of newspapers that also contained the *Imperial Weekly Journal, Times, Evening Mail* and *Pilot;* and, for some odd reason, the provincial *Ipswich Journal* and *Chester Chronicle.* "Set your fears at rest. Bat is rich enough to buy an abbey."

"And, in fact," murmured Hubert maliciously, "has been barely restrained from doing so!"

Gwyneth, reminded of the purpose of their visit, hastily intervened. "We have come upon a matter of the gravest importance, dear Baroness, a matter of great delicacy."

"*You* have," corrected Hubert, smoothing a flawless sleeve. "I merely agreed to lend you countenance."

Gwyneth was tempted to quarrel with this unchivalrous

attitude, but Dulcie gave her no time. "Out with it," advised the Baroness. "What is this matter of such great import?"

A lady less stalwart, or less devious, might have been dismayed by this unsympathetic attitude, but Gwyneth plunged bravely on. "I must see Austin!" Her hands were clasped devoutly in her lap. "Surely it is a mother's privilege to visit her only son? I beg that you will intervene with Dickon on my behalf!"

"You waste your time." Unimpressed, Lady Bligh opened the *Post*. "It is my policy never to interfere." Hubert looked as though he might challenge this remark.

Gwyneth's green eyes flashed wrathfully. "You are very anxious to court scandal. I have already consulted a barrister concerning Dickon's treatment of Austin!"

The Baroness yawned prettily. "You may confer with Lucifer himself, and I shall raise no protest." The Countess Andrassy wore a stone-colored walking habit trimmed with swansdown. A sealskin hat and muff, black kid sandals, white stocking and black gloves completed her dashing ensemble. "I must quibble, however, with the manner of your attire. You look as though you are prepared to set out for Siberia."

"You'd like that, wouldn't you?" Gwyneth, in high dudgeon, ignored Hubert's amusement. "I'm sorry to disappoint you, but I'm going nowhere without my son!"

"Then you shall be with us quite some time," mused Dulcie. Her gaze moved to Hubert, who resembled nothing more than a walking pincushion, so laced and padded was he. She closed her eyes and wrinkled her nose. Hubert exchanged a glance with the Countess and meaningfully tapped his head. "Mr. Crump," intoned Lady Bligh, without opening her eyes, "why are you hovering in the hallway? Do come in!"

No bit embarrassed at being caught blatantly eavesdropping, an act far more profitable than squirming on the uncomfortable hall chairs that awaited the unexpected visitor, Crump stepped across the threshold. Gibbon, distraught, hovered at his heels.

"I tried to stop him, my lady." Gibbon's left eyelid danced wildly, a sure indication of extreme distress. "But he threatened to haul me off to Bow Street!"

"Aye, and I may yet." Crump was distracted, his attention having fallen upon Hubert, dazzling in a combination of bright yellow coat and lime green pantaloons of ribbed kerseymere, worn with Hessian boots. "For a more guilty-looking specimen I have never seen!" Gibbon gulped.

"Shame, Mr. Crump! You must not terrorize my butler or he will retaliate by denying you admission here." Gibbon's visage brightened perceptibly. "We can't have that, can we?"

"No, indeed, Baroness." Crump gazed about the marble chamber, surely enough to take a man's breath away. Crump could never visit the Bligh mansion without recalling large, once handsome houses where thirty or more people of all ages now inhabited a single room, squatting, sleeping, copulating on straw-filled billets or mounds of verminous rags that were the only furniture. Just the previous evening he had visited a cellar home, fetid and damp with sewage, to talk with a sharp-eyed woman who fended rats away from her infant's face and fingers as they spoke. His gaze returned to the Baroness. It was unlikely that Lady Bligh had ever glimpsed this extremely enlightening side of London life.

"I'm glad you called," remarked Dulcie, behind whose roguish eyes resided all sorts of unexpected knowledge. "Allow me to introduce you to more of my family." Her butler received a reprimanding look. "Gibbon, tea."

"I'm sorry to intrude." Crump exhibited an unusual humility, inspired by Dulcie's unexpected cordiality. "I was passing by and thought I'd stop in for a friendly chat." He did not add that he had been skulking about London, lurking in doorways, alehouses, and near gentlemen's clubs, in hope of surprising Lord Dorset; or that his visit was due to unbearable curiosity aroused by the crêpe that liberally adorned the Bligh residence. To the best of Crump's knowledge, no one of any significance had recently departed this vale of tears.

"Your timing," said the Baroness, "is most opportune." She presented her companions, both of whom suffered no small surprise at her acquaintance with this common little man who committed the unpardonable sin of wearing a moleskin waistcoat. "Mr. Crump," she added, as Mary brought the tea, "is from Bow Street." With Mary came Casanova, who took instant interest in the tassels that dangled from Hubert's cane.

Putting aside his question about the crêpe, Crump took out his Occurrence Book and concentrated on these new sources of information. He had hoped to meet the Countess Andrassy who, since her return to London, had plunged into a reckless orgy of levees, breakfasts, dinners, card parties and routs, spending money as easily as if the Hungarian Count to whom she was now wed could lay claim to something more valuable than his illustrious name, which, it was well known, he could not. Crump pondered the significance of this sudden change in fortune. "I, too, have questioned that," remarked Lady Bligh. Crump glanced askance at his hostess, but was distracted as Mary, grinning, swished gracefully from the room.

"Gwyneth," said the Baroness, recalling Crump to his duty. "was an intimate of dear Arabella's and, I understand, very much in her confidence. Perhaps she can be of assistance to you." Crump supposed he should not be surprised to learn that Lord Dorset's ex-wife and mistress were the best of friends.

"I doubt it," Gwyneth replied, too hastily. "You will recall that I have been out of the country for several years."

"You are too modest!" protested Hubert, intent on stirring up mischief. "Arabella may well have mentioned something of importance in that voluminous correspondence she maintained with you!" Crump missed none of Gwyneth's fury at this reminder; the lady looked ready to chew nails. Hubert smiled.

"She told me little enough of interest." Gwyneth reflected upon her recent visits to linen drapers, silk mercers, dressmakers and milliners, none of whom had yet been paid, and thought it might behoove her to cooperate with Bow Street. "What is it you wish to know?"

Crump hastily withdrew his fascinated gaze from Hubert's yellow coat which had, in addition to a padded breast, huge plated buttons, French riding sleeves, and skirt tails that reached below the knee. With this were worn a frilled shirt and a waistcoat of light cashmere. On the gentleman's knee sat a very small flat hat. "Very little is known about Lady Arabella's background. Perhaps you can tell me more."

Gwyneth shrugged indifferently. "Arabella was a country girl who took the *ton* by storm and married a wealthy and elderly Duke. I don't believe she ever discussed her origins." It seemed to Crump that Gwyneth was on the verge of saying more, but Hubert intervened.

"The Duke," added that Exquisite, "died disillusioned, leaving poor Arabella with nothing more than her clothing and her jewels." Malicious eyes observed Crump over the wall of starch and muslin that served as a cravat. "You see how it was necessary for her to wed again as speedily as possible." Lady Bligh sat enthroned in her chair as if enjoying a command performance.

"I understand you were one of Lady Arabella's admirers." Crump watched warily as Casanova stalked Hubert's tasseled cane.

"It was my honor." Hubert twirled his moustache tip. "Arabella was a lovely creature, Mr. Crump. Those of us who appreciated her beauty lament the day when she came to Dickon's notice." He turned to Gwyneth. "Forgive me. I know that mention of Dickon can only bring you pain."

It was true that the bronze-haired beauty seemed to labor under some strong emotion. "My marriage was an unhappy one," she murmured. "I was but an innocent child, with no notion that a man could be so depraved."

"Loath as I am to interrupt this moving drama," commented Dulcie, "I must protest that 'depraved' is too extreme." She propped dainty feet on a velvet-covered stool.

"Where Dickon is concerned," Gwyneth flashed, seeing yet another way in which she might recoup her losses, "nothing is too extreme! I could tell tales of my life with Dickon that would surpass belief."

"I don't doubt that for an instant," said the Baroness. Crump viewed the Baron's portrait, then quickly looked away. Save Dulcie, few could long meet that hawklike gaze, even in muted painted form.

"Come, come, aunt!" Hubert was a demon of discord. "Even one so partial as you cannot deny that Dickon has the most diabolical disposition. I have always deprecated his tendency toward violence."

"Poor Arabella!" sobbed Gwyneth, into the handkerchief. "Dickon truly deserves to be punished for his sins."

Crump expected the Baroness to intervene, but she merely applied herself with gusto to her tea. The somber hue of her garments, which contrasted admirably with her silver hair, reminded Crump of the inexplicable signs of mourning that were everywhere. Casanova, thwarted by the tassel that dangled just out of reach, sat back on furry haunches to reconnoiter.

"He does deserve punishment," Hubert agreed. "The man is a veritable scourge, wreaking havoc and ruin, leaving brokenhearted desolation in his wake."

"Fie, Humbug!" The Baroness deposited her teacup in its saucer forcefully. "To speak of your cousin so!"

"Your fondness blinds you, Dulcie." Hubert might have

been a sympathetic mentor of elderly years. "Consider the many unfortunate females he has ruined. Now poor Livvy will be next, and you do nothing to prevent yet another catastrophe." Sadly, he shook his well-tended head. "I do not understand you, aunt. Where is Livvy, by the bye?"

"I understand *you,* Hubert," Dulcie retorted, "only too well!" To Crump, this sounded remarkably like a threat. "Livvy is happily engaged in selecting her trousseau."

Crump cleared his throat. "Let's get back to those unfortunate females."

"Of course." Hubert counted on slender fingers. "They are legion, Mr. Crump; I know not where to begin!"

"I doubt that will stop you," ventured Lady Bligh.

"There have been opera-dancers and actresses, females of every station and walk of life, left by my heartless cousin to sink into declines, and worse." Hubert's audience was spellbound; even Gwyneth, well-acquainted with the extent of her ex-husband's dissipation, stopped crying to listen. "Of Arabella, I need not speak, we all know Dickon treated her most callously."

"Almost as callously as Arabella treated her husband," Dulcie observed. "Continue, Hubert, we are all ears." Casanova, amber eyes fixed on golden tassels, tensed to pounce.

Hubert was in a playful mood. "Dear Gwyneth is the greatest sufferer of all. She exists in a state of constant alarm and occasional fainting fits. I fear she will never overcome the consequences of Dickon's influence; she has been corrupted by him, made familiar with infamy and vice."

"Vice!" shrieked Gwyneth shrilly. "How dare you speak so of me, you ungrateful cur!" Casanova leaped upon the cane and brought it crashing to the floor.

"Gwyneth!" Hubert turned pale. "Don't fly into a tantrum! We must assist Bow Street."

"I'll show you vice and infamy!" gasped Gwyneth, engaged

with Casanova in a tug-of-war for possession of the cane. Gwyneth won the honors, but Casanova retained the golden tassel.

"My stick!" wailed Hubert.

"Assist Bow Street," raged Gwyneth, brandishing the ebony cane, "will you? Then tell the Runner that you've known Arabella since her earliest days! Tell him how furious it made you that she ignored you whenever Dickon was around!" Giving Hubert one vicious thwack, she made for the door.

Arms above his head in ineffectual defense, Hubert rose hastily. Despite his dire predicament, he managed a bow that was only slightly lacking in its usual elegance. "I'll be back," Gwyneth promised, panting from her exertions, "and before long, Dulcie Bligh! If you don't want to see your dirty linen washed in public, you'll think over my offer most carefully." Crump watched fascinated as, bellowing like a fishwife, she chased Hubert from the room.

"My nephew," remarked the Baroness, "is a trifle liverish. Gwyneth took his meddling in ill part, did she not?" She was serene. "As you may have observed, my family is not without eccentricities." Crump goggled at this understatement.

"Gwyneth seeks to replenish the family purse," Dulcie continued, "and thinks that if she behaves with sufficient atrocity I will buy her off." Casanova worried the golden tassel as if it were a mouse. "She may be correct. I don't know that I can tolerate a great deal more idiocy."

Crump murmured sympathetically and wondered how to broach the subject uppermost in his mind. He was not given the opportunity.

"Now to business," said the Baroness, sitting upright. "You have not made much progress, Mr. Crump. The jewels have not resurfaced among the lower elements, nor did you find them in my nephew's house." A bright eye fixed on him. "I might have told you that searching Dickon's lodgings would prove a waste of time, but you would not have listened to me."

"How," inquired Crump suspiciously, "did you know I had?" It appeared the Baroness had stolen a march on him.

"A good investigator," retorted Dulcie airily, "does not reveal her sources. I take it you have also learned that Sir William is on the verge of bankruptcy?"

Crump's expression was dour. "Yes." It was uncanny, the way that Lady Bligh managed to stay a step ahead of Bow Street. Perhaps she was not quite as dotty as she seemed.

"Good!" Dulcie settled back in her chair. "Let us compare notes. Is there anything you care to ask me?"

Crump grasped his opportunity. "Yes, Baroness, there is." He was forced to be direct. "Excuse my presumption, but why are you in mourning?" Lady Bligh's face fell.

"Calypso." Dulcie's mournful gaze moved to Casanova, sleek and undeniably well-fed. "I came upon the dreadful scene too late." Crump stared at an arrangement of yellow feathers and crêpe, displayed tastefully under glass. "It is a shocking world, Mr. Crump, wherein even an innocent canary falls prey to the forces of villainy."

Crump, revolted, stared at the orange-striped cat.

"Arabella a blameless victim?" mused the Baroness. "An intriguing notion, Mr. Crump, but I think not."

Chapter Eight

LIVVY FOUND SIR William in the library, seated at his desk and sunk in deepest gloom. Hitching up her skirt, she dusted off the brandy bottles, adopted an attitude of imbecilic servility, and knocked timidly on the open door.

"Come in, come in!" Sir William hastened to remove her burden and closed the library door. "I've been wanting to speak with you, Primrose," he added, with a playful pinch, "but you've been avoiding me."

"Oh no, sir!" Livvy was coy. "Your mama keeps me very busy, poor invalid that she is. I knew you wouldn't want me to neglect her, so I waited 'til I was free." She strove for a glance simultaneously innocent and aware. From the lecherous expression in Sir William's bloodshot eye, she achieved a tolerable success. "Why did you wish to see me, sir?"

"No hurry for that!" Sir William pulled a chair closer to his desk and gestured for Livvy to be seated. "Just an informal little chat, you know." He enthusiastically assaulted one of the bottles purloined from Luisa's private stock. "Drink a bumper with me, Primrose, and tell me what you think of Arbuthnot House."

"Truly, I could not!" Livvy's horror was genuine, inspired not so much at the suggestion of consuming spirits as by the invitation to air her opinion of the Arbuthnot menagerie. Sir William patted her knee.

"Of course you can!" His affability grew. "You must oblige me, Primrose; I cannot drink alone."

Reflecting that Lord Dorset would not even be properly grateful for the efforts made in his behalf, Livvy meekly bowed her head. "As you wish, sir."

"No one will ever know." Her host brought forth two glasses, none too clean. "No matter if they did! I am the master of Arbuthnot House, and my word is law." Livvy hoped that Bertha did not learn of this *tête-à-tête*, lest she determine to whittle away at her competition with a carving knife.

Sir William leaned back in his chair. "Well!" His fondness for the bottle might, perhaps, have been an inherited trait. "You've been with us only a few days, yet already you seem a member of the family, so well do you fit in! What do you think of us, eh, Primrose?"

Livvy stifled a rebellious impulse to answer honestly. "Madame Arbuthnot is very gracious, very amiable." She sipped her brandy and gagged, wondering how Luisa managed to consume such vast quantities of the loathsome stuff.

Sir William, briefly distracted from his fell purpose, namely the seduction of his mother's companion, gazed mistily upon a miniature. "Poor Madame! She has not had a happy life, I fear, and the fault is entirely mine."

Livvy blinked to hear a man speak of his mother in such sottish tones, and inspected the gold-framed miniature that he pressed into her hand. Luisa, in her heyday, had been an amber-eyed, black-haired beauty with generous proportions

and a sultry air. "She was lovely," Livvy commented honestly.
"My fault," mourned Sir William, with a lugubriousness that made Livvy suspect that he was already drunk as an owl. "I crippled her, Primrose, and never will I forgive myself for it."

Considering Luisa's tyrannical disposition, it was not likely her son had ever been given the opportunity. "How dreadful," murmured Livvy sympathetically. "How did it happen?"

"Madame told me I was too intoxicated to safely take the reins, but I would not listen." Sir William sighed. "The off-leader shied at a hen flying across the road, and we tumbled into a ditch. The horses were in an awful tangle, kicking and struggling so much I thought I'd never calm them." His eyes were glazed, his tone mechanical. "Madame swears that I did more damage getting her out of the coach than was done in the accident itself." He looked at Livvy, for all the world like a dog wishful of a bone. "Her back, you see."

Livvy was repelled. Sir William's pudgy features were streaked with perspiration. She grasped the brandy bottle and filled his glass to the brim. "How tragic."

"Even Prinny admired Madame. He is, you know, in the way of being an intimate of mine." Sir William shook his head, jiggling his various chins. "Poor Prinny! Have you heard the latest *on-dit* concerning the Princess of Wales?"

Livvy, schooled to patience, made a negative gesture. The Princess was a querulous, restless lady with coarse manners and a marked partiality for food and drink and low company; she had reputedly taken one of her own footmen as a lover. With little interest in the goings-on of royalty, Livvy wondered how to turn the conversation to her own ends.

"She is engaging in ostentatiously displaying a child whom she claims she adopted from a docker and his wife, but which everyone believes to be hers!" Sir William peered at Livvy but saw no maidenly blush. "As a result, she has been banished from royal society and is to leave immediately for the Continent."

"Shocking," murmured Livvy, and filled Sir William's glass once again.

"What's this? You're not drinking, Primrose!" He watched as Livvy bravely sipped the vile brew. "I tell you in strictest confidence that it is true that the Princess does not bathe as frequently as she should."

Livvy inhaled Sir William's characteristic odor of combined bandoline and perfume and heroically withheld comment. "Would you not," inquired her would-be seducer, "like to meet the Prince, Primrose? To mingle with the *ton* and rub shoulders with royalty?"

It was doubtful that Sir William's patronage would gain anyone *entrée* to the haunts of the Upper Ten Thousand, but Livvy adopted a thrilled expression. "Oh, sir! Such a thing is hardly possible."

"Nonsense!" Sir William preened. "I am not without influence, my dear." An unpleasant thought presented itself to him. "No matter what Brummel may say!"

"Brummel?" Livvy briefly forgot her mission. "What *does* he say?"

Sir William again wore a look of gloom. "Nothing to me, curse the man. He does not dare!" The heavy lips pouted. "To others, he not only remarked that I am as plump as a dumpling, but went on to insult my coat."

Livvy choked back laughter. "You place too much importance on Mr. Brummel's words," she protested. "Do you forget that he is merely the grandson of a valet?" She grasped the opportunity. "It is your grief for your wife, no doubt, that makes you so sensitive."

This time it was Sir William who grasped the brandy bottle. Livvy hastily moved her glass out of reach. "Poor Arabella. That was my fault, I fear."

"Your fault?" Livvy was alert. "How can you say so?"

"I wouldn't listen to her." Sir William's eyes filled with easy tears. "I thought it was just another of her tales, that she was merely trying to get around me." The damp eyes focused on Livvy. "Arabella had no notion of money, you see. She thought she had only to hold out her pretty hand and whatever she wanted would appear." He touched his false sidewhiskers. "Madame told me how it would be, but I wouldn't listen. Now look what it's come to! Arabella dead."

"You have had much to bear." Livvy nudged the second bottle into view. Sir William opened it.

"Hah!" Slurred tones indicated the extent of his inebriation. "You don't know the half of it, Primrose. I shall again be forced to visit Jew King in Clarges Street—a moneylender, you know." The mournful gaze brightened. "*You* don't care if a man's pockets are to let, eh, Primrose? I knew from the moment I clapped eyes on you that we'd suit right down to the ground."

"You are too kind," Livvy replied, with every evidence of flattered gratitude. She marvelled at the man's lack of discrimination; with her hair brushed ruthlessly severe, and wire-rimmed spectacles affixed to the bridge of her nose, Livvy appeared, if not exactly plain, extremely spinsterish.

"Nothing of the sort." Sir William ponderously slid his chair closer. "You're not averse to plain speaking, are you, Primrose? No reason to be missish, after all!"

"You will have Lady Arabella's jewels," Livvy said nervously. "Surely they will be swiftly recovered and returned to you."

Sir William exhibited rare good humor. "Arabella's jewels! That's a good one, Primrose. I'm to be saved from debtor's prison by my wife's jewels, and I didn't give her one of them!"

"They were presented to her by her first husband, then?"

Sir William looked confused. "Her first husband? Oh, you

mean the Duke. One thing I'll say for the old goat, he was generous." He gazed appreciatively upon his companion. "Damn, Primrose, if you don't have lovely hair!"

"I understand," Livvy persevered, "that you have suffered various thefts." Sir William's face fell.

"My manuscript," he mourned. "It was to restore our fortunes, and now it's gone." One fat hand found Livvy's knee. "My memoirs, you know. You'd have found them interesting."

Livvy, her spine rigid, did not recoil. "Perhaps," she offered, through clenched teeth, "it was stolen at the same time as Lady Arabella's jewels. Could someone have learned of its value?"

"No one even knew of its existence." Livvy offered thanks to heaven that Sir William was so easily distracted. "Poor Arabella! Snuffed out like a candle in the prime of life. She was sorely burdened, and I did nothing to ease her load."

"You must not blame yourself! I am sure Lady Arabella understood."

"That," retorted Sir William, withdrawing his hand, "she did not! She came to me with a cock and bull story about being blackmailed and expected me to fix it up all right and tight. Well! Any man would be suspicious, and so I told her." His florid features were irate. "Understand! Never have I seen anyone kick up such a dust."

"Calm yourself, sir." Ruthlessly, Livvy poured more brandy. One thing could be said of this repulsive man: his capacity for liquor was stupendous. "Who threatened your wife, and why?"

"She wouldn't say." Sir William shook off unpleasant memories. "Let us talk of happier things, Primrose." He leered. "Such as you and me."

Quickly Livvy rose. "I fear your mother will be calling me. It has been a pleasure to talk with you, sir; I hope we may do so again." But she was not to escape so easily.

"You can be sure we shall!" Sir William clasped her arm in

a grip that was surprisingly strong. "Primrose, you forget yourself! I have not yet dismissed you."

"Sir William, you go too far!" Livvy struggled to free herself from an ardent embrace. "Release me at once." Her spectacles went flying across the room.

"Playing hard to get?" inquired her admirer, delighted at this game. "By Gad, you're a damned good looking woman, Primrose! Why didn't I notice it before?" With a most unladylike oath, Livvy wrenched free and darted to the door. Behind her came a resounding crash as Sir William, in hot pursuit, collided with the library steps. Cautiously, Livvy approached the prostrate body, but he did not stir.

Livvy was not a timid soul, but even she was not sufficiently stout-hearted to stoically await developments, which would likely involve an embarrassing visit to Bow Street. Without a second moment's thought, she exited Arbuthnot House in a manner as furtive and hasty as that of the most cowardly criminal. Through congested streets she scurried, taking notice of neither mettlesome horses nor startled pedestrians, oblivious to the clattersome danger of iron hoofs and wheels. With a sigh of vast relief she spied the Bligh mansion. Slipping through the servants' entrance, Livvy made her way upstairs. Casanova, looking unusually disgruntled, climbed out of an umbrella stand to accompany her.

Lady Bligh's bedchamber also showed the Baron's perverse influence. Commonly known as The Seraglio, the spacious room boasted stained glass windows that depicted scenes from the *Decameron* of Boccaccio. The Baroness stood before a remarkably fine wardrobe with matched oval panels of beautifully figured mahogany veneer outfitted with bands of herringbone inlay, rummaging through an extensive array of evening attire. "Lavender," she remarked, unsurprised, as her companion burst into the room. "Welcome home. You've just missed Dickon; he left not five moments past."

Livvy, panting, sought to catch her breath. "Sir William," she gasped, "is a candidate for Bedlam! He has the soul of a baboon, the body of a hippopotamus, and the wit of a wooden spoon!" Lady Bligh's tinkling laughter pealed. Livvy pressed cold hands to her hot cheeks and, for some inexplicable reason, burst into tears.

Making soothing noises, Dulcie led her companion to an alcove that was fitted up with cushions in the form of a Turkish sofa, with a drapery curtain in front. Firmly installed in the midst of this Sybaritic luxury, Livvy abandoned herself to melancholy, while the Baroness murmured comfortingly.

At last the storm subsided. Feeling extremely foolish, Livvy opened her eyes and found herself the subject of an intense scrutiny. A brilliant blue bird, on a perch as thick as a broomstick, was craning its neck at her in a distinctly vulturelike manner. "Dinna fash yerself!" advised the parrot, sidling to the extreme edge of the perch and fixing its eye on Livvy.

"Dulcie," said Livvy weakly, staring at the wicked curved beak, "*what* is that?" Casanova approached warily.

"A Hyacinth Macaw," the Baroness replied. "The largest and most beautiful of the parrot family." She bestowed a caress upon the huge bird. "Alexander the Great had pet parrots three hundred years before the birth of Christ." Casanova, envisioning gastronomic delights, leaped into Livvy's lap.

"Frigging landlubber!" screamed the bird, in tones so harsh and strident that Casanova leaped straight up into the air, resembling a startled acrobatic porcupine, and beat an ignoble retreat.

"I suspect," Dulcie commented, "that Casanova has met his match." The parrot bestowed upon her a velvety look.

"That bird," gasped Livvy, cautiously removing her hands

from her ears, "certainly has an extensive vocabulary! How did you come by it?"

"Not it, him." The Baroness was reproving. "Bluebeard is most sensitive." Livvy gazed upon the bird's large head, and the wings that must have measured at least forty inches tip to tip. "A grubby urchin brought him, with no explanation other than the wish that Bluebeard would help atone for our sad loss." Dulcie settled herself more comfortably among the pillows.

"You're holding out on me." Livvy was acquainted with that demure look. "Confess, Dulcie, you know where that bird came from." Bluebeard cocked his bright head to observe them inquisitively.

"Of course I do." Lady Bligh assumed a yoga position. "But Mr. Crump would be dreadfully embarrassed if I thanked him for his thoughtfulness, so I shall say not a word."

Livvy's thoughts were proceeding in an extremely disorderly manner. "*What* sad news?" She was afraid she knew.

"Alas, poor Calypso." Dulcie sniffed the air. "Lavender! Do I smell *spirits* on your breath?"

Livvy hiccoughed, only too easily imagining the little canary's fate. "You do. You must give me thirty-five pounds beside."

"Bribing the servants, Lavender?" inquired Lady Bligh. "I do not know where you come by these shocking habits."

"It was that," Livvy sniffled, "or enter into a life of sin. I did not think you would wish me to go that far."

"No?" The Baroness considered. "It is for a good purpose, after all." She laughed merrily. "Darling Lavender, you have put up with a great deal for my sake, and it is not kind of me to tease you."

"No, it isn't." Livvy stared down the length of her reddened nose. "Especially when I suspect I am quite shockingly drunk!"

Her eyes filled again with tears. "Dulcie, I have left the spectacles behind!"

"Blow me down!" cried Bluebeard. Having engaged the ladies' attention, he executed a neat somersault. Livvy subsided into watery giggles.

"Don't fret, you silly girl, you shall need those spectacles no more." Chuckling, the Baroness took her sodden companion into her arms. "Tonight you made your debut as Dickon's bride-to-be."

So far was this promised treat from cheering poor Livvy that she buried her head in Dulcie's shoulder and sobbed heartily. Life had suddenly turned from a placid and peaceful affair into a maddening and frightening game of chance. Livvy was not foolish enough to dream that she might win the coveted prize.

Lights flared at the entrance to the Royal Patent Theatre at Covent Garden, casting eerie shadows across crowded pavements. Fashion had long ago deserted the area, leaving the great houses around the Piazza to either rot away or become home to every imaginable viciousness. Heavily painted ladies of the evening lurked at alley corners and in the theatre's entryway. Bursts of laughter escaped from opened doors on the side streets. Child prostitutes dodged after prospective clients, mouthing lewd suggestions, plucking at rich sleeves; and raddled matrons conducted a brisk trade in virgins, earning profits of £100 and more, pandering to the belief that deflowering a virgin was the one infallible cure for venereal disease.

Beyond the Doric portico, the theatre was crowded with every possible example of humankind. Courtesans paraded side by side with glittering aristocracy in passages and saloons, displayed themselves advantageously on the grand staircase that led nowhere, lounged seductively in the greenroom.

Inside the auditorium, where three thousand people might

be seated in varying degrees of comfort, notorious demireps took front-line seats, at £200 a season, as shopwindows for their charms. This evening, however, immorality decked out in silk took second place in interest to the mysterious Mrs. Lytton, who had so suddenly snared London's most elusive, and most unpredictable, unmarried gentleman. More than one lady, Cyprian and Duchess alike, gazed upon the Earl's dissolute, detached countenance, and speculated mightily upon how the thing had been done.

Even those high-sticklers who had raised eyebrows at Mrs. Lytton's appearance or delivered her a snub stared curiously at Lord Dorset's betrothed, who was dressed in a dashing gown of clinging lavender silk with an extremely low neckline, adorned with Lady Bligh's magnificent matched pearls. Hubert gazed with approval upon her dark hair, combed *à la* Titus with a center part in the disheveled curls. "You are beautiful," he murmured. "How can you waste yourself on an unappreciative clod like my cousin?"

Livvy's well-being was not ruffled by Hubert's audacity. "I've a notion to become a Countess," she explained. "You are talking fustian, you know. Your cousin is well enough." In an opposite box, Gwyneth, abandoned, seethed with ill-tempered annoyance.

"Such lukewarm tones," mused Hubert, "yet you are quick enough to defend Dickon." He cast a cautious eye at his aunt, deep in conversation with Sir John. Lady Bligh, in contrast with her companion, looked almost severe in a high-necked, long-sleeved gown of rust-colored velvet. "I ask myself, why."

"I wish you would not." Livvy bestowed upon her interrogator an impish smile. "It is none of your concern."

"I suspect that you are up to your pretty ears in intrigue." Hubert wore an unusually animated expression. "No doubt of my aunt's devising. How lowering to reflect that I have underestimated Dulcie for so many years."

"I haven't the faintest notion of what you're talking about." Livvy watched with interest as, in a neighboring box, a languishing barque of frailty was introduced to an admiring gentleman. "Would you care to explain?"

"I think not." Hubert rose as Lord Dorset, who had departed in search of refreshment that he vowed was necessary for the maintenance of his equanimity, reappeared. "You are involved in a deadly game." His foppish air had gone, leaving him unexpectedly sincere. "Should you find yourself in difficulty, I beg you will come to me. Strange as it may seem to you, Livvy, I will be happy to stand your friend." With a slight nod to his cousin, Hubert left them, leaving Livvy staring after him with the liveliest curiosity.

"Why such astonishment?" inquired Lord Dorset. Clad in deepest blue, he was a diabolically handsome man. He was also in the devil of a temper, as Livvy well knew, having been the recipient of his scathing opinions of the theatre's devotees, players, and program of entertainment. "What has Humbug been saying to you?"

"Well you may ask." Livvy wondered at this possessive attitude. It would not do, of course, for the Earl's betrothed to display marked favor for another man, particularly one whom Lord Dorset held in such enmity. "Hubert speaks in riddles, like the Sphinx."

Lady Bligh turned her golden head. "Humbug," she commented, "knows a great deal more than he will tell." She smiled, with great effect, upon the Chief Magistrate. "You might bear that in mind."

"You are a schemer, Dulcie." Sir John was uncertain how, against both his will and common sense, the Baroness had persuaded him to join her party. "What devious ploys have you in mind?"

Dulcie turned to him, thus dispelling her air of prim propriety, for the velvet gown molded itself superbly to a body unfettered by either artifice or age. "Dear John, do you fear to compromise yourself by being here with us? It is very dull of you." Carelessly, she touched his hand, and Sir John discovered that the theatre had grown uncomfortably warm. "The world is more likely to think that you are here to keep Dickon under close surveillance than to believe you are biased in his favor."

"I hope you are correct." Immune to the allure of candle-lit drama, the Chief Magistrate gazed about him. He had not visited Covent Garden since the Old Price diversions several years before, when some of the more ingenious members of the opposition contrived to introduce live porkers into the theatre, then pinched their ears at intervals when a variation of the disharmony of protest was required.

"When," inquired the Baroness, with a toss of her topaz-colored head, "am I not? You are a great deal too serious, John. Can you not forget your wretched Bow Street just this one night?"

"Apparently not." Despite his uncompromising tone, the Chief Magistrate was sufficiently abstracted to wonder how far Dulcie would go to insure his compliance with her nefarious schemes. She sat entirely too near for his peace of mind, her sweet perfume invading his nostrils and wreaking absolute havoc with his processes of thought. "I cannot so easily put aside the puzzle of Lady Arabella's murder."

"It *is* perplexing, is it not?" Dulcie leaned even closer, inspiring Sir John with a strong desire to take her in his arms, to the edification of the entire Covent Garden audience and the detriment of his career. "John!" As if she read his intention, the Baroness blushed like a schoolgirl. "Keep your mind on the matter at hand, if you please!"

"I do *not* please," retorted the Chief Magistrate. "You are no less a vixen than you were thirty years ago, Dulcie Bligh!"

"Shocking, is it not?" inquired the Baroness. "Especially in a great-aunt!" In imperious tones, she called her nephew to attention. "Dickon! I strongly recommend that you bring Austin to town."

Lord Dorset's affability vanished. "So that he may see his mother? Think again, Dulcie! Austin is far better off where he is."

Lady Bligh wore a thoughtful expression. "I have the oddest feeling, Dickon, that you are mistaken." The Earl's countenance darkened. "However, I shall not quarrel with you tonight. We will discuss the matter at some other time."

Livvy inhaled the mingled scents of oranges, sawdust, and humanity. It was her first visit to the theatre, and she had sat rapt through Shakespearean tragedy, renderings by a popular vocalist, and conjuring tricks; and had thoroughly enjoyed *The Gamester*, heedlessly clutching Lord Dorset's sleeve when Mrs. Beverly threw herself, in hysterical despair, into her husband's arms. The Earl had proven remarkably patient, even suffering in stoic silence this assault upon his immaculate person. "Pray remove that atrocious scowl," Livvy murmured. "All eyes are upon us, remember? I do not wish to be accused of provoking a lovers' quarrel."

Dickon raised a quizzical brow. "No? But you do provoke me, Mrs. Lytton, at every opportunity."

"Nonsense!" Livvy touched her borrowed pearls, the finest gems it had ever been her privilege to wear. "It only seems so because you are accustomed to being indulged by all the world." In the pit and gallery, the *ton* strolled and visited, quizzing each other and gossiping about the fortunates currently in favor with the Regent and the luckless who were out.

"How long," Dickon inquired, his arrogant features melting into a heart-stopping smile, "have you wished to deliver that set-down?"

Livvy considered the question. "Since first we met, I suspect. I must warn you that I am one to bear a grudge!"

"Did I insult you?" asked Lord Dorset. "It seems to be a habit of mine. Shall I offer my apology?"

"I should not accept it." Livvy was discovering that intimate conversation with the Earl had an effect almost as giddy-making as Madame Arbuthnot's brandy. She hoped the after-effects would not be as severe. "You offered observations on my personality and appearance that were both unsolicited and unflattering." She could well remember her chagrin. "But there! You who are born to the purple cannot be expected to consider those less fortunate with anything but contempt."

"My words rankled, did they?" The Earl exhibited every indication of enjoyment. "I do apologize, and regret my lack of discernment. You are a diamond of the first water, sweet Livvy, and cast every other woman here quite into the shade." His manner was provocative. "I include the Paphian sisterhood."

Livvy studied her long white gloves. "I was not angling for a compliment," she said quietly. The theatre audience, grown restive at the long interval, gave vent to various forms of protest, including catcalls, hisses, and the thudding of canes against the floor.

"Had I thought you were," Dickon replied, sapphire eyes twinkling, "I would not have paid you one." Livvy looked up shyly. "As you rightly pointed out on that occasion, I am a monster of inhumanity."

In the manner of females from time immemorable, Livvy changed her mind. "You are not," she protested. "It was unforgivable of me to say such a thing."

"It was," agreed the Earl cordially. "And you thus revealed yourself to be of as reprehensible a character as I."

Livvy was determined to wear sackcloth and ashes. "I am surprised that you do not read me a terrible scold."

"In public?" inquired Lord Dorset. "It would be extremely foolish of me, particularly in view of our circumstances. If it will ease your merciless conscience, I will endeavor to box your ears in private by and by."

"Wretch!" snapped the widow, good resolutions flying out the window.

The Baroness turned her head. "Children!" she intervened. "Can you not cease billing and cooing, even temporarily? The farce has begun."

"So besotted am I with my darling Livvy," said the Earl with sickening ardor, "that any other matter must seem a dead bore." The object of his affections received a sly wink. "I find that I can concentrate on nothing but the approaching nuptials."

"Ah, young love," sighed Lady Bligh. "How well I remember." So, with nostalgia, did Sir John. "In consideration of those of us who have outlived such excesses, pray keep your voices down!"

"I suspect," murmured Livvy, who found better entertainment in the Earl's nonsensical conversation than in what transpired upon the stage, "that you are laying it on much too rare and thick! You will have the world thinking that I have taken your fancy to a most alarming degree."

"You have, my darling!" Dickon played his part with an expertise born, Livvy suspected, of long practice. "Believe me, I am driven wild by thoughts of you."

"Palaverer!" retorted Livvy. She glanced surreptitiously at the fourth member of their party. "Do you seriously expect Sir John to believe you are suddenly anxious to settle in matrimony?"

"It is an odd thing," Dickon murmured thoughtfully, "but I anticipate little difficulty in that regard. It is from other sources that incredulity will come." His proud features were amused. "With your compliance, dear Livvy, I cannot but succeed."

"You are as bad as Hubert for speaking mysteriously! I have

agreed to help you." Livvy decided to ponder Dickon's cryptic remarks at some other time. It was typical of the man to offer no thanks for efforts undertaken, however unwillingly, in his behalf. "I suspect the lot of us will speedily find ourselves in hot water." She recalled Newgate's forbidding facade. "Or worse!"

"Such a lack of courage!" Lord Dorset mocked. "Reflect that almost overnight you have been pitchforked into the midst of the *ton*. Polite society watches with fascination as I assiduously court you."

"It has never been my ambition," Livvy retorted, "to make a byword of myself." She thought of the *ton*'s reaction when this playacting was done and Lord Dorset deserted her to pay court to ladies more in his style. Polite society would then be less kind. "Let us talk of other things." She eyed him curiously. "Why are you so determined that your son should not come to town? London must hold incomparable delights for a child."

The Earl's brows lowered but he made no attempt to avoid the question. "I do not care to have Austin involved in this thing, nor would I expose him to curious eyes. My son does not speak."

"I'm sorry." Livvy found herself disarmed by Dickon's obvious devotion to the boy. "I should not have pried."

"There is no reason why you should not know." The Earl studied her. "In view of our supposed betrothal, it would be odd if you did not. The doctors find no reason for Austin's silence. It resulted from an accident that occurred when he was in Gwyneth's care."

"I see." Livvy could not imagine the Countess Andrassy in a maternal role. She wondered if this accident had anything to do with the subsequent divorce. "You do not think Gwyneth would be a beneficial influence on her son?"

"I think," Dickon replied seriously, "that the sight of her would send Austin into hysterics. It has happened before."

"Does anyone know," Livvy wondered, "what has brought her back to London at this particular time?"

Lord Dorset grinned. "Pin Arabella's murder on my ex-wife and I will be forever in your debt! No reward will be adequate."

Livvy, intrigued by the notion of holding the Earl thus enthralled, gazed pensively about the theatre, magnificently rebuilt after the fire that had, in 1808, resulted in the deaths of twenty-odd people and the destruction of £15,000 worth of properties. Sir William was, thankfully, not in attendance that evening. In the opposite box, Gwyneth observed Livvy as Hubert looked on. The Earl was leaning close to whisper in his fiancée's ear, and Hubert laughed spitefully at Gwyneth's expression.

"A penny for your thoughts," Dorset murmured. "I find myself intrigued, Livvy, by the secrets that hide behind those lavender eyes."

"No secrets, I assure you." It was much too easy to forget the reason for this masquerade. Livvy reminded herself sternly of the Earl's perverse character. Many another lady who had earned the Earl's warm regard had lived to rue the experience. "I am a very ordinary person, with ordinary thoughts."

"I doubt that very much. Dulcie would have little interest in such a nonentity." There was laughter in his voice. "Now you are the one who frowns and forgets your role." Livvy smiled ferociously. "No, no!" the Earl protested. "Your expression must be gently triumphant, as befits the lady who finally caught me."

"Had I caught you," Livvy retorted, striving for the requisite air, "I should have speedily thrown you away!" Lord Dorset roared with laughter, a feat that Gwyneth during several years of marriage had never managed to perform. From across the width of the theatre, the green-eyed beauty studied her successor speculatively.

Lady Bligh, exhibiting no concern at these various indications that her rakeshame nephew meant to get up a real flirtation with Lavender, leaned conspiratorially toward Sir John. "I believe that an exchange of information might prove beneficial to us both." Her dark eyes were compelling. "Will you oblige me, John?"

The Chief Magistrate knew that he would come out on the short end of any such exchange. "What sort of information?" he inquired cautiously, abandoning his efforts to overhear the Earl's murmured conversation. Sir John was pleasantly surprised in Dickon's fiancée, for Mrs. Lytton was several cuts above the Earl's usual conquests. The Chief Magistrate, whose vast knowledge of humanity had inspired him with little faith in the durability of the tender emotions, wondered how long the infatuation would last.

Lady Bligh was undismayed by his lack of faith. "You might explain to me the functions of a receiver of stolen goods."

This seemed an innocent enough request. "What notion have you taken into your head? Never mind! I'm sure I'd rather not know." Sir John frowned. "It's simple enough. A fence moves stolen property back into circulation, whether it's clothing, trinkets or jewels. Identifying marks must be removed, of course; in some cases, others are substituted."

"I see." The Baroness gazed innocently upon her escort. "Where would one find such a creature?"

"Dulcie!" Sir John grasped her arm. "I won't have you prying into such matters!"

"Dear John." Her tone was close to a caress. "Will you also take it upon yourself to see that Dickon does not hang?" Silently, the Chief Magistrate released her. "I thought not. You may set your mind at rest; I ask simply to be sure." Still he did not speak. "If you do not oblige me, John, you may be sure that Gibbon will!"

"Very well." Even a man as dedicated as Sir John sometimes

grew weary of hearing cases and making decisions that meant life or death, but an evening in Dulcie's provocative company could hardly be considered a restful interlude. "They are often connected with small businesses licensed to deal in gold and silver." Her expression was intent. "You're up to something, and I don't like it. I'll tell you no more."

"You need not." The Baroness was unperturbed. "Such a fussbudget you've become, John! Relax and enjoy yourself, if you can remember how."

"Relax?" repeated the Chief Magistrate incredulously. "When I expect you to be momentarily dragged into Bow Street?" He spoke with little hope of being attended to. "Well, and what information do you have in return for me?"

Dulcie pinched his cheek. "Nothing now, for I cannot be sure. Hush, John, or we shall miss the play." As if she had not a single care, Lady Bligh leaned forward, the better to observe the stage. Sir John sighed heavily, victim of a fleeting impulse to throw the Baroness over his shoulder and vanish into the night, leaving murderers and thieves to wreak havoc as they would while he exacted from her a singularly sweet revenge.

Chapter Nine

LORD DORSET'S CITY residence was a superb stone-fronted townhouse, constructed by Adam, in Cavendish Square. Gwyneth gazed about the first floor drawing room, a chamber fourteen feet high with a finely moulded ceiling, in which were discs of lunettes painted by Antonio Zucchi, wedded to woodwork with carved swags and wreaths, medallions, vases and paterae. "This, at least, you haven't changed." The room contained eighteen oval-backed chairs, numerous wall mirrors and candle scones, a large sideboard, countless tables, and a couch covered with striped horsehair.

The Earl was bored. "It is not a chamber that I use frequently. Out with it, Gwyneth! What has brought you here?"

The Countess Andrassy settled on the couch. "I hope I may call upon my own husband without exciting undue comment!" She presented a flawless profile. "I thought it time that we spoke privately."

"Your divorced husband," Dickon amended, unmellowed by memories of connubial bliss. He lounged against the delicate worked Carrara marble mantelpiece. "What is it you want? I did not imagine that we had much to say to one another—at least of an amiable nature."

Gwyneth brought forth her vinaigrette. "How quickly you forget!" Almost in Dickon's presence, she forgot the purpose of her visit. "It is otherwise with women."

"It is?" Lord Dorset inquired. "I have never found it so." Indifferently, he inspected his visitor. "These lachrymose airs do not suit you, my dear. You are of too robust a figure to sink easily into a decline."

Gwyneth's brief weakness, inspired by the almost overwhelming masculinity of her onetime spouse. abruptly vanished. She waved the vinaigrette. "I loathe you!"

"Much better," commented Dickon. "Far more convincing than your imitation of a watering pot."

"Mrs. Lytton is of a less emotional disposition, I daresay!" It was galling, just when one contemplated an amorous interval, to suffer insult. "I wonder at you, indeed I do! But it is none of *my* concern if you wish to shackle yourself to an icicle."

"Hardly that." The Earl was amused. "Mrs. Lytton suffers no excess of sensibility, but I have seen in her no indication of a lack of passion." He regarded a vase-shaped knife-box that sat upon the sideboard. "It is a matter that I cannot yet discuss with any exactitude, you understand."

Gwyneth's humor grew increasingly sour. "What's this? You worship at the feet of your goddess instead of stealing quick embraces in conveniently darkened rooms? How odd! You were never one to observe the proprieties." Green eyes narrowed spitefully. "Either your nature has changed beyond recognition or Dulcie is proving a strict chaperone."

Though the Earl's mouth twitched at this notion of the

Baroness in the role of duenna, he preserved his sanguine air. "You speak of the past; my eyes have been opened at last. If my treatment of Mrs. Lytton perplexes you, Gwyneth, you must reflect that I have never felt for any other female what I feel for her."

"I see." Gwyneth was further provoked by his lazy, careless smile. "I pity the wench, then, for you are bound to make her miserable."

"I doubt that Mrs. Lytton would have much use for your sympathy," observed Lord Dorset with aggravating smugness.

Abruptly, Gwyneth rose. "You may fool all the world, but you shan't fool me! That insipid female means nothing to you."

"Insipid." The Earl tested the word, in apparent ignorance of the fact that Gwyneth approached him with lustful intent. "You may call my sweet Livvy a number of things, but hardly that." He eyed his ex-wife calmly. "Still waters run deep, my dear. I find myself much more intrigued by fires as yet unlit than by volcanoes who spill molten lava upon all who come near."

"So you've turned chicken-hearted! Was Arabella too spirited a handful for even the legendary Dorset?" Gwyneth's tone was sulfurous. "It is no use to speak to you! You are unwilling to recall even the happy moments that we shared."

"Ah, but they were so few. As you have pointed out innumerable times, we made a ghastly mistake." Dickon carelessly flicked Gwyneth's cheek. "You may spare yourself the travail of enacting me any more tearful scenes, nor need you bring Arabella into this. You will not be permitted to see Austin."

Pale with anger, Gwyneth shoved his hand away. "You underestimate me, Dickon. I *will* see my son, with or without your consent." With grim determination, she strode to the door. "I will go to any lengths to insure that Austin is placed in my care, as I will do my utmost to see Arabella's killer hanged."

"It is not Arabella's killer that you wish to see apprehended, but myself brought low; just as it is not Austin that you covet, but control of his fortune." The Earl was at his most blasé. "You seriously delude yourself if you believe I shall allow you to touch either."

"His fortune?" Gwyneth's fury was arrested. "So the eccentric uncle *did* make Austin his heir! Oddly enough, that thought had never entered my head." Her smile was triumphant. "Thank you, dear Dickon, for an extremely enlightening interview!"

It was not surprising, considering this prelude, that Crump found Lord Dorset in a most unamiable mood. He had expected to interrupt the Earl in a gentleman's usual morning pursuits, holding colloquies with his tailor, bootmaker, and dog fancier, or perfecting the creases of his pristine cravat; instead, the whole household was a-tiptoe, as if the slightest strident noise might bring the structure tumbling down about their ears.

Lord Dorset, on the verge of departure, did not greet his visitor with any great affability. "The button," he remarked. "I thought we should get around to that. Be seated, Crump." A thought struck him. "Or would you prefer that I accompany you to Bow Street?"

"There's no need for that, your lordship." Obediently, Crump selected one of the oval-backed chairs. "Not just now, anyway." The Earl dropped carelessly onto the couch, muscular legs stretched out before him. "Since you brought up the matter, perhaps you'd like to explain that missing button of yours."

"I'd like to very much." Lord Dorset appeared remarkably

sincere. "Alas, I cannot! It is extremely unlike my man to be so careless." One eyebrow rose. "It is a pretty puzzle, is it not? I am missing a button from an evening coat. You have found a button, from a similar evening coat, at Arbuthnot House." The eyebrows lowered. "How extensive is your knowledge of mathematics, Crump?"

"Broad enough to know that two and two make four!" The Runner did not care for this condescending attitude. He thought of the great John Townsend, hired by fashionable people as protection against pickpockets, and wondered if Townsend suffered equal frustration on those many occasions when he was paid handsomely to mingle with haughty aristocrats. "*Was* it your button, Lord Dorset?"

The Earl remained unconcerned. "How should *I* know? Ascertaining such details is your job. If it *is* my button—and I am far too ignorant to venture an opinion on the matter—I can assure you it was not, er, torn from me on the night of Arabella's death." The dark features were mocking. "I was with my fiancée, if you will recall. Believe me, Crump, the last place I'd take Mrs. Lytton is to Arbuthnot House!"

"You may not've taken her there," Crump retorted, recalling all too vividly his most recent interview with Sir William, "but she's been at Arbuthnot House all right, and recently."

"You intrigue me, Crump," said Dickon. "I did not imagine Mrs. Lytton would feel it necessary to proffer sympathy."

"So far was Mrs. Lytton from extending condolences that she left Arbuthnot House in a worse case than she found it!" The Runner couldn't decide whether Sir William was more upset about the death of his wife, the theft of his papers and her jewels, or the disappearance of his mother's companion. "Did you not know she went as a servant to Madame Arbuthnot?"

Lord Dorset's surprise dissolved quickly into amusement,

"Livvy is a very enterprising young lady." Crump was treated to a comradely wink. "A good woman is beyond price, Crump. I am a fortunate man."

Crump believed that the Earl was luckier than he knew, or deserved, since so many people were determined to clear his name. It was understandable that Mrs. Lytton would wish her future husband cleared of any suspicion of murder, at least until her claim to his wealth was assured. Crump had entertained suspicions about Primrose's identity ever since Sir William had drawn a precise, if unflattering, word picture of the missing servant; Lord Dorset's reaction proved his conjectures correct. Never had Crump known the like! An Earl's betrothed passing herself off as a servant! "Will she lie for you as well?"

The Earl considered the question. "I do not know," he said at length. "You must ask her, if you wish to know. I must warn you, however, that Mrs. Lytton is apt to take offense."

Crump wished that he'd fortified himself with more than a quartern of gin before attempting this interview. "You still stick to your story that you were with Mrs. Lytton on the night of Lady Arabella's death?"

Lord Dorset accepted this temerity with godlike aplomb. "I do."

"At Vauxhall, was it?"

"I believe so." The Earl surveyed a gleaming boot. "My memory for such things is shockingly remiss."

Lord Dorset drinking heavily and far into the night, had once won so staggering an amount at the whist table that White's doors had almost closed permanently. Crump began to see how the thing was done. The Earl's composure was nothing short of formidable. "Trysted often, did the two of you?"

"Crump!" Dickon was pained. "I cannot allow you to cast aspersions on the lady who is soon to become my wife!"

"Seems to me," Crump retorted testily, "that you behave

queerly for a man wishful of protecting a lady's name! No sooner do you get involved in murder than you engage yourself to her and make her an object of great curiosity."

"You seem to believe," Lord Dorset murmured thoughtfully, "that I have done Mrs. Lytton a grave disservice. Perhaps you are correct." The habitual impatience reappeared. "Make haste, Crump! I have an appointment to view the prettiest little filly one might ever wish to see."

"A woman called at this house," Crump said, with an equal lack of good temper, "on the night in question. I would like to know her identity."

"You have been told who she was. Must we belabor the subject?" The Earl scowled. "It is hardly your concern if Mrs. Lytton was so anxious to see me that she could not await the appointed hour."

"On the contrary, it's very much my concern." Crump was hot on the scent. "The lady was heavily veiled, but she could not disguise the color of her hair." He paused dramatically. "May I point out that Mrs. Lytton's hair is black, not brown?"

"You hardly need remind me of the color of Livvy's hair." Calm as a bestilled ocean, Dickon smiled. "Lovely, is it not? In view of our circumstances, we thought it best she not be easily recognized." Gracefully, he took snuff. "The explanation is simple: Mrs. Lytton wore a wig."

Crump hooked his thumbs in his waistcoat. "Then where," he demanded, "did Lady Arabella vanish to on the night she died? More than three hours are unaccounted for!"

"Have you ever witnessed a séance, Crump?" asked the Earl helpfully. "You must speak with my aunt. She is well up on such things."

"A séance?" Crump was confused. "I'd appreciate it if you'd explain."

"I'm amazed." Lord Dorset looked particularly diabolical.

"Have you never attended one of those convivial gatherings? I recommend it strongly! You might have your answers straight from the horse's mouth." He smiled. "So to speak."

"Horse?" Crump repeated weakly. He felt like he'd fallen into a vat of molasses, or a spider's web.

"The purpose of a séance," explained the Earl kindly, "is to call up the dead." He closed the enamelled snuffbox with an expert flick of his wrist.

Crump's brows snapped together in a terrible frown. "You'll be having your little game, guv'nor." His glance was buzzardlike. "Why did you slash Lady Arabella's portrait to shreds?"

Dickon was caught in mid-motion. "I beg your pardon?" For the first time, Crump saw Lord Dorset without a mask. "Arabella's portrait?"

Crump was disgruntled, for his tactics had shocked the Earl into betraying nothing more damning than astonishment. "It was your knife, all right, same as it was your knife found stuck in Lady Arabella's er . . ."

"Bosom," supplied the Earl. "An unattractive word, but suitable. It always reminds me, somehow, of deflated balloons."

"We're getting off the subject," Crump persevered. "I haven't heard a reasonable explanation of that knife."

"Ah, the knife." Lord Dorset looked, Crump thought, like a man with secrets. "You are not the only person to be intrigued by that knife. I have received a veritable avalanche of mail."

"Mail?" Crump realized, with disgust, that he sounded like a bloody mocking bird.

"Letters," Dickon explained patiently. "Few are of an admiring tone. Not only do my anonymous fans exhibit great interest in my knife, some have gone so far as to express a wish for my blood." The Earl pondered. "I wonder what they mean to do with it."

Crump tried a diversionary tactic. "What do you know of

the mysterious gentleman who first appeared some months ago at Arbuthnot House?"

"Gentleman? I would hardly call him that." Lord Dorset smiled benignly. "You refer, of course, to Arabella's long-lost cousin, so miraculously restored to her?"

"Her cousin, is it?" Crump had not expected such an obliging reply.

"So she called him, though I seriously doubt the validity of the relationship. If a cousin, not one held in any great esteem." Crump waited hopefully as Dickon consulted his unreliable memory. "I only observed this so-called cousin once, and then briefly. Arabella was most anxious to whisk him out of my sight. The name, I believe, was James."

"She didn't want you to talk to him?" The puzzle grew. "Didn't that strike you as queer?"

"Not at all." Lord Dorset rose. "Arabella's cousin bore more resemblance to a Captain Sharp than to one with any pretentions to gentility. He was memorable only for the vulgarity of his attire." The Earl's gaze rested eloquently upon Crump's Jockey waistcoat, which boasted vertical stripes of gaudy hue. "Which calls to mind another person of whom, I think, you have not taken sufficient heed."

"Who might that be?" Crump regretted the necessity of treating Lord Dorset with kid gloves, but the Chief Magistrate had made it painfully clear that no charges were to be brought until the murderer's identity was unquestionable.

"My estimable cousin, of course. Hubert was not only among Arabella's admirers, he has suffered recent financial reverses." The Earl observed the Runner's face. "You disapprove of my frankness? I collect you are not well acquainted with Humbug. He would be only too happy to serve me an equal turn." A gold watch came into play. "You must forgive me for terminating this fascinating interview, but I must tend to my filly before someone else snaps her up."

Crump doubted this excuse. It was far more likely that Lord Dorset's engagement was with one of the pretty horsebreakers known by such appellations as Brazen Bellona or The Queen of Tarts. Scowling, he followed the Earl into the long hallway. "I wonder if you might tell me how Mrs. Lytton managed, on the night she came here, to look both shorter and more opulent of figure than she actually is."

"Ask her!" Lord Dorset advised. "Considering that you haven't the slimmest shred of evidence against either Mrs. Lytton or myself, your interest seems a trifle excessive, does it not? But my horses grow restless." He paused in the front doorway, which was surmounted by a semi-circular light with a straight-rayed fan tracery. "I wish you luck in your further investigations, Crump, and advise you to tread cautiously!"

Crump crammed his hat upon his head and strode vengefully away, more determined than ever to prove the guilt of the maddening Earl.

While Lord Dorset sought distraction from his various afflictions among cronies at Tattersall's, that grand mart for everything concerned with sports of the field, the business of the turf, and equestrian recreations, his indomitable aunt was engaged in an undertaking of a far less respectable nature. Gibbon swallowed hard as they skirted the ground level opening of an underground slaughterhouse, its walls inches thick in putrefying blood and fat, into which sheep were hurled to be, broken legged, knifed and flayed by the men below.

The Baroness displayed no revulsion at either the carnage or the bloody stench. "Remove that offended expression at once!" she hissed. "You forget who we're supposed to be."

Gibbon, gazing down upon the tattered smock that proclaimed him a none too sanitary country laborer, grew even more morose. "As if I could, my lady." His white hair, matted with dirt, clung closely to his high-domed skull. "Never have I been so mortified." It was a sensation he experienced anew each time Lady Bligh set out with him upon one of her forays into London's less prosperous areas.

"Would you prefer," Dulcie asked, "to see Master Dickon rot in jail?" The Baronees, in a rusty black gown, looked like a particularly malevolent crone. Straggling locks of lank gray hair peered from beneath the stained shawl that covered her head and shoulders. "It is not an impossibility. He could also be transported—or hanged."

"Not Master Dickon, my lady." Gibbon thought of the various methods of discipline that awaited hapless criminals. Flogging was a mild punishment compared with the treadmill, the shot drill, and an ingenious engine of torture referred to, in hushed tones, as the crank. "May I remind you, my lady, that you are not without influence?"

The Baroness mingled easily with street screamers, thieves, and running patterers crying hoarsely of assassinations, seductions, alarming accidents. "May I remind *you* of where we are?" Her tone was reprimanding. "You do me no great favor by using my title here."

Gibbon offered no apology, being too busy removing his mistress from the path of a herd of cattle being driven through the street. Never had Gibbon suspected, when first he entered Lady Bligh's employ, that he would be called upon to conduct his iron-willed mistress upon regular excursions into the worst of London's rookeries. He gazed bleakly upon the decaying piles of tenements that lined black, dilapidated streets where children played in gutters that were no more than open sewers. It was a scene that he once thought to forever leave behind, a setting for drunken violence and a breeding place for crime.

They stopped before a tall, crazy house that verged on imminent collapse. "Step lively, Gibbon!" Resigned, the butler preceded his mistress through the gaping doorway, as ominous and foul as must surely be the gates of hell.

A crafty-eyed slattern leaned against the wall. "Look alive, slut," Gibbon said roughly. "We're wanting the mot of the ken."

The woman spat. "Think you're the only ones?" She reeked of gin. "Jael won't be trafficking with the likes of you." Silently, Gibbon held forth a coin. The woman bit it, shrugged, then stepped aside.

The house was filthy and ill-ventilated, a stopping place where transient wayfarers might sleep, huddled together regardless of age and sex, eighteen and twenty to a room. For a penny deposit, they might hire knife or fork with which to eat their greasy food. Grim-faced, Gibbon ploughed through the muck on the staircase, the Baroness in his wake, and led the way to the back of the house where two evil-visaged men guarded a closed door. The Baroness drew aside the concealing shawl and held forth two gold coins. Recognizing her as a regular, and open-fisted, visitor, the men moved aside.

Stepping through that forbidden doorway was like passing into another country. Here was none of the stifling heat and revolting smell that permeated the rest of the house, no sign of disease-ridden poverty. Well-executed prints hung on pristine walls above furniture that might have graced the abode of any successful businessman. Gibbon, a figure of silent condemnation, took up a watchful position beside the door. Lady Bligh moved toward a massive chair where the matron of the establishment and unofficial regent of the entire rookery was enthroned.

Jael was an eye-catching, dark-skinned woman of perhaps thirty-five, with unbound jet-black hair and pale grey eyes. If not for the thin scar that ran from left cheekbone to chin, she might have competed with the most successful courtesan. "You're got up clever, Baroness." Bare feet peeped from beneath a bright-hued skirt as Jael rose. "It's not necessary; no one would dare harm you here."

"Wretched girl," remarked Lady Bligh, seating herself at a table. "Do you mean to spoil my fun?"

"From what I hear, you've been up to as many tricks as a barrelful of monkeys." Jael picked up a desk of garish cards and placed herself opposite the Baroness. "Take care, Dulcie. There's only so much I can do for you."

Gibbon remained impassive only through great effort. Not only must Lady Bligh associate with this brazen creature who, it was rumored, had been mistress to royalty before the mysterious assault that had left her both embittered and scarred, but must speak to her as an equal as well. Once the relationship had been conducted on a more businesslike basis, with the Baroness paying dearly to have her fortune read, but this state of affairs had abruptly altered on the infamous day when Dulcie saved the gypsy from a long prison incarceration. Jael paid her debts, for good or ill, as many a luckless offender speedily learned.

"You can read the cards," the Baroness retorted, "and spare me any further lectures. It is a sublime case of the pot calling the kettle black!"

Jael laughed, revealing perfect teeth. No small force in London's underworld, the gypsy was well-known to Bow Street, where the standard practice was to leave her strictly alone. "It's more a case of leaping from the frying pan into the fire, if you take my meaning!" She shuffled the cards. "There's those who mean to see Dorset hang, and they won't take kindly to interference."

"They shall have to." Dulcie cut the cards to the left, frowning with concentration. "Name the person behind it, Jael."

"I can't." This in itself was ominous; a considerable force of pickpockets, prostitutes, cutthroats and worse were at Jael's disposal, sharp-eared creatures who were well rewarded for information received. "There is vague talk, but no names." Jael set out ten cards in a Celtic cross. In the center sat the Queen of Wands, a staff in her right hand and a sunflower in her left, at her feet a sinister black cat.

"What of Arabella's jewels?" The Baroness studied the cards. So often had Gibbon observed this ritual that he thought he might himself lay out the cards, could he but gather sufficient courage to touch the wicked deck.

"Paste!" Golden earrings danced as Jael tossed her head. "That lady had deep dealings, and not just at the gaming table. Her baubles have been turning up regular as clockwork." The pale eyes rested on the Baroness. "There is a first-rate milliner on Bond Street, an establishment most respectable on the outside."

"And inside?" There were not many anxious to meet Jael's cold gaze, as eerie and bone-chilling as a midnight cemetery.

The gypsy smiled. "You are an innocent, Baroness. Inside are Paphian intricacies available not only to bits o' muslin but to married women and their lovers. The cost is a mere guinea or two."

"Arabella was a client?" Dulcie absently twisted the fringe of her shawl. "How enterprising, to be sure."

"The owner of the place engages in discreet blackmail. From all accounts, hers wasn't the only hand in Lady Arabella's purse." Jael leaned across the table. "Never fear, it wasn't Lord Dorset she met there. Idiot woman! I'd have met him there myself, had the opportunity come my way in an earlier day!"

Lady Bligh, untroubled by this frank disclosure, frowned at the table. "The cards."

A Ten of Swords lay across the Queen of Wands. "Your question concerned Dorset? Ruin and pain surround him, affliction and tears."

Gibbon, to whom the dissolute Earl had never spoken an unkind word, shifted positions uncomfortably. He could not take the reading of the Tarot seriously, except in Jael's commanding presence, listening to her hushed and somber tones.

The gypsy looked puzzled. "Has Dorset any children?"

"One," the Baroness replied. "That I have been apprised of."

"A son." Jael cracked the knuckles of one surprisingly elegant hand. "The boy will take an unexpected journey. He is threatened by selfishness and greed."

"That may be," Lady Bligh remarked, "a gross understatement. Pray continue."

"Justice, reversed: legal complications and excessive severity." The gypsy regarded her visitor. "I warned you. Dorset has powerful enemies."

"Powerful in what way?" Dulcie was equally serious. "Surely not politically. How, then?"

"Evil, but no creature of mine. Only a fool would kill for imitation jewels." The mocking smile flashed again. "If it's fools you hunt, then look among the nobs! Any true thief would immediately know the difference between paste gems and the genuine thing."

"The last card, the outcome, if you please."

"The Nine of Wands, reversed. Obstacles and delay." Jael settled back in her chair. "You will not have an easy task. I wish you luck of it!"

The Baroness sighed heavily. "Well you may, for I know not where to begin." Gibbon perked his ears; he knew that feeble tone. "It seems that now I must determine what became of the real gems as well as the copies, and why!" She bowed her head. "Perhaps I am foolish, and waste my time. Perhaps Dickon truly *is* guilty of the crime."

"Ah, he'd die damned hard and bold as brass." For the first time, Jael's manner was sympathetic. Gibbon wondered what artful scheme his mistress was embarked upon. "Will you abandon him so easily, Baroness? What if I tell you it's a certainty Lord Dorset is guiltless as a new-born babe?" The gypsy laughed. "At least in this affair!"

"Truly, I believe in his innocence." The Baroness grew even

more frail. "What can *I* do, an old woman, alone? Particularly when, as my nephew Hubert informs me, I am thought to be wandering in the wits?"

Jael, recipient of a mournful stare, snorted. "A royal scamp, *he* is!" Gibbon wondered what this denizen of the underworld knew of the exquisite Hubert. Humbug might warrant some investigation of his own. "You're pitching it too rum, Baroness! Do you think to so easily pull the wool over my eyes?" Jael rose and moved to an iron-bound chest.

"I had hoped," Dulcie admitted, abandoning her elderly air, "to do something of the sort. In a mad quest like this, one needs whatever help one may obtain."

"You'll meddle once too often, Baroness." Jael's smile was blood curdling now, a strong reminder of the fact that even the most hardened criminals held Jael in awe. Gibbon moved quietly to his mistress's side. It was commonly known that the gypsy concealed a small arsenal of weaponry in her gaudy attire, instruments of violence she was not reluctant to use. "Perhaps one fine morning we'll fish your body out of the river, along with all the other riffraff who've pried where they should not."

"I sincerely hope not," remarked Lady Bligh, sublimely unconcerned. "I'd hope for a more decorous end."

"May it be granted you." Jael reached into the chest. Gibbon, with a speed unsuggested by his cadaverous frame, darted forward to grasp her wrist. He next found himself in an ignominious position, sprawled upon the hard floor. The gypsy watched with great amusement as the Baroness hauled her butler to his feet.

"I appreciate your concern, Gibbon, but you must learn not to interfere." Dulcie's tone was as stern as if she had not spent her entire adult life poking and prying with uninhibited glee.

Jael shook with laughter. "God's bones, but I like you,

Dulcie Bligh!" She extended a handful of sparkling gems. "Here, take these before I change my mind."

The Baroness gingerly inspected the diamond necklace, once judged to be of sufficient brilliance to grace the young Arabella's elegant neck. "You have only this piece?"

Jael nodded. "It's bloody queer. Sir William was so besotted that he ate out of Arabella's hand; why, then, did she have to sell her gems? He'd have fetched her the moon, by all accounts, if she asked him to." The gypsy looked at the diamonds regretfully. "I must be daft! Those are the finest stones I've ever laid hands upon." Gibbon, sulking, thought that Jael had probably collected no small store of unlawful merchandise. He'd have given much to learn the trick by which she'd laid him out so easily.

Dulcie tucked the necklace into the bodice of her ragged gown, causing her butler to blush crimson with embarrassment. "You'll be well paid, Jael."

"I expect to be." The gypsy returned to her thronelike chair and reached for a long-stemmed pipe. "Go away now. I'll waste no more time on you." It was not tobacco that she smoked, but the opium that had once numbed her hunger pains.

"One more question." Lady Bligh's glance was stern. "Where are the rest of the gems?"

The gypsy surveyed her visitor through a cloud of sweet smoke. Few dared to speak to Jael in that imperious tone. "You've a nose like a bloodhound." She decided to be amused. "I've told you all I know."

Gibbon hovered at the door, hopeful of a speedy exit, but the Baroness was not done. "You're lying," she said bluntly. "Why?"

Jael's eyes narrowed. "Damned if you aren't a feisty one! You dare venture into *my* territory and order me around like you were a grand duchess and I was a scullery maid. Men have died for less!"

"Well?" Dulcie was polite. Gibbon quaked in his boots, seeing the two of them floating face down in the foul Thames.

"God knows what's to be done with you!" Jael muttered. "They say the Lord protects fools." The cold eyes rested on Lady Bligh with a grudging respect. "We will see, won't we? Look for a down-at-the-heels gambler known as Slippery Jim."

Chapter Ten

LIVVY'S SCRUPLES HAD been overcome. Lady Bligh, having at last found a perfect excuse to deck out her companion in a dashing style, had set out on a whirlwind shopping expedition that culminated in vast quantities of silk stockings, French gloves, satins and brocades, Indian muslins, tippets of fur and feathers, plumes of every kind, ribbon and lace and fancy trimmings, all in the latest mode, and countless new costumes to be delivered with all possible speed. Livvy could no more have stopped the Baroness than she might stave off a full-scale hurricane. At length she had given up the unequal struggle and sat back, with only a small pang of conscience, to relish her unaccustomed luxury.

"You are enjoying yourself?" Lord Dorset wore a long-tailed coat of sky blue cloth, polished top-boots, a jaunty hat and gloves; and he was exercising the practiced charm that had led so many ladies to cast prudence to the wind.

"I am." Livvy gazed upon a street sweeper, a painfully

ragged urchin who darted forward to remove horse dung from their path. "I should not, I know, but I have never before had an opportunity to discover that London is so interesting." She realized that she had been caught off guard, tricked into speaking frankly while favorably comparing Dickon's moderate shirt points with the neck-stretching cravats preferred by the dandy set, and waited for the inevitable ridicule.

Dickon did not oblige, but led her firmly past an Italian organgrinder with a hurdy-gurdy slung from one shoulder and a chattering monkey perched on the other. "Poor Livvy! You have a Puritan conscience and an irreverent soul." The harsh features were amused. "Which will triumph, I wonder?"

From the corner of her eye, Livvy caught her image in a dirty shopwindow. She wore a carriage dress of white poplin with a deep blonde flounce and a blue levantine pelisse edged with floss silk. Covering her dark curls was a cottage bonnet of blue twilled sarcenet tied with a large ribbon bow. "I do not know." Foolish to condemn the Earl's profligacy when, given the opportunity, she would doubtless prove every bit as dissipated as he. She cast him a mischievous look. "It is the Dashwood blood, I fear."

"The devil!" Lord Dorset's amusement increased. "You are a descendant of Sir Francis?" That gentleman, an accomplished and industrious rake, had gained posthumous fame not only as an inept statesman and patron of the arts, but for the perverse eccentricity that led him to work with Benjamin Franklin on a revision of the Book of Common Prayer while simultaneously conducting sinister and bizarre satanic rites at Menmenham Abbey, which he owned.

"It is not something of which I boast," Livvy replied, wondering if she should have so recklessly acknowledged her infamous ancestor. "I do not know why I told you at all! Let us make haste, lest Smirke think I do not mean to keep my appointment with her."

The Earl chivalrously refrained from pointing out that their tardiness was due to Livvy's fascination with a circus menagerie, which he had not been able to persuade her to abandon until she had viewed the quantities of stock and equipment laden on long, lumbering wagon trains. Her enthusiasm extended to the caravan owners, who were engaged in cooking, like so many tinkers, in black pots outside the wagon train, and it had taken all Dickon's diplomacy to finally lure her away. "Smirke will wait," he replied. "She will not bypass an opportunity for profit."

"It is an avaricious world," said Livvy, allowing herself to be escorted into a coffeehouse. She looked about with interest; this too was a new experience. In the center of the narrow room were dozens of padded armchairs, and a table bearing journals and newspapers secured by long chains. Sawdust covered the floor. "It is kind of you to accompany me to this meeting, though Mary or Gibbon would have done as well."

Dickon frowned. "That they would not." He conducted her to a high-backed seat. Each of the booths that lined the walls bore the likeness of a different great man in literature and art, ranging from Ben Jonson to Gainsborough. "You forget your position. Ladies do not venture into surroundings such as these, even with their servants' protection."

"Your presence, however, makes it right with the world?" Livvy scowled at a likeness of Fielding, sharply reminded of Dickon's peril. "I thank you for your efforts to lend me countenance!"

"Not right," Lord Dorset corrected, "but permissible." He was sardonic. "You must know that I am expected to lead you into depravity."

Livvy was stricken mute by the startling discovery that this was a path she would very much like to tread, with Dickon as her guide. Resolutely she placed her errant heart under closer guard. Lord Dorset played a game with her, nothing more; his passionate nature must chafe at the restrictive bonds of this mock betrothal. He was only flirting with her to alleviate his boredom.

"Did you know," inquired the Earl, "that your face is a perfect mirror for your thoughts?" She stared at him, aflame with guilty embarrassment. "Sweet Livvy, you worry needlessly."

"Mrs. Lytton?" A plain, middle-aged woman stood by the table. "I am Smirke. Bertha told me I was to meet you here."

Livvy thought, as the abigail joined them, that this woman would never succumb to frivolity. Smirke's unfeminine severity was strongly reminiscent of Dulcie's abigail, Culpepper; perhaps it was characteristic of the breed. For herself, Livvy was content with Mary's pert mischievousness. A stout apron-wrapped individual deposited a tray of coffee and biscuits on the table, then bustled away.

"I saw a hanging at Tyburn once," Smirke volunteered, helping herself to biscuits as if she had not eaten for a week, "when I was a child. A grand thing it was, too, with people everywhere! I was eating bread dipped in mutton fat when they put the black hood over the highwayman's head." The guant face was ghoulish. "The executioner drove off the horses and left the villain kicking in the air." She gave the Earl a grisly grin. "He was a long time dying. There was no one to pull on his body, and hasten his end." Idly, she scratched her head. "I still have a copy of his dying speech."

"It is a pity that such spectacles are no longer held at Tyburn," the Earl remarked, as calm as if he were not threatened by the same fate. "They were remarkably edifying."

Having disposed of the biscuits, Smirke leaned back on the hard wooden seat. "Mind you, I don't care if Lady Arabella's murderer hangs or not. When I was her abigail, many was the time I wished to squeeze the life out of the hussy with my own hands!" She looked at Livvy. "I beg pardon, ma'am! She turned me off without a reference and it still fair makes my blood boil. I can tell you, I've seen hard times since then."

This had to be true; Smirke looked like walking death. "Why did she dismiss you? Were you not with her a good number of years?"

"I was, since her marriage to the Duke. Then she met Sir William." Smirke was sullen. "First she said she no longer had need of my services, but I wasn't about to take that lying down, not from her!" The woman's mouth twisted viciously. "When she saw I meant business, she accused me of stealing from her, and threatened to turn me over to the magistrates."

"*Did* you steal from your mistress?" The Earl was mildly curious.

"A woman," whined Smirke, "has to live. You needn't think that Lady Arabella was generous." Her shifty gaze settled on him. "*You* know what she was!"

Livvy's high spirits suddenly evaporated in a struggle with searing jealousy. Arabella had enjoyed the Earl's admiration, a pleasure that, to Livvy, might more than compensate for a tragically premature demise.

Then her thoughts took a new turn. She had not considered the possibility of Dickon's prior acquaintance with Arabella's ex-abigail. Suddenly suspicious, she wondered if he hoped to prevent Smirke from revealing information injurious to him. "When were you first taken into Arabella's employ?"

"Just before she wed the Duke." Smirke was spiteful. "A brazen hussy she was, even then. What she wasn't was virgin, though she fooled the Duke well enough." She cackled. "The besotted old man was properly taken in."

"Where was Arabella from?" Livvy asked quickly, not eager to learn further details of the lady's marriage bed.

"Coward!" murmured the Earl.

Smirke shrugged. "A country village, I can't recall the name."

"Try," advised Lord Dorset, reaching into a pocket. Smirke's face brightened.

"Lady Arabella was a wild girl. There was some sort of scandal; I never learned what. Her aunt raised her after her parents died."

"That won't do." Lord Dorset withdrew his empty hand. "We must know the village name." Livvy half wished Dickon had dealt with Bertha. It would have been an interesting battle between wit and greed.

Smirke's greasy forehead wrinkled with the effort of sustained thought. "I'll ponder on it." She glanced up hopefully. "I doubt the family was well-off. Arabella was as feckless as someone who'd never had money of her own. She had enough after she came to London, though, and deposited herself on the grandmama's doorstep."

"I don't understand," Livvy interrupted.

"Lady Arabella's father," Smirke explained, "was an adventurer. He married above himself, and his wife's family cast her off. Later Arabella's grandfather came into a title, and a fortune. I reckon they didn't know of Arabella's existence, and when she showed up they took her in." Smirke's tone was faintly admiring. "Arabella fooled them too, for a while, though when they learned of her carrying-on they washed their hands of her." There was no need to add that the final straw had been Arabella's indiscreet liaison with the Earl. "They're all dead now."

"You astound me," remarked Lord Dorset. "I had not realized Arabella was of so confiding a nature."

Smirke laughed. "You should know better, my lord! I've always been one to keep my eyes and ears open, as they say." Mirth faded. "That's why she sent me away, I'll wager; I knew too much for her peace of mind."

This conversation was affecting Livvy oddly; she felt like she was being stuck with white-hot pins. "Was Lady Arabella afraid of anyone?"

"Afraid!" Smirke was dumbfounded. "She had no fear of the devil himself! Bold as brass, she was."

Arabella's unease, then, did not precede her marriage to Sir William. Livvy's interest quickened.

"Your wife was the one Arabella confided in," Smirke added, following another train of thought. Livvy was subjected to an unflattering appraisal. "Your first wife, that is!" The narrow gaze grew speculative. "I wonder how curious you are about your son's accident."

Though Lord Dorset retained his impassivity, Livvy, with her newly heightened sensitivity, was aware of his tension. "Very, very curious," he replied. "What might you know about that?"

Smirke knew she'd struck a nerve. "Make it worth my while," she suggested. "They talked in front of me like I was a piece of furniture." Carelessly, Dickon dropped a gold coin on the table. Smirke grabbed it; then, with a familiarity that inspired Livvy with a wish to throttle her, patted the Earl's arm. "I know about the argument that followed, too, when your lady went for your face with her sewing shears but caught only your hand."

Livvy sat rigid with shock, and Lord Dorset's expression darkened. "The accident, if you please!"

Smirke had blundered badly and sought to make amends. "It was no mishap. Lady Dorset slapped her son and knocked him down the stairs." The expression on the Earl's face was blood chilling. "No need to look that way, my lord! The boy took little harm from it. What frightened him more was when she locked him in that dark closet for days at a time, feeding him bread and water and telling him tales of wicked children burning in hell."

"Dear Lord," whispered Livvy, through stiff lips. As if awakening from a nightmare, the Earl looked at her.

"I was a fool," he said, "to try to force Gwyneth into a maternal mold. Her temper is vicious, but I never suspected she had gone so far. I assume the servants were too afraid of her to come to me, or were bribed to remain silent."

Smirke had little interest in the Earl's personal problems. She quickly drew the conversation back to matters which might be of profit to her. "You're not the first ones to come asking questions about Lady Arabella. There was a man some months ago, wanting to know about her past."

Livvy reflected that Arabella was certainly a prime candidate for blackmail. "Who was he, do you know?" She thought it might be Crump, though Bow Street would hardly investigate a crime that had not yet occurred. "Did he wear a striking waistcoat and reek of tobacco?"

Smirke shook her head. "Not him. He was a shabby little person who looked like he needed a square meal." She pondered. "Nor was he a thief-taker," she added, well-acquainted with that breed.

"What did you tell him?" Dickon asked, emotionless.

"Little enough." Smirke picked at crumbs. "*He* hadn't the wherewithal to loosen my tongue." The Earl gestured and a fresh supply of biscuits appeared. "I don't think he knew what he was looking for." Smirke chewed busily. "He didn't know anything about Arabella, not even what questions to ask." She paused, mouth open. "Sapping! That's the village where she's from. It came to me just like that!"

"Sapping," mused Livvy, and rose in response to Dickon's nod. She watched as Smirke received a handful of gold coins. "Am I mistaken, or does Hubert's home not lie near there?"

"You are seldom mistaken," Lord Dorset replied, escorting her to the door, "except in matters concerning myself. Humbug is more and more drawn into this thing. I believe it time my foolish cousin and I have a serious talk." He frowned. "Then, Gwyneth."

"Dickon!" Forgetting her various noble resolutions, Livvy clutched his arm. "She has been exceedingly wicked and cruel, but you must not seek revenge!"

"You upset yourself unduly." The Earl's hand closed over hers. "If Gwyneth's death could alter what she has done to Austin, I would dispose of her summarily—but it will not."

"What do you mean to do?" Livvy tried in vain to pull her hand away.

"I shall call upon Gwyneth." Dickon led his fiancée into the sunlight. "And inform her of what I have learned. She will be forced to abandon her schemes concerning my son, or find herself involved unhappily with the law. I doubt that Gwyneth will remain in London long."

"Will she offer Austin further harm?" Livvy did not think the Countess Andrassy would be so easily routed.

"Austin is well protected." The Earl helped Livvy into his sporty curricle. "Thank God I did not listen to my aunt and bring him to town."

Livvy, unreassured, sank onto the well-upholstered seat. None knew better than she that it was foolish to ignore the Baroness's forebodings. "Cheer up, sweet Livvy!" Dickon took the reins. "We shall earn Dulcie's highest praise, for we bring her revelations of the most extraordinary."

But Livvy was not listening. She had received a shattering revelation of her own, a realization of her unsuitability for the role she played. Even if Lord Dorset overcame the disillusionment that had attended his first experience with the joys of matrimony, he would never woo an impoverished widow without claim to even a good name. He was engaging in this charade purely to save his own skin. Then it occurred to Livvy that, were not Arabella's murderer quickly found, Dickon's future might be entirely hypothetical. "What will become of Smirke?" she asked.

"Nothing good, I imagine." Lord Dorset was concerned only with guiding his carriage through the crowded streets. "She will probably be dead of the pox in a few years' time, if she doesn't starve first. She is not the sort of wench to attract the attention of more discriminating gentlemen."

"I see." Livvy wore a secret little smile.

"What amuses you?" asked Dickon. "Most ladies of my acquaintance would swoon away to learn that they had spent the past hour in conversation with a whore."

"I was thinking of my father." Livvy looked into the past. "He was so pious that he must now dwell among martyrs and saints. I cannot imagine what he would say to his daughter's acquaintance with a lady of easy virtue!"

"Does it matter?" the Earl asked, interested.

"Not in the least!" Livvy retorted briskly. "He and I disliked each other most cordially."

A man of more virtuous character might have been offended by this bluntly unfilial attitude, but Dickon laughed aloud. "My adorable girl!" Livvy's wide eyes flew to his face. "How could I ever have thought you strait-laced?"

"It does not signify," Livvy snapped irritably. "I thought *you* an arrogant, overbearing boor." Whatever transpired, the Earl must never suspect that her affections were seriously engaged. "My opinion, I must add, has not altered one iota."

"I thought it had not, little hornet." Dickon's smile was wicked. "What a splendid time we shall have!"

Sea-coal smoke from countless domestic hearths hung low over busy London thoroughfares. Crump, tired of his fruitless vigil, breached the walls of Tattersall's, at Hyde Park Corner, headquarters of the Turf. Though there was no sale scheduled this day, Tattersall's was thronged with sporting gentlemen engaged in the examination of horses' merits or defects and the exchange of related intelligence.

An excellent painting of Eclipse hung over the fireplace. Sir William's nasal tones were raised in strident argument concerning the invaluable properties of his favorite setter. He was an eye-catching figure in a curly-brimmed beaver, drab benjamin, a tightly fitting coat of superfine, sporting waistcoat, and yellow buckskins. When his red-rimmed gaze fell on Crump, he abruptly moved away from the circular counter. "What," he demanded, "are you doing here?"

"Looking for you, guv'nor," Crump replied genially, listening to the recitation of a carriage horse's pedigree. "We need to have a little talk, you and me."

"Not here." Sir William glanced about him and hustled the Runner outside. He nourished improbable aspirations to membership in the Four-in-Hand Club run by Lords Sefton and Barrymore, Colonel Berkely, Sir John Lade and the Marquis of Worcester; an intimate association with Bow Street would hardly advance his cause. " 'Tis a nice day for a walk," Crump suggested, and led the way into the park.

Sir William, no enthusiast of gently aimless strolls, deposited his vast bulk on a marble bench. "You've results at last? You've found the jewels?"

Crump surveyed the florid gentleman. It was a ticklish situation, for matters of law had changed little since the previous century when almost all prosecutions were initiated by private persons and conducted in accordance with their wishes. It was Sir William who had called in Bow Street, just as it was Sir William who offered a reward; and, though Crump might dislike the fleshy fool, and doubt his ability to render monies due, he must proceed with a certain amount of tact. "Well?" demanded Sir William impatiently.

"No jewels yet, guv'nor." Crump smoothed his lime green waistcoat. "The thief is lying low." He observed Sir William's darkening countenance. "No need to fly into a temper, sir! We'll find him soon enough."

"Is *that* all you have to tell me?" Sir William bellowed wrathfully, attracting the interest of a nursery maid with chubby child in tow. Briefly distracted, he followed her well-rounded figure with an appreciative eye. "I am far from satisfied with the efforts of Bow Street."

Nor was Crump complacent about the meager facts that he had thus far upturned. "It begins to look," he offered cautiously, "that Lord Dorset may not be our man."

"Devil take you!" roared Sir William, startling the birds out of various nearby trees. "Dorset is guilty as bedamned, and I mean to see him dangle in the sheriff's picture frame!" His heavy jowls quivered. "How has Dorset got around you? Did he offer you a bribe?"

Crump experienced a sneaking sympathy for the luckless Arabella. Given a spouse like Sir William, it was not surprising she chose to alleviate her boredom with Italian music masters, actors, even the corrosive Earl of Dorset. "There may be some members of Bow Street," he replied coldly, "who can be bought off. I am not one of them."

Sir William smiled nervously. "No need to take offense! You can understand a man's natural grief, I'm sure." He rested damp hands on one pudgy knee. "What *have* you learned?"

"Not enough to invite Lord Dorset into the Palace of Newgate." Crump had no intention of sharing his carefully gathered information with this fat clown who would immediately blab it all over the town. "Though it seems likely that he spent some time with your wife on the night she died."

Oddly, Sir William showed little surprise. "I could have guessed that! She was forever sneaking off to meet him, I'm told. If only I had known sooner, I might have avoided a nasty scandal." Gloom sat heavy on him. "Damned if I know why you must dither, man! You can be certain that Dorset has the jewels."

"We have searched his home. There was no sign of them."

"Look again!" Sir William thought of the post-obit bills stuffed away in his desk and wiped perspiration from his brow. "Dorset's a clever rascal. We must lull his suspicions, then close in quickly for the kill."

Crump found this conversation distasteful, even though the

Earl could hardly be considered easy prey. "Very well. It will be as you say."

"What have you learned of my missing papers? Or my mother's companion?"

"Primrose?" Crump took his figurative hat off to the courageous Mrs. Lytton, who was as plucky a female as he'd ever seen, even if very foolish in matters of the heart. "Not a sign."

"Find her!" Sir William's venom toward the unaccommodating Primrose almost equalled his hatred of the wife-stealing Earl. "I mean to bring charges against the wench for assault."

"I wouldn't advise it." Crump thought of the Chief Magistrate's reaction were Lady Bligh's companion dragged into court. "You've told me already that it was an accident, and nothing was stolen."

Sir William pouted. "She led me on, enticed me into extending confidences! You do not know what she intended, probably to murder us all and make off with the family valuables."

Crump was more interested in what Livvy might have learned. "One can't be hanged for one's intentions." He smiled. "Fortunately." Considering Sir William's intimate acquaintance with various pawnbrokers, there was probably little enough left at Arbuthnot House to steal.

Sir William fidgeted. "Is that all? I can't see why you dragged me out here. You have told me nothing I didn't already know!"

"It wasn't my idea, guv'nor." Crump retained his composure. "I could have as easily spoken to you at Tattersall's! There is one other little matter that I meant to mention to you." He paused, very aware of Sir William's discomfort. "On the night in question you were in attendance at the Cyprians Ball, is that so?"

"I don't see what business that is of yours." Sir William was flustered. "You overstep yourself!"

"Lord love you," replied the Runner, unmoved by this reminder of his lowly social status, "I don't care what you do with your time." Thus might a tiger smile before it pounced. "Except for the hour and more that you were absent from the Argyle Room."

Sir William gaped like a landbound fish, his eyes threatening to pop out of his head. "After," Crump added, "receiving an urgent note delivered by hand."

"Nonsense!" said Sir William weakly. "Whoever told you such a cock-and-bull tale?"

"A number of people." Sir William was not of a figure to slip unobserved from a gathering. "No point in trying to bamboozle *me,* guv'nor! I wasn't born yesterday." Crump no longer appeared jovial. "Let's have the truth without the bark on it! Where did you go?"

"I shan't tell you." Sir William was petulant. "A lady is involved. I must protect her good name."

If Sir William's conquests included ladies, they were of Covent Garden variety and probably only too happy to have their names flaunted before the world. "Bow Street has ways of finding out such things."

"Don't be a nodcock!" Sir William sought to awe his interrogator. "Is it likely I'd call Bow Street in if I had a hand in Arabella's death?"

Crump was very interested in this reaction. "I didn't make any accusations, did I?" He rocked back and forth on his heels. "That's an intriguing notion, guv'nor, that you've put into my head. You had more than enough time to sneak back to Arbuthnot House, kill your wife, then return to the Argyle Room."

"The devil fly away with you!" cried Sir William, close to apoplexy. "To think that I would harm a hair of Arabella's head!"

"And then," persisted Crump relentlessly, "to call in Bow

Street to make it look like you had nothing to do with the crime." He gazed upon the stricken man. "Brilliant strategy, if I may make so bold."

"Moonshine." Sir William's voice was faint.

Crump was inclined to agree; this clown lacked sufficient wit to evolve such a complicated scheme. The fact remained, however, that the florid gentleman obviously had something to hide.

Sir William cleared his throat. "No need to say anything about this little matter to your superiors, Crump, no need at all! It has nothing to do with Arabella's death, my word on it." Encouraged by the silence, he regarded the Runner hopefully. "We'll keep it between ourselves, eh? And I'll make it worth your time."

"Ah, you'll be pulling my leg, guv'nor." Crump's geniality turned sinister. "You knowing already that I'm not one to take a bribe." Turning on his heel he strode jauntily away, leaving behind a trembling mountain of panic-stricken flesh.

Chapter Eleven

SIR JOHN LOVED his London and its people, from scarlet-coated porters laden with bags, and hawkers with bandboxes on poles, to country milkmaids with yokes across their shoulders and the manure of rustic cowsheds on their feet. White-aproned bakers added cries of "Hot loaves!" to the medley of dustcart bells and newsvendors' horns. A little ballad-singer, sharp eyes alert for a new fancy-man, crooned the tale of a highwayman who paid for his sins with his head; pale-faced merchants' clerks hurried to their countinghouses. On the pavements, apprentices removed shutters from bow-fronted, multi-paned windows while ragged urchins leapfrogged over posts.

Unlike the City, the fashionable West End was not yet awake. Here were no brewers' drays, drawn slowly by draught-horses as large as elephants; no carts with hay for the London marts or drover-driven bullocks on the way to Smithfield. The Chief Magistrate, who had already that morning sentenced several deserving criminals to death, made his way to the Bligh mansion.

Mary, a mob cap covering her carroty hair, perched dreamily in an upper-story window, taking refuge from the battle royal raging within the walls of the Baron's home. The strife was initiated when Pudding, the merry cook, had let fall an unwise, and somewhat vulgar, observation concerning the progress of Culpepper's romance with the whiskey-swilling watchman. The argument had ended in fisticuffs and tears. Mary surveyed the approaching visitor with a connoisseur's discriminating eye, then, waving to catch his attention, gestured toward a pathway that led around the side of the house.

Sir John found Lady Bligh in one corner of a walled garden, the perfect setting for clandestine intrigue, gazing pensively at a circular pool bordered with lilacs, tulips, jonquils, acacias, and syringas. Here the Baron's fancy, held firmly in check by his wife, had found expression only in statuaries, the most exceptional pieces being a bronze Apollo and Daphne, and a sleeping Morpheus in plaster.

The Baroness looked like a woodland nymph in a morning dress of cinnamon jaconet, its sleeves tightly buttoned at the wrist, and its hem embellished with a broad, embroidered flounce. Her hair was a stunning shade of palest peach. "John," she said, holding out her hand.

Sir John was stricken with guilt. Dulcie must be driven half-mad with worry about her nephew's predicament; never had he seen her so melancholy. The Chief Magistrate could not know that Lady Bligh had spent a large portion of the night staring intently at a piece of parchment with a blacked-out name.

"How good of you to call!" The Baroness gestured to a great oak bench designed in the shape of a shell. "Pray be seated."

"I do not like to see you so blue-deviled." Dulcie's tantalizing scent surrounded him, a combination of frankincense, mastic, benzoin, cloves, pine-nut kernels and a half-dozen other things, and sold under the impressive banner of Imperial Water. "What has happened, Dulcie? You are usually more cheerful."

"I try," sighed the Baroness, "to be brave. Time marches on, dear John, and inexorably." Her mournful gaze rested on her guest. "Madman Mott once snatched a kiss from me in Marylebone Gardens, more than thirty-five years ago."

Sir John was more than a little startled at this disclosure, though it should not have surprised him that Dulcie had been embraced by, among others, a notorious free-trader. "Forgive me, but that is hardly a reason to be in the dumps."

"Madman Mott long ago hanged for his sins. Now even the Gardens are gone." Lady Bligh opened her fan, vellum stretched on ivory sticks and decorated with amorini, goddesses, shepherds, fruits, flowers and leaves in wrought gold. "And I, alas, am no longer young."

"Twaddle!" retorted Sir John, with some justification. The Baroness looked like little more than a girl. "You are an incurable dissembler, Dulcie! What do you want from me?"

"I want," Dulcie said somberly, "Dickon cleared of suspicion! It is a black cloud hanging over us all." She touched his arm. "No, I am not asking you to do anything you should not! I only want to know what I may expect if my efforts in Dickon's behalf are in vain."

At least it lay within his power to offer a glimmer of hope. "Prinny is among your admirers. You could probably secure a pardon for Dickon, regardless of his guilt." The ability to gain a pardon was recognized as a mark of importance among the rich and propertied, though this went on at the highest levels only and was kept hidden from the poor.

"I do not care to be so deeply in Prinny's debt." Lady Bligh winked in a manner that inspired the Chief Magistrate with a burning resentment of his Regent. "You are very frank, John. How can you justify this connivance at setting a possible villain free?"

"I am not frank, madam, but damned imprudent!" Sir John scowled. "I trust you know that my forebearance in this matter could make an end to my career."

"In that event, you will select a suitable wife and settle down to the life of a leisured gentleman. It would be the best thing in the world for you, John!" The Baroness sighed. "We will not discuss your foolish aversion to gaiety. I know that only Prinny's support and your intervention have kept Dickon from jail, and I am more grateful than I can say."

Sir John refrained, with effort, from taking the Baroness in his arms and demonstrating how she might best express her gratitude. "There are vast inequities in our legal system," he said. "Only last week a man who stole a piece of honeycomb tripe and a cow-heel, worth ninepence, was jailed and sentenced to forfeit his whole property. Another man who beat a girl and threw her over a parapet was sentenced to a mere ten months of hard labor. The wench fell ten feet. She lost an eye."

"John!" Dulcie was horrified. "Cannot you do something?"

"What? I am only the chief of Bow Street." Sir John knew he was being manipulated most adroitly yet, in Dulcie's charming presence, he didn't care. "You begin to understand, I think. I find little in Dorset to admire, but that does not mean I can sit by idly while he is convicted of a crime that I am not at all certain he committed." Were it not for the great amount of public interest in Lady Arabella's death, Sir John would have paid little attention to that particular crime. In an age when lonely turnpike keepers were robbed and beaten to death, gangs of smugglers and poachers engaged in constant battle with keepers and revenue officers, and that damned impudent rascal known as The Gentleman embarked upon highway robbery as blithely as if no law enforcement agency existed at all, the assassination of another willful beauty was not of much significance.

"I admire your ethics," said the Baroness wryly, snapping shut her fan. "I have lately come into possession of an item that may prove of interest to you."

Sir John stared at the diamond necklace. "Arabella's," Dulcie explained.

"How the devil did you come by this?" Sir John's brows beetled. "Dulcie, I begin to suspect you of the deepest chicanery."

"Of all the unfair things to say!" Dulcie's dark eyes twinkled. "You are only annoyed because I have been more clever than you."

"You have not answered my question." The Chief Magistrate did not voice his gnawing worry that the inquisitive Baroness might come to harm. The city teemed with traps for the unwary. Pickpockets lurked in the doors of coaching inns; crowds of thieves swept through busy streets emptying pockets, snatching purses and whatever else came to hand. Nor was murder uncommon. Sir John gazed upon the countless amber beads that adorned the Baroness. Despite her intense vitality, Dulcie would be no match for a determined ruffian.

"I do not intend to." Lady Bligh rose to pace restlessly. "The necklace was given to me by someone totally unconnected with the crime."

"Who?" demanded Sir John, with little hope.

"It is not part of the killer's loot." The Baroness broke off a choice bloom. "I must tell you that the gems stolen from Arbuthnot House that night were worthless. Everything of value was sold off previously."

"Paste!" The Chief Magistrate wasted no more time seeking explanations. "Not robbery, then, but made to look so. I wonder why."

"I applaud your acumen." Dulcie fastened the flower to Sir John's somber coat and resumed her position at his side. "What can you tell me of a dubious character known as Slippery Jim?"

The Chief Magistrate was pleased beyond all reason by Lady Bligh's casual intimacy. "A magsman, a professional swindler with a silver tongue. Why?"

"*I* am asking the questions, John!" The Baroness was stern. "You will have your turn. Continue, please!"

"I know little enough about the man; he's too clever to come in the way of Bow Street. He knows all the tricks, from thimble-rigging to cogged dice and marked cards, but is fondest, I believe, of the E.O. stand."

"And his current occupation?"

"I do not know." Sir John searched his encyclopaedic memory. "I believe the rascal has dropped out of sight." He frowned at Dulcie, so close that he could see the tiny laughter lines around her fine eyes. "Do you think to pin Lady Arabella's murder on him? It isn't likely. Slippery Jim has too great a regard for his own skin."

"You might have Crump look into his movements." Dulcie was confiding. "I believe this uncouth individual may have been Arabella's puzzling cousin."

"How did you know about *that?*" Sir John removed the flower from his coat and idly plucked off petals, one by one. "Ah, the enterprising Mrs. Lytton, alias Primrose. So Crump was correct."

"Crump is more astute than he appears." Lady Bligh did not approve. "We must learn more of Arabella's relationship with her visitor." She pursed her lips. "Tell me, what do you think of the notion that there may be someone else behind the crime, someone who employed minions to carry out his grand design while he remained safely in the background?"

"It is fairly common," the Chief Magistrate admitted, "but

not likely in this case. The more people involved, the less likelihood of maintaining any secrecy."

"Hmm," replied the Baroness, in a tone that made Sir John wish the Baron would speedily return, although there was no guarantee that even Max could curb his wife's headstrong foolishness. He sought diversion.

"I will tell you, though I should not, that Crump has conceived a severe dislike for Sir William."

"He offered Crump a bribe? The fool!" Dulcie's foot rhythmically tapped the ground. "I suppose it was about his inexplicable absence during the Cyprians Ball."

"You know entirely too much!" Sir John was testy. "I wish I could convince you that this is a murder investigation, not a parlor game!"

"Your concern is most flattering." Lady Bligh's smile was warm. "It takes me back, John, a great many years. But we digress! Your diligent little Crump is also determined to prove that Dickon was with Arabella on the fatal night, and that simply will not do."

"You may ask only so much from me," he said stiffly. "I will see that Dickon is treated fairly, but I will go no further."

"How stuffy you are! As if I would ask you to do anything dishonorable!" The Baroness was indignant. "You are far too proper to consider such a thing—a pity, since it would make my task much easier, but there it is." She pressed his hand. "Never mind, I don't hold it against you, John."

"How good of you!" retorted the Chief Magistrate caustically. He began to understand how one might be driven to murder the object of one's affections.

"I don't think that's what happened to Arabella," Dulcie commented, reading him perfectly. "There is much more to this thing than you have begun to suspect." Her smile was dazzling. "I keep you from your duties, and I must not. Discover what you can learn about the elusive Slippery Jim!"

So buffeted by emotion was Sir John that he did not quarrel with this peremptory decree. He rose. "And you?"

"I must speak with my rakeshame nephew." The Baroness was pure mischief. " 'Tis vastly amusing, I vow, to watch him fall victim to Cupid's levelling dart!"

The Chief Magistrate was left to find his own way back into the harsher daylight of reality. He felt as though he'd fallen prey to a skinner, a villainess who lured small well-clad children into deserted corners, then stripped them of all attire. It was not terror, however, that left Sir John so bemused. Before her abrupt departure, Lady Bligh had risen on tiptoe to kiss his cheek, as lightly and elusively as a butterfly.

Livvy was a lovely sight in a violet mantle trimmed and lined with white swansdown worn over a dress of flower-strewn muslin, and a velvet bonnet trimmed with graceful ostrich plumes. "Tell me," she demanded, "whom *you* hold responsible for Arabella's death. I have never heard you venture an opinion on the matter."

"That is because I don't have one." The Earl was apologetic. The Green Park, province of browsing deer and cattle, was thronged with people. So thick was the press of bodies that the white-stuccoed Ranger's Lodge, set among sprawling shade trees, was obscured from view. "I rather fancy Humbug as the culprit, but honesty forces me to admit it an unlikely eventuality."

"Hubert?" The Royal Parks had been thrown open to the public in a gala celebration of Wellington's most recent victory at Waterloo. Gambling and drinking booths dotted the scene. "Why should a fashionable fribble be suspected of violence?"

"Humbug," retorted Lord Dorset, "is not so negligible as he may seem. His chosen role is that of a thorn in the flesh, and he plays it over well."

"You do not mean to tell me what you think." Livvy

remembered Hubert's promise of friendship. "Very well! I refuse to believe that you have given no thought to a matter that so directly concerns you, but I shall tease you no further."

"Other matters have concerned me more, sweet Livvy." The Earl guided her toward a sham castle, before which was being staged the storm of Badajoz, complete with mimic three-deckers and frigates on the Serpentine. "It is not remarkable, surely, that a man so near the altar should have little thought to spare for anything but his beloved?"

Livvy shot his lordship a darkling glance, and sighed, wondering if there existed a magical potion to purge a misguided heart.

The crowds, orderly and good-humored, picnicked under the trees while young and more adventurous spectators perched in leafy branches. "What is *your* opinion?" inquired Dickon. "If you will not have Hubert as our villain, who?"

Livvy gazed upon the Castle of Discord, one hundred and thirty feet high. "I am not sure," she said demurely. "I hesitate to point this out, but no one else had both your motive and opportunity."

"I see." Dickon wore his satiric look. "You play a dangerous game, do you not? Take care, my darling, lest I also decide to dispose of you."

Livvy could cheerfully have bit off her tongue. "I spoke in jest, Dickon, and without thought. Pray forgive me. I do not believe you were in any way connected with the thing."

"Nor would it matter if you did, so devoted are you to my aunt." The Earl was distant. "It is an excellent opportunity, also, to bring yourself to the notice of the *haut ton*. What is to be your reward for this service? Has Dulcie promised you gold? Or to find you a suitable husband among her various tradesmen?"

"No!" Livvy's eyes filled with tears of rage. "My motives are not yours to question, nor have I been offered a reward." She glared at him furiously. "Nor need you think it is any fondness for you that makes me lend myself to this absurd charade, for I find you contemptible!"

Lord Dorset's wintry gaze had cowed many a stalwart soul. "Then I shall remove my unwelcome person from your presence." He turned on his heel and strode away.

Livvy stared blindly at redcoats with blackened faces creeping through the dark with glittering bayonets, and diabolical Frenchmen gesticulating on the battlements of the Castle of Discord. "A lover's quarrel, eh?" came a voice behind her. "I've timed our meeting well!"

"Sir William!" Livvy's first, craven impulse to flee was frustrated when he gripped her arm.

"Think you'd seen the last of me?" Livvy realized, with sinking heart, that the florid widower was hopelessly drunk. He dangled the abandoned spectacles under her nose. "You left these behind. We have a number of things to say to one another, Primrose."

Livvy dug in her heels and refused to budge. "I think not, Sir William. If you do not release me this instant, I shall scream!"

"No, you won't." Fat jowls wobbled. "Think of the scandal! Wouldn't want the world to know you'd been posing as a servant, would you?" With difficulty, he focused on her ashen face. "Why did you run off, Primrose? Just when we were getting to know one another! There was no need to behave so shabbily just because I dropped a hint or two. We'd have dealt well enough together, you and me."

"Sir, you go too far!" Frantically, Livvy wondered what to do.

"Gad, but you're a damned fine looking piece!" Sir William's eyes were hot. "I've always had a weakness for a pretty face. Tell you what, let's let bygones be bygones." Livvy clenched her teeth as he leaned closer. His false sidewhiskers had come partially unglued. "The offer's still open; name your price!"

"William!" Lord Dorset was a thundercloud. "You are speaking to my future wife!" Sir William released Livvy as abruptly as he might a potato hot from the fire.

It was a scene that might, at some future date, be recalled with amusement. The Earl looked as grim as a vengeful demon; Sir William ran a finger under a neckcloth suddenly grown suffocating; and Livvy glowered with equal loathing at both the gentlemen. "The minx led me on," said Sir William, in a fine blend of contrition and cowardice. "What else was I to think but that she was for sale to the highest bidder?" He shrugged, attempting nonchalance. "No harm done."

"There will be, and to you, if you are tempted to repeat this performance at another time." Thus might a merciless magistrate sound. "Do I make myself clear?"

Sir William recalled his position as a wronged husband. "Who'll care for the little lady when you're dangling from the nubbing cheat?" He leered at Livvy. "I can wait til then!"

Livvy stamped her foot in rage. "Stop it, both of you! You are quarrelling over me as dogs might a bone."

Sir William was bewildered. "I have yet to see a female who didn't want her mind made up for her! Don't worry, my pretty, you'll be free of this rogue before long." At an impatient exclamation from the Earl, discretion seemed the best course; Sir William melted into the crowd.

"Furthermore," said Livvy, turning her fire on the Earl, "my experience with matrimony leaves me with no wish to ever re-enter that reputedly hallowed state!"

"What then?" Lord Dorset refrained from violence with only great effort. "You have too much passion for a nunnery, and too much principle for a courtesan. I shall overlook your apparent lapse into intrigue with that fat idiot."

"I care not a fig for your opinion!" Livvy snapped. "Lord, but men are an arrogant lot!"

"Are they not?" The Baroness Andrassy was in remarkable good humor for a lady who had a few hours past tried her hand disastrously at *Rouge et Noir.* "Particularly Dickon." Livvy wondered how long Gwyneth had lurked within earshot before making her presence known. "But easily enough managed if one exercises tact." She obviously thought Livvy unlikely to ever master this art.

Livvy turned away, her anger with the Earl so great that she wished to tear him limb from limb. Four of the model ships were ablaze, to the shrill dismay of the Serpentine swans. "Have you missed me?" Gwyneth's voice was smooth as syrup, and extremely smug.

"No." The Earl was brusque. "I would prefer your absence to continue indefinitely."

"Would that it might!" Gwyneth agreed quickly. "I would happily never set foot on British soil again, had I sufficient funds to sustain myself abroad."

If this was an example of Gwyneth's tact, Livvy wasn't impressed. She maintained a disapproving silence.

"That horse won't run," remarked Lord Dorset. "I've no interest in your financial affairs."

"You should develop one!" Gwyneth retorted. "It is the only way you'll be rid of me."

This was too much; Livvy forgot her anger in outrage. She stared at the audacious beauty, swathed in a Spanish pelisse of shot sarsenet trimmed with Egyptian crepe and embellished with antique cuffs. "Can it be," Gwyneth added, with a provocative glance, "that I have misread your sentiments, that you do *not* wish me gone?" She smiled at Livvy. "I regret that you should hear me speak so plainly, my dear, but we must be blunt. Dickon was ever a fickle lot."

"I have not found him so." Perversely, Livvy placed a possessive hand on Dickon's arm. Beneath the fabric of his coat, she felt taut muscles and bone.

"Nor will you," murmured the Earl. Quick to resume the game, Livvy thought.

"It is as well, then, that I have another string to my shaft."

Gwyneth was vindictive. "You will be interested to learn, dear Dickon, that I have spent the past few days becoming reacquainted with my son."

It was a moment of victory never before achieved during the entire history of her long and tempestuous acquaintance with the Earl. Gwyneth gazed triumphantly upon her one-time husband, damnably elegant in his brown coat, frilled shirt, and drab kerseymere Inexpressibles; and experienced a brief regret that he was not more kindly disposed toward her. Count Andrassy might be of a sunnier disposition but his expertise in matters of matrimonial intimacy was far inferior. "I shall take Austin with me," she added, moving safely beyond Dickon's reach, "when I return home. It is not what he is used to, I suppose, but I see no reason to mollycoddle the boy."

Dickon's expression gave even Gwyneth pause. Livvy clutched the Earl's arm as if to anchor him firmly to the spot and thus prevent the enactment of bloody mayhem in the midst of Prinny's victory jubilee. "I trust," said Dickon, in chilling accents, "that you jest. Every harm that you inflict upon Austin will be returned to you tenfold."

"You will discover soon enough whether I am in earnest." Gwyneth's laugh was brittle. She turned to Livvy. "Do what you can to make him see reason! It will not go easy with either of you if I am forced to publish what I have learned; nor will it go easy with Austin if he must live with the Count. My husband is not fond of children." Jauntily, she walked away.

"What a horrible woman!" Livvy, assured that Dickon did not mean to set out in murderous pursuit, released his arm. "She has been busy, it seems. What will you do?"

"I doubt that she has seen Austin, but I do not mean to call her bluff. Dulcie was right; I must bring the boy to town." Lord Dorset was wrapped in thought. "I will set out immediately after I have apologized for my unforgiveable treatment of you."

"Pray do not!" Livvy's voice shook. "It was as much my fault as yours, a foolish misunderstanding. Let us forget it."

Dickon captured her hands. "Hush, and listen to me. I am behaving like the rawest schoolboy—a lowering reflection, I assure you!—and you are entirely to blame. Even my dreams are haunted by censorious lavender eyes."

"This is hardly the moment for flirtation." Livvy tried to free herself from both Dickon's grasp and the dizzying effect of his bewitching smile.

The Earl was not to be dissuaded. "My dear girl, the world will tell you I am a most polished flirt, and would be greatly amused to hear me stammer so! This is something quite different, and quite new." His hands moved to her shoulders, with electrifying effect. "Tell me that you find me repulsive, Livvy, that you will not consider my suit, and for once in my life I will endeavor to behave like a gentleman and will trouble you no more."

"You must not say such things to me," Livvy whispered, in a last-ditch defense.

Abruptly, she was released. "I have presumed," said Lord Dorset ruefully. "It will teach me a lesson, I suppose."

"Dickon!" Livvy, feeling tragically bereft, stared at him with comical dismay.

"Why so woebegone?" inquired the devious Earl. "You have just said that you will have no more of me."

"No! I did not!" In the midst of hot confusion, Livvy noted his growing amusement. *"Damn you, Dickon!"*

With a deafening explosion, brilliant fireworks streamed across the sky. Roman Candles and Girandoles, Jerbs and Gillocks exploded in a thousand dazzling lights. The canvas walls of the Castle of Discord lifted to reveal a revolving Temple of Peace lit with countless colored lamps, and water flowed from lions' jaws into golden basins. In attendance were a choir of Vestal Virgins in transparent draperies; while, on the roof of the Temple, a detachment of embarrassed Foot Guards held aloft the Royal Standard and gave voice to three self-conscious cheers. The crowd gaped at the spectacular display.

Mrs. Lytton cared nothing for the Regent's tribute to the hero Wellington. Her spectacles lay forgotten on the grass as the Earl of Dorset drew her, unprotesting, into his arms.

Chapter Twelve

ON A GREEN plot in the middle of Cavendish Square stood a statue of the Duke of Cumberland, second son of George II, mounted on a prancing horse in the military costume of his day. The rear view of this work of art was even more eye catching than the front, for the Duke, affectionately known to his contemporaries as The Butcher, was of remarkable corpulence. Livvy grinned.

Lady Bligh had no time to stand and stare at the Duke's great girth spread across a saddle. Resolutely, she approached a small but elegant stuccoed building with sweeping Ionic columns, situated on the south side of the square. She did not enter the house itself but walked briskly through the gardens to a building in the rear. "Once," the Baroness remarked to her giddy companion, who was so contented that she wore a smile similar to Casanova's after the Calypso feast, "this garden commanded an excellent view of the meat carts that passed along Oxford Street carrying condemned prisoners to the Tyburn gallows." Livvy's smile vanished. "Many is the time I saw them, for I often visited here as a girl."

Livvy smoothed the sleeves of her merino pelisse and wondered at the extent of her employer's perspicacity. She also wondered what the Baroness would say if her nephew's sham betrothal became, in fact, reality, for Lord Dorset's marriage to a penniless widow was nigh unthinkable. Livvy then chided herself for foolish dreams. A passionate kiss, no matter how satisfactory to both participants, did not necessarily betoken wedding bells.

"You are not to worry." Without knocking, Lady Bligh opened a door. "Though it is best to bear these things in mind. We still face heavy odds."

Hubert was not pleased to receive visitors. "You must not blame your servants," said the Baroness. She inspected the studio, converted from the coachman's rooms and a hayloft into a long gallery. Painter's paraphernalia was everywhere. "I'm sure they would have told us you weren't receiving visitors, had we not neatly circumvented them."

Livvy was more astounded by Hubert's appearance than by his unexpected artistry, for he was clad in a brocaded dressing gown, liberally spattered with paint, and a pristine cravat. On his feet were Turkish slippers; on his brown hair, a domed skullcap with a tassle. The effect was indescribable.

"Since you have found me out," Hubert said gracelessly, "you might as well come in." The studio was large and sparsely furnished, with countless windows that admitted bright sunlight. Paintings were stacked against a wall, tubes of paint and other supplies strewn across a large table.

The Baroness, resplendent in a Rutland half-robe, with striped zephyr shawl and formidable turban, settled herself upon a plain wooden chair. "How nice," she said, dark eyes darting inquisitively from canvas to canvas, "to see in you such evidence of industry! It is hardly what one expects from a Tulip of Fashion."

"Your approval overwhelms me." Hubert quickly covered an easel stand, but not before Livvy had glimpsed a half-finished study of a scantily clad woman with wild black hair and a thin white scar on her cheek.

"I am impressed." Livvy beheld canvases depicting witches, devils, and other scenes equally macabre. "May we see what you are currently working on?"

"Loath as I am to appear disobliging, I fear you would not approve." Hubert placed himself in front of the easel, shielding his masterpiece from violation by prying eyes.

"Now that we have observed the amenities," the Baroness interrupted, "perhaps you will be so good as to tell me what you and Arabella discussed on the night of her death."

"You are determined to distract me, I see." Hubert wrenched the skullcap from his head and tossed it onto the cluttered table. "I wonder if you realize, dear aunt, how fragile and elusive is the artistic mood."

Lady Bligh's dark eyes rested on a depiction of a voluptuously collapsed young woman to whom grotesque succubi appeared. "My good temper," she retorted, "is equally elusive. Answer me!"

Hubert placed his fingertips together. "I have not said that I saw Arabella on the fatal night. Indeed, I spent that night at White's, sitting up until the last gambler had gone." He smiled. "I wished to ascertain the truth of the rumor that Raggett sweeps the carpets himself in order to retrieve any gold carelessly scattered on the floor."

"*Is* it true?" Livvy asked.

"It is, dear Livvy. Raggett is a wealthy man."

"Don't confuse the issue, Hubert!" Lady Bligh was not so easily sidetracked. "I do not intend to budge from these premises until you have confessed."

Hubert circled the Baroness, who was as firmly planted as the Rock of Gibraltar, and reconsidered. "Dulcie, there are times when I find your obstinacy a grievous trial. Very well! Arabella was in sore need of financial assistance—why, I do not know. One might fairly say that she was desperate."

"And your reply?"

"Alas, I was unable to oblige." Hubert perched on the table and dangled an elegant leg. *"I'm* not the member of this family who can pay a thousand guineas for a thoroughbred."

"Sour grapes!" commented Lady Bligh. "So you advised Arabella to apply to Dickon?"

"It seemed most logical." Hubert was apologetic. "Your pardon, Livvy, but why should Dickon not pay for favors received?"

"He may pay all too dearly!" Dulcie snapped. "I wonder at you, Hubert. You would stand by idly and watch your cousin drown for want of a rope."

"Is that the fate reserved for Dickon?" Hubert exhibited interest. "I rather thought he might dangle from the deadly Never-Green." He plucked at his moustache. "Imagine the spectacle! All the riffraff of London, drunk on gin and horrors, shouting themselves senseless as Jack Ketch cuts the body down. I must arrange for a front row seat."

"You detestable beast!" cried Livvy, all too easily imagining this horrid scene. She advanced on Hubert, clutching a palette knife, with the express intention of inflicting irreparable bodily injury. Hubert prudently took shelter behind his aunt's chair.

"Call her off!" he begged. "My valet cannot tolerate the sight of blood."

"Control yourself, Lavender," advised the Baroness, without severity. "Hubert was not serious." Livvy paused, but did not relinquish the weapon.

"Actually," said Hubert, righting his robe, the sash of which was oddly mismatched, "I was not, though I expect you will find that difficult to believe. Think of the scandal were one of the family to hang!"

"Hubert, you are the strangest mixture of scoundrel and perfect idiot that I have ever known!" Dulcie turned to her companion. "And you, Lavender, must strive for some control! Dickon will not benefit from Hubert's mutilation, my child."

"Not materially, perhaps." Lord Dorset, grim-visaged, stood in the door. His coat and breeches were dust-covered, as if he'd ridden hard and far. "It would, however, afford me great spiritual satisfaction." Livvy was numb; the palette knife clattered to the floor.

"How delightful!" Hubert recovered sufficient aplomb to speak maliciously. "It is not often that my morning hours are enlivened by a family deputation." Livvy, wondering if the Earl's savage countenance was in part inspired by a revulsion of feeling for her, stood rooted to the floor.

Hubert was not destined to long retain his poise; the Earl grasped his padded shoulders and lifted him straight into the air. "Tell me where Austin has been taken!" He shook Hubert as a terrier might a rat. "Or I shall mutilate you myself and with only my bare hands!"

"Unhand your cousin at once!" demanded the Baroness, in the unemotional tones of one who has witnessed countless similar scenes. "If Humbug knows anything of value, an unlikely event, he is hardly in a position to divulge it."

Hubert was released abruptly. He picked himself up from the floor. "So Austin is gone," mused Lady Bligh. "I anticipated as much."

"And Humbug and Gwyneth as thick as two thieves." No witness to this scene could doubt Lord Dorset's capacity for violence. "You would be well advised to tell me what you know, cousin, before I am driven to silence you permanently."

Hubert inspected himself for broken bones. "Have you taken leave of your senses?", he demanded indignantly. "As if I'd connive to do Austin harm!"

"I have seen little indication that you would not." The Earl's contemptuous eye measured his unhappy cousin from top to toe. "Did you consider Austin easier prey than I? What share of the ransom money did Gwyneth offer you to ensure compliance with her schemes?"

"Ransom," Hubert murmured thoughtfully. "Is that what she intends?"

"I assume so." Lord Dorset was impatient. "Don't pretend that you don't know!"

"Enough!" decreed the Baroness. "Suppose you tell us, Dickon, precisely what you discovered at the Hall?"

"The whole place in a panic, and Austin nowhere on the grounds." Dickon paced the floor. "I finally found a servant willing to admit he'd seen a strange woman approaching the house several days before. After that, it was easy enough to piece together what had happened." He hit the table with his fist, causing several objects to bounce into the air. Hubert winced. "Gwyneth has the boy, and God only knows what she will do to him!"

"I thought," remarked Lady Bligh, "that Gwyneth was not to be permitted access."

"So did I." Lord Dorset picked up the knife and Hubert turned pale. "It seems my retainers are not impervious to bribery. It is not a matter that will recur." Livvy spared a thought for those unfortunates.

"Why lock the stable when the horse is gone?" murmured Hubert, then moved again behind Dulcie's chair as he caught Dickon's murderous stare.

"I believe Hubert tells the truth," the Baroness interjected, perhaps in hope of forestalling further disruption of the peace.

"At least in this instance. You waste time here, Dickon. I assume you found no trace of them?"

The Earl tossed the knife onto the table and strode toward the door. "No, but I shall." His tone promised that the meeting would not be a pleasant one.

In silence, they listened to his fading footsteps. "My hot-tempered cousin may not have murdered Arabella," remarked Hubert conversationally, "but I wouldn't wager a guinea on Gwyneth's continued survival." Weak-kneed, Livvy dropped into a chair.

"Don't dare to berate Dickon for his temper," she warned, unsteadily. "I do not think I can tolerate any more of your beastly nonsense today."

Hubert turned to his aunt with bewilderment. "What ails the creature?" he inquired. "As if Dickon's violence was unnatural in the present case!" He smoothed the dressing gown. "I only wish that my cousin would refrain from engaging in a brangle with me every time he is out of sorts."

"Popinjay," commented the Baroness, as her least favorite nephew unknotted his odd-looking sash. "What are you up to now?"

"Forgive me, aunt, but that's a damned silly question." For one startled moment, Livvy wondered if Hubert meant to disrobe. "I happen to be fond of my nephew, and believe I may be of some assistance there."

"Humbug!" Dulcie rose. "Do I behold in you a noble sentiment?"

"I must disappoint you, dear aunt." Hubert smiled. "I am motivated by a wish to put Dickon's nose out of joint. While my cousin is racketting about the countryside, endowing the rustics with admiration for as clipping a rider as ever they've seen, *I* shall take matters in hand. Imagine Dickon's chagrin! He will not like being indebted to me for Austin's rescue."

"He will be more likely to murder you," Livvy said hopefully.

"Balderdash." Lady Bligh studied Hubert enigmatically. "I wish you luck; you will have need of it! Come along, Livvy, we must leave Hubert to his efforts, no matter how unworthy their motivation. Austin's safety must have priority."

Livvy followed her employer outside. She recalled Gwyneth's threats, and the disclosures made by Smirke. A woman who would mistreat her own child was capable of any wickedness.

"I do not believe she will harm him," Dulcie said, "though her mere presence may cause severe damage. Austin is terrified of his mother."

"And with reason," Livvy murmured. "Dulcie, is there nothing *I* can do?"

"Did I not tell you?" The Baroness was contrite. "You are to go to Sapping and dig into Arabella's past. There is a mystery there." She paid no heed to her companion's muttered protest. "Pray remember, Lavender, that Austin's disappearance is not the only matter of concern! Too much hangs in the balance; Dickon may yet wear a halter round his neck." She frowned. "Perhaps that is what someone intends. I fancy Gwyneth had assistance."

Livvy, wrenched from the vision of a mute child in Gwyneth's unmaternal hands to an image of Lord Dorset dangling from the gallows, meekly agreed. Sleuthing about a country village might prove distraction for her unhappy thoughts, not least among which was a sickening awareness that the Earl had awarded her no more interest than a stick of furniture, addressing to her not a single word.

Crump had been busy, and to good effect, venturing even into Tothill Fields and Seven Dials where, by tacit agreement, neither watchman nor Runner ordinarily trespassed. There, among the thousand thieves and their female consorts who lived in tumble-down houses and narrow courts reeking with ordure, he had found a woman willing, after various dire threats, to identify Lord Dorset's mysterious lady visitor. Crump was vindicated: he had not for a moment believed that the brown-haired woman had been Mrs. Lytton in disguise.

It was Crump's habit, when faced with a dilemma, to idly wander the London streets with pipe in hand. Thus was he presently occupied, wondering how to tactfully inform the Chief Magistrate that Lord Dorset was as guilty as bedamned. Not only had Crump established, beyond a doubt, that Dorset had been among the last to see Lady Arabella alive, but a second search of the Earl's lodgings had unearthed the missing gems.

Crump frowned; he was not satisfied. Easy enough for the Earl to gain access to Arbuthnot House and dispose of his paramour, but only a fool would hide stolen jewels in his own home, particularly when he was under close watch by Bow Street. Crump could not determine why anyone would bother to pilfer baubles made of paste, unless to throw hunters off the scent, nor could he fathom the mystery of the jewels' odd reappearance. He had followed Sir William's instructions, with faint hope of success, and had found Lady Arabella's gems in a wall-safe that, during his previous search, had stood empty. Crump was seized by a conviction that, though the acerbic Lord Dorset might be easily guilty of murder, he was innocent of theft.

The Runner was further intrigued by the odd behavior of his suspects, who were travelling about in the queerest way. The Countess Andrassy was in and out of town with perplexing frequency, and no one could guess where she went on her secretive jaunts; Hubert Humboldt had departed London, hours previously, in a spanking equipage; Lord Dorset had been seen, riding hell-for-leather, on the Great North Road; while his fiancée had set out only moments past in Lady

Bligh's elegant travelling carriage for an unknown destination. Crump pushed back his hat and scratched his balding head, while gazing upon the facade of a hospital for the insane, enlivened with gloomy statuary of Melancholy and Raving Madness. If this case was not soon solved, Crump would be a likely candidate for admission. He envied his fellow Runners, involved in a city-wide search for that pesky highwayman, known to friend and foe alike as The Gentleman, who with great daring and increasing regularity divested the wealthy of their more portable treasures. This impudent rascal would doubtless be easier trapped than the crafty Earl. Crump leaned against a lamp post and chewed the stem of his pipe.

With a sudden flurry of hooves, a carriage drew up at a house opposite where brightly lit windows framed nodding feathers and starry chandeliers. A tall liveried footman leaped down. Powdered gold-laced servants lined the mansion steps, and staring, starving crowds massed at the doors. Crump thought of the delicacies doubtless on display inside to tempt the jaded palates of the aristocracy: Périgord pie and truffles from France, Indian sauces and curry powder, hams from Westphalia and Portugal, Russian caviar, reindeer tongue from Lapland, Spanish olives, cheese from Parma, Bologna sausages. Gluttony was one of the many vices reserved for the Quality and denied to the pallid, emaciated poor who eked out a crowded existence amid rotting heaps of garbage.

Crump turned away from such profitless reflection. One more matter had to be dealt with this day, though he would have much preferred to while away his time sampling a quart of mulled claret and sharing the favors of a willing serving girl. Instead, he had to speak with the Countess Andrassy, whose reported activities filled him with curiosity. Unless Crump was greatly mistaken, Lord Dorset's one-time wife was playing a deep game.

Pondering the Earl's diverse taste in ladies, from the voluptuous and ill-tempered Lady Arabella to a well-brought-up young woman like Mrs. Lytton, the Runner made his way to a small and elegant hotel on the south side of St James's Street. With no eye for such marvels as walls of Norwegian marble in light greens and yellow and pinks, stately columns and Oriental rugs, he made his way to a suite of rooms on the second floor.

The Countess was not in. Crump, not one to bypass an opportunity, scanned the empty hallway, then withdrew from his pocket a strange-looking instrument. Within seconds, he was fumbling through dark apartments in search of candles.

Gwyneth could not by any standard be considered neat. Clothing was strewn about carelessly, hanging from half-opened drawers. Crump inspected a dressing table veneered with satinwood and decorated with oval panels, silver mounts, and festooned flowers painted in natural colors. On the dusty surface were innumerable powders, oils, washes, soaps and cosmetics, among them Magnetic Rock Dew Water, guaranteed to give a youthful appearance even to ladies of the greatest antiquity.

The Runner moved on quickly to a slender writing table. Although the Chief Magistrate would not be likely to sanction his endeavors, Crump opened the tambour shutter that enclosed pigeonholes and drawers. An unfinished letter lay in plain view, crying to be read. Bow Street Runners had few scruples. Crump carried this missive to the light and squinted at spidery handwriting.

"You will know by now," Gwyneth had written, *"that I have Austin. He will be returned safely to you upon my receipt of 100,000 pounds."* Crump whistled silently; the lady was ambitious. *"The money is to be handed to me at 5 o'clock in Hyde Park on Friday, two days hence. Dream not of revenge, dear Dickon, for I will not be alone."* Crump recalled the Earl's legendary temper, and decided that Gwyneth was foolishly bold.

"Do not ignore this letter," the Countess went on. *"Consider the many unfortunate accidents to which a child may fall prey! I trust I need not say more."* The paper was splotched and smeared with ink.

Crump stared at the writing table, where an inkwell stood uncovered, his agile brain working furiously. Gwyneth had been interrupted in her labors, but by whom? And where had she gone? A thorough search of the apartments revealed no clue. The Runner's scalp prickled. Only one place remained. He threw open the door to the ornamental wrought iron balcony.

There, at last, Crump found the Countess Andrassy. Even Magnetic Rock Dew Water would not avail her now. Gwyneth lay sprawled on the balcony floor, a brocaded sash knotted tight around her neck, her swollen tongue protruding impudently.

Chapter Thirteen

LIVVY HAD ALMOST forgotten the English countryside. It was an endless landscape of emerald downs and meadows dotted with lazy sheep and fat cattle, neat hedgerows and chestnut coppices stretching into blue sky. Rainbow blooms wreathed cottages; classical country houses with cool, ivy-framed windows nestled among lawns and trees. Corn mills and hop yards rubbed shoulders with ancient churches and barns.

Sapping, birthplace of the last Arabella Arbuthnot, had none of the amenities that had brought other English villages booming prosperity and fame. It boasted no aquatic displays, so popular at Sadler's Wells; it lacked the healthful waters and octogenarian populace of Bath, where bands played almost continuously while crowds promenaded in the Pump Room; it was without the architectural magnificence of the Regent's favorite, Brighton by the sea.

Livvy, doing justice to a breakfast of cold pigeon pie, boiled beef and ham, grilled kidneys and bacon, and hot buttered muffins, washed down with quantities of tea, gazed through an open window upon a painted hay wain with straked wheels and tilted bow. It was difficult to imagine the flamboyant Lady Arabella in so bucolic a setting. From outside came the rattle of carriage wheels and the loud voices of quarrelsome coachmen and linkboys.

Mrs. Lytton was posing as a wealthy widow at this bustling coaching inn, where, thanks to Mary's clever hints to the staff, she was treated with amazing deference by the proprietor, and with awe by ostlers and waiters, chambermaids and boots. Livvy remained in determined ignorance of whatever clankers Mary may have told to achieve this happy state.

That resourceful young lady, flushed with success and the overtures of a handsome young yardboy, stepped into the room. "If you don't look moonstruck, Miss Livvy!" she said impudently. "Master Dickon has a way about him; none can naysay that!"

"That will be enough, Mary." Livvy tried to look aloof, though she would have liked nothing better than to pass an hour in discussion of the Earl's better qualities. "What have you learned?"

Unrepentant, Mary grinned. "Lady Arabella lived here sure enough." She bit into a cold muffin and gestured vaguely toward the window. "A wild one she was, by all accounts! Her aunt's still here, in that house on the Common."

"I must call on her." Livvy had little enthusiasm for the task. It was an overcast morning, with strong intimations of impending storm.

"Her name is Rebecca Baskerville, and they say she's as close mouthed as an oyster." Mary's eyes held a devilish glint. "Think how grateful Master Dickon will be if you solve all his troubles!"

Livvy rose, with an attempt at dignity. "I have told you I do not wish to discuss the matter."

"Pshaw!" Mary was blithely oblivious that she violated every rule of conduct that governed a lady's maid, not only in her lack of subservience, but in her attire. Abigails were not supposed to wear heels several inches high, or white muslin gowns, or sport riotously curling hair. "You're just like one of those big birds that's always burying its head in the sand. Anyone with half an eye can see that Master Dickon's properly smitten! If you'd just make a push, Miss Livvy, you could be a ladyship for real."

"You read too many romances, my girl, and are likely to find yourself without a place if you keep on in this vein!" All of Lady Bligh's servants, willing or not, learned to read and write. Seeing the maid's downcast countenance, Livvy relented. "Never mind, Mary. I promise that you shall dance at my wedding, if ever it comes about." Before she could be offered further well-meant advice, Livvy made a quick escape. Outside, Livvy straightened her plumed plush bonnet and inspected her embroidered muslin gown and cottage mantle of gray cloth. As ready to confront Arabella's aunt as she would ever be, Livvy stepped out into the dreary day.

Sapping, despite its unpretentiousness, enjoyed local fame. A strategic position and adventurous inhabitants made the village a perfect center for the smuggling trade. Cutters from France and Holland were met, three or four miles from the coast, by local boats which carried the goods ashore, there to be hidden in the most unlikely places imaginable. The entire populace connived at smuggling out wool and bringing in tea and brandy, to the eternal frustration of the revenue officers. Consequently Livvy attracted little attention; the villagers were inured to strangers, who usually turned out to be customs officers in ambitious disguise or London dealers anxious to reap the harvest of the local trade.

Rebecca Baskerville viewed her visitor with as much suspicion as if Livvy were an excise man. Nor did her distrust decrease when the purpose of the visit was announced, but she grudgingly led her guest to an oval drawingroom furnished with mock bamboo. "Well?" demanded Rebecca, picking up a piece of needlework. "What's the little wretch done now?" Faded eyes examined Livvy thoroughly. "Did she run off with your husband? If so, it's nothing to me."

Livvy was startled. Rebecca Baskerville looked the perfect virginal spinster who would never allow an impure thought to cross her mind or an improper word to sully her lips. She wondered how to tell the woman that her niece was dead.

"Cat got your tongue?" inquired Rebecca. "I might inform you I haven't seen the chit for nigh onto ten years. Nor are you the first to come asking questions about her."

Livvy took a deep breath and plunged into a highly edited version of Arabella's passing, one that portrayed the dear departed as a paragon of virtue most tragically cut down in her youth. "We were all devoted to Arabella." Livvy sniffed into her handkerchief daintily, in a fair imitation of Lady Bligh at her most demure. "And we are most anxious to see the murderer brought to justice."

"I don't believe a word of it." Rebecca shook her salt-and-pepper head. "Not that someone would murder Bella, for I always said she'd come to a bad end; but that she was beloved of all her acquaintance." The eyes, behind their spectacles, were shrewd. "Unless she underwent a great change after she left me, Bella was fortunate to have been allowed to live so long."

Unwilling to retreat from her lie, Livvy plunged ahead. "We thought the past might yield a clue to the villain's identity. Will you tell me why Arabella left your home?"

"Plagued if I see why you're so concerned," said Rebecca suspiciously, but when Livvy moved to answer, she raised a thin, imperious hand. "Quiet! I must deliberate."

Livvy was as noiseless as a mouse venturing into Casanova's territory. It seemed that Arabella and her outspoken aunt had not existed in a state of amity.

Rebecca nodded decisively. "I will tell *you*, though I quickly showed my earlier questioner the door. Perhaps what I know of her can help you to find her murderer." The frail hands busied themselves with needlework. "Bella was a willful girl, with a tendency to let passion get the better of reason. I believe her mother was the same."

"Arabella's father was your brother?" It was obvious that the lady's legendary warmth was not inherited from her aunt.

Rebecca nodded her head. "He was, and Bella greatly resembled him. There was nothing my brother dared not do, including the seduction of a lady of good family. I must admit that Bella managed to keep *her* virtue reasonably intact until she encountered that accursed Dragoon." The well-modulated voice had become husky. Rebecca firmly pushed her ill-fitting spectacles back up to the bridge of her nose. "The reason for his presence in Sapping, a place far removed from the gaieties of the metropolis, I cannot say; though I would guess it concerned the local livelihood."

"Arabella fell in love with him?"

Rebecca snorted. "Bella fell in love at least once a week, with everyone from stablehands to the vicar's son! Scandalous!" She sighed. "In this case, it was no surprise, for young James was a deuced handsome rapscallion."

"James?" Livvy quivered with excitement. "What was his surname?"

Rebecca, caught up in unpleasant memories, shrugged irritably. "I'm sure I couldn't say. I remonstrated with Bella, not meaning to question her conduct but to put her on guard against scoundrels who will callously ruin a girl's good name." Here was no high opinion of the male species. "Bella was besotted—she was determined to become a lady, you see, and saw in her Dragoon the perfect opportunity to marry advantageously."

"He was of good family?"

"He was rumored to be." Rebecca, it seemed, disapproved of gossip. "I never believed it myself. To make a long story short, Bella eloped with him."

"Eloped!" Livvy started. "Believe me, I knew nothing of this. What happened?"

"You could say as easily as I." With only a faint tremor, Rebecca folded the needlework away. "Mind, no one but ourselves know of this. My neighbors think I packed Bella off to London when she became too much for me. She had a reputation for wildness and that's remembered, but none can claim she blackened her good name!"

Livvy felt a pang of compassion, guessing that Rebecca made such careful preparations in the hope that her renegade niece would eventually return. "Perhaps Arabella truly married her Dragoon."

"Legal or illegal, the connection could come to no good end, and so I told her." Rebecca was fierce. "You've said Bella was married to a duke and a knight, so I can only assume she was *not* wed to her accursed James." The thin hands knotted. "When I had no word from her, I believed my worst fears confirmed."

Livvy could inflict no more pain. She rose to take her leave. "I will trouble you no more, and am sorry to have been the bearer of sad news. Thank you for seeing me."

Rebecca accompanied her caller to the door. The top of her lace-capped head came only to Livvy's shoulder. "Bella's been dead to me for a good many years," she said gruffly. Suddenly, she clutched Livvy's arm. "I don't know why you're so interested in my niece, but I'll be forever in your debt if you catch my Bella's murderer!"

"I shall," Livvy promised recklessly, not explaining her own reasons for wanting to apprehend the villain. With relief, she escaped into the daylight and wandered aimlessly along the Common. Rebecca Baskerville was not what Livvy had expected, and she experienced a strong sympathy for Arabella's misused aunt. A chapel half-hidden in a grove of trees caught Livvy's attention, and she wandered closer to investigate, recalling Rebecca's comments about the vicar's son.

The chapel was an incongruous structure, far too grand for so mundane a setting, with an interior like a Gothic cathedral, fitted up in crimson and gold. Livvy glimpsed jeweled reliquaries and gilded statues in every niche, and wondered how much of this splendor was paid for out of the profits of smuggling.

"Overwhelming, is it not?" said someone behind her left shoulder, and she started nervously. "My name is Beame." An extremely unctuous individual, he gazed about the chapel with complacent pride. "Visitors to Sapping always find their way here. Note that the pulpit and reading desk are opposite to each other, an excellent arrangement." Beame folded ascetic hands. "Are you interested in antiquities, madam?"

Livvy ignored this delicate attempt to learn her name. This too agreeable man with pasty skin that apparently never saw the sunlight reminded her of one of the less pleasant characters in a horror tale. "Vastly, sir. How splendid it must be daily to view such beauty, such inspiring relics of the past!" She hoped she wasn't overplaying her part.

"We have managed to retain most of our treasures, unlike so many other shrines of this sort." Beame smirked. "Note the richly carved canopies that form the seats of the Earl and Countess of Lansdale—the title has long since lapsed, alas."

"You are well versed in local history. Are you a native, sir?" Livvy could not imagine Arabella encouraging so obsequious a swain.

"No, to my regret." Beame was conspiratorial. "The living became vacant several years past; there was some scandal regarding my predecessor's son. Shocking, you will say, but even men of the cloth are subject to human frailty." He cast an anxious look at the doorway. "I was fortunate enough to secure the place."

Livvy had a distinct impression that Mr. Beame's attention was elsewhere. "How long ago was that?"

"Why, ten years." Pale eyes slid to Livvy, then away.

"The former parson and his son—" Livvy displayed kindly concern. "Had they anywhere to go, anyone to shelter them in their time of need?"

"We must trust to the Lord." Beame grew increasingly jittery. "Are you also interested in local history? I have some fascinating old registers—but there! I've left them in my study." Livvy was speedily bustled outside. "Perhaps you will call again. Services are held daily!"

Livvy stood on the church steps, so lost in thought that she was oblivious to the raindrops that had just begun to fall. Perhaps Beame had wished her gone so he might offer spiritual succor to some members of his flock. But Mr. Beame did not strike her as a spiritual man. Livvy smiled. It was far more likely that the chapel's custodian was engaged in the neighborhood trade, with tea hidden in the relic chests and brandy stashed beneath the pews. A thought, dazzling in brilliance, struck Livvy and she eyed the unpretentious residence that stood nearby. It could only be the vicarage. With cunning born of long acquaintance with the Baroness, Livvy walked aimlessly in that direction. Luck was with her, if not the weather; the study lay at the back of the house, commanding a view of gently rolling hills. Livvy was less interested in this rustic panorama than in the fact that not a single soul was in sight. Forcing open a window, she hiked up her skirts and clambered over the sill. There was little doubt that, in some richly merited afterlife, Livvy would inhabit that portion of Hades reserved specifically for ladies of insufficient decorum.

Papers evidencing Mr. Beame's industriousness were strewn across a plain wooden table. Livvy, wondering what esoteric and scholarly quest had resulted in such chaos, carefully skirted piles of paper and ancient manuscripts. Without the vaguest notion of what she sought, she leafed through the record book for the year of Arabella's departure from Sapping. No practiced housebreaker, Livvy did not realize the folly of turning her back to the door.

"Just what do you think you're doing, miss?" Livvy jumped and spun around, instinctively thrusting the register beneath her mantle. She was confronted by Beame's housekeeper, and irate indignation was written large on the latter's plump face. "Answer me or I'll be fetching the constable!" She advanced on Livvy, brandishing a mop in one capable-looking hand. "I never thought I'd see the day when an honest man isn't safe from the likes of you."

Livvy sidled around the table and backed toward the window. It appeared that she had been mistaken for an enterprising lady of joy. "Where, precisely, am I?" she queried, in good imitation of Lady Bligh's convenient vagueness. "Who are you?"

The housekeeper's eyes narrowed with suspicion but she made no further move. "I'll have no more of your nonsense!"

Livvy raised a hand to her brow. "I must have lost my way." She stiffened, listening. "What's that I hear? Someone calling? How wonderful if it is my dear Beame!"

The housekeeper was confused. Perhaps the stranger was no common trollop, but the purpose of her presence remained to be seen.

"We have known one another forever," Livvy added helpfully, "though I have not set eyes on my friend for ten years—since, in fact, he took the living here. How good it will be to see him again!" Slightly reassured, the housekeeper lowered her mop. "Do make haste, you foolish thing, and bring my dear Beame to me!"

The woman, conditioned to obedience, cast a wary eye on

her odd visitor before peering into the hallway. Quick as lightning, Livvy vaulted over the windowsill and was away, approaching the inn by an indirect route and praying that the natives would find nothing remarkable in the London lady who chose to stroll about their village in a pouring rain.

Mary was engaged in pressing frocks. "Lawks!" said she, staring at Livvy's flushed face and wet attire. "How have you got in such a state?" She grinned. "Did you know that Master Dickon has seen fit to join us here?"

Livvy tore off her bonnet and her mantle, both liberally splotched with rain, and dropped the register onto the bed. "Dickon? *Here?*" She smoothed her hair with icy hands. "Never mind that, Mary, start packing. We must leave immediately!"

Thunder cracked and Mary stared. "In this storm? Miss Livvy, we'll end up in a ditch."

"It's a great deal better than being apprehended by a constable." Livvy was on her way out the door. "Do as I say, Mary! There is no time to lose."

Lord Dorset was preparing a bowl of punch, a noble concoction of steaming port and roasted lemon, when his disheveled fiancée burst into the private parlor. "My good girl!" he said, with evident surprise, and poured a glass of the brew. "You look to be at wit's end. Sit down, and tell me all."

Livvy fought to catch her breath. Even in her anxious state, she noted that the Earl looked remarkably fine in the tailed riding coat, tight breeches and boots that constituted country dress. His expression was withdrawn and brooding and Livvy wondered, sinkingly, what new calamity had struck. "I cannot tell you, not now!" Reaction had set in. "I have done the most terrible thing!"

"Drink," commanded the Earl, his expression lightening. Displaying an expertise gained through exploits that Livvy did not care to consider, he rearranged her disheveled curls. "I do not mean to contradict you, but I doubt that any action of yours could be so very bad."

"You don't know the half of it." Livvy thought glumly of the various vengeful individuals who were doubtless hot on her trail. "Dickon, I must leave at once or all will be undone!"

As Livvy swallowed her punch in one gulp, the Earl, like Mary, surveyed the bleak weather. "Very well," he said abruptly. "I will admit it does not suit me just now to be seen in so public a place."

Livvy was given little time to ponder this queer remark. Lord Dorset was remarkably efficient, and in no time worth mentioning, they were firmly ensconced in Lady Bligh's carriage. Lightning forked across the sky, and Mary huddled in her corner, the cheerful, freckled face as pale as death.

"What can I be thinking of?" Livvy wiped raindrops from her face. "Have you found Austin? Why are you here?"

The Earl placed his tall, curly-brimmed hat on his knee. "No. He was briefly in the keeping of a woman who boards unwanted children, but disappeared yesterday. The trail ends there, I fear, though my man still searches that particular neighborhood." His voice was grim. "I am here, sweet Livvy, because Dulcie deemed it the most prudent course of action to take."

"I don't understand." It was plain that Dickon's presence was not inspired by an intolerable longing to view his ladylove.

"I returned to London on the chance that Austin might have found his way there. The boy is extremely precocious, despite his lack of speech. Gibbon intercepted me before I reached my home—most fortunately, as it turns out." Livvy, with dire premonition, braced herself. Lord Dorset regarded her somberly. "Gwyneth has finally driven someone to murder her."

Livvy was stricken dumb. It was quite marvelous that, on a subject so enormously dreadful, the Earl should appear so cool and deliberate. "Coo!" said Mary, briefly distracted from visions of being fried alive by a lightning bolt. "Now we're really in the suds."

"Are we?" Livvy pulled her mantle tighter against sudden cold. "I mean, are you suspected of this also?"

"I didn't think it prudent to call at Bow Street to inquire." The Earl was caustic. "Austin's safety is my first concern, and I can do nothing about that while answering Crump's incessant questions or sauntering about London with you in an effort to keep up appearances."

Outside, the storm raged. Mary, all else forgotten, began to pray. "Stop that mawkish drivelling!" snarled Dorset. "We will shelter at my cousin's home, and will arrive there momentarily."

"Hubert?" Livvy blinked. "Is *he* here, too?"

"I devoutly trust not!" The Earl, at this mention of his cousin, looked even more saturnine. "Mary has the right of it, however; we cannot travel all the way to London in this downpour." Thunder punctuated his remarks and Mary whimpered. Livvy took her hand.

"How," she asked, wishing she didn't have to know, "did Gwyneth die? Could it have been an accident?"

"It is a trifle difficult," Dickon retorted, "to strangle oneself." His features were strained. "We can console ourselves that Gwyneth would have been delighted with the drama attendant upon her end. The people in the streets talk of nothing else, even the mob, and I am afraid everyone sees my own conduct in the most unfavorable light." He did not sound particularly regretful. "Take heed, sweet Livvy. I am looked upon as one not fit to associate with respectable persons."

"I fear," said Livvy glumly, "that I will soon be in like case. At least I have thus far avoided publicizing my true name while running afoul of the law!" She sighed. "Although I should not be surprised to find myself heralded in the newspapers as the 'Wicked Widow of Sapping.' "

As she had hoped, the Earl was intrigued. "You fascinate me," he remarked. "What were you up to in that dull place? And, now that I think of it, why?" He raised a hand. "I know:

Dulcie! Never was there a female so determined as my aunt."

Livvy could not quarrel with this. As she explained her mission, Lord Dorset's eyebrows rose. "This does not sound at all nefarious. Why, then, did we depart with such undue speed?"

Livvy might have been in a confessional. "I stole a parish register," she admitted gloomily. "To make the matter worse, I was caught in the very act! Only by the skin of my teeth did I make my getaway."

"Livvy, you delight me!" Dickon's laughter was muted, but sincere, and Livvy congratulated herself. "Do you think you might explain why you committed this heinous crime?"

"I thought Dulcie might find the register pleasant reading!" Livvy retorted. "Of all the absurd questions, Dickon! You might as well ask me why I've done anything this past week."

"You will have to do better than that." Lord Dorset looked out the carriage window. "Explanations must wait until later, though; we have arrived."

Hubert's country manor seemed very grand for a gentleman who lived with the constant spector of the debtors' prison at the Fleet. It was a massive medieval structure, covering a vast area of land, with a great central tower that soared high into the air.

"Heavens!" said Livvy as they were admitted into a marble entrance hall as lofty as a Roman basilica. "It quite takes one's breath away."

"An inadequate appreciation." The Earl gazed about him without interest. "In its glory, this place required a minimum of eighty-seven servants to run. Humbug has closed off most of the rooms, though I believe he still burns perfumed coal in the fireplaces."

"Ah, I am all extravagance." Hubert strolled into the hallway and smiled benignly upon his startled guests. "How delightful that I should be here to greet you!"

Lord Dorset had taken one menacing step toward his cousin

when a small and energetic whirlwind launched itself into his arms. Hubert watched the reunion complacently, taking snuff while Dickon and his son embraced, but fell back a step when Dorset, after the initial joy of reunion, raised a face of murderous wrath. "You must not leap to conclusions!" Hubert said quickly. "Things are not what they seem."

"For your sake, cousin, I hope they are not." The Earl trembled as he spoke, and Livvy wondered how far, in this mood, he might go. Hubert, who shared her morbid curiosity, blanched.

One member of the audience was not in awe of the Earl's rage. Reaching up, Austin tugged impatiently at his father's sleeve. There was a great resemblance between them, Livvy thought, and it was odd to find in the face of a nine-year-old child those fathomless eyes.

"You must not curse at Hubert," Austin informed his warlike parent. "I was having a tremendous adventure and Cousin Humbug rescued me!"

Chapter Fourteen

THE SENSATIONAL MURDER of the Countess Andrassy had instantly become the talk of the town. Newspapers were crammed with fact and rumor, and the recent assassination of Lady Arabella Arbuthnot was vividly recalled. Even the celebrated scandal of Lady Caroline Lamb, who had burst into Lord Byron's rooms disguised as a carman while he was intimately entertaining another lady, took second place in the popular press.

"Damn your eyes!" said Madame Arbuthnot conversationally, raising her glass. "We must have this business settled straightaway." Her golden eyes were uncomfortably similar to those of Casanova when he was preparing to pounce. Crump wondered if that accursed feline had yet met its comeuppance, and what Lady Bligh thought of the huge blue parrot that had been the boon companion of a privateer who had met a well-deserved fate at the hands of his mutinous crew.

"We are progressing with all possible speed," he replied stiffly. "One cannot rush these things. It is a matter of tracking down and apprehending your criminal by means of observation and logic and the consideration of evidence."

"Pshaw!" Luisa brandished her bottle. "While you ruminate upon your so-called evidence, your criminal is free to misbehave as he will. Not that it's anything to me!" She drank deeply. "I hope Dulcie has greased your palm well, not that it will avail her anything in the end. Young Dickon will be a great deal the handsomer for his neck being stretched by an inch or two!"

In a time when even the most respectable people drank themselves under the table without shocking anyone, Luisa managed to become scandalously drunk. "If you don't mind," Crump ventured, with no desire to see the lady fly into a temper, "I'd like to ask you a few questions."

"Ask away," Luisa retorted, draining her glass in a most vulgar manner. "Not that I promise to answer you! It's a ridiculous waste of time to badger a helpless old woman while Dorset makes a clean getaway, but no one cares what *I* think!"

Crump, too, doubted that this visit would serve any purpose, but the Chief Magistrate's orders had to be obeyed. "Bow Street has received information that Countess Andrassy called on you the day of her death. Would you mind telling me what you talked about?"

"Of course I mind!" Luisa snapped. "Is a body to have no privacy? But it shan't be said that I didn't cooperate with the authorities." She smiled in a most unsettling way. "Gwyneth came to talk about Arabella, or so she said. She was set on stirring up scandal, of course, and I very soon sent the silly twit on her way with a flea in her ear."

This was more than likely, in the literal sense. Madame Arbuthnot's chamber was as dark as the pit, and slovenly enough to house countless species of unwholesome occupants. Crump repressed a shudder. "Did she say anything that might shed light on her subsequent death?"

"Gwyneth?" Luisa was derisive. "That one had more hair than wit, and an extremely disobliging nature beside." She grew irritable. "Why do you plague me, man? Go and apprehend Dorset, for he's your culprit."

"You feel very strongly on the matter. Could I ask your reasons?"

Luisa gave vent to an exaggerated sigh. "Must I do your thinking for you? Very well!" She ticked off her salient observations on swollen fingers. "One, everyone knows Dorset was with Arabella on the night of her death; two, there is the matter of his button and his knife. Additionally, he could easily gain access to this house and Arabella's boudoir." Madame wore an evil smirk. "Then we come to Gwyneth, with whom Dorset was on the most unamiable terms. They quarrelled in public frequently; I suspect you will discover that Gwyneth sought to extort money from him." She mournfully surveyed her empty bottle. "I further suspect that you will find she was strangled with the sash of *his* dressing gown."

Crump chose not to quibble with this deduction, though he doubted greatly that the impeccable Earl would be caught dead in that gaudy article. On the sideboard he found more brandy.

"Now, Mr. Bow Street Runner, you may answer a question for *me*. Have you yet turned up that revolting girl who attacked my William?"

"No, ma'am," Crump answered politely. "We are still making inquiries."

"Don't play the innocent with me!" Luisa snarled suddenly. "I cut my eyeteeth before you were born. Dulcie Bligh might think she bamboozled me, but I knew all along who Primrose was." She cackled. "I kept her guessing! And ran her off her feet. It's a pity the chit turned tail and ran so soon, for she had many a treat in store!" The unsightly head nodded. "I'll say this for Dulcie: she knows just how close she can sail to the wind without disaster." The hooded eyes closed. Luisa's head dropped; from her mouth issued lusty snores.

Crump, unhappy, did not know whether to go or stay. There were far more important matters that demanded his attention, such as the ascertaining of Lord Dorset's whereabouts, but the Runner's trusted intuition told him that Madame Arbuthnot could, if she chose, say a great deal more.

Longing for his pipe, Crump settled back in his uncomfortable chair and consoled himself with Sir William's promise of a handsome reward. The Runner wondered if Madame Arbuthnot knew that Arabella's stolen jewels were only paste. Happily, those tidings were not his to disclose, and Sir John was keeping unaccountably mum.

The residences of both Lord Dorset and Lady Bligh were under constant surveillance, though the watchers had thus far turned up little enough of interest. Mrs. Lytton and Hubert Humboldt had returned to the City, bringing with them Lord Dorset's son, a lad that Crump would have greatly liked to interview, had he not been denied all opportunity. He had also been disappointed in Lady Bligh's servants, for only the plump cook would give Bow Street more than the time of day, and that merry individual, though a rare gossip, had little enough of interest to impart, save fulsome reminiscences of the Baron. Crump knew enough about that erratic peer to fill a book, and shocking reading it would be. The Runner scowled. The cook had also told him the identity of Lady Bligh's sole caller, in recent days, an indigent relative who interested him not at all, being an elderly female of shabby appearance, overly tall and broad of waist, who had thrown herself upon the Baroness's mercy.

"This time even Dulcie's machinations will not serve," Luisa announced abruptly and with great satisfaction. "Beware of her: she is an artful woman who will take you in, as far as it lies within her power."

Crump could not argue. "About the Countess's visit," he prompted gently.

"Gwyneth did say one thing that was queer, hinting that she had learned something that would prove beyond a doubt that Dorset murdered Arabella. No doubt she gave him the opportunity to buy her silence." Luisa's smile was malicious. "Instead the hussy was silenced permanently. I dislike your methods, Crump! You waste time with me while Dorset flees the country, no doubt. What stake have you in this that you would wish him to go free?"

Crump rose. It grew obvious that, whatever Madame Arbuthnot might know, he would learn no more. "You are convinced of his guilt. Bow Street, however, requires more concrete evidence. I assure you, madam, that justice will be served." Crump bowed as he spoke, prepared to exit.

"Certainly, when pigs will fly!" It was seldom that Luisa was denied the last word. "The wheels of justice turn exceedingly slow, it seems. Take care that they don't grind *your* bones!"

In the hallway, with Madame safely behind a closed door, Crump pondered his next move. Someone had to track down the elusive Lord Dorset, and though Crump had no great love of horses, he would have to avail himself of one of the pair kept in constant readiness for Runners who were called out of town. He set out for his lodgings to pack and prepare his brace of holster pistols. In his present frame of mind, Crump looked forward with pleasure to discharging those instruments into the first man to offer him further affront. He hoped that first offender might be the pestilent Lord Dorset, for since the Earl's entrance into Crump's orderly existence absolutely nothing had gone right.

The exhausted travellers had returned safely to London unmolested by Bow Street, vicars, or irate villagers. Only Austin had remained sufficiently nonchalant to appreciate the horse fairs and tramping pedlars, sleepy country towns and prize rings that the procession passed by, and even he had lapsed into sulks when his fond, if irritable, companions denied him a closer look at the Flaming Tinman. In all, it was a somber party that had made its various ways into the Bligh mansion, and though they were now reunited after supper in their rooms, the mood had not noticeably improved.

They were gathered in the Music Room, a large chamber embellished with windows of Mexican onyx, rose-garlanded friezes, Pompeiian ceilings, Persian tiles and a spectacular Roman fountain. Livvy, gowned in cambric muslin with waggoner's sleeves and a cottage vest of green sarcenet laced across the bosom, sat at a magnificent grand piano inlaid with ivory, mother-of-pearl, and tortoise shell. Casanova perched meekly beside her on the bench, his exemplary behavior inspired by Bluebeard, who, when provoked, had a habit of swooping down upon the indignant feline as a hawk might its prey.

"Uncle Max," commented Hubert, surveying his environment through a quizzing-glass, "must do all in the grand style. He ships home entire Grecian temples as others might china sets!" Since the room was graced with bronze Floras, muses, hermaphrodites, bulls and harpies; a crystal lustre from which darted aerie creatures in attitudes of flight; and a bright blue carpet ornamented with birds, flowers and insects, there was, perhaps, some justification for his dismay.

"We are not here to discuss Bat's foibles," reproved the Baroness. Austin, leaning against her knee, looked up inquiringly. "No, child, I don't know when he will be home. At last count his caravan included seven Green servants, a *maître d'hôtel*, four manservants, a cook, a scullery boy and a stray dog. Add tents, camels and horses, and Bat must appear to have a perambulating circus in tow." She ruffled the boy's hair. "I'll wager that he'll return to us soon."

"Famous!" Austin's young face was bright with anticipation.

"Uncle Bat brings back such nacky things." Lord Dorset looked as if he would disagree, but he was silenced by the ignominy of his disguise.

" 'Tis a great pity you are already spoken for, cousin!" Hubert was in splendid spirits. The Earl was a feast for the eyes, clad in a frowsy gray wig, a dress that threatened to burst its seams at any moment, and a dowdy all-encompassing shawl. "Seldom have I set eyes on a wench more artistically draped."

"If you don't curb your tongue, Humbug, I shall give myself the privilege of breaking your blasted neck!" growled Dorset unappreciatively.

"Like Mama?" piped Austin, with interest. Livvy's hands fell from the piano keys.

"Yes," said the Baroness thoughtfully. "It is time we got down to the business at hand." She wore a fetching robe of satin and lace, and held in one bejewelled hand a sheaf of parchment. On her lap was the pilfered parish register. "Tell us once more, Austin, exactly how your mother contrived to steal you away."

"I don't remember much," Austin replied, with all the ghoulish gusto of an adventurous young soul who has been most satisfactorily kidnapped and drugged. "Mama came in the middle of the night, and then there was that nasty woman, and then Cousin Humbug came and we ran away." Austin eyed the Baroness hopefully. "I didn't have near half enough to eat."

"In a moment." Dulcie frowned. Her hair, whether by accident or design, achieved a remarkable brindled effect. "Do you know what your mother meant to do with you?"

Austin screwed up his features. "Not exactly. She either meant to take me away or to do away with me, but I can't remember precisely what she said." He was apologetic. "It's all fuzzy, you see."

This calm announcement struck its various auditors dumb

with horror. Lady Bligh recovered first. "To whom was she speaking, Austin?" Livvy dropped one shaking hand to Casanova's furry back, seeking warmth. The cat rumbled with almost as much violence as one of Mr. Trewithick's mechanical contrivances that ran on rails.

"I don't know." Austin was perplexed. "It was a man, I think, but I never saw him." In atonement, he offered a further fact. "I guess Mama didn't expect me to speak, because when I told her she was an evil, nasty witch, and I disliked her above all things, she shrieked like a banshee. Then she gave me that rotten medicine that made me sleep."

"Laudanum," murmured Livvy. "How *could* she?"

"Easily," retorted the Earl harshly. "Gwyneth was unhampered by ethics of any sort." He tugged impatiently at the bodice of his gown. "That will do, Austin. I daresay if you go to the kitchen, Pudding might find you some syllabubs and cream."

In a flat second, Austin was across the room and on his way out the door. Livvy felt a queer little wrench in the area of her heart; so must Dickon have looked at a similar age. "I also told Mama," Austin added, "that if she hurt me, you'd do for her. It didn't scare her like I thought it would. She said you'd likely hang instead." Suddenly, he was a very frightened little boy. "That's not going to happen, is it?"

"Most assuredly," said the Baroness firmly, "it is not! Now be off with you." They were silent as his footsteps echoed down the marble hall.

"I begin to think," Hubert remarked, "that Gwyneth was hardly worth the price of a man's neck." He lounged against a chimney piece representing Apollo and the Muses, copied from the sarcophagus of Homer. "It is a pity Bow Street doesn't award medals for the extermination of such vermin, but I suppose the law must be upheld."

"You showed a certain regard for the lady while she was

alive." Lord Dorset yanked the wig from his head and ran supple fingers through his disheveled hair. "Explain that, Humbug! If you can."

Hubert was all startled innocence. "It is as plain as daylight, cousin! When have I ever bypassed an opportunity to irritate you? It is my ruling pleasure and has the added felicity of costing me not one cent."

"Enough!" Dulcie held up a hand. "We have no time for these petty squabbles." Her dark gaze rested appraisingly upon Hubert. "I wonder how you knew precisely where to find Austin."

Livvy marveled at Hubert's composure, for he blinked not an eye. "Intuition and useful contacts, dear aunt." He made a mocking bow. "The virtue of both which I have learned from you."

The Baroness was not disarmed. "Humph. Your useful contacts may well land you in the basket, my boy! However, we are not here to discuss your likely fate, but Dickon's." Papers rustled. "I have asked you to attend this conclave because you are so closely involved, more than you realize. You will, of course, keep secret anything you may learn."

"Trust me." Hubert observed his cousin with ironic glee. "Not for the sake of Dickon's blue eyes, you understand, or even because of Austin's lamentable adventure, but because it promises to be vastly diverting." He twirled a white-thorn cane and ostentatiously surveyed Dorset's costume. " 'Tis better even than a play."

Livvy did the same, and had to repress an untimely giggle. At that, Lord Dorset smiled ruefully.

Dulcie plopped the register on a table and opened it to a certain page. "Arabella," she announced, "was married in 1804 to one James Worthington." There was a hint of a satisfied smirk on her face as she rang the bell.

"So she *did* marry him," Livvy mused, as Gibbon appeared.

"And in the village itself. How odd! I wonder that no one knew."

"Send Culpepper to me," Dulcie ordered, and Gibbon left silently. "It will all eventually come clear, Lavender. Hubert, you continue to insist that you knew nothing of this?"

"I did not." Hubert so far forgot his cultivated languor as to peer over Dulcie's shoulder at the register. "You know I spend as little time as possible at my estate. I heard some vague rumor of Arabella's misbehavior, true, but was never sufficiently interested to learn exactly what it was she'd done."

"How unlike you, Humbug!" Lord Dorset dripped sarcasm. "You ordinarily have a nose for mischief a mile away."

"Not," Hubert protested, pained, "when it concerns schoolgirls, and hoydenish ones at that." He snickered. "You wouldn't know, of course, but there was nothing remarkable about Arabella at that age."

Lady Bligh wrinkled her elegant nose. "Arabella only cultivated Hubert to gain an introduction to Dickon," she informed Livvy. "It's a pity Hubert wasn't quick-witted enough to see through her scheme! We'd have been spared a great deal of trouble." Culpepper silently entered the room. "There you are! What do you know about James Worthington?"

Culpepper's ability to retain odd facts gleaned from society journals, particularly those concerning the more scandalous exploits of the aristocracy, was her greatest source of pride. "Worthington," she repeated absently. "Of good family but bad reputation—a black sheep, in short. There was some rumor of a marriage, a *mésalliance,* but it was quickly hushed up, and he was reported killed in action shortly thereafter."

"What family, Culpepper?" Lady Bligh was intent. "Give us a name."

"Rumfoord," Culpepper replied promptly. "Younger brother, if memory serves, to the present Marquis."

"Excellent!" Dulcie deliberated. "The Marquis is a starched-up sort; I wonder if we should throw him into a tizzy with inquiries about brother James." She nibbled her lower lip in a manner that presaged great discomfort for the unfortunate peer. "Yes, I believe we shall! That is all, Culpepper; you may go." Lady Bligh gazed triumphantly upon her audience. "It begins to make sense now."

"Oh?" inquired Hubert. "Damned if I see how."

"That is because you are not in possession of all the facts." As Dulcie waved the parchment, Bluebeard stretched and opened an interested eye. Casanova, seeking protection, molded himself to Livvy's thigh.

"Do you intend to enlighten us?" Lord Dorset was not in an equable mood. "I am going to offer someone violence if I am forced to skulk about much longer in this asinine attire."

"You must look on the bright side, darling," Livvy said mischievously. "You may come and go as you please, and indulge in all sorts of activities unsuited to an Earl, and not one of your acquaintances will recognize you."

"I may also accompany you to any number of places, without either scandal or chaperone, for everyone will think me your maid." The Earl smoothed his skirts. "Sweet Livvy, I rapidly become resigned."

Livvy, suddenly envisioning the Earl invading her bedchamber, offered no comment. "To continue," announced Dulcie. "Arabella married her Dragoon, by name James Worthington, but it availed her little." She turned to Livvy. "As for how she married in the village and yet no one knew, I'll wager the thing was clandestine, and at Worthington's insistence. The vicar's son also comes to mind; perhaps the vicar performed the ceremony hoping that Arabella would leave town."

"Was it legal?" Livvy found it difficult to keep her thoughts on a properly elevated plane. She might have been pinched with hunger, and Lord Dorset a sumptuous meal. "The marriage, I mean?"

"Perfectly." The Baroness spread out one sheet of parchment, Arabella's marriage lines. "As you can see, Arabella, in a fit of belated prudence perhaps, crossed out her husband's name. The document, however, is perfectly legitimate. It is odd that she would keep such damning evidence as I suspect this certificate may be, but the poor thing was unblessed with wisdom, after all."

"Forgive me, aunt, but I fail to see why this marriage should be so guilty a secret." Hubert was condescending. "We have already learned that Worthington is dead. Despicable, perhaps, that a widow should pass for maiden but it wouldn't be the first time a bridegroom was deceived by spoiled goods." Livvy blushed. "Forgive me, darling Livvy! I did not mean to malign *you.*"

"Wise of you," commented the Earl, dangerously.

"Lavender," said Dulcie, waving the second piece of parchment, "is not to be compared with Arabella in any way." Livvy quietly closed the piano. She and Arabella had at least been sisters under the skin, both seduced by the ecstatic, if transient, raptures of being the Earl's light-o'-love. Like moths to the flame, Livvy mused, and marvelled at the ineffectiveness of her strict upbringing. The road to ruin stretched out ahead and her only rational thought was that Lord Dorset would make a splendid guide.

"Lavender!" The Baroness stared astonished at her companion.

"I wish I knew," Hubert lamented, "what is going on here!" Livvy stared mortified at the splendid carpeting.

"We may conclude," continued Lady Bligh, "that Arabella's marriage did not prove blissful. Worthington departed quickly enough to resume his neglected military duties, leaving Arabella to fend for herself. Where she did so, or how, I cannot say, but I doubt it is of significance."

"Then he was killed," Livvy guessed, pushing her unladylike

thoughts firmly aside. "Had Arabella no awareness of his family? Why didn't she go to them?"

"I daresay she would have liked to, but she was offered a considerable sum to refrain from doing that very thing." The Baroness tapped the letter. "It was the most Arabella could hope for, since Worthington was disinherited when the family learned of his marriage."

"So she cut her losses and came to her mother's family, blithely neglecting to inform them of the true state of affairs," Hubert murmured. "And soon enough married her Duke. I had no notion that Arabella was so enterprising!" He gazed speculatively upon his aunt. "Nor do I see how this helps Dickon." He draped himself gracefully against the marble fireplace. He seemed a spectator at a play and Livvy wondered what, if anything, might engender an honest emotion in this mincing mannequin.

"I have told you," growled Lord Dorset, crossing his legs in a manly way and exposing feet encased in satin slippers, "that I had no chance to speak with Gwyneth after our encounter in the Park, which Livvy was witness to. It's true that I called at her hotel several times, but she was always out. I assume she was arranging for Austin's kidnapping."

"Is it not fortunate?" Hubert inquired brightly. "Someone saved you the trouble of disposing of her! I vow, you should be grateful, cousin."

"I might be," retorted the Earl, "were it not for persistent visions of my head in a noose!"

"Never mind," soothed the Baroness. "A few hours more and Bow Street will be off on a different witch hunt."

"I hope you may be correct." The Earl modestly fussed with his bodice. "I begin to think that hanging would be a great deal more comfortable than this damned dress."

"No," Livvy breathed, but he heard her and smiled.

"Never fear, sweet Livvy, I do not mean to adorn the

gallows tree." His glance was warm. "I find there remain a great many things that I have yet to do."

Hubert had no interest in sentimental digressions. "I must confess," he admitted, "to a certain curiosity. How do you propose to set about Dickon's miraculous rescue, dear aunt?"

"Not I," retorted the Baroness, "but you." All eyes turned to Hubert who stared at his aunt with startled disbelief.

"I do not mean to contradict you," he said cautiously, "but indeed I must protest! What could *I* possibly do that would have bearing on Dickon's plight?"

"You need do nothing at all," Dulcie replied blandly, "a course of action that you follow remarkably well, although I give you credit for the effort that led to Austin's rescue. Matters, in this case, are already out of our hands."

Hubert refrained from pointing out that a way of life that included playing faro from early evening until the candles glittered pale in dawn's early light, and intricacies of toilette that involved the passage of several hours, not to mention time passed in the usual pursuits of a fashionable gentleman, could hardly be considered effortless. "You are developing a habit of speaking in riddles, Dulcie, and in a way that fills me with the liveliest dread. Pray enlighten me!"

"Certainly." Dulcie stroked Casanova in a practiced manner that caused the tomcat to roll over on his back, all four paws extended heavenward in absurd ecstasy. "I meant only that suspicion of murder is about to swing from Dickon to you."

"This," announced Hubert, indignantly and with uncharacteristic forcefulness, "is the outside of enough! Family feeling is all very well in its place, but I balk at the notion of saving Dickon's skin at the expense of my own!"

"Never fear, Humbug," murmured the Earl. "I shall exert fully as much effort on your behalf as you have on mine."

"Hubert?" asked Livvy, with a heady sense of relief, "why?"

"Yes," agreed that shaken individual. "Why me? I admit myself avid for your reply!"

"If you hang, Hubert, it will be entirely through your own carelessness." The Baroness did not appear particularly concerned. "Although I daresay I might arrange to have you merely transported instead."

Hubert had turned a ghastly hue. "I swear to you that I had nothing to do with either of the deaths. For God's sake, Dulcie, why should Bow Street come after me?"

"This faintheartedness does not suit you, nephew! I know exactly what you have and have not done." Hubert quailed under her astute eyes. "Gwyneth was strangled with the sash of your dressing gown."

Chapter Fifteen

ALONE IN HIS office, Sir John lingered over his evening meal. Once six servants had waited on him at dinner, while the housekeeper and butler hovered around the door in case he wanted for anything not provided. But Sir John did not pine for his pampered life. The Bow Street office, bare and unpretentious, was more homelike to him than his luxurious mansion had ever been, the street people more fascinating than all the Dukes and Duchesses in the realm. He thought of Lady Caro Lamb, last glimpsed prancing about in green pantaloons at a Watiers Club masquerade in honor of Napoleon's defeat, and compared her unfavorably with fiery-eyed Billingsgate Moll, a guttersnipe who defended her dubious virtue furiously. Caro, forced to live by her wits in London's brutish streets, would not survive a single day.

Those outcasts of society lived by other standards, obeyed other laws. Why should they not take what they might from the indifferent rich who battened on them; who sent their children into factories and mines, there to sicken and die while the owner's plump purses grew fuller still; who hanged a man if he dared steal a crust of bread to ease his belly's gnawing hunger?

Footsteps sounded on the worn floorboards in the hall and Sir John pushed away his tray and steeled himself for the encounter. While he would have liked nothing more than to beguile away an hour with the intoxicating Lady Bligh, he did not look forward to this meeting.

She was dressed in a gown and pelisse of white muslin, with a delicious concoction of ribbon and ostrich feathers perched jauntily on multi-colored curls. With her was a gypsy clad in flaming scarlet and countless golden chains. Sir John could not imagine why or by what means Lady Bligh had persuaded the legendary Jael to set foot in Bow Street headquarters, but the gypsy's sulky expression hinted that coercion might have been used.

"John!" The Baroness dropped onto a wooden chair and smiled graciously. "I have decided the time has come for frankness, and am prepared to lay my cards on the table." The Chief Magistrate exhibited no great delight. "I have learned any number of things that will prove of interest to you."

"My primary concern at this moment is with the whereabouts of your nephews." Sir John wondered why the gypsy eyed him so appraisingly, unless to calculate how far she might pursue her criminal activities before Bow Street intervened. He saw no reason to inform Jael that her career was likely to continue unchecked, since officers and patrolmen alike were convinced of her ability to administer the evil eye. The Chief Magistrate, surveying that savage countenance, thought this a talent that even he would not like to put to the test.

"Dear John, I have so many nephews that I cannot count them all, let alone account for their whereabouts!" Lady Bligh was aghast at the prospective task.

"You might begin with Dorset," said Sir John, resisting her blandishments. "I would not like to instigate a city-wide manhunt for him."

"Could you?" Dulcie's eyes were wide. "I had no notion you had such vast resources at your disposal, John. Are not the great majority of your men engaged in searching for that brazen highwayman? I hear he has most recently divested a most indignant dowager duchess of a magnificent inlay set." Jael moved to the window, from which vantage point she commanded both an excellent view of the doorway and an excellent, if somewhat dangerous, avenue of escape.

"I've no time for these games." Sir John's mood was not improved by this reminder of his failure to entrap The Gentleman.

"Games, John?" Dulcie was wounded. "I'm sure I don't know what you mean. Do you wish to speak with Dickon? Merely say so and it will be arranged."

"Don't play the innocent miss with me, Dulcie," he said shortly. "Dorset's ex-wife and current mistress are both found murdered, and Lady Arabella's jewels are discovered in his house. Anyone with half a grain of sense would see that his whereabouts must be of utmost interest to Bow Street."

"Yes, but I thought you bright enough to see that Dickon could have had nothing to do with either event." Dulcie delivered the insult gracefully. "Dickon was not even in London at the time of Gwyneth's death."

"I should prefer to discover that for myself," the Chief Magistrate replied in frigid tones. "I suppose that Hubert Humboldt is no more readily accessible? Before you pitch me any more gammon, *I'll* inform *you* that he was seen entering your home."

"You have my permission to search." The Baroness was martyred. "Disrupt my household, if you must, terrorize my servants. I will not stop you—indeed, I cannot! I am only a poor defenseless female with no one to protect her against such outrage."

"Balderdash!" Despite his resolutions, Sir John could not help but be amused by these antics. From the window, Jael watched impassively. "It is perfectly clear that neither Dorset or Humboldt is on the premises, or you would not be so willing to cooperate with the law." His brief amusement ended. "It all comes to the same thing. We will have the murderer in the end."

"I trust so," the Baroness said briskly, "though it is taking you an unconscionably long time." She deposited a paper-wrapped parcel on his desk. "I truly do not know Humbug's whereabouts, though I anticipate that we will encounter him ere long." She resumed her seat, leaving Sir John to regard the package as one might a coiled serpent. "Hubert is not your culprit, John. I suspect him of a great number of things, few of them praiseworthy, but I sincerely doubt that murder is among his vices."

The Chief Magistrate gingerly unwrapped the package. "I am surprised that you defend him."

"Frankly," said Lady Bligh, "so am I! It is the oddest thing, but I find myself developing a grudging affection for my waspish nephew. Humbug may act exceedingly foolish, but he does it with style."

Jael spoke abruptly. "He is not so great a fool as you may think, Baroness, not by half." Sir John regarded the gypsy with interest, but she volunteered no more.

Under the intent scrutiny of both women, the Chief Magistrate examined both the parish register and the stolen documents. "Very interesting," he said at last. "Have you considered that these may be a screever's work?" Such individuals, who in happier times were employed as clerks and lawyers and even clergymen, eked out a fair living by drafting bogus documents.

"Not those." Jael knew whereof she spoke. "There's no question that they're legitimate."

Sir John was not pleased to be told his business. "The conclusions are obvious, but hardly of monumental import."

"You are far off the mark," retorted the Baroness gleefully. "Tell me, what have you learned of Slippery Jim?"

His brows lowered. "Nothing. We haven't found a trace of the man."

"Infallible Bow Street!" jeered the gypsy, and moved from the window to perch impudently on the edge of Sir John's desk. "What if I were to tell you Jimmie's whereabouts, down to his exact address? What would be in it for me?"

"Avaricious hussy," remarked Lady Bligh. "You've already been handsomely paid."

"More than handsomely, and I'd take nothing more from *you*." White teeth flashed. "But Bow Street has offered a reward for information, and I mean to claim it as my own." Her chill and emotionless gaze rested on Sir John.

The Chief Magistrate, inhaling a not unpleasant scent of musk, wondered where Jael had received her obvious education, an unusual accomplishment for a denizen of the underworld. Tales about the gypsy were legion, and macabre; gazing upon the scarred visage, he couldn't doubt that they were also true. "Very well, the money's yours, providing that you earn it."

Jael laughed bitterly. "Don't fret, I shall, every ha'penny and more beside!" She paced the floor like a caged wildcat. "Mind you, it's only because of the Baroness that I tell you this and even at that, I suspect I'm made." She scowled. "What's it to me if a damned aristo hangs? Best hang the lot of them, I say, for a bunch of bloodsucking leeches! The Frenchies had the right idea when they lopped off noble heads with Madame Guillotine."

"That'll be enough!" snapped Sir John, considerate of Lady

Bligh's sensibilities. He might have spared his efforts; Dulcie was undisturbed by rampant bloodthirstiness. "Get on with it."

"All right then. Jimmie lives in Marylebone, in that slum district of narrow courts and mean alleys between James Street and Stratford Place."

Sir John knew the area, rife with crowded rookeries stretching as far as Orchard Street. Irish laborers filled every cellar and garret, spilling over into the labyrinth of underground passages and footways that were once tributaries of Tyburn brook.

"Jimmie's come into funds of late," Jael added. "He's been laying low, hiding from someone or something, and threatening at the least mention of Bow Street to jump right out of his skin."

"Very enlightening," commented Sir John, "but what connection does this have with the other thing?"

"I'm disappointed in you, John." Dulcie returned to the present. "It should be obvious. Continue, Jael."

The gypsy shrugged. "There's little more." She smiled at the Chief Magistrate with malicious triumph. "Save that Jimmie's made a proper fool of himself trying to sell jewels made of paste!"

"It would be interesting to speak with Slippery Jim," Lady Bligh remarked as Sir John digested this unpalatable tidbit. "I suggest we do so without delay. Jael will escort us to him."

"Us?" repeated Sir John doubtfully.

"I will?" inquired the gypsy, in the same tone. "I must have windmills in my head! What do you plan for me, Baroness, when you have made it impossible for me to return to my old life? I'll likely be strangled myself some fine night when certain people learn I've been cooperating with Bow Street!"

"I would not have thought you a coward," remarked Dulcie, earning a fierce Romany scowl. "Well, John?"

"By all means, I must speak with the man," the Chief

Magistrate was firm, "but not until tomorrow when it is daylight and I may see who is at my back. Nor will you accompany me."

"You might recall that old adage about tomorrow being lamentably too late! We will be safe enough tonight in Jael's company."

The Chief Magistrate was adamant. Beguile him as ever she would, he had no intention of escorting Dulcie into that particular part of Marylebone. "The best-laid plans of mice and men," murmured the Baroness. "John, you are muleheaded. And, unless I am mistaken, you are about to be visited by an even greater fool."

"I demand to see the person in charge!" came a high-pitched, heavily accented voice, excitable in tone. The Chief Magistrate sighed, anticipating a futherance of confusion, and Count Bela Andrassy, followed by a protesting Crump, burst into the room.

So splendid was the Hungarian gentleman that on initial appearance he dazzled the eye and temporarily silenced the most garrulous tongue. Of a perfection that would make even the immaculate Hubert appear a dowd, the Count was dressed in a wide-brimmed hat, high and tight cravat, superbly cut coat worn wide open to display a rose-colored waistcoat and snowy cambric shirt, and skintight pantaloons. Further adorning his person were jewels and fobs, chains, spotless gloves and boots so highly polished that they might serve as looking glasses. Count Andrassy was not unaware of the impact made by his perfection. He paused to allow his observers to absorb the full effect of his splendor, and observed them condescendingly.

Lady Bligh did not remain mute for long. "This," she explained kindly to Sir John, "has to be Gwyneth's second husband, and I daresay he has come to enact us a Cheltenham tragedy." She regarded the intruder with as little appreciation as a gardener might a particularly hardy variety of weed. "I suggest you leave him to me."

Count Andrassy drew himself up to his full stature, approximately five feet three, and inspected the Baroness through a gold-rimmed monocle. "Who is this pernicious creature?" he demanded, of no one in particular. Crump, anticipating a rare set-to, positioned himself by the door, one bright eye fixed warily on Jael. "Never have I been offered such insolence! Had I anticipated that you English would prove so odious of manner, I should never have set foot off my native soil."

"Why did you?" inquired Lady Bligh, with calm curiosity. "Did you seek to help your wife further her avaricious schemes? Or did you find it expedient to escape indignant creditors?"

The Count was briefly discomposed, for both remarks were true. His recovery was quick. "You please to taunt me, madam, but it is insignificant." One could almost imagine a batallion of spectral ancestors standing firmly behind this last member of their ancient, if degenerate, line. "I shall not be drawn into crass argument with one so obviously inferior."

"Popinjay!" retorted the Baroness, the light of battle in her eye.

"Count Andrassy," said Crump, in reluctant response to Sir John's fulminating look, "has come to inquire about his wife." The Runner had little liking for foreigners, with their finicky ways and incomprehensible speech. "He just arrived in London and was understandably startled to be told that she is, er, dead."

"Murdered!" mourned the Count, thus reminded of his mission, and staggered broken-heartedly toward a chair. "Gwyneth, my pearl beyond price, my treasure, my wife! It is unthinkable."

"That's all very sad, Count Andrassy, but what brought you to London?" Sir John could bear no more histrionics. The

Count Andrassy swiveled to observe his interrogator. "How prodigiously unfeeling you English are! It was the anguish of separation that led me to follow my beloved wife to this cold, unsympathetic land." He carefully removed his hat. "Imagine my sentiments when I arrived only to learn that my darling Gwyneth had been launched into eternity. My angel!" He ceased his lament long enough to survey Sir John with disapproval. "And no effort made to apprehend the *bâtard* who delivered her death blow!"

Dulcie, bestowed on Count Andrassy the full impact of her enigmatic gaze, with the effect of causing the gentleman to shift positions uncomfortably. "Did your wife have any enemies," she asked, "anyone who would wish her harm?"

"Only one," replied the Count, directing his vision heavenward. "My wife was of a disposition that made her beloved of all she knew."

"Fustian," murmured Lady Bligh. Crump, recalling his brief acquaintance with the Countess, silently agreed.

"Put a name to this unappreciative individual," Sir John suggested, with little doubt of the reply. Count Andrassy did not disappoint him.

"The Earl of Dorset, my angel's previous husband who treated her so abominably."

Lady Bligh addressed the emotional Hungarian with a degree of civility that seemed remarkable to Crump. "Are we to assume that your wife was unhappy in her previous marriage, then? Is it not odd that she should return to London and seek out Lord Dorset, if he caused such sad memories? And even odder that you should allow her to do so without your protection and support?"

Count Andrassy had no inkling of this annoying female's identity, but he wished her to blazes all the same, and with her that gaudy gypsy who laughed so immoderately. "I could deny my angel nothing," he replied sadly. "Never shall I forgive myself! But Gwyneth deemed it more prudent that I remain behind, for she feared I could not restrain myself from challenging Dorset to a duel." Soulfully he surveyed his hat. "Gwyneth was the most forgiving creature, willing to let bygones be bygones, no matter how grievously she was abused."

While acknowledging that Count Andrassy would have made a remarkable success at either Covent Garden or Drury Lane, Sir John wondered at the purpose of this monologue. "Why did Countess Andrassy return to London?" he asked forthrightly. "Did she seek a reconciliation with Lord Dorset?"

"Never!" The Count bristled with offense. "She had vowed to avoid everything that could remind her of him, never to mention his name again or inquire after him, and if possible never to think of him again!"

"Indeed?" The Baroness was bland. "Did she break all her vows with equal ease?" Crump chuckled appreciatively at this facer. It was the worst of these foreigners that they talked volumes around a question and never answered it.

"Madame!" Count Andrassy rose. The gypsy moved to stand, arms crossed like a sword-bearing bodyguard, behind the insolent woman's chair, and her scarred, hard face inspired him to quickly resume his seat. Indignantly, the Count addressed Sir John. "Surely you do not intend me to tolerate such disrespect."

"I expect you," retorted Sir John, who had experienced an impulse similar to the one that had inspired Jael's unprecedented protectiveness, "to answer the question! What brought your wife back to England after an absence of so many years?"

"Her son," Count Andrassy replied sulkily. "She was concerned that his character might be ruined by the sort of upbringing that Dorset would provide."

"Wasn't this concern a trifle belated?" Sir John's quick question effectively forestalled the Baroness. "The boy is already some nine years of age."

Count Andrassy had an answer for everything, it seemed. "It

was Dorset's scandalous *affaire* with Lady Arabella Arbuthnot that caused my wife's concern. A man who spends his time in pursuit of married women is hardly of proper moral fiber to satisfactorily rear a son."

The Chief Magistrate was rapidly coming to agree with Crump's opinion of foreigners in general. This particular gentleman was, additionally, a damned cool specimen. "How did your wife expect to persuade Lord Dorset to give up his son?"

"First by an appeal to reason," the Count replied wearily. "Then, if reason did not serve, she meant to publish his infamy to the world." His expression was tragic. "Forgive me! I endeavor to bear with resignation my irreparable loss, but it has been a sad blow. My darling Gwyneth lies brutally slain, and the authorities do nothing at all."

"On the contrary," remarked Sir John, to whom a decent night's sleep was an almost forgotten thing, "the authorities have already accomplished a great deal."

"Dorset," protested Count Andrassy, wild of eye, "goes free! Is this your famed English justice? I give not a fig for it!" With such a gesture might his ancestors have sentenced a head to roll. "I am prepared to offer a generous reward to the man who brings Dorset to the gallows!"

"One wonders," remarked Lady Bligh, "where you intend to come by such a sum. Everyone knows the Andrassys haven't a penny to their name."

"*Who,*" demanded the Count, livid with rage, "is this abominable female?"

"Yes," agreed Dulcie. "Do introduce us properly, John."

"The Baroness Dulcie Bligh." Sir John awaited Count Andrassy's reaction. "Aunt to the aforementioned Earl of Dorset and great-aunt to your wife's son."

Dulcie focused her razor-edged gaze on the sputtering Count. "You have treated us to a great deal of nonsense, my man, for your account has been nothing but a tissue of lies from start to finish."

"I must protest!" gasped the Count, goggling.

"I suppose you must," Crump remarked, "but listen you will, along with the rest of us."

"Thank you, Crump!" The Baroness smiled and turned to Sir John. "I believe you'll discover that Count Andrassy arrived in London at the same time as Gwyneth, and indeed travelled with her. His presence was kept secret since it might have hindered Gwyneth's schemes."

"Utter nonsense!" The Count had turned an uncomfortable shade of pink. "What schemes were these, madam?"

"Why, to bilk my nephew of as much of his fortune as possible." Dulcie adjusted her bonnet with a businesslike air. "Gwyneth might have been more successful with a more astute accomplice but Hubert, though happy enough to help her annoy Dickon, would have balked at Austin's kidnapping. Therefore, she was forced to rely on the Count, which no doubt contributed to her downfall."

"Infamous!" sputtered Andrassy. Crump watched with fascination as the Count's self assurance crumbled.

"Yes," agreed Lady Bligh, "it is." She meditated. "I perceive that Gwyneth first meant to reclaim Dickon's affection, in which case her current husband would have been very much in the way. Have you ever considered, Count Andrassy, what would have been your lot if Gwyneth had succeeded?" The Count looked surprised, then stricken. "I thought not! But it did not serve; first Arabella, then Lavender, stood in the way."

"Surely you don't mean to suggest," Sir John protested, "that *Gwyneth* killed Arabella?"

"No." The Baroness frowned. "Although the notion did, at one point cross my mind. When her plan to seduce Dickon failed, Gwyneth determined to extort money from him, first to ensure her departure from these green shores and then, when that failed, to guarantee Austin's safe return."

"This is pure conjecture," the Count protested, with more assurance than he felt. "The product of an overheated mind." He tried to smile in a comradely manner at Sir John. "You have no proof of any of this!"

"We shall have a confession, which is worth a great deal more." Behind Lady Bligh, Jael stirred. "You never meant to return Austin, of course, whether Dickon paid the money or no." Dulcie's dark eyes bore into her victim. "You must have been shattered to learn that Gwyneth had been killed before the first ransom note had ever been delivered, and even more distraught to discover that Austin had fled his temporary hiding place."

"Never have I heard such a ridiculous tale!" Count Andrassy's desperation was plain to all. "Do you suppose I meant to return to Hungary with a brattish schoolboy hanging round my neck?"

"No." Dulcie was deceptively calm. "I suppose it was *your* idea to dispose permanently of Austin, for even Gwyneth would not do that. How did you mean to set about it, Count? To inform Gwyneth that her son was being safely conducted to his father, then to dispose of the body in a manner guaranteeing that it would not soon be found?" The Baroness was as mesmeric as a cobra. "It might have served you very well, had not Gwyneth gotten herself killed by meddling in what didn't concern her."

"I repeat, you have no proof." Count Andrassy had begun to perspire copiously. "Nor shall I ever admit to such infamy."

"All is at an end, you know." Lady Bligh rose and adjusted the folds of her pelisse, as if concluding an unexceptional morning call. "You made a grave error when you spoke in Austin's hearing, for the boy will easily recognize your voice."

The Count's control snapped then, broken by the matter-of-fact way in which this damnable Englishwoman had ruined all his plans. With murderous fury, he lunged across the room, hands outstretched as if to snap her fragile neck. Sir John and Crump stared in frozen horror, but Jael was less civilized. Count Andrassy found himself flying head over heels through the air, to land most painfully atop Sir John's desk with Jael beside him, her sharp-edged knife against his neck, her dark face looming over his own.

"You'll talk, my culley," promised the gypsy, her face alive with pleasure. "You'll sing like a bloody little bird." Neither Sir John or Crump felt the slightest urge to interfere with Jael's sport, not even when her knife pressed harder against the Count's neck, bringing forth a drop of blood. Lady Bligh moved to the window and gazed out pensively upon the deepening dusk.

Count Andrassy was of ancient lineage and unscrupulous character, and his delicate constitution could stomach no thought of personal injury. It took only the warm wet sensation of his own trickling blood to inspire him to speech. "I'll tell you everything!" he gasped. "I swear!" With a contemptuous oath, Jael released him, upon which he was promptly collared by Crump and dragged ignominiously away. Sir John released a long pent-up breath and hastily averted his eyes as Jael restored her knife to its hiding place, in the process of revealing a shapely thigh. "Let me know if that one gives any more trouble," the gypsy remarked. "I'll slit his gizzard for you."

"Dear John." The Baroness crossed the room to stand beside his chair. "You've had a trying day." Her sweet perfume encompassed him, comfortingly. "You might thank me, ungrateful man! I've given you not one new suspect, but two."

Chapter Sixteen

LEISURE WAS *de rigueur* for the monied upper class: no gentleman boasted of worthwhile accomplishment; no lady dared be caught doing what someone else could do for her. Gentlemen of fashion rose late in the morning, breakfasted largely, then strolled up St. James's Street to loiter for an hour or two in their clubs, hearing the latest *on-dits* and surveying their world. Later might come a ride in the park or an afternoon call. The evening hours were amply filled with dinner parties, the Opera or theatre, perhaps a ball; then back to the club for some supper until four or five a.m.; and at last home to bed.

Hilary, Lord Rumfoord, was a perfect example of a leisured gentleman. Accepting Brummel's dictums on matters of fashion as unquestionable law, he eschewed perfume, but sent his linen to be washed and dried on Hampstead Heath; his impeccable attire was fashioned by Weston, the tailor whose reputation, and fortune, the Beau had made; and he had acquired the knack of being unspeakably rude in the politest possible way. The Marquis was reserved of manner, but not sufficiently cold natured to forego the companionship of the opposite sex, and so he kept under his protection a sprightly, full-bosomed high-flyer whose embraces he repaid with a house in Montpelier Square, a box at the Opera and a smart cabriolet, most recently utilized to drive down to Brighthelmstone for a week's amorous relaxation. Now his practiced gaze rested on Livvy in an impersonal yet calculating manner that made her feel her flaws and virtues were being assessed for some future market day. "My felicitations, Dorset," he said at last. "I believe they are in order?"

"They are," replied the Earl. They were in Lord Rumfoord's house in Harley Street, a large mansion of brown London brick with delicate balconies and tall sash windows. Wrought iron railings guarded the deep, narrow basement area and marched up a short flight of steps to the solid, double front door, which was graced by a bevelled fanlight. The mansion exuded a dignified air of respectable solidity as did the Marquis. In fact, Lord Rumfoord, the epitome of reserved aristocratic elegance, appeared out of place in his drawing room, which was decorated *à la mode* in shades of terra cotta and citron in the Egyptian style. Friezes painted with figures representing pharoahs and Egyptian deities enhanced the walls, as did hieroglyphic paper with an ibis border. Sumerian lions supported the furniture, and odd items were fashioned as pyramids and obelisks. Livvy was seated on a couch in the shape of a crocodile, an item in execrable taste that looked as though it might at any moment snap open its jaws and devour her alive.

"I appreciate your predicament," the Marquis said, seating himself in a square-backed armchair. "However, I fail to see how I might assist you."

Lord Dorset was not put off by this uncooperative attitude. "Let us not be evasive, Hilary! We know that Lady Arabella Arbuthnot was once married to your brother James."

"I see." Lord Rumfoord gazed pensively into his fireplace. "You know, of course, that my brother is dead."

Livvy watched the Marquis carefully, wondering if Lady Bligh had been correct when she predicted that he'd lie.

"Come, come, Hilary, do not waste our time!" Lord Dorset was brusque. "We know perfectly well that your brother is alive." This was a shot in the dark, undertaken at Dulcie's request.

Lord Rumfoord regarded his interrogator with haughty disapproval. "You forget yourself, Dorset! This unconsidered behavior verges on impertinence."

So chill a tone might have awed unruly servitors, but on the Earl it had little appreciable effect. "Damn me as you will," he replied indifferently, "but I will have the truth." His smile was unamiable. "The matter is of considerable interest to me."

"I can see that it might be." Lord Rumfoord looked away from Dorset to gaze upon a bookcase which had spinxes' heads carved on the pilasters that separated the doors. "I have no wish to be caught up in the scandal that invariably follows in your wake." His impersonal attention moved to Livvy. "Your pardon, Mrs. Lytton; I speak only the truth."

"The choice is yours." Dickon was unmoved by these observations on his character. "You may either be frank with me, or leave it to Bow Street to delve into the affair. You might consider which method is likely to prove the least disastrous."

As if in search of superhuman guidance, Lord Rumfoord raised his eyes to a lotus-bowl chandelier. "My brother," he said abruptly, "was not of strong character. He was incapable of resisting any woman that wanted him."

"As Arabella did," put in Dorset.

"She was a woman of strong passions, and she indulged them with great latitude." The Marquis made a *moue* of disdain. "Her consuming passion was a lust for money, and she saw in James not only a personable young man but an opportunity for fortune and social standing beyond her most ambitious dreams."

"But it did not serve," Livvy prompted gently, as the Marquis threatened to lapse into reverie.

"No, as she quickly learned." His vindictive satisfaction was so blatant that Livvy looked away. "I'm not a pigeon to be so easily plucked! I'll say this for the wench: she accepted her blood money and stuck to her part of the bargain."

"Was that not unlike her?" Livvy inquired. "You have said Arabella was both ambitious and acquisitive."

"But not totally without principle," commented Dickon, in reluctant eulogy. "Bella had a certain code of honor; she kept her promises." He came to stand behind Livvy's couch. "As a result, she was also most reluctant to give her word."

"She was very young," Lord Rumfoord remarked. "I imagine she later regretted settling with me so quickly, for she must have realized I would have paid thrice the sum to insure her silence." He wore the air of one who had successfully concluded an important business transaction. "It took her no time at all to bring her Duke up to snuff, and then she devoted all her efforts to bleeding him dry."

"Why," asked Livvy curiously, "were you so anxious to keep the marriage secret? Arabella was of respectable enough birth, if a trifle wild."

"Respectable!" The Marquis was haughty. "The daughter of an adventurer! I had her background checked thoroughly when James first fell under her spell, and it quickly became apparent that the relationship was unthinkable." His lip curled. "Better the young fool had given her a *carte blanche* and be done with it, but no! She held out for marriage and James was so besotted that he obliged, without a thought for what was due his name."

Livvy stared incredulously at this tall, thin, and autocratic man who had been more concerned with family pride than with the prospective happiness of his own brother. Disbelief passed quickly, leaving her deflated; it was not an uncommon view. There were many, no doubt, equally aghast at the announcement of Lord Dorset's intended marriage to a mere commoner.

"Arabella made no move to approach you when she came to London," Dickon mused. "I assume you realized who she was."

"You *pre*sume, Dorset!" The Marquis rose to pace restlessly, coming to stand beneath a portrait of his wife, shown strolling in the park with spaniels snapping at the ribbons that dangled from her garden hat. Lady Rumfoord was a very forceful woman who was reported to have said that she would prefer the company of packhorses to other females. Nor did she appear to enjoy masculine companionship, since she and her husband lived happily apart.

"Your refusal to recognize her must have been a terrible blow to Arabella's pride." Livvy angled blindly for information.

"I doubt that Arabella shared your delicate sensibilities." Lord Rumfoord was patronizing. "She certainly seemed to labor under no sense of ill usage, but contrived to make constant appearances at dances and social gatherings, cheerfully making enemies wherever she went." Annoyed at his visitors' perseverance, he returned to his chair. "She should have known that we would not acknowledge the connection; it was no more than she deserved."

"Deserving a thing does not often lessen the pain of it," Livvy retorted.

Lord Rumfoord was unaccustomed to such impertinence. "Arabella was a brazen hussy," he said pompously, "with bold and outspoken opinions calculated to shock the prudish and the sensitive. I imagine that she would be amused at your sympathy for her."

"You imagine a great deal," Dickon commented, "about a lady whom you admittedly never met." Livvy was not exhilarated by his defense of his dead mistress. "It was in your best interests, was it not, to keep her discreetly under your eye?" He smiled. "Think of the scandal were it to become public that Lady Arabella Arbuthnot was a bigamist, her legal husband being James Worthington, scion of the venerable Rumfoord line!"

Livvy stared. She had not previously grapsed the implications of Dulcie's theory. It would be a pretty kettle of fish if Arabella's Dragoon was still alive.

The Marquis's indignation was fearsome to behold. "You would not dare publish so discreditable a thing!"

"Frankly, Hilary," Lord Dorset apologized, "there is little I would not do to save my neck from the noose! Arabella had an absolute desire, amounting almost to an obsession, to broadcast her *affaire* with me to as many people as possible. Consequently, my position is not exactly comfortable." This was an understatement; Livvy had expected them to be apprehended by the law before they reached Harley Street.

"This is plain-speaking!" said Lord Rumfoord, with a startled glance at Livvy. "I am surprised that you would want to admit your liaison in front of your fiancée."

"Dickon and I have no secrets from one another," Livvy lied calmly, with apparently no greater concern than the smoothing of her elegant satin pelisse, of a shade that brought out the blue lights in her hair. "My main concern must of necessity be the establishment of my lord's innocence."

"I wonder," mused the Marquis, finding Lord Dorset's betrothed worthy of his belated interest, "how far you will go."

"My interest," Dickon remarked, "remains unsatisfied. If I

may be blunt, Hilary, I believe that your brother is not only alive but in London at this very moment."

"Damn your eyes!" The Marquis was shaken by the prescience that he attributed to Lord Dorset, but which actually belonged to Lady Bligh. He leaned back in his chair. "What do you propose to do about it?"

"As I have told you, whatever I must." The Earl would clearly tolerate no more delaying tactics. "Come out with it, Hilary, or I will not answer for the consequences!"

"That sounds remarkably like blackmail." Lord Rumfoord gazed upon Dickon's stern face. "Very well, though I'm damned if I know how you've learned of a secret that I paid dearly to see well-kept! James did not die in action, but deserted, taking with him various regimental funds. He has been paid a handsome allowance to stay out of England these past many years. All in all, my brother has cost me considerably."

"Yet you allowed Arabella to think him dead!" Livvy was horrified.

"James wished it as well as I." The Marquis, his defenses battered down, looked both exhausted and ill. "Don't deceive yourself that there was a sentimental attachment! All that ever existed between my brother and Arabella was passion and a certain greed. Their union was one of expedience and, I imagine, was speedily regretted by both. James was not reluctant to abandon his blushing bride, nor did she seem loath to have him go. Arabella evinced little regret for my brother's presumed death."

Dickon regarded the Marquis steadily, willing him to continue. "I will spare you the anguish of further inquiries," murmured Lord Rumfoord, in response to that watchful attitude. "In reply to the question that you are doubtless burning to ask, my brother is indeed in London." He leaned his head on his hand. "I cannot tell you his precise address, but James follows the ancient and dishonorable profession of a Captain Sharp, battening on unsuspecting youths with too much money and not enough wit."

Livvy was too soft hearted for this line of work; left to herself, she would have tiptoed quietly away and subjected Lord Rumfoord to no futher harassment. Dickon, who labored under no such handicap, leaned forward. "When did he return?"

"I sincerely regret," the Marquis retorted, raising his head, "your interest in my affairs! Since you will learn the truth eventually, I prefer that it should be from me. I first became aware of James's presence in the city over two months ago." His gaze was remote and passionless. "I doubt that Arabella escaped his notice for long, given her elevated position in the world."

"The mysterious visitor!" whispered Livvy, breathlessly.

The pavements were thronged with citizens of all varieties: men with big noses, lantern jaws and resolute mouths; loose-limbed young giants and girls in tawdry elegance; matrons with painted faces and corseted physiques. Old men with grog-blossom complexions jostled against sharp-faced, nimble-fingered children, while workmen in padded leather jackets hastened home. Ancient women sold canaries from wicker baskets on church walls. Indifferent to this cross section of humanity, the ancient carriage barreled by, its passengers oblivious to even raree-show men carrying on their backs the mysteries of their trade.

Soon enough there were no more shop windows with silks, muslins and calico, china and glass-ware, jewels and silver, to tempt the passing eye. "Are we not," inquired Lady Bligh, ignoring her companions' ill-temper, "travelling by a circuitous route? I begin to suspect, John, that you have another object beside the apprehension of our Dragoon."

"I've granted your wish; you can ask no more." The Chief Magistrate's heavy brows were drawn into a straight, angry line. "Since you are so determined to accompany me, the consequences are on your head."

The Baroness smiled placatingly. "Believe me, there is need for haste. Tomorrow will be a great deal too late."

In a corner of the unmarked coach, which had been selected by Sir John to alleviate any suspicion that Bow Street was making an official call, Jael brooded. "Too late?" she mimicked. "Aye, if we live to see the morn! 'Tis a dangerous place we visit, Baroness; they'll cut out your liver for a pastime, and commit murder for the joy of it. The way they look at it, you can't hang twice, and most of their lives are already forfeit."

"Pooh!" said Dulcie airily. "I'm perfectly safe as long as I'm with you." Grimacing, the gypsy lapsed into silence.

Not long past, the isolated and lonely Marylebone Fields had been a regular haunt of highwaymen, as had Hounslow Heath, Barnes Common, Hampstead Heath and Epping Forest. Since 1805, when numerous men had been organized under one inspector with the objective of clearing the London roads of such pestilent vermin, the menace had notably decreased, though few actual captures were made. Despite these advances, the danger of highway robbery was not totally removed. Sir John thought with disgust of the manhunt now underway. Even with the help of constables and volunteers, Bow Street men and magistrates had not apprehended The Gentleman, a fact that Sir John suspected might have to do with his officers' respect for their own skins. He was most anxious to interview, at great length, that impudent knight of the road.

"I am not convinced," said Lady Bligh, "that James Worthington is our murderer. Let us consider the evidence yet another time."

Though Sir John was fast under Dulcie's spell, there were

moments when her erraticisms inspired him with intense frustration. No sooner did she present him with a potential villain than she set out to establish the rogue's innocence. "Then why this determination to seek him out tonight?" he asked. "It is an endeavor more wisely undertaken in the light of day."

" 'Tis the truth, begod!" muttered Jael, eyeing Sir John's pistols with approval. "Praise be you've sufficient wit to bring your barking irons." It was a rare occasion when Sir John found himself in such wholehearted agreement with a member of the underworld.

"Cowards, the pair of you," announced the Baroness. "You must take my word that it is important that we apprehend the man tonight. Now let us discuss Arabella, whom the French would undoubtedly have described as *une veuve fringante,* a gamesome widow. She was also a reckless fool!"

"As are the lot of us!" Jael sighed gloomily. "I'd be much happier about this night's work could I have a bracing noggin of lightning. That a quartern of gin to *you,* Baroness!"

"Tsk!" The coach rattled and jostled its passengers in a most uncomfortable way. "As I began to say, there is something deuced odd about the disappearance of those gems."

"That's the devil of it." Sir John briefly forgot his irritation with the Baroness. "Nothing was known of the robbery until the newspapers got hold of it, nor was the jewelry expected in any of the flash houses where stolen property is received and disposed of. It appears that the thief knew the gems were worthless and made no effort to rid himself of them."

"Keeping them instead until he had an opportunity to hide them most conspicuously." Lady Bligh ruminated. "Have I told you, John, that an unknown tradesman gained access to Dickon's home the day before Crump undertook his second search? He fitted the description of Slippery Jim." Jael, in her corner, listened attentively. "I think we must assume that

Arabella's jewels, the real ones, were disposed of sometime previously."

"Have you not already determined," Sir John asked, with a return of irritability, "that Arabella sold her jewels to pay off her blackmailer? It seems to me that we're covering familiar ground."

"I'm not so sure." The coach gave a great lurch, sending Lady Bligh into the Chief Magistrate's lap. He caught her instinctively. The Baroness righted herself. "I suspect, John, that you have several surprises yet in store for you."

The Chief Magistrate was in no mood to be teased. "It is not necessary," he snapped, "for you to be so damned mysterious! It's obvious that the murderer disposed of the jewels because we were getting too close to the truth."

Lady Bligh gazed reproachfully at Sir John, as if he were a servant caught in some rude act. "We?" she repeated frigidly. "I beg you will recall who brought the Dragoon to your attention, who figured out his involvement with Arabella and ascertained his whereabouts! You, of course," she said graciously, "may take full public credit for the rogue's apprehension."

Unwisely, Jael laughed, drawing the Chief Magistrate's fire. "Watch your tongue, gypsy, or you'll find yourself charged with compounding a felony! I've sufficient wit to guess where Dulcie came by that diamond necklace."

"In which case," Jael retorted, "*you'll* be found with your neck slit from ear to ear!"

"A truce!" demanded Dulcie. "Where was I? Ah! Arabella's jewels were stolen only to throw dust in our eyes. Arabella did not die because she interrupted a robbery." Jael and Sir John waited, their curiosity aroused, for her next deduction. "Yet someone went to great lengths to make it appear like robbery, even to disarranging her chambers and mutilating her portrait.

There is also the matter of Arabella's precise activities on the night of her death."

"She was with Dorset," Sir John interrupted, "as you very well know."

"Briefly, perhaps, but not for long." Dulcie was clearly annoyed at his observation. "Then we come to the nondescript little man whose inquiries preceded my own. I want very much to learn more about him."

"You are mighty interested in Arabella." Sir John, though he would never admit it, was equally curious about this elusive little man. "May I remind you that Gwyneth also met an unfortunate end?"

"Unfortunate, perhaps, but remarkably well-timed. I take it Count Andrassy continues to vehemently protest that he had nothing to do with his wife's death?" Sir John nodded, and Dulcie graciously explained. "Find Arabella's murderer and you will also find Gwyneth's. She learned too much for her own good, sought to use it to advance her own ends, and thus signed her own death warrant." Sir John might have chosen to argue with this bland assumption, had not fate intervened.

It had come to Jael's notice that they were nearing a notoriously dangerous stretch of land, where a thick and gloomy copse stood to one side, with another thick bank of forest atop a nearby hill. A fatalist, she was not at all surprised when the coach skidded to an abrupt halt, sending Lady Bligh tumbling to the floor.

In the midst of the chaos, as frightened horses screamed and reared and earsplitting oaths filled the air, the carriage door was wrenched open. "Stand and deliver!" demanded The Gentleman in the languid drawl that had earned him his nickname, and found himself staring straight down the barrels of Sir John's pistols. The Chief Magistrate discharged the first of his weapons, intending not to kill but to confuse. A dead man could not be handed over to justice, and Sir John meant to capture The Gentleman alive. "I don't aim to get *my* neck cricked!" cried the highwayman's accomplice, and took speedily to his heels. But the rogue himself, in a last desperate effort to avoid capture, dragged Sir John from the coach.

Suddenly the copse was thick with men. Sir John, engaged in desperate combat with the criminal, fired again into the air as the highwayman sought to wrest the second pistol away. Crump, delighted by his scheme's success, pounced from behind and slipped a choking forearm around the rascal's neck. Sir John, with great satisfaction, applied the butt of his pistol to the miscreant's skull. "Into the coach with him," he panted. "I wish to have a word with this blackguard." He wondered why Jael had not defended herself, for she was legendarily abrupt with those who threatened her, dispatching them summarily with no questions asked. Instead, the gypsy wore a ferocious scowl.

"We shall be a trifle crowded, I fear." The Baroness picked herself up from the carriage floor as Crump and Sir John settled onto the opposite seat, the unconscious highwayman secured between them. "It will not be the first time indignity has been suffered so that the law may claim its own. I suppose this encounter means further postponement of our visit to Slippery Jim?"

"The law is not to be trifled with," Crump announced, elated to be in on the capture of this notorious brigand. "This is a dangerous ruffian and the quicker he's locked up all nice and tight, the safer we'll all be."

"Such excessive caution!" mocked Jael. "This cutthroat of yours never hurt anyone and, what's more, never stole from those who couldn't stand the loss."

"You're mighty quick to defend him." Crump was immediately suspicious. "What's this gallowsbird to you? Can it be you've been trafficking in stolen goods?"

Jael did not consider this worthy of reply. "Aren't you curious about his identity?" she said quietly. "Take off his mask and let's have a look at him!"

The highwayman stirred, drawing their attention. He was a slenderly built man, dressed in filthy laborer's clothing, with a scarf covering his chin and a makeshift mask disguising his eyes. Crump reached over and pulled the villain's battered hat further down over his face. "He'll keep! Until we reach a place where we can have a closer look at him." Inexplicably Dulcie sighed. Sir John wondered why The Gentleman was of such consuming interest to Jael and Lady Bligh, for both ladies' silent attention was centered on the villain, but attributed this intensity to a typically feminine appreciation of the macabre.

In silence the triumphant party wound a tortuous route through eastern Marylebone, where prostitutes flourished in such picturesque places as Night Pit and Wrestling Lanes. Further west, the elite demimonde lived in their own houses, exacting as much as a hundred guineas for a night passed in voluptuous arms. Sir John was regularly sent a list of these damsels, complete with such pertinent information as places of abode, stature, the most circumstantial and exact details of the ladies' appearances, and the qualifications for which each was remarkable. A similar catalogue was published every year and sold under the piazza of Covent Garden.

The coach passed by the Workhouse and Infirmary, an extensive range of buildings with their main facade on Northumberland Street, and arrived at last at the Marylebone Watch House. Herein were contained living accommodations for the beadle, or parish officer, cells for apprehended criminals, and a court or vestry room.

Sir John roughly hauled The Gentleman from the coach. Lantern-bearing night watchmen in greatcoats flocked round the carriage, welcoming any excuse to delay their nightly patrols of the neighborhood. His vision totally obscured by his hat, the villain stumbled. "You must be made an example of," Sir John announced in tones of pending doom, "a warning to like-minded rogues that our highways will be kept safe for honest travelers. Prior to your trial, you will be lodged at the Fleet."

"I think," remarked the Baroness, alighting from the coach, "that you are being much too hard on the boy."

"Aye, such an innocent lamb it is! Let's have a look at him." Arms folded across her chest, Jael looked like an Amazon warrior.

"I seem," remarked the villain, "to have attracted a remarkable crowd! Do you think one of you might remove this wretched hat? Not only does it place me at a great disadvantage at this, the most monumental moment of my entire career, but it is damned uncomfortable."

Crump recognized that waspish tone and stepped forward, visited by an uncontrollable urge to commit mayhem. "Crump!" Lady Bligh adjusted her bonnet, which had slid rakishly over her forehead. "Moderate your manner, pray!" Ignoring both Crump and Sir John, Jael stepped forward suddenly and, with the air of one performing a splendid trick, whisked away The Gentleman's disguise.

"Aunt!" Hubert regarded the Baroness reproachfully. "How could you serve me such a trick? Have you no feeling for the family?"

"You might recall," Dulcie retorted, apparently not at all lacerated by her nephew's shame, "that I warned you to abandon your pursuits before you came to this very end. More than that I cannot do for you."

"Blame not the Baroness, but Bow Street." Jael smirked at the representatives of the law. "What will you do, my coveys, now that you've caught your man? It would make far too great a carnage in elite circles if you hung every errant son of the rich who tried his hand at highway robbery to pay his gambling debts!"

"Dear Jael!" cried Hubert gratefully. "To think that I have hitherto lacked sufficient appreciation of your sterling qualities!"

"You'll appreciate them even more," Lady Bligh predicted, as the gypsy laughed maliciously, "before this thing is done." She observed the Chief Magistrate, whose initial astonishment had rapidly turned to rage. Crump, ready to spit nails, vowed to do his utmost to see this damnable clown transported to Botany Bay.

Chapter Seventeen

THE NEXT MORNING Sir John reflected gloomily that if matters were not soon resolved he would share the fate of the Chancellor of the Exchequer who, when attending divine service at the Millbank Penitentiary, was bombarded with stale bread by aggrieved lady inmates. If the Chief Magistrate knew his discontented Londoners, they would not be satisfied with such innocuous pellets, but would hurl rotten vegetables and horse dung. He sighed heavily, totally unamused by the raree-show that was being enacted before his weary eyes.

Ironically, it was Hubert who appeared the most alert, as if only he had been granted the deep and restoring sleep of innocence. He was also looking quite fresh, having been permitted—against Crump's express wish—to exchange his shoddy attire of the previous evening for something more suitable. Jael's gray eyes were smudged, which added a touch of vulnerability to her savage features. Sir John was not pleased to discover that the gypsy had returned, evidently having overcome her dislike of Bow Street. She perched on the windowsill, a vivid picture in violet satin, and the Chief Magistrate wished mightily that he might summarily shove her out of doors.

Lady Bligh showed no signs of fatigue, but looked instead as if she'd passed the night in orgiastic celebrations of the most satisfyingly intemperate sort. Sir John wished that he might have joined in this debauch, rather than pacing the floor for endless hours while pondering this tangled mystery, receiving for his pains only an aching head.

"My reputation," uttered Hubert woefully, "is in ruins!" One tragic eye lit on Sir John. "For years I have cultivated tardiness, until I have accomplished the invariable habit of being late for every appointment; yet here I am, at your command, and even before the appointed hour!"

"You are fortunate," growled Sir John, "that you were not taken out and shot." Jael yawned, and he realized suddenly that the gypsy's countless golden chains and baubles weren't imitation but real, and extremely valuable.

"Shot?" asked Hubert, with mock horror. "Makes it any difference if my preference is to hang? I have a horror of firearms, you see. Even better would be transportation, though I would shudder to join the company of gentlemen with, er, perverse appetites."

Sir John was in no fit frame of mind to appreciate either Hubert's artful ways or the incongruity of a highwayman who feared guns. "There's one man already on his way to the gallows for this business!" he snapped. "Have a care you don't go with him!"

"You are of choleric temper this morning, dear John!" Lady Bligh spoke in the amused, unshockable tones she reserved for her mature men friends. "Lady Jersey snared the Prince when young, and put Epsom salts in his bride's soup on his wedding night. It is no wonder Prinny's marriage does not thrive."

Sir John neither welcomed nor needed this reminder of Dulcie's privileged standing with the Regent. He observed the provocative lady with intense, if fleeting, disapproval. "Do you think," he inquired awfully, "that we might proceed with the matter at hand? I might remind you that this is not a social gathering."

"Of course!" Dulcie was kind. "My nephew is possessed of a tremendous capacity for compromising genially with circumstance; I believe you will find him perfectly cooperative."

"Indeed!" agreed Hubert, whose impeccable appearance was slightly flawed by a livid bruise on his forehead, souvenir of his encounter with Sir John's pistol butt. "You have but to ask, dear man!"

"Thank you," said Sir John caustically. "There *is* one thing I would like to ask. You were seen in heated argument with the Countess Andrassy on the day of her murder. What did you quarrel about?"

Hubert was pained. "Not a quarrel, precisely, but a mere difference of opinion!" His features were mournful. "You are determined to expose me, I see. So be it. I told Gwyneth that I would have no more to do with her efforts to secure Dickon's comeuppance." He winced delicately. "Her methods were so crude."

"You understate the case," said Sir John bluntly. "Observers report that you were quite vehement."

"You should not listen to gossip," Hubert chided. "It is invariably elaborated upon most tediously."

"It is you who are tedious, Humbug," the Baroness observed. "If you keep up in this manner, we shall be here all day."

"You were also," continued Sir John relentlessly, "well-acquainted with Lady Arabella Arbuthnot. Must I point out that you are in serious trouble, Master Highwayman? These airs and graces will not benefit you here!"

"You accuse me of clouding the issue." Hubert wore the

woebegone look of one grievously misunderstood. "I must say, aunt, that given my present circumstances, I am most grateful for your company."

"You needn't be," Lady Bligh retorted. "You need a harsh lesson, Humbug, and if John chooses to administer it I shan't make the slightest move to interfere."

"I see how it will be." Hubert cast a mournful glance at Jael. "Brief but splendid has been our acquaintance, my dear! If I extricate myself from my present difficulties, I shall return to you with the greatest satisfaction; but if not, it would be better if you set eyes on me no more!"

The Chief Magistrate was shocked that Hubert, who despite his discreditable habits was of impeccable birth, should speak in so fond a manner to a female as reprehensible as Jael. It was just more of his nonsense, of course, but nonetheless in the worst possible taste. "Cease your infernal prose!" he bellowed.

"You are so *stuffy*, John!" the Baroness complained, as the gypsy scowled.

"I am in a sad case," Hubert mourned. "I have not even power left to repel impertinence, and I have met with it."

"What you have," Sir John snarled, "is an excessive love of talking! Pray direct your conversation to an explanation of why you wished to rob me."

"Believe me," Hubert replied with utmost sincerity, "had I the least notion that carriage was yours, I would never have ventured near it!" The Chief Magistrate's expression prompted him to continue hastily. "I must, incidentally, congratulate you on the clever trap you laid for me, giving out that the coach would be unguarded and carrying valuables. It seemed a trifle obvious, and I asked myself why such a precious cargo should be treated so carelessly, but I could not resist so promising an opportunity. Considering various recent developments, I had begun to think that a change of climate might be advisable. Hence my efforts to replenish my sadly depleted purse."

"It is a pity," Lady Bligh commented, "that you never

learned to practice economy." She spoke with the righteous censure of a lady who in all her life never had to render an accounting of her debts. "It is a greater pity you were inspired to flight just when we were so close to the Dragoon."

"We will get the Dragoon later," Sir John interrupted, feeling as though he presided over a quarrelsome nursery. "Right now I'm more interested in this imbecile's activities."

"I doubt," remarked the Baroness, "that you will get to the Dragoon at all." She ignored her admirer's mounting wrath. "You have underestimated his importance all along. Consider the possibility that Arabella spent the greatest portion of her last evening in that rascal's company."

The Chief Magistrate considered the possibility of clearing his office of all but the hapless Hubert, but was not granted the opportunity. The door burst open and Lord Dorset, wearing his thunderstorm expression, strode imperiously into the room. Behind him came Mrs. Lytton, in a state of extreme agitation, and Austin, expressing unmitigated delight at his surroundings. "*There* she is!" crowed the boy triumphantly. "I *told* you Dulcie was all right!"

"Austin," remarked the Baroness, as her great-nephew came to lean against her well-formed knee, "has more wit than the rest of you combined."

"Unremarkable," murmured Hubert, with a malicious glance at his cousin. "Austin is untroubled by love's young dream."

"Nor is he distracted by visions of himself dangling from a gibbet," retorted the Earl, not at all displeased to see Hubert take his place in the suspect's seat.

Dulcie ignored her squabblesome nephews and smiled at Austin, who had just whispered something in her ear. "Yes, your Uncle Max is returning home. I believe the decision was made when he was feted by an Emir, who recently had three nephews blinded in case they aspired to his throne, and found himself in the inescapable position of dining upon a raw sheep.

The house in which he stayed belonged to a local politician who, upon the Emir's orders, had been strangled the day before." Austin's eyes were wide. "I daresay he will bring you a splendid present. We can only hope it will not be something totally unsuitable, like a dancing-girl."

Livvy had no interest in the Baron's adventures. "Dulcie!" she cried. "Wherever have you been? We were dreadfully worried when you failed to come home last night!"

Lady Bligh regarded her devoted companion with disfavor. "And so you rushed to report my absence to Bow Street? Foolish girl! I would not be so hasty to take action were *you* bold enough to pass a night away from home." Livvy gasped, not in indignation but at the accuracy of Dulcie's thrust, for the idea had more than once occurred to her. "It would probably do you a great deal of good. You are looking shockingly peaked, Lavender."

"I will thank you, Dulcie," the Earl intervened, "not to put thoughts into Livvy's head." Idly, he tweaked a blue black curl. "I intend to personally oversee her descent into depravity."

"Sits the wind in that quarter?" inquired Hubert, with great interest. "I had thought it all a sham. Cousin, I applaud your intelligence!"

"Magnanimous of you," observed Lady Bligh, "though you are a trifle premature." Having effectively silenced her retinue, she turned again to the Chief Magistrate. "I concede the floor to you, dear John. Continue!"

"Thank you." The Chief Magistrate, wondering how the Baroness had passed the night, since she had not been home, was unappreciative. "We come now to the matter of Hubert's dressing gown."

Hubert evinced lively curiosity. "My dressing gown? Prithee, sir, what is this concern with the niceties of dress?" He itched for his quizzing-glass. "I would not have thought it of you!"

Livvy was impressed by Humbug's dramatic abilities, but

she was even more intrigued by the stony-faced gypsy who perched precariously in Sir John's window. The woman was not only most impressively flamboyant, but oddly familiar. It was a pity that her face was scarred, though, once one had gotten used to it, it detracted little from her wild allure. Livvy looked quickly at the Earl, that notable connoisseur of feminine beauty, and received a warm glance that cast her into blissful confusion.

"Describe," said Sir John woodenly, "your dressing gown."

"I am at a total loss," Hubert apologized. "I possess several such garments, you see. Do you think you might give me a hint?" Dickon leaned indolently against a wall.

"This is no time to play off your airs." The Baroness was censorious. "John refers to that abominable creation in which you dauble with your oils."

"Ah, *that* dressing gown!" Hubert glowed with enlightenment. "I shall overlook your insults, both to my art and my attire, though I wish you would not speak of that particular garment in such derogatory tones. It was a gift from an admirer, and has great sentimental value."

"You amaze me, Humbug!" Lord Dorset's sardonic features did not display that particular emotion. "I did not know you were so relentlessly pursued by the gentler sex. Who is this unknown admirer, so smitten as to come bearing gifts?"

"You presume, cousin, indeed you do! I cannot recall ever asking *you* to reveal your more intimate relationships." Hubert smiled. "Not that I need to, of course, considering your unfortunate propensity for announcing your *affaires* to the world."

"How odd," Livvy remarked, "that a highwayman should be so considerate of the proprieties."

If Sir John felt affinity with anyone in the crowded room, it was with Austin, who listened to this family conversation with uncomprehending awe. "The dressing gown!" he bellowed, hitting his desk with a violence that made Livvy flinch nervously.

"This seems an excessive interest in an unremarkable object," Hubert said, with perplexity and a lack of any desire to assist Bow Street.

"You wear it with an unmatched sash," the Baroness prompted, in tones she might have employed to inspire Austin to recite his alphabet.

"Ah!" Hubert beamed. "How clever of you to note, dear aunt, that the sash has been misplaced. Can this be the information that our good magistrate has been searching for? How much less time-consuming to have asked the question outright!"

The antics of Dulcie's clan did nothing to ease Sir John's throbbing head. "Poor John!" The Baroness rose and crossed the room to place healing fingers on his temples.

"How long has this sash been missing?" asked the Chief Magistrate, striving vainly to ignore her cool touch.

"Some few days, I believe." Hubert was once more apologetic. "I've a poor head for details, I fear! I cannot think what happened to the accursed thing; it might as well have vanished into thin air."

Sir John dropped, as he thought, his explosive. "The item was found draped most artistically around the Countess Andrassy's throat. Explain *that*, if you can!" He thought it highly curious that not a single member of his audience exhibited the least surprise.

"Cousin Hubert is mighty careful of his person," remarked Austin, branding himself irrevocably as one of Bligh blood, "and mighty careless about everything else. Even I could steal half his possessions and he'd never know the difference."

"Lamentable, but true." Hubert regarded Austin appreciatively. "And very well-said, nephew."

"Enough!" Jael slid from her perch with a muffled thud of

unshod feet on bare wood. The Chief Magistrate tensed as the icy-eyed gypsy approached him. With a comforting pat, Lady Bligh moved away, abandoning him to his fate. "Are you suggesting that Hubert had anything to do with that damned Gwyneth's death?"

"Damned she certainly must be," Dulcie remarked, resuming her seat, "without any help from us." Jael made an irritated gesture and even the Baroness subsided. Livvy watched the gypsy curiously.

"Answer me!"

Sir John wondered whether, if Jael gave way to violence, he would receive assistance from anyone in the room. It seemed extremely doubtful. "I am stating facts," he equivocated. "Hubert was seen in urgent argument with the Countess Andrassy, and that same day she was found strangled with the sash of his dressing gown. The conclusions are obvious."

Jael settled on the edge of his desk and proceeded to clean her nails with her wickedly sharp knife. "Equally obvious were the conclusions drawn from the presence of Lord Dorset's belongings on the scene of a previous crime."

"A very astute observation," commented Lady Bligh. Jael nodded graciously. "Someone appears to harbor a strong dislike of my family."

"Gwyneth emerged from her encounter with Hubert obviously unharmed," the gypsy continued, "since she later called at Arbuthnot House. So much for your deductions!" Her smile was both victorious and menacing. "You shan't pin this on our fine fribble, for he spent the rest of the day with me."

"May I ask," inquired Sir John, in a shocked tone, "why?" Jael was as protective of Hubert as a bitch of her litter, and he wondered at it. It was not like the gypsy to act altruistically.

"Sir!" Livvy was in the process of developing an unsuitable admiration for the dangerous, insolent Jael. "Does Bow Street now mean to inquire into a lady's more intimate moments? The shame of it!"

"Darling Livvy," murmured the Earl. "You are a source of constant delight."

"For once," commented Hubert, "I am inclined to agree with you." He eyed Sir John, who appeared on the verge of choking. "It distresses me beyond description to refuse, but I believe I shall not answer that."

"How chivalrous of you to spare my reputation!" Jael spat, in no need of anyone's defense. "Hubert is painting my portrait, and is devoting much time to the project. It is true that we were alone in the studio that day, but Hubert's servants were very much aware of my presence." Her smile was derisive. "They always are. You may verify the matter, if it suits you." Livvy stared, recalling now the painting she had briefly glimpsed in Hubert's studio, and the subject's state of near undress. It was a curious association, the gypsy and the fop.

Sir John was left with the wind taken out of his sails, a fact he did not appreciate. "My treasure!" cried Hubert, greatly moved. "At the risk of your own good name, you have absolved me of all suspicion of the iniquitous act! How can I ever express my gratitude?"

"You might start," Jael suggested sourly, "by refraining from behaving like a bloody fool!"

"*Truly* a treasure," said the Earl, as Hubert scowled. "Where did you find her, Dulcie?"

"Alas," replied the Baroness, "I did not. Rather, she found me." She glanced at the doorway. "It is a tale that I will relate to you at some future time."

Crump hovered on the threshold, startled to find the Chief Magistrate presiding over such a large gathering. Jael paused in her nail-scraping, the point of her evil dagger aimed at the Runner. Crump felt like a virgin sacrifice being sized up for the kill. Then Lady Bligh intervened.

"Ah, Mr. Crump!" Dulcie radiated welcome. "We all wait with bated breath to learn of your latest discoveries." The

Runner cast a questioning eye at his superior. Resigned, Sir John indicated assent.

"The Dragoon," said Crump, "was absent from his lodgings, where he hadn't been seen since yesterday." The Baroness nodded, decisively. "In the course of my investigations, I obtained a detailed description from the fence to whom Slippery Jim tried to sell Lady Arabella's jewels, the imitation ones. The description of the gems matches perfectly with those found in Dorset's home."

"Very clever," mocked Jael, flipping her dagger into the air and catching it artfully, "and very much a waste of time. *I* could have given you your description, had you thought to ask!"

"Oh!" Livvy reached into her reticule. "I almost forgot. Lord Rumfoord kindly loaned us this likeness of his brother James." She resolutely refused to look at Dickon, for Rumfoord had not been all that obliging and Livvy had resorted to sleight of hand. She did not imagine that the Marquis would quickly miss his detested younger brother's miniature.

"To shorten a long story," said the Earl, "there remains little doubt that Lord Rumfoord's brother, Arabella's first husband, Arabella's mysterious cousin, and Slippery Jim are all one and the same man, and that the knave was Arabella's blackmailer."

Crump seized the miniature, consoling himself that, were he not required to cope with the meddling of so many amateurs, he would have reached these conclusions on his own. "It doesn't appear that Jimmie-boy knew the gems were paste, and was most anxious to dispose of them."

"Jimmie-boy," murmured Hubert, "seems to have been a bit of a fool. What now, dear aunt? We return to the motive of robbery."

Sir John grew weary of allowing the Baroness to run the show. He gazed sternly at Jael, still seated impudently on the edge of his desk. "Those jewels, the real articles, must be placed in the custody of the law. As the Chief Magistrate of

Bow Street, I now call on you to deliver them up to me."

"You're off, my covey!" Jael's smile flashed as bright as her sinister weapon. "I've handed over the necklace and that's all that came my way, and that honestly. You might as well save your breath; you've nothing on me!"

"I've quite enough against both you and Hubert," snapped Sir John. "*If* I choose to use it."

Crump cleared his throat. "After exhaustive investigation," he announced, "I did find the suspect." Genially, he observed his rapt audience.

"Don't beat about the bush!" Sir John's tone was withering. "Where is the scoundrel? Did you question him?"

"More to the point," interrupted Lady Bligh, "*where* did you find him?"

Crump surveyed the Baroness more appreciatively, for this was the opening he desired. "Floating face down in the Thames," he announced baldly, "as the result of a violent argument, last night, with a husky figure wrapped in a cloak and a large-brimmed hat."

"That lets me out," observed Hubert gleefully. "Since I passed the evening with the Marylebone patrol." His tone was malicious. "Over to you, dear cousin!"

"Do you mean Papa is under suspicion again?" asked Austin. "Well, that can't be! Papa spent last night with Livvy and me at Dulcie's house, and there wasn't an instant when he wasn't safe by one of our sides."

"Dear Lavender." Lady Bligh's devoted companion blushed bright red. "Your efforts on behalf of the family are quite laudable." She regarded her fascinated nephew. "I don't mean to rush you, John, but wasn't there some mention of Austin identifying Count Andrassy?"

"See to it, Crump." The Runner was delighted at the prospect of scaring the accursed foreigner right out of his skin. Without even token protest, he took Austin in hand.

"Don't look so glum, the lot of you." Jael surveyed the

various downcast countenances. "Jimmie may be dead, but that doesn't mean he wasn't your murderer, merely that he ran afoul of someone he should not."

"A good try," remarked the Chief Magistrate, almost as distressed as his companions at having this last suspect so conveniently removed, "but I doubt the scoundrel had the wit to mastermind these crimes."

"Wit?" scoffed the gypsy. "When it's been a comedy of errors from start to end?" She was almost amiable. "At least you're rid of one nuisance, for it was Slippery Jim, not Hubert, who was the Gentleman!" Sir John frowned.

"I am reluctant to confess to failure—" Hubert was not slow to catch a hint—"but, alas, it's true. My career as a highwayman was excessively short lived. My first effort at highway robbery was in fact my last, and prompted solely by the exigencies of my situation and my empty purse."

"Oh?" inquired the Chief Magistrate, who didn't believe a word of it. "You've learned your lesson now, I suppose?"

"Humbug!" cried Lord Dorset gleefully. "A bold move, to be sure!"

"Neither your murderer nor your highwayman," observed Jael contemptuously, "merely a misguided aristo driven to desperate means. Look at him!" Hubert quailed. "Have you ever seen a less likely brigand?"

Sir John thought it unnecessary to reply. "I *might* be willing," said the Chief Magistrate carefully, "to consider last night's frolic as devilment and let it pass as such, if you in return give me a sworn and true account of your activities on the day of the Countess Andrassy's death."

Hubert looked pained. "*All* of them?"

"All." Sir John was firm. With a watchful eye on Jael's sharp knife, he brought forth paper and pen and indicated that Hubert should be seated at the desk.

"If I must," sighed Hubert, taking Sir John's chair. "How do I begin?"

"Given in the presence of Bow Street by me, and your name."

Hubert paused in his activities. "Dear creature," he remarked to Jael, "I find I do not know your surname."

The gypsy nibbled thoughtfully at her dagger's tip. "Leaman," she said at length. " 'Twill serve as well as any other, I suppose." Pained, Sir John closed his eyes.

"You are mighty equable, my treasure." Hubert regarded her speculatively. "I wonder why."

"I might as well hang for you as another." Jael flipped her dagger in the air, dexterously catching it by the hilt.

"We must hope it doesn't come to that," the Baroness commented. "We're all in this together and if one swings, so will the rest." Sir John wished briefly that this might come to pass; he'd not give a brass farthing for the lot of them, with the exception, of course, of Lady Bligh.

The silence was broken only by the scratching of Hubert's quill. Jael, who could not only read but could do so upside down, watched its progress intently, occasionally correcting a point. Then Crump returned, in obvious good spirits, with a grinning Austin skipping by his side. "You were successful," the Baroness deduced.

"We had a grand game," confided Austin, draping himself over the back of her chair. "That silly man was Mama's husband, did you know? We told him I knew he'd been in on my kidnapping and could identify him."

"Could you?" asked Livvy, her character so far corrupted that she found nothing untoward in this dishonorable manipulation of the unfortunate Count.

"No, but *he* didn't know that." Austin stared at Hubert, secure in the seat of authority. "Why is Cousin Humbug sitting there?"

"Writing my memoirs, nephew," replied Hubert, with a flourish of his pen. "Perhaps, if you are very good, you may read them some day."

"That reminds me," murmured the Baroness, tapping a front tooth thoughtfully. Despite the interest of her family, she said no more.

Crump moved to the window. "Anything?" asked Sir John. The Runner shook his head.

"He squawked like a plucked chicken, but nothing to the purpose. It's my belief he truly doesn't know anything about his wife's murder."

"I suppose I shouldn't be surprised." Sir John lowered his voice so that only Crump could hear. "I want you to have a man follow Humboldt; I am going to release that damned fop"—Crump turned pink with barely suppressed indignation—"but want him under surveillance at all times. I am most curious to know what he will do."

"There!" cried Hubert, with a final flourish. "I have told all! See how anxious I am to oblige? What is your next command?"

As Crump left the room on reluctant feet, Sir John wearily took the document. "Do you swear this to be the truth, by Almighty God?"

"If I must," said Hubert.

"*I'll* swear to anything you like," offered Jael magnanimously, dangling a slender foot. "It's no skin off *my* nose!"

"Then so write, and sign." Hubert, all eagerness, complied.

"I thought," said Austin suddenly to the Chief Magistrate, "that you wanted to talk to Papa. Have you changed your mind?" Livvy winced and the Earl awarded his son a stern glance.

"He has," answered Lady Bligh. "Dear John has come to realize that our family is only circumstantially connected with this thing."

"That's as may be," growled the Chief Magistrate, reclaiming his chair. "I freely admit that there's something very disturbing about the way clues point so determinedly and indiscriminately to one or the other of you." His brows bristled. "Not that I exonerate any of you from all blame; if nothing else, you have done your combined best to thwart Bow Street at every turn!"

"Moonshine, John!" Dulcie was impossible to chastise. "You must own that we have been of great service to you."

"I would be more appreciative had you presented me with the murderer!" Then he noticed Lady Bligh's smug look. "Dulcie, what are you up to now?"

"Do not abandon hope!" Dulcie smiled demurely. "You may recall that in the last century a Scotch court accepted the supernal testimony of a murdered man's ghost."

"A ghost!" Austin's eyes were round. "Can you conjure up Mama?" He did not appear pleased at the prospect.

"Gwyneth? No." She patted his curly head. "Even I have no influence where she's gone."

Sir John felt as though someone had taken a woodsman's axe to his weary brow. "My aunt will not explain herself," Lord Dorset explained kindly. "Nor are you alone in your misgivings, but she will listen to none of us."

Hubert had little interest in his aunt's future plans. He regarded Sir John anxiously. "Pardon, I beg, but may one assume that one is to be released from custody?"

"One may," the Chief Magistrate conceded grudgingly. "You are strongly advised to speedily mend your ways. If you are ever brought before me again on any pretext whatsoever, I will show you no mercy." His voice rang with sincerity. "The penalty for highway robbery can be hanging or at least transportation, and you may be sure of that, if you are again apprehended in that activity, I will speedily commit you for trial, with perhaps a flogging in the bargain, gentleman or no!"

"*Extremely* well said," approved the Baroness, gathering up her various belongings. "I hope you realize, Hubert, what an extremely narrow escape you have had."

"Oh, I do!" Hubert retorted fervently, shaking Sir John's hand with vigorous enthusiasm. "I feel as if I had just waked up from a horrid dream. I am overwhelmed by my good fortune, so much so that I am going to make our good magistrate the present of some information that may prove of use to him."

"I'd think," muttered Jael, sliding from the desktop, "that you'd be content to leave well enough alone."

"How little you know Humbug," commented the Earl. "My cousin brings to mind the adage that fools rush in where angels fear to tread, only Hubert's case is so extreme that he would venture even on quicksand were there a possibility of doing mischief thereby!"

"That was also well stated," remarked Hubert indifferently, "but this once I was serious. Ah, I see you all wait anxiously for the pearls of wisdom that I may let fall!" Jael snorted.

"Out with it!" demanded the Baroness.

Ignoring his unappreciative audience, Hubert addressed Sir John. "You earlier mentioned a diamond necklace that Jael most generously handed over to the law. I can tell you more about that item, if you're interested."

"I gave it to the Baroness," Jael amended. "Damned if I'd give it up to the law!" She looked daggers at the Chief Magistrate.

"I'm interested, all right," said Sir John. "What do you know about the gems?"

"Quite a bit." Hubert preened. "Since it was I who gave them to Jael."

"Nincompoop," sneered the gypsy. "We no sooner extricate you from one mess than you land yourself in another."

"Silence, wench! I am being cooperative." Hubert gazed blandly upon Sir John. "I had it from a jeweler; you will be interested to learn that he purchased it in good faith, with no idea that there was anything questionable about the deal."

"Why," inquired Austin, "did you give it to *her?*" He regarded the gypsy with bright curiosity. Jael tossed her head.

"I will explain that to you later," the Baroness intervened, to Hubert's obvious relief. "Now, don't interrupt."

"I immediately suspected something odd," Hubert continued, "from the jeweler's description of the person who'd sold the gems to him." He paused expectantly.

Livvy did not disappoint him. "Why?" she asked. "That person was Arabella, surely?" Hubert grinned maliciously.

"Enlighten us!" demanded Sir John. "Before I throw you back behind bars."

"Tsk! Such impatience." Hubert was sheer impudence. "But I shall tantalize you no longer! It was not Arabella who offered the necklace for sale, but her devoted spouse, Sir William Arbuthnot."

Chapter Eighteen

WANDERING THROUGH THE gallery where Dulcie displayed the Blighs' works of art, Livvy reflected dismally that there had been a time when she found pleasure in simple things. Once she would have been happy to spend a half hour wandering through a Ladies' Bazaar, shopping for trifles, or rambling along the wide flagstoned pavement of Oxford Street, where streetlamps were enclosed in crystal globes and elegant shops offered every variety of merchandise. Now such innocent pastimes held no allure. There was no pleasure anywhere save in Lord Dorset's company.

Even Dulcie's priceless treasures could not capture her attention. Every great mansion had such a gallery, to house the collection of paintings, marbles, and bronzes that some ancestor or other had begun accumulating on his Grand Tour, and Bligh House was no exception. Livvy, moving aimlessly among these riches, came upon a portrait of the Baroness, executed when Dulcie was eighteen years of age. Even this masterpiece had no power to raise Livvy's flagging spirits. She felt she had aged ten years in as many days.

She was surrounded by columns of Derbyshire alabaster, white and purple veined, supporting a ceiling that resembled the one found in Henry VII's Chapel in Westminster Abbey. Crimson Norwich damask graced the walls, and Moorfield carpets lay upon the floor. A painted glass window bore the Bligh coat of arms. Livvy sank onto a plump festooned settee covered with blue and white striped linen, and abandoned herself to misery. She wished almost that she had never been rescued from her former existence of unrelieved drudgery. So accustomed had Livvy been to apathetic gloom that she had accepted it as her lot, one that she had heedlessly traded for heart-numbing anguish that would doubtless be her lifelong punishment for loving unwisely and much too well.

Annoyed at herself for this unaccustomed descent into self-pity, Livvy rose. Her restless pacing brought her to another portrait—the Baron and Baroness with their two most noteworthy nephews when Dickon and Hubert were near Austin's age. Hubert leaned against his aunt's chair while Dickon stood, aloof and unsmiling, at her other side. Dulcie looked enchanting, while the Baron's bronzed features conveyed extreme boredom. Livvy wondered briefly at Hubert's favored position, and concluded that he must later have fallen from grace.

It was Dickon, of course, who captured Livvy's attention, as he always did, though she had fought a bitter struggle against his fascination. He was a born intriguer of the boudoir sort, a man whose very nature was opposite to all in which Livvy had thought she believed, and she loved him madly, to distraction, and with the subsequent upheaval of all her higher principles. But Livvy was no fool. Much as she might wish to throw all caution to the winds and dance along the primrose path with the Earl, she was not yet lost to all propriety. Lord Dorset's next Countess would not be a penniless widow of humbly respectable origin but a dazzlingly beautiful socialite who possessed both fortune and a noble name. That left for Livvy only the role of *petite amie,* and this she would become for no man, even if her refusal damned her to eternal regret. Far better she had never become involved in Dulcie's machinations, and had thus been spared a closer acquaintance with the devastating Earl. She sighed.

"So pensive, sweet Livvy." Lord Dorset closed the gallery door behind him. "May one ask why?"

Livvy scowled, aware of looking her worst in an old, unstylish dress and with her curls uncombed. "One may not," she retorted. "I believe you will find Dulcie consulting with Culpepper in the morning room."

"I do not wish to find Dulcie." The Earl crossed the wide, long room. "I wished to speak privately with you."

"I see." Livvy clasped her hands and attempted an unconcerned air. Dickon's mouth twitched. "Do not disturb yourself, my lord; I know why you have sought me out and I agree."

"You relieve me," said the Earl, apparently finding this conversation a source of rare amusement. "I had feared you might prove difficult."

"I'm sure I don't see why." Humiliated, Livvy sought defense in indignation. "We entered into this charade at Dulcie's prompting, and its purpose is fulfilled. It is little wonder that you would wish to be freed from an obligation that is meaningless. Your name, to all purposes, is now cleared; we may dissolve our spurious betrothal without exciting undue comment."

"So I am to be jilted." Livvy's eyes dropped under Dickon's brilliant gaze. "It will serve me right, or so the world will say. No one will be the least surprised that you have had second thoughts about marrying me."

Livvy found it difficult to breathe. "I imagine that the world will be more likely to think you have had a fortunate escape, and not just from the accusation of murder." She turned away.

"What nonsensical notion," inquired the Earl, firmly seizing her arm, "has got into your pretty head? What does it matter if some busybodies consider you unsuitable?"

Overwhelmed by an impulse to burst into tears, Livvy could only remain silent.

"I see what it is." Dickon retained his hold. "You have been playing fast and loose with me, offering me false coin, throwing out lures like the most heartless lightskirt, while all the time you meant to ultimately cast me into despair."

"I did not!" Livvy blazed, then belatedly, resumed her air of nonchalance. "It is hardly a moment for levity, my lord. Would you prefer to be the one to cry off, or shall I?"

"Neither, my peagoose." Dickon grasped her shoulders and Livvy's pulse hammered loudly in her ears. "I have a most decided partiality for you, sweet Livvy, and have no intention of allowing you to slip so easily away."

"Pray, don't!" Livvy cried, certain that she was about to be offered a *carte blanche* but not certain that she would have sufficient resolution to refuse. She pressed cold hands to her flaming cheeks.

"There is some mystery here," observed the Earl and tilted her face up to his. "I trust I am sufficiently, er, experienced to know when a female is not indifferent to me!" Livvy glowered. "A crude way to put it, perhaps, but I seem to have misplaced my usual eloquence. What troubles you, Livvy? Do you hesitate to entrust yourself to a man with my history?" His smile was crooked. "That's a thing of the past, my dear."

Livvy blinked back tears. "Say no more, I beg! I cannot deny that I have a certain regard for you, nor that I have excessively enjoyed our relationship these last weeks, but I will not become your mistress, Dickon!" So severely were Livvy's withers wrung that she cared not even that she had betrayed herself.

Lord Dorset wore his devastating smile. "I don't know why you should think I want you to be my ladybird," he remarked huskily. "I have expressed myself badly, I fear." He brushed an errant tear from her cheek. "My adorable Livvy, I want you to *marry* me!"

Gibbon had seen a great many strange sights during his service with Lady Bligh, and thus exhibited little surprise when he threw open the door of the gallery and found Livvy in Dickon's arms. Nor did Bertha, who had witnessed shocking displays while in Arabella's employ, find it remarkable that Mrs. Lytton was pressing her lips to the Earl's scarred hand.

"I beg your pardon," Gibbon said stiffly. "This person is desirous of speaking with Mrs. Lytton." He gazed down upon Bertha, his thin nostrils flaring with offense.

Lord Dorset swore fulsomely and reluctantly released his captive, who sniffled. "Bertha," she remarked, dazed. "Do come in. What brings you here?"

Bertha settled onto the settee, her homely features apprehensive. Gibbon, disapproval wrapped around him like a greatcoat, withdrew. "I'm sure I didn't mean to burst in on you," Bertha said, "but I've left Arbuthnot House and I thought you'd like to know." She waited hopefully.

"Are you seeking another position?" inquired the Earl, his lack of interest calculated to quash all pretentions. Livvy held her breath. "You must speak with my aunt, though I doubt she can do anything for you."

"No, sir; it was Mrs. Lytton I wished to see." Humility did not come easily to Bertha. "On a matter of interest to both of you."

Despite her dislike of the treacherous maid, Livvy felt Dickon was a bit too harsh. Bertha obviously suffered no small distress. "What is it, Bertha?"

"It will cost you." Bertha's apprehension gave way to greed. "Since I'm out of a place, I must have the means to live."

"First, the information." Lord Dorset was not in the most sanguine of moods. "Then we will determine its worth." Bertha stared narrowly at the Earl, then grinned.

"No flies on *you*, eh, Lord Dorset?" she remarked. "Well, I'm game. It's about that button of yours that caused such a to-do. It wasn't found outside the window, like everybody said."

"Oh?" Bemused Livvy dragged her attention away from the Earl. "Then where *was* it found?"

"Maybe I shouldn't say, in front of you." Bertha considered alternate avenues to the greatest profit. Dickon made an impatient movement and she continued quickly. "But I daresay you know what men are! I found the button, in Lady Arabella's dressing room, several weeks before she died." She quailed at Lord Dorset's expression. "How was I to know it was yours? I thought it was William's and gave it to him and nothing more was said."

"How do you know it was the same button?" asked Livvy bewildered.

"I saw it again, after Lady Arabella died." Bertha cracked her knuckles nervously. "We were all asked about the button, and if we'd seen it before."

"By Bow Street, I presume?" asked Dickon coldly. "You said nothing?"

"I should think not!" Bertha was shocked. "I hope I know what side my bread's buttered on! It would've been as much as my job was worth, and I didn't want to come afoul of the old crone."

"Why," inquired Livvy, "are you telling us this now? And why did you leave Sir William's employ? Were you turned off?"

"I was not! I doubt they've any notion that I'm gone." Bertha might have been sitting on a pincushion, so fidgety was she. "*I*'ve no wish to end up floating in the Thames!"

"Heavens!" cried Livvy. "Do explain."

Encouraged by this invitation to unburden herself, Bertha relaxed sufficiently to scratch her thigh. "I told you, miss, that I draw the line at being cozy with a murderer."

Livvy was no longer amused. "William a murderer?" she whispered numbly, remembering how far she had pushed the gentleman's tolerance. "Are you sure?"

"Sure enough to hustle my tail out of there!" Bertha was pale. "I saw that picture in the newspaper, the sketch of the man they found drowned. He was the same person who came to Arbuthnot House claiming to be Lady Arabella's cousin. And the Countess Andrassy came to Arbuthnot House before *she* died. Believe me, miss, I'm not one who can't see what's right in front of her nose!"

"Sir William knew of this man?" asked Lord Dorset abruptly. "The 'cousin'?" Livvy, chilled, absently rubbed her arms.

"He had to. Madame Luisa saw the man and was mighty curious, especially when Lady Arabella took to carrying on." Bertha's reddened nose twitched as if filled with the bitter dust of crumbled dreams. "It's not likely she wouldn't have told Sir William about it; Madame was always stirring up trouble between them."

"If William recognized my button," Dickon mused, "he must have suspected Bella's relationship with me some time before her death."

"Suspected, maybe," Bertha was dour, "but he's not one to face facts. Madame made it very clear to him the day that Lady Arabella died; I heard her. She said William was so namby-pamby that he allowed himself to be cuckolded without raising a hand to stop it, and that it was a sorry day when she realized her son was less than a man." Bertha repeated Luisa's comments with awe. "A regular dragon, Madame is! Sir William was in a terrible rage. Then Lady Arabella came in and there was a flaming row."

"Did Sir William return to the house that night after he'd left for his club?" asked Dorset. Bertha wore a sullen expression, as if she feared she'd gone too far, but the jingle of gold coins in the Earl's pocket speedily loosened her tongue. Livvy realized belatedly that she'd been granted her wish to see Dickon deal with this avaricious girl.

"He did." Bertha was now truly terrified. "He doesn't know I saw him, and I haven't dared breathe a word." She peered about the gallery, as if expecting retribution to step out from behind a statue and deal her a killing blow. "Not only was he in the house, he was with Lady Arabella in her rooms."

"Did they quarrel?" Livvy whispered. It was all well and good to discover the murderer but she would have preferred him to be someone she didn't know. Faint traces of the bruises left by Sir William's pudgy fingers still remained on her skin.

"I couldn't say." Bertha obviously wished herself elsewhere. "Madame called me and set me chores to do. I don't know how long he was in the house."

"Dulcie had better know of this," the Earl commented. "She'll never forgive us if we deliver information of such monumental importance secondhand." Livvy moved to the doorway, there to collide with Culpepper, who stared with astonishment at the widow's flushed face. Austin, grinning impishly, was hot upon her heels.

"Dulcie," said Livvy. "Where is she?"

"Why, I'm sure I don't know." Culpepper was startled, not only by Livvy's harried haste but by her employer's absence. "I thought she was with you!"

"*I* know," Austin interrupted, pleased to claim the limelight. "Or, I don't know where she went, but Dulcie slipped out of the house more than an hour ago. She was all dressed up like a real quiz." His face fell. "I forgot! I promised her I wouldn't breathe a word."

Livvy had experienced too many shocks in succession. Imagining the dauntless Baroness engaged in a battle of wits with a desperate criminal, she fainted dead away.

St. James's Street, Piccadilly, Bond Street and their environs were the most exclusive shopping districts in London. Here were found Berry Brothers, famous for its selection of teas and coffee, tobacco from the New World and spices from the Far East; Clark and Debenham of Cavendish House, where one might browse happily among a large assortment of cottage twills, stuffs, bombazines, sarsenets, and satins; and Gunther's, the celebrated Berkeley Square confectioner's. It was, however, not for the sake of a spendthrift orgy that Lady Bligh had eluded her retainers and friends.

The Baroness was dressed in flaming orange unsubtly embellished with countless yards of black lace, a low-cut creation that clashed hideously with her shocking red coiffure. With her rouged and powdered countenance imperfectly concealed behind a loo mask, Dulcie looked like an ambitious Jezebel. The Baroness paused for a moment to admire White's narrow brick facade, and then entered the club—an act that, were it to become known, would cause great consternation in Polite Society, for no lady who valued her reputation dared venture unaccompanied into this eminently masculine territory. White's bow window was empty, at this early hour, of the famed inner circle who posed and preened there in company with Brummel, the club's special oracle.

A startled doorman was too taken aback to deny the Baroness entrance, and the hall porter suffered a similar lapse. Stopping for a moment to survey the notice board in the lobby, where ladies of pleasure often posted cards, Dulcie gazed kindly upon the turbaned Negro page who was goggling at her, and allowed him to conduct her to the Visitor's Room.

Deep in a game of whist, Sir William was not pleased to hear that a brazen lightskirt had not only gained access to these most hallowed premises, but especially desired speech with him. He had been going down heavily, ill luck that he could scarce afford. With a vague notion that his caller might be some little demirap impressed from afar by his air of sporting elegance, Sir William entered the Visitor's Room, prepared to pack her off. At the sight of Dulcie he stared open mouthed, then turned crimson as he recognized the package that she bore.

"Do stop gaping, William," commanded the Baroness in the authoritative tone of one who has known her subject from his salad days, "and close the door." Even if he had not seen through her disguise, Sir William knew that voice. Speechless, he obeyed.

"Have you ever witnessed a hanging at Newgate?" Lady Bligh inquired, seating herself comfortably. "The gallows are draped in black, and the condemned faces death supported only by the executioner and a man of God." Sir William swallowed hard. "The bodies are carried to the Butcher's Hall or to hospitals for surgical experiments." Clinically she examined Sir William's corpulent figure. "I imagine that medical science would find *your* corpse extremely edifying."

Sir William was of a temperament that could deal with only one crisis at a time. His frightened eyes were drawn as if by a magnet to the bulky package in Lady Bligh's lap. "Yes," said the Baroness, tapping the item. "Your missing memoirs. Shocking, and I don't believe a word of it. I am very disappointed in you, William."

Sir William made a gurgling noise and reached for the manuscript. Dulcie slapped his hand away. "All in good time! You may reclaim this nasty piece of work only after answering my questions."

It occurred to Sir William that a man of his standing need not be intimidated so easily. "Who are you to dare address me in this manner? May I remind you that you risk your reputation by daring to enter here?"

"You are impertinent," the Baroness retorted coolly. "Furthermore, you know perfectly well who I am. Were you to use the wit God gave you, you might also guess why I am here. Let us return to the matter at hand!" She smiled in a manner that made his skin crawl. "To wit, one pornographic manuscript."

Sir William blanched. "You go too far!" he blustered, resolutely approaching her. "You've interfered in my life once too often, you and your damned family. Meddling in my affairs, introducing your spies into my home! Now I find you've removed my personal belongings." His heavy features were purple with rage. "You're nothing but a common thief, Dulcie Bligh, and I demand that you hand over those papers now!"

The Baroness was undisturbed. Sir William's hot eyes glazed as he stared at the small but businesslike pistol that was pointed square at his stomach. Instinctively, he sucked in his breath, as if to present a slimmer silhouette. "You will have your manuscript back, all in good time," said Dulcie, very much in control of the situation. "We shall now return to the subject of your misdeeds. The game is up, William: you may as well confess."

"I'm sure I don't know what you're talking about," Sir William said sulkily.

"Have you a wish to dance the Paddington frisk? Before your corpse is summarily dissected, it will serve any number of purposes. Splinters from your gallows will be taken to cure toothaches, wood chips will be worn in bags around the neck to cure the ague." Her gaze was uncomfortably direct. "However, if you choose so ignominious an end, it is none of my concern, even though Luisa will hardly approve. I might add that if you do *not* answer my questions, I shall take your so-called memoirs to her immediately."

Sir William turned to the window. "What alternative do you offer me?" he inquired bitterly. "It seems I must answer your questions or be damned."

"You are a murderer," Dulcie observed. "Persons of your sort are damned as a matter of course."

"I knew I wouldn't get away with it." Sir William thought furiously, seeking some means of escape from this dreadful predicament. "How did you know?"

"We will discuss alternatives later," the Baroness continued, ignoring his question. "You need not consider escape, William; I am an excellent shot and would feel no compunction whatsoever about disposing of you. Nor do I suggest you consider trying to overpower me, for the same reasoning applies. You would be dead before you ever laid a hand on me."

"I wouldn't think of such a thing!" Sir William tried to appear sincere. "I'm not proud of what I've done; to say the truth, I'm glad to see it end."

Lady Bligh remained unmoved. "Should you not cooperate, we will proceed immediately to Bow Street. Were I you, William, I would prefer to preserve as much of my honor as I could."

Sir William sat down heavily, the picture of a defeated man. "I didn't think," he said gloomily, "I'd be so easily done for. I'll tell you, I've been all of a muck of sweat these past days."

"Poor William." Lady Bligh held her pistol steady. "You are certainly the most unfortunate of beings. To business now! You returned secretly to Arbuthnot House on the night Arabella died. Tell me what occurred between you then."

"We quarreled." Sir William's manner was far from calm. "I had perceived the extraordinary attention paid to my wife by Dorset and had remonstrated with her, but it did no good. She laughed at me." He held out pudgy hands, palms up, and gazed at them. "I am by nature a very passionate man. I left my wife in a temper, too angry myself to listen to more, but returned later to try to reason with her." His face was as ashen as if he relived the ghastly scene.

"And in the meantime she discovered that you'd been selling off her jewels," Dulcie prompted. "How did she find out? Did she seek to dispose of something only to learn that it was paste?"

Sir William goggled. "How did you know *that?*" Lady Bligh gestured impatiently. "Arabella was forever demanding money, until I had no more to give. I guess it was then that she thought of her jewels." Sir William clasped his hands so tightly that the knuckles showed white. "She took them to the very man to whom I'd sold the originals, worse luck! That did it; the fat was in the fire."

"She would not listen to reason?" In the excitement of the conversation, Dulcie's atrocious wig had slipped to one side.

"No." Sir William found the subject painful. "She threatened me with exposure, even though I'd given all the money from the sale of the gems to her. I lost my temper, I'm afraid. That's when all came to an end."

"With *poison*, dear William?" The Baroness caught him up sharply. "That is hardly a spur of the moment thing!"

Sir William looked haunted. "I could not have laid a harmful hand on my wife! It was the only way. She was going to leave me, and publish my infamy to the world! Her damned cousin had promised to take her away with him."

"How did you administer the poison?" Lady Bligh's relentless interrogation would have put the Chief Magistrate to shame.

Sir William's forehead was beaded with perspiration. "We shared a bottle of wine. It was easy enough to do."

"I see." Dulcie's tone was dry. "You drank, perhaps, to the future?" Sir William's cravat was suddenly too tight. "I shan't quibble about that. Having disposed of Arabella by this very odd means, you proceeded to implicate my nephew."

Sir William eyed the pistol nervously. "It seemed only fair, since he cut up my peace!" The Baroness snorted. "His knife was there—Arabella had it from him as a love token, or so she said. I suspected the button was his."

"You set the scene and then sat back and watched the fun." He flinched at her tone. "So we come to Gwyneth. That, too, was by your hand?"

"She knew." Sir William stared at the floor. "Don't ask me how, but she did. There was no choice; she had to die."

"It is not up to us, but to the Almighty to determine these things." Lady Bligh was pious. "Then, when Gwyneth called at Arbuthnot House, she spoke with you?"

"Yes." Sir William shifted uncomfortably in his chair. "She wanted me to buy her silence, but I could not. There was nothing else to do. I agreed to take the money to her later, at her hotel."

"Where you strangled her instead. Yet no one saw you."

"You are not the only one who can go disguised." He grew increasingly desperate.

"Control yourself, William," the Baroness advised. "Remember that I wouldn't have the least qualm about shooting you. Let us return to the matter of the jewels. Why make it look like robbery when you sought to blame the thing on Dickon? Or did you intend Arabella's so-called cousin as the second string to your bow? It was to him, of course, that you gave the imitation jewels, bribing him to place them in my nephew's home."

"Damned if I know how you figured this!" Sir William was briefly his old self, indignant and blustering. "I thought I'd covered my tracks most carefully."

"Carelessly, in fact, but I don't doubt you did the best you could." Dulcie irritably pushed at her wig, which had slid over one ear. "You were hardly in a position to think coherently. Arabella had introduced you to her cousin? How could you be certain he would do as you asked?"

Sir William's laugh was short and ugly. "I know his kind.

He cared not for Arabella, nor she for him. I suspect the fellow sought to take advantage of her social position."

"You are wrong. He was blackmailing her, and probably thought it a miraculous windfall when you calmly handed the jewels over to him besides."

Sir William, despite his dire predicament, was awed by his captor's acuteness. "He was practically on the doorstep and I decided to make use of him. I told him that Arabella had changed her mind, and wouldn't see him again. He didn't find out until later that she was dead."

"A lucky meeting," mused the Baroness, "at least for you. I daresay Worthington had demanded more money, and thus inspired Arabella's fateful meeting with your jeweller. It's certain, at least, that she and Worthington met that night." She pursed her lips. "Or perhaps he truly did mean to take her away with him. Her supposed fortune in jewels would have been an inducement sufficiently powerful to reawaken old desire. When did you have copies made of those gems?"

"Is there nothing you don't know?" Sir William would find the Recording Angel easier to face. "Soon after our marriage."

"You knew," continued Lady Bligh, firing her questions like cannonballs, "that this so-called cousin was nothing of the sort?" Sir William was obviously startled. "I thought not! He was, in fact, her legal husband and you were no more married to Arabella than the man in the moon. You were cleverer than you knew when you implicated Worthington. He was told to place the jewels in Dickon's lodgings?"

Sir William nodded, speechless.

"But you failed to inform him that they were paste." Dulcie's mind worked with awesome precision. "Then you tidied up here and returned to the Cyprians Ball, hoping that your absence had gone unnoticed." He glowered sullenly.

"Worthington panicked when he heard she was dead," the Baroness continued. Sir William, thinking her distracted, made a slight movement. "Instead of disposing of the jewels immediately, he held on to them; then, desperate, took them to a pawnbroker. I imagine he was dumbfounded when he learned that they were paste." Dulcie did not seem to notice that Sir William had tensed to spring. "How did you get him to cooperate?"

"Money," said Sir William. "The fellow had no scruples."

"When Gwyneth died, he must have been truly terrified, recognizing your handiwork. One who so long lived off his wits must surely have realized he was dangerously involved." Lady Bligh frowned in deep concentration. "What then? I assume he tried to blackmail you."

"He wanted money to leave the country." Grimly, Sir William smiled. "And leave the rascal did, though not in the way he'd intended."

The Baroness was deep in thought; her gun lowered fractionally. "Just how much of this does your mother know?"

"Madame is a feeble, crippled woman!" Sir William's denial was vehement. "The blame is entirely mine."

Lady Bligh did not question this. "Were you responsible for the investigator who delved with such determination into Arabella's past?"

"What investigator?" Sir William was desperately planning his last-ditch effort to save his skin. Despite her bravado, Dulcie was neither young nor muscular. She would be easily overpowered. "I know nothing of that."

"I see," murmured the Baroness. Encouraged by her abstraction, Sir William lunged. He could not have anticipated that Dulcie's long acquaintance with the gypsy Jael had exposed her to various of the Eastern methods of self-defense.

"Foolish boy," the Baroness chided. Sir William flinched away from the cold steel pressed so ruthlessly against his temple. Dulcie's left arm was hooked around his neck, pressing against his windpipe in a manner that threatened to resolve on the spot the question of his fate. "You can hardly commit murder here and hope to escape." She released him and he dropped his head into his hands. The manuscript lay forgotten on the floor. Dulcie picked it up and pressed it on him. "I suggest you dispose of that prurient and puerile essay."

Sir William stared blindly as she moved toward the door. "What do you mean to do?"

The Baroness considered him thoughtfully. "I shall go to Bow Street, travelling by a roundabout route that will allow me to call upon your mother." Sir William looked hopeful. "It will not benefit you, William; believe me, your race is run. It's all over, William. You have played your game neither wisely nor well. I shall apprise Luisa of what has happened here today."

"Madame," said Sir William helplessly.

"I will be gentle with her." Dulcie raised the mask. "Better from me than another, don't you agree? Your mother sets such store by the Arbuthnot name."

Sir William sighed heavily. "Then this truly is the end. I am surprised that you let me go."

"I have no wish to act as your executioner." Lady Bligh's voice was as metallic as the gun that she still held. "You had what you thought was good reason for the things you did."

"I've failed," muttered Sir William, at the end of both endurance and hope. "All my life I've tried so hard, yet failed at everything."

"You have an hour," the Baroness was emotionless, "in which to make one more attempt." Sir William sobbed helplessly as she turned away.

Chapter Nineteen

"THE LAW IS," said Sir John, "that thou shalt return from hence to the place whence thou camest, and from thence shall remove only to the place of execution, where thou shalt hang by the neck until dead." He might, for all the emotion he displayed, have recited an oft-told nursery rhyme. "May the Lord have mercy upon thy soul."

The shackled prisoner snarled and spewed abuse upon his prosecutor. Sir John blinked not an eyelid as the miscreant was dragged from the room, to be taken to the condemned cell at Newgate. In death he would become an awful testimony to the majesty of the law and, one hoped, a dreadful example to others. In practice, however, although the impression made by the execution of a person of position and property was deep and long lasting, the conviction of so common a felon as this would serve mainly as excuse for a holiday.

The Chief Magistrate reluctantly made his way back to his bare office, where visitors awaited him. He would have preferred to have the Arbuthnot murderer in the dock, or at least to have had sufficient evidence to issue a warrant for an arrest. Sir John had various resources under his control: the Horse Patrol, which guarded the roads approaching the metropolis from highwaymen; the Foot Patrol, whose territory was the center of town; the Dismounted Horse Patrol, which policed the area between the other two. Yet, even with the additional efforts of his Runners and the Day Patrol, the assassin remained at large. Perhaps it was true, as one wit snidely claimed, that Bow Street was fit only for such menial tasks as attending the Bank of England when dividends were being paid, guarding foreign envoys and valuables in transit, and protecting aristocratic revellers from pickpockets.

Sir John accepted a folded note from a whey-faced underling. It was a sad comment on the state of English justice when his best Runners spent the majority of their time playing nursemaid to the frivolous Regent or attending routs and balls. Sir John unfolded the note. As he read the few scrawled lines, his eyebrows rose. Then he gave word that Dorset and Mrs. Lytton should be admitted.

Livvy herself was in a state of severe disorder, prompted partially by Dulcie's sudden disappearance and partially by a gift that she had received from Lord Dorset, a dainty memento from a previous century that bore an extremely moving, and improper, sentiment expressed in French. Some ladies might have been shocked by the tiny scent bottle, on which was depicted a minuscule cupid drumming enthusiastically upon a pair of luscious breasts, but Livvy was not among their number. She gazed with some trepidation upon Sir John's unwelcoming scowl.

"To what," inquired the Chief Magistrate, dropping heavily into his chair, "do I owe this unexpected visit? I warn you, I am in no mood for further of your games." Surely, at a time when all Society waited with bated breath to see how Lady

Caro Lamb would react to the announcement of Lord Byron's engagement to Miss Milbanke, anticipating that Caro might even transcend her antics of the year before when she slashed her wrists with broken glass at a fashionable ball, Lady Bligh's annoying family could find more promising diversions than meddling in Bow Street affairs.

"To my aunt's disappearance," replied the Earl calmly. Sir John looked upon this sensual and short-tempered gentleman and wondered just how much Mrs. Lytton knew of Lord Dorset's reckless way of life, and if Livvy was so sanguine that Dickon's disgraceful divorce didn't signify.

"This is the second time you have come to me on that pretext." Sir John massaged his careworn brow. "Dulcie makes a habit of giving you the slip. What reason have you for assuming that she has fallen into a scrape? It seems more likely that she merely wished to be about her business without an interfering chaperone."

"Dulcie," retorted the Earl, "has an infinite capacity for stirring up mischief, and no more prudence than the merest babe!" Sir John was startled to see that Lord Dorset was sincerely concerned.

"We have reached certain conclusions," Livvy interrupted hastily, lest Dickon antagonize the Chief Magistrate, "that I am sure Dulcie must share. We are afraid that she may have taken matters into her own hands, and may encounter grave danger even now!" She made a splendid beauty in distress. "I beg you, help us find her before it is too late!"

Sir John knew what was coming, and smiled almost jovially. For once in the course of this damnably convoluted affair, he had the upper hand. "You'd take me off on another wild-goose chase, would you? Not this time!" He leaned back in his scarred chair and crossed his arms. "First tell me about these conclusions, and then we'll see what we may do."

"I hope," remarked Lord Dorset grimly, "that you may be

moved to action before my aunt has been dealt her death blow." His tone did not bode well, in that event, for the Chief Magistrate's well-being.

Sir John smiled. "I have often thought patience the most difficult of all the virtues to acquire." With a scowl that indicated no appreciation of this profundity, the Earl moved to the window and stared bleakly down into the street.

"You *must* help us!" Livvy cried, twisting her gloves. "Dulcie may be in great peril at this very moment!"

Only severe worry could bring Mrs. Lytton out into the public eye in such a shabby state. Sir John considered the possibility that these amateurs might possess information that he did not, and his brief sense of well-being was abruptly dissipated. "Tell me these conclusions that so distress you."

"Truly there is no time!" Livvy's beautiful eyes were suspiciously bright. "You must find Sir William before he does Dulcie harm."

The Chief Magistrate relaxed, his apprehension gone. "If you are so anxious to see Sir William, why did you call here instead of at Arbuthnot House?"

"You don't understand," Livvy wailed. There was no question of the sincerity of her distress. "Sir William is the murderer!"

"Calm yourself, my love." The Earl stood behind her, one hand resting on her shoulder as if to impart strength. "I suspect Sir John is not unfamiliar with these views." His gaze was speculative. "We did call at Arbuthnot House, but William was not in. We also called upon my cousin Hubert, but he had not seen my aunt." Dickon did not add that they had surprised Hubert in the practice of his art, and Jael *en déshabille*. "You begin to understand our anxiety?"

"They could be anywhere!" Livvy had grown calmer, and the glance she gave the impatient Earl spoke volumes to Sir John. He had thought this betrothal a diversionary tactic instigated by the devious Lady Bligh, but even the most accomplished actress would be hard pressed to sham a look so sizzling as the one that had just passed between Mrs. Lytton and the Earl.

"True," said the Chief Magistrate, with a nostalgic thought of his own youthful amours, "but they are not. Sir William, at least, has been accounted for."

"Thank God," whispered Livvy. "Are you sure that he can offer Dulcie no harm?"

"Reasonably." Sir John's tone was dry. "Since he hanged himself not an hour past, an occurrence that has scandalized the entire select membership of White's." He surveyed their faces, Livvy's startled and ashen, Dickon's merely thoughtful.

"So William was our murderer," mused the Earl, as Crump silently entered the room, "and in a fit of remorse took the matter of his justice into his own hands. How neat!"

"I suspect," Sir John commented wryly, "that you may now guess at your aunt's activities this day. She has driven men to distraction, and inspired them with fine madnesses, but never before, I think, has she prompted one to suicide."

"No." Livvy was unable to accept this. "Surely the agony of remorse that Sir William suffered as a result of his crimes led to a temporary derangement of the mind, during which he put an end to his own life. It is unthinkable that Dulcie may have had a hand in his suicide." Lost in her own confused speculations, she did not see the meaningful glance that passed between Lord Dorset and Sir John. Crump cleared his throat.

"I'll own I'm glad to see this thing cleared up," admitted the Chief Magistrate, with an odd reluctance to hear the news that Crump was evidently anxious to impart. "Even though Bow Street's efforts hardly produced praiseworthy results." The Runner's expression was one of chagrin. "Sir William was more clever than commonly acknowledged. I doubt if anyone seriously suspected him of being the murderer."

"As to that," Crump interrupted bravely, determined to vindicate himself and consequently not at all reluctant to throw a spanner in the works, "it seems that we may have all jumped to conclusions, and the wrong ones at that." Crump's audience watched with unanimous amazement as he ruffled the pages of his worn Occurrence Book. Sir John's expression indicated that he might happily see this too zealous subordinate immersed in boiling oil. "I've found the gentleman who investigated Arabella in Sapping, and a curious tale he has to tell. It was not Sir William who hired him, but Madame Arbuthnot." Crump threw open the door and a humble, shabby little man, features twitching like a rabbit's, stepped shyly into the room.

Madame Arbuthnot surveyed her visitor, who was looking like a tart smothered in all the jewels she could borrow, hire or steal, and whose heavy rouge gave her the appearance of some hybrid fruit, half flesh-toned and half red. "You're in fine looks!" cackled Luisa. "Fetch me another bottle so I may celebrate your cleverness. You're slipping, Dulcie: it should not have taken you so long!"

Lady Bligh, despite her queer garb, moved through the cluttered room with undiminished majesty. "It is a compliment to you, Luisa, that it *did* take me so much time. You displayed great virtuosity in kicking dust in my eyes." She set a battered tray on the stained chairside table.

Luisa's magnificent eyes rested on the tray. "Two glasses?" she inquired. "Sweet Lord, am I expected to drink to your triumph?"

"Come, Luisa!" The Baroness strolled across the room to idly inspect her startling reflection in a flaking mirror. "Do you mean to be a poor loser? You disappoint me. I had expected you to accept defeat philosophically."

Those golden eyes had once intrigued the adventurous Baron Bligh, and had wept to see him make a younger woman his wife. They looked inward now, as Luisa's hands moved automatically toward the bottle. "Still, it is a shame about William," Dulcie remarked, moving to stand at a window, her back to Madame Arbuthnot. "I am not pleased with the way that turned out."

Luisa snorted. "Don't fret over William!" Glasses clinked. "That boy was a constant disappointment to me. He had no more wit than a pea-hen! I have often wondered how I came to have such a nodcock for a son."

"So you know." Lady Bligh moved to stand beside her hostess. "I am truly sorry for you, Luisa, but it was a great deal better this way than that he should have stood his trial."

Luisa closed her eyes, the only sign of grief that she would ever display for her unfortunate offspring. The Baroness busied herself with the glasses "So be it." The golden eyes snapped open, brimming with malice and some other undefinable thing. "I never thought I'd have reason to be grateful to you, flibbertigibbet! Here, take your victory cup." Dulcie obliged and perched on the love seat. "At last I'm forced to concede to you, Dulcie Bligh."

"It seemed the tidiest thing," agreed the Baroness, and her hostess joined in this bizarre toast. They were relics of a generation that valued the truth with no gloss on it. Faced with a crisis, they did what they had to without recourse to either vapors or vinaigrette.

Madame grinned. "You had a few bad moments yourself, when it seemed like your precious Dickon would hang! I'll tell you it was a rare pleasure to contemplate your distress, one of the few I've had from this wretched affair."

"Why Dickon?" Lady Bligh savored her brandy. "I thought at the time that it seemed a trifle extreme to implicate him so seriously merely because Arabella nourished a *tendresse* for him. He was not her only lover, after all."

"William didn't know about the others." Luisa grimaced. "I said he was a nodcock! But Arabella was so pleased with her conquest of Dorset that she was mighty indiscreet, flaunting the relationship before the whole world."

"And *that* you could not forgive, since it made William look a fool. So you made sure William was aware of Dickon's involvement with Arabella." Lady Bligh might have discussed the weather, such was her *sang froid*. "What did you hope to accomplish?"

"My motives were purely altruistic." Madame was a grotesque parody of innocence. "Dorset possesses the most vicious nature and falsest heart that man ever had, as witnessed by the *débâcle* of his first marriage. Could I sit back and see my daughter-in-law ensnared by such a rogue?"

"Pooh!" retorted Lady Bligh. "You would have happily watched Arabella entangled with Satan himself without lifting a finger in her aid." She raised her glass. "Nor were you always so condemning of rakish gentlemen!"

Luisa laughed rustily. "I detest you, Dulcie! And yet you have been more faithful to me, in a way, than those upon whom I had claim."

"It is because we speak the same language." The Baroness accepted the backward compliment gracefully. "You misjudge Dickon, you know: people claim he is hard and mocking, unappreciative of delicacy and romance; but he has a splendid talent for living and enters with zest into every pleasure."

"Every debauchery, you mean," Luisa retorted. "Dorset is damnably self-assured and careless of convention. He has the further disadvantage of being *your* nephew."

"I rather thought that might be it." Dulcie studied her glass. "It was not Dickon that you wished to see suffer, but me."

"Contemptible, ain't I?" inquired Luisa, unrepentant. "It comes from being tied to this damned chair. I led your silly Primrose a merry dance! The silly twit was terrified lest William take her unawares and commit rape most foul." Luisa cackled. "Nor did she fancy playing dogsbody to me."

"Lavender is a dear girl, and will be well rewarded for her

services." Lady Bligh appeared to suffer no pangs of conscience from her companion's grievous misuse. "If ever she overcomes her wretched principles, she will make Dickon an admirable wife."

"Is that the way of it? I wish the chit joy of her task." Luisa sighed heavily, rather like a horse blowing into its feedbag. "I knew it would only be a matter of time when that damned Bertha got the wind up and fled."

"Oh?" Dulcie raised heavily penciled brows. "You were wrong, Luisa; I arrived at the truth without aid of your maid's confidences. What inspired her flight?"

"I'm sure I couldn't say. Who can understand how these commoners think?" Luisa hunched her shoulders, vulturelike. "The stupid wench knew the truth of that button, and that William returned secretly to the house on the night Arabella died."

"William," remarked Dulcie, "was kept busy. The other two deaths were an outgrowth of the first."

"Greed is a dangerous vice," Luisa retorted solemnly, "one that all three of the unfortunates shared. Gwyneth was sure she knew the truth of Arabella's death and had to be silenced for it; while Worthington was a coward whose panic made him dispensable."

"Such men make dangerous tools." Lady Bligh might have been discussing the merits of a good servant. "How did you learn who he was? I assume you knew."

"I have my sources." Luisa was superior. "Don't make the mistake of thinking my brain has atrophied along with my legs!"

"You wished me to think that very thing." The Baroness set down her empty glass. "I own I do not see why you chose to use Worthington. A risky gamble, was it not?"

"Needs must when the devil drives," Luisa snapped, refilling her own glass. "It wasn't as if there was a wide assortment of accomplices from which to choose! Worthington would at least keep silent or find his own neck in a noose." Her tone was vicious. "Had he followed his instructions, instead of succumbing to avarice and fear, this affair might have seen a different outcome."

"You left those papers in Arabella's room for me to find." Dulcie surveyed her hostess as a spider might a fly.

"You or another!" Luisa cackled. "I tell you I was mighty disappointed in Bow Street. 'Tis downright amazing how they overlooked so many things that were right under their noses."

"That has puzzled me," the Baroness confessed. "It seems a trifle odd that William should commit murder and then promptly call in the authorities, engaging them, in fact, to apprehend himself!"

"A neat stroke, that." Luisa grinned. "Need I add that it was *my* idea?"

"No." Dulcie grimaced, then rose to walk the floor. "I have never underestimated your abilities, Luisa. It is a pity you did not put your talents to some better use."

Luisa's hooded eyes followed her guest's every move. "I think you may have underestimated me," she said, "but let that pass for now. I haven't had it all my way, you know, and have been forced to prodigious compromise. For example, I didn't know William had sold off Arabella's jewels; and I didn't know she was married to Worthington, despite the extensive inquiries that I had made, until the night she died. She was going to run off with the rogue and, she threatened to reveal the whole story if William attempted to stop her." Luisa shuddered. "Think of the scandal!"

"She would never have done it," Dulcie remarked, leaning against the back of the loveseat. "Arabella would never have cut off her nose to spite her face, no matter how angry she may have been."

"Perhaps not." Luisa frowned. "It was a chance I dared not take."

The Baroness let this startling remark pass by. "Is the scandal that you now face so much less? William is dead, and by his own hand."

"You think your dratted nephews are in the clear." Luisa exhibited little distress at this reminder of her son's lamentable end. "William's death is easily explained; his mind was unhinged by his wife's terrible murder. That leaves Dorset and Humboldt as prime suspects."

"Ah, yes, Hubert's sash." Dulcie was inquisitive. "How did you manage that, Luisa? It was a brilliant ploy."

"*You* know servants ain't impervious to bribes." Luisa shifted awkwardly in her chair. "Hubert isn't one to inspire loyalty in his staff."

"Not in his servants, perhaps," Lady Bligh mused, "but Humbug is not without friends. Do you realize that you have admitted Gwyneth's murder was a well-thought-out thing? William called upon her with Hubert's sash in his pocket and with murder firmly in mind. It suggests a purposefulness that he seldom displayed."

"He had no choice." Luisa laughed at Dulcie's widened eyes. "I know what you're thinking, but it don't signify! He told you Arabella's death was a crime of passion, didn't he? The fool! All three of those murders were well and coldly planned, as will be the fourth."

"How do you plan to cover *it* up?" the Baroness asked. "I fear, dear Luisa, that you have depleted your resourcefulness."

"Not I!" Madame's expression was evil. "I would've preferred Dorset to swing for my cleverness, but he threatened to escape my net. That was when I thought of Humboldt; you ain't fond of him but his hanging would have made you squirm." She gazed upon her visitor with malevolent interest. "I wonder whom I shall contrive to blame for *your* death. Tell me, Dulcie, if you aren't feeling a little faint?"

"I find," retorted the Baroness, adjusting the ill-fitting wig, "that I have little heart for this sort of thing. So you planned it all, Luisa; *you* poisoned Arabella, then called William home to disarrange her quarters and plant the false evidence."

"I did." Luisa was complacent. "I couldn't let Arabella leave. She threatened to raise the devil of a dust when she learned William had sold her jewels."

Lady Bligh dropped, as if weak-kneed, onto the loveseat. "You forced him to commit the other murders, for William was always firmly under your thumb. Poor man! What agonies he must have suffered for your sake. It is a pity there was no other course but that he had to die."

"As must we all," remarked Luisa, with rare glee. "It don't matter now what you know, since you'll have no time to pass your knowledge along."

"You are mightly obliging, Luisa." Dulcie's voice was faint. "I wonder, how do you mean to dispose of me, now that your henchmen are gone? A corpse in your drawing room may prove a trifle difficult to explain."

"I'll own you forced my hand; I did not expect you quite so soon." Luisa's frown turned into a grimace of pain. She pressed a trembling hand to her abdomen. "You *wretch!* What have you done?"

"I believe," said the Baroness, with a resumption of her brisk manner, "that our murderer will never be found. Your heart failed you, Luisa, upon receipt of the information of William's tragic death. It will create a furor, but the gossip will soon die down. I do not see that it would serve any purpose to reveal you as the author of three assassinations."

Luisa's hands clenched the arms of her chair. "You switched the glasses." It was no more questionable than her ultimate destination in an imminent afterlife. "I could hardly have turned my back on you; it seems I should also have refrained from closing my eyes."

"It has ever been *your* greatest error to underestimate me." Lady Bligh was sympathetic, but firm.

"You will show me no quarter." Even in this last desperate moment, Luisa would not plead. "Indeed, I suppose I should think the less of you were you suddenly to develop feminine sensibility." Her voice was harsh, as if she spoke around strangling fingers clenched at her throat.

"No more mercy than you showed three fools." Dulcie's hands were clasped in her lap; her fine features were strained. "I would not have wished this upon you, Luisa, but you determined your own fate. Since it has meant so much to you, I vow that I shall do my best to not besmirch your name."

Luisa's laughter was a ghostlike mockery of her old malevolent mirth. "A fitting end you've granted me!" she gasped. "I could ask for no better." Her hands clawed at her belly as she was wracked by another spasm of pain. "Sweet Lord! More than any friend, I loved you, Dulcie Bligh."

The golden eyes would gaze viciously no more upon a world to whom their possessor had long been only a half-forgotten memory. Dulcie slipped silently from Luisa's tawdry tomb.

Chapter Twenty

CARRIAGES THRONGED THE street outside Bligh House. Some of the more daring coachmen, trying to force their vehicles through the congestion, unhappily locked wheels. Elegant equipages were stuck as fast together as Siamese twins. Terrible venomous oaths split the air.

This confusion did not extend to the gardens, which were transformed for the occasion into a vista of Arcadian delight. Hothouses were tapestried with moss of every possible shade; the ground was thickly strewn with new-mown grass, out of which flowers seemed to grow. Walks were illuminated by colored lamps, glittering like gaudy jewels. In the background stood a beautiful transparent landscape complete with moonlight and water, and a band concealed in the shrubbery played sentimental tunes.

"Soon," murmured Dulcie to her great-nephew. The Baroness was a delightful vision in an evening dress of shockingly transparent muslin and strategically placed pearls and ostrich plumes. Golden ribbons were woven through her copper curls, and she wore a fortune in intricate and ancient jewels. "He will come bearing splendid gifts, as I promised you."

Austin smiled blissfully, his contentment unsurpassed. Not only was he permitted to attend this very grown-up function, but he had earlier been granted the opportunity of witnessing, in Culpepper's austere company, a balloon ascent from Green Park. A gallant lady accompanied the balloon and released a dove from the heavens as a symbol of peace. No event in Austin's young life, save his kidnapping and subsequent rescue, could compare with that splendid moment when the ropes were cut and the balloon sprang into the air.

"I still don't understand one thing," he said, taking advantage of the prevailing mellow mood. "Where *are* Lady Arabella's jewels? The real ones?"

The Baroness studied the boy, then seemed to decide that he'd earned a reply. "They were sold by Sir William, piece by piece. I doubt that they will ever come to light now." She pinched his rosy cheek. "Run along and find some mischief to get into. I must speak with Sir John."

Austin obligingly scampered off toward a large tent, decorated on the outside with half-moons and covered inside with chintz.

"The lad seems to have survived his adventures tolerably well," remarked Sir John to Dulcie.

"Of course!" The Baroness was serene. "You must know, John, that all of Bat's blood thrive on calamity and intrigue."

"Yes," agreed Sir John. "And so do some who share his name, if not his blood." He knew well that Dulcie had enjoyed every moment of this ridiculous caper; nor did he deceive himself that she would, as reward for his long-suffering efforts on her nephew's behalf, fall into his arms. In perfect understanding, they strolled for awhile along the flower-strewn path.

Those fortunate enough regularly to attend Lady Bligh's

spectacular galas knew to expect the unusual, although her efforts were less flamboyant than those of her spouse, who had on one memorable occasion provided fighting gamecocks with silver spurs for the edification of his guests. Dulcie's brilliance was less savage; it lay in the intermingling of unlikely people, such as Arabella's aunt, Rebecca Baskerville, and Lord Rumfoord, who were happily engaged in verbally vivisecting the characters of their fellow guests; and Crump, engaged in jolly conversation with Pudding, who had emerged from her domain to speculate upon the visitors' capacities for appreciation of her culinary extravaganzas, which included a fantastically iced sugar cake exactly three feet high. Sir John's amused glance moved on to Lady Caro Lamb. He wondered if it was true that she had offered herself in payment to any youth sufficiently bold as to challenge Byron to a duel. Thus far, according to rumor, she'd had no takers.

"Poor Luisa," murmured Dulcie, in a tone that put Sir John immediately on guard. "Think how unhappy she must have been! One might almost say that Arabella drove her to murder, as did Gwyneth and that idiotic Dragoon. It is good of you to agree that her exposure would serve no purpose."

"I have *not* agreed," retorted Sir John, "though you have contrived to spread the story that her heart failed when she learned of her son's death." His terrible scowl was inspired by the thought that Dulcie herself had barely escaped the grim reaper's scythe. "It amazes me that you will go to such lengths to shield a woman who tried to murder you."

"Pooh!" The Baroness was maddeningly nonchalant. "Had the situations been reversed, I daresay I would have acted much as Luisa did, though with a great deal more finesse." She frowned. "All the same, John, we must contrive to see that the Arbuthnot name remains blemished by nothing more odious than suicide."

"So you say." Sir John hoped fervently that Lady Bligh

would never turn her clever mind to the successful enactment of a crime.

They approached a group of people and Dulcie pressed closer against his arm. Sir John's temperature rose appreciably. "None know, save ourselves, of William's villainy; already the furor has begun to die down. Let it remain our secret, Arabella's previous marriage and its distasteful consequences. Bertha will not talk, for I have secured her a position with one of my innumerable relatives on the understanding that she holds her tongue. Nor will any of *my* people gossip about the affair." She smiled roguishly. "All that remains is for *you* to warn Crump and the detective Luisa employed to keep silent. We will allow Slippery Jim to pass as the murderer; that can cause no harm since only we few know of his connection with Hilary Rumfoord."

"You have," the Chief Magistrate retorted acidly, "an odd notion of justice! Were anyone else to dare make such a suggestion, he would feel the lash of my tongue."

"John!" The Baroness cast him a languishing look. "I *do* adore an authoritative man." Perhaps it was the heat of the lanterns that made Sir John's head swim. "Do I often ask favors of you? Surely you can find it in your heart to do this one little thing!" Gibbon, bearing crystal glasses on a silver tray, saved Sir John a reply. "Ah, refreshments." Dulcie's voice was low and amused. "I fear that you do not properly value my efforts, sir! Never mind. You will in time come to appreciate my services to Bow Street." Sir John blanched; this sounded ominously as if Lady Bligh meant to become Bow Street's patroness.

With hands that shook, Gibbon extended the tray. His pallor was thrown into high relief by the lantern light, making him appear a decomposing specter invoked by the Baroness expressly to cater her fete. Recent events had left their mark on him, but no trial had been so severe as the one he now endured. Jewels glittered everywhere, and Gibbon was sworn to appropriate none. The Chief Magistrate drew forth his pocket watch and Gibbon swallowed, hard.

"Well-met, Sir John!" Hubert, stunning in emerald green, removed two glasses from the tray. "Do you still bewail the fact that I shall be tossed no nosegays from balconies while on my way to the gallows tree?"

"Dressed," added Jael, clad in claret silk and countless gold baubles and exhibiting a surprising ease of manner amid exalted company, "in your winding sheet." Gibbon turned away. Temptation had proven too great; Sir John's treasured watch rested snugly in the butler's hand.

"That is my one regret." Hubert's satiric gaze rested on Sir John's disgruntled countenance. "I should have dearly loved to design my own shroud." Artistically, he pondered. "Black, of course. But embroidered with silver stars and moons."

"Popinjay!" Lady Bligh's patrician nose twitched. "Do you fancy yourself an alchemist, Humbug, or a magician of old?"

"There is magic in these fingers." Hubert surveyed his hands with satisfaction. "I can, after all, transform the merest dross into gold."

"You'd be well-advised, my covey," Jael remarked calmly, "to better guard your tongue." Never had Sir John seen the gypsy so equable.

"Ah, no." Hubert's well-tended fingers traced her scar. "No derogatory word concerning *you*, my treasure, has ever passed my lips!" Jael tossed her head, and Sir John's eyes narrowed speculatively as he pondered the obviously easy terms between this disparate pair.

"I should hope not," commented Dulcie, not at all discomfited by her nephew's marked attention to a female of no background and even less reputation. "Jael saved your skin, after all." She manipulated the fan. "Speaking of which, I believe we are to congratulate you. I trust you will not play ducks-and-drakes with *this* inheritance."

Hubert froze, in the act of taking snuff. "Confound you, Dulcie! Am I never to be allowed the gratification of surprise?" Only Hubert's creditors knew that his sickly and irascible godfather had, in a moment of pique inspired by the vulture-like hoverings of his family, made Humbug his heir; or that, before rational thought had reasserted itself, the old gentleman had died.

"I doubt it greatly, Humbug." The Baroness was kind. "You are not precisely unpredictable. Do take that oafish expression off your face; you are beginning to resemble one of Bat's statuaries!" Since these were most vacuous examples of the stonecutter's art, she paid him no compliment.

"I remind myself," said Hubert magnanimously, "that you have expended a certain amount of effort on my behalf, and shall therefore refrain from taking offense. I understand that you have told young Austin that my uncle is momentarily expected home?" He turned to Jael. "The kings and queens of Europe perambulated through their lands in medieval days, taking with them the whole court and conducting business from whatever site took their fancy. It is a tradition that my uncle follows, with all the grandeur of that long dead royalty."

"He is returning." The Baroness surveyed her many guests, but none displayed a tendency to misbehave. "Having journeyed extensively through the Middle East, surviving the permanent strife between the Turkish overlords and their subjugated peoples, and periodic waves of destructive plagues including a swarm of locusts that covered trees and houses so thickly that they appeared painted bright green, Bat has decided to return to England's calmer shores."

Hubert raised his glass in the direction of Bligh House. "What architectural marvel will my uncle next create?" he asked thoughtfully. "I anticipate a harem with barred and latticed windows, an extensive garden and a marble swimming pool."

"Do you?" The Baroness seemed to look upon vistas invisible

to ordinary mortals, and Sir John was stricken with severe jealousy. "I, Humbug, anticipate a great deal more."

"My aunt," explained Hubert, as Crump joined them, "delights in posing us puzzles. It is part of her ineffable charm." Lady Bligh rapped his knuckles smartly with her fan.

Crump did not know if his sense of vast relief was due to the closing of the damnable Arbuthnot case, or the five hundred Yellow Boys that he had received from Lady Bligh as a reward for his efforts, or his immeasurable consumption of fine champagne. He was suffused with a rosy affection that encompassed even the acid-tongued Hubert and the steely-eyed Jael. Filled with the milk of human kindness, the Runner beamed upon them all.

"So, Hubert, your fortunes have been repaired," observed Sir John, anxious to turn the conversation away from the irritating topic of the fifth Baron. "I am glad to hear it. Perhaps now you will no longer be tempted to masquerade as a highwayman."

Hubert shuddered convincingly. "Not I! The ghastly vision of myself dangling from a rustic gallows was a sharp enough lesson for me."

Jael was not particularly interested in further discussion of Hubert's change of fortune. "What happened," she asked abruptly, "to that confounded Count? Gwyneth's husband?" Her tone left no doubt that this gentleman had aroused her antipathy. Despite the gypsy's good humor, Crump did not doubt her capacity for gross, and cold-blooded, butchery.

"He is on his way, I trust, to his home in Hungary." Sir John was cautious; Jael's moods were mercurial. "I thought it best for all concerned if we simply let him go, since no formal charge was made."

"God's bones!" Jael's golden earrings danced with the force of her annoyance. "Better you had turned him over to me."

"Such bloodthirst, my treasure!" Hubert retained his aplomb. "Never mind, we shall find some deserving individual and you shall make mincemeat of him." Jael looked as though she might purr with pleasure in anticipation of the treat. "Although I find myself in such sunny temper, inspired by Dame Fortune's caress, that I rather wish you would refrain."

It had crossed the Runner's befuddled brain that Jael was an even unlikelier attendant at this spectacular celebration than he was himself. He peered at the gypsy appraisingly. "Hubert," explained the Baroness, "has received a much-needed inheritance. We trust it will inspire him to speedily mend his ways."

Hubert smiled, sublimely unconcerned that every member of the small group knew him to be the infamous Gentleman. "Dear cousin Bertram," he murmured. "I'll own I never expected him to come up to snuff!" He noted various puzzled expressions. "My godfather, you know. He was the most redoubtable old gentleman, a veritable old Tartar with an adder's tongue."

"One hardly needs add that Humbug was the only relative whom Bertram could tolerate." Lady Bligh, with little evidence of approbation, regarded her shameless nephew. "Like attracts like, they claim. What now, Hubert? I have a persistent notion that you will bask in the Spanish sun."

Jael's cold eyes gleamed. "You're a witch, Dulcie Bligh!"

"Were it some previous time," Hubert agreed, "it might take our combined efforts to save you from the stake, dear aunt! But yes, I have decided that a change of scenery might be beneficial to my health." His irrepressible gaze rested upon Sir John. "I do not mean that the august authorities might change their minds, but I believe it might be wise to temporarily place myself somewhere beyond the reach of the law's long arm."

"You've a portrait to finish." Dulcie pinched Sir John. "Jael, of course, will accompany you."

"*My* health," said Jael, "is far more precarious than that of this dandy fellow!" She studied Lady Bligh. "I've made a lot of enemies for your sake, Baroness!"

"Not for mine, I think," Dulcie retorted. Crump, who had finally assimilated the startling fact that Hubert meant to go off in the company of the disreputable gypsy, was filled with profound shock. Jael did not suit his notion of a gentleman's light-o'-love.

"It is amazing," Hubert mused, "how much tragedy evolved from Arabella's youthful indiscretions. But I have promised to say no more of that!" He took Jael's arm. "Come, my treasure! Our trials are now ended. Let us wander among the *beau monde* and raise such eyebrows as we may."

"One moment, gypsy." Sir John could no more withstand Dulcie than the march of time. The troublesome diamond necklace changed hands. "Arabella's aunt considers this to be rightfully yours."

Jael, the diamonds securely tucked away, cast Dulcie one last glance. "Someday," she said, "*you* must read the Tarot for me, Baroness!" Crump stared indignantly as the gypsy turned to Hubert with a sultry smile. "You promised me fireworks! So far I've seen none."

Humbug's voice, for once, was totally devoid of satire. "If it's fireworks you wish, my treasure," and he led her, unprotesting toward a more secluded portion of the gardens, "then it's fireworks you shall have!"

"There are unexpected depths to Hubert's character," remarked Sir John, only slightly less startled at this relationship than was Crump. "Forgive my curiosity, but just what is that female to him?"

"Dear John." Dulcie smiled, with the effect of a thousand candles springing into light. "I will forgive you anything! Jael has been Humbug's mistress for a good many years, though she wished the connection kept secret. She could hardly command the respect of her minions if they knew of her liaison with an aristocratic gentleman, or so she claimed. I suspect it was actually concern for Hubert's reputation that prompted her reticence; Jael's experience with the Upper Ten Thousand has left her with few illusions concerning them."

"An embarrassing couple, surely?" asked Sir John. They continued their wanderings, leaving Crump behind to absorb further quantities of champagne. "I'm surprised you condone a relationship that many would consider ruinous."

"Good heavens, I'm no prig!" The Baroness was offended. "It's not as if he meant to marry her—in fact, I doubt Humbug will ever wed, not fancying himself in a patriarchal role. As for the other, they are remarkably well-suited, and Hubert has shown Jael a devotion that I would not have thought possible in him. He first admired her when she was the ruling belle of the *demimonde,* and was quick with assistance when she fell upon hard times." Dulcie touched her copper curls, already threatening to come unpinned. "Naturally, I am not supposed to know the tale."

"Naturally." Sir John was wry. "Sometimes, Dulcie, I think you know too much for your own good! It was Jael who initiated Hubert into the mysteries of highway robbery?"

"I think not." They passed a cluster of more notable guests, among them the incomparable Brummel and the Prince Regent himself, for once on amiable terms. "Jael would not wish Humbug to embark upon a career so unsuitable to one of his birth, though she is hardly the sort of female to seek to dissuade him from any chosen course."

Sir John, blinking as he observed Austin and Culpepper engaging in a game of tag among the stately trees, reflected upon the endless unpredictable actions of the Bligh family. "And I," added the Baroness, firmly closing the subject, "am quite fond of Jael, who is possibly the one proof that Humbug possesses a modicum of sense." Her air was reflective. "Odd, isn't it, how evil may bring good? If not for Luisa's machinations, Dickon might never have discovered the delightful character of my dear Lavender, and Jael might still be hiding, so to speak, in the woodwork. And there is Austin, who now chatters like a magpie as if to make up for the years in which he did not speak at all."

"That's all very well for Dickon," observed Sir John, "but what of Mrs. Lytton?"

"Dickon," retorted the Baroness cryptically, "is fast mending his ways. I hope he does not mean to become a model of propriety!" She frowned at Bligh House, then turned again to the Chief Magistrate. "I think I will see to it that Mary becomes Livvy's abigail. They get on well, and if nothing else, it will give Gibbon some peace." She cast a melting look at Sir John, who was preparing to depart.

"I suggest, dear friend, that you have a word with Gibbon before you take your leave."

Visited by a terrible suspicion, Sir John felt for his pocket watch. Dulcie's attention wandered again to a certain candle-lit window of Bligh House. She screwed up her exquisite features as if, by intense concentration, she might visualize the scene being played within the confines of that chamber.

Livvy and Dickon were not the only occupants of the Feather Room; Casanova and Bluebeard also sought refuge from the furor that swept through Bligh House. The Feather Room was one of the Baron's earlier efforts and, though unusual, it fell short of the extraordinary effects that he later achieved. Three round-headed Venetian windows were set, like a triptych, within relieving arches; large canvas-mounted frames, displaying mounted feathers collected from every conceivable and unwilling source, hung upon the walls.

Mrs. Lytton wore a gown of richly figured pale blue French gauze over white satin and a large quantity of Lady Bligh's fabulous collection of sapphires; the soft candlelight struck pewter sparks from her blue black curls; and her woebegone expression might have befitted the most miserable matchgirl. Lord Dorset, clad in fashionable evening attire that set off his muscular physique to perfection, paced the floor as restlessly as a caged jungle beast. His expression was equally fierce. Livvy's tear-blurred gaze rested indiscriminately on peacock plumes, pheasant tails, and cock's feathers.

"Confound it, Livvy!" the Earl exploded. "What more can you wish me to do? I have demonstrated my affection for you in every imaginable way, both proper and not; I have proposed to you on bended knee!" Livvy sniffled. "Yet all you do is weep into that damned handkerchief and tell me it will not do."

Livvy sought to regain her poise. "Well, it won't! If you would only admit it, you know that as well as I." Casanova leapt into her lap and Livvy clasped the huge, orange cat, heedless of the damage to her gown. "I regard you far too highly to marry you."

The Earl swore a terrific oath and hurled an inoffensive pillow across the room. Bluebeard, perched on the back of a tapestried chair, clucked reprovingly.

"Never did I think that *you* would turn missish, Livvy!" Quailing, she refused to meet his eye. "You have treated me to a rodomontade worthy of the flightiest schoolgirl!" The Earl was saturnine. "Never did I expect to find myself a mawkish figure of romance."

"No." Livvy had achieved a semblance of calm. "Nor of tragedy." Her first wild ecstasy at Dickon's proposal of marriage had succumbed to an onslaught of common sense. If Lord Dorset was not aware of the unsuitability of this match, she was; if he had no regard for his position in the world, then she must. "Do not plague me, Dickon; I have made up my mind."

"I see." The Earl's expression was unreadable. "It is my accursed reputation, I suppose. You fear that one with my libertine tendencies will cause you only distress."

"Rubbish!" Livvy retorted succinctly. "You think me a

milquetoast lady, to be sure!" Her caress was so ungentle that Casanova growled. "Acquit me, at least, of that! Our marriage will not take place due to *my* unsuitability, not yours."

"I see." For a thwarted and rejected lover, Dickon was inordinately meditative.

"You are," continued Livvy, encouraged by his receptive attitude, "a gentleman, one of impeccable background and lineage, despite your divorce. It is unthinkable that you should ally yourself with a female like myself who has neither fortune, family, nor beauty to recommend her. Far better, Dickon, to regard our acquaintance as nothing more important than a pleasant interlude."

It was not difficult to understand why the Earl was known as a most provoking and unpredictable man, for he greeted this soul-baring honesty with the faintest twitch of his lips and a slightly elevated brow. "So in future when we meet, I am to greet you with a polite indifference? You expect me, in short, to forget that I have held you in my arms?" He met her scowl with innocent eyes. "I only ask enlightenment, sweet Livvy, so that I may know how to go on."

"The occasion will not arise." Livvy wondered why nobility of action was so invaribly dispiriting. "I am leaving Dulcie's employ. After tonight, Dickon, we shall not meet again."

While not expecting her impatient suitor to accept this information without protest, she had not anticipated that he would yank her roughly to her feet, sending Casanova tumbling to the floor. "You," snapped Lord Dorset, "are talking gibberish!" Livvy stared fascinated at his furious face. "I am no polite cavalier, my darling, to obey your least command, particularly when it would mean a great deal of discomfort to myself. You have given me no good reason why our marriage should not take place, but have instead mouthed a great deal of nonsense that is totally unlike you." Dickon's sapphire eyes were black with the force of his rage. "I have in my pocket a special license; I have every intention of marrying you. And I don't intend to let you out of my sight until the thing is done!"

Most young ladies would have been stricken dumb by the implications of this last determined remark, but Livvy merely regarded Dickon with something approaching awe. "Did you mean what you said?" she asked. "Earlier?"

"Which?" inquired the Earl, for one of the few times in his life bewildered. "All of it!"

"That you would be uncomfortable if I went away." Livvy, in contemplation of her own unhappiness, had not considered that Lord Dorset might suffer a similar distress.

"Uncomfortable?" Dickon echoed with disbelief. "Sweet Livvy, I should be wretched, which is precisely why I do not intend to let you go!" He shook her, not ungently. "Don't you understand yet, you silly girl? I love you, I want to share my life with you, to make up to you all that you've been denied." Livvy blinked rapidly and he drew her closer into his arms. "Never has there been a woman like you, Livvy, and never will there be again. If you will not marry me, I shall doubtless turn into a crusty old curmudgeon whose foul temper is the terror of his acquaintance and whose profligate excesses are the talk of London. Could you have it on your conscience to condemn me to such a fate?"

"I suppose," murmured Livvy into his shoulder, "that it would be a terrible thing." She fought a last battle with her conscience. "Perhaps it will not matter to you when people say you have contracted a shocking *mésalliance;* or that I am a heartless fortune hunter who has caught you in her toils; or recall that I drove my last husband to take his own life and predict a similar fate for you."

"Not a bit," the Earl retorted cheerfully. His warm breath touched her curls. "They've said far worse." He held her away from him. "More important, will it matter to *you?* I would not have you hurt, sweet Livvy, but there is no question that marriage to me would make you a rare tidbit for the scandalmongers' feast."

"I never regarded it for myself," she said softly, "only for you." She felt as though she could fight dragons or, at least, walk on air. "But Dickon, I haven't the faintest notion of what being a countess involves!" Lord Dorset's prompt reaction clearly demonstrated to both parties that any gaps in Livvy's education would be speedily filled.

"Papa!" Austin bounded into the room, nearly colliding with Casanova, and Bluebeard squawked. "Uncle Bat's come home!" He paused, and stared. "Why are you cuddling Livvy? Is she going to marry you?" He watched their disentanglement with an interest worthy of Hubert. "Dulcie said she would."

"You see," murmured Dickon as they followed a scampering Austin outside, "my son's priorities. We rate second, I fear, to my fascinating relative."

Earlier that year, the British army had advanced onto French soil from Spain, and the armies of Russia, Prussia and Austria had marched on Paris. All those splendid, gallant troops combined commanded not half the attention rewarded, justly, to Maximilian Bonaventure Bligh. Turkish Pashas had bowed to him; the Sultan had called him friend; and the Prince Regent now took one look at the swashbuckling fifth Baron and felt like a dirty-eared schoolboy again.

A tall and slender man, the Baron moved through the crowd with the lithe and regal grace of the born athlete, acknowledging greetings with a bored indifference that put to shame the most haughty of aristocrats. He wore a Barbary outfit of purple and gold, and thrown across his shoulders was a magnificent brocaded Turkish cloak. Gray streaked his dark hair and beard. He was a figure of incredible magnetism, a disdainful marauder, a splendid barbarian who inspired more than one prim and proper lady with fantasies of burning desert sands, wicked sheiks, and ravishment. Maximilian had experienced what others dared not dream about, and the knowledge was written on his arrogant, weathered features, gleamed from those heavy-lidded and seductive eyes. Livvy looked at him and gasped.

Her reaction did not surprise Dickon, who had many times observed the Baron's effect. "You behold my legendary Uncle Max." Austin darted heedless through the crush, tipping more than one guest momentarily off balance, and tugged at the Baron's sleeve. He was swung, shrieking with laughter, high into the air. "Max is highly intelligent, witty, cultivated, exceedingly rich," Dickon went on, as Livvy continued stunned. "He also possesses the devil's temperament and a tongue as feared as the sword. Only Dulcie dares engage him in a verbal duel." The Earl smiled, stopping Livvy's heart and bringing Livvy's full attention back to him.

"How did Dulcie meet him?" The crowd parted before the Baron as once had the Red Sea for another man.

"Max was pheasant-hunting, and Dulcie was breaking in a horse. He emerged from the woods and saw her, praised his good fortune and vowed that she must be a divinity. What happened next I cannot say, but Dulcie claims she was lost from that moment on." Dickon was rueful. "I do not mean to distract you, sweet Livvy, from bestowing upon Max the admiration that is his due, but the matter of our future has not yet been resolved."

The haughty features that Livvy had come to love so well were humble and anxious. Her scruples went down to a resounding defeat. "I will be pleased," she said breathlessly, "to become your wife." It was a mark of the Baron's hypnotic presence that not one of the other guests, even those strictest sticklers to propriety, noticed that the Earl of Dorset was so lost to sanity that he engaged his fiancée in a most passionate public embrace.

No less than the *ton*, the various Bligh retainers suffered conflicting emotions at the Baron's return. Countless servants scurried to and fro, laden with boxes and parcels of great variety and intriguing dimensions. Culpepper, with an excited Austin held firmly by his jacket collar, oversaw these complicated activities. Gibbon, while content that Bligh House would no longer suffer from an absence of the masculine element, quailed to think of the Baron's reaction were his butler's recent lapses into petty thievery to become known; and Mary, on her mettle, swished her hips experimentally. Even in the nether regions of Bligh House the event was felt, as Pudding delved frantically into her cookbooks in search of delicacies to tempt the Baron's finicky appetite.

Sir John watched Maximilian's leisurely approach. The eccentric Baron had a profound disregard for the polite world that so toadishly fawned on him. Of too restless a disposition to pass more than brief moments in one place, Bat was renowned for his habit of suddenly appearing in a roomful of guests, where he would make a few genial remarks, reveal considerable erudition, and as abruptly go away. With regard to polite society, at least, the Chief Magistrate and the Baron felt the same. Gibbon, his white hair wildly disheveled with the force of his emotions, bobbed along in his master's wake. Silently, Sir John held out his hand. Equally wordless, Gibbon dropped the pocket watch onto that extended palm.

Gibbon need not have feared; the Baron's attention was all for his wife, who had assumed an attitude of charming helplessness that contrasted beautifully with her scandalous gown. The Baron broke off in the middle of the song he had been humming beneath his breath, a delightful Romany air concerning the poisoning, and subsequent devourment, of a fat and juicy pig. Sir John, well acquainted with the stratagems of his dear and aggravating ladylove, slipped away quietly, preferring not to witness the outcome of this particular meeting.

Maximilian bowed with an expertise envied by all who saw. Lady Bligh inclined her head and regarded her husband soulfully, as if she beheld in him the personification of countless crumbled dreams. "I have missed you damnably, my dear," said he. The Baron's deep, rich voice had sent delicious shivers along many a maiden's spine.

"If only I could believe that!" The Baroness raised a languid hand to her brow. Her copper curls, loosened from their pinnings, tumbled down her back. "But no! You are an utter beast, my husband, and have broken my heart so many times that it must resemble an old, discarded piece of crockery."

There was a diabolic twinkle in Maximilian's perceptive eye. "I am excellent at mending old pots," he remarked and without further ado swept his wife up into his arms.

"An old pot!" Lady Bligh abruptly abandoned her fragile air and buried her fingers in his thick hair. "You truly *are* the prince of rogues!" Her words were almost a caress.

"I am," agreed the Baron, striding unconcerned through the fascinated throng.

The Baroness wound her arms more securely around his neck and nibbled experimentally on a well-shaped ear. "Which recalls to mind the fact that I am not speaking to you!" Provocatively, she smiled.

He bent his handsome gray-streaked head until his lips brushed hers. "For what I have in mind at this particular moment, *dulcinea,* you needn't say one word." Dulcie's delighted laughter, drifting back to her spellbound guests, was the tinkling of a hundred silvery bells.